GRI[illegible]

At last the orc took notice, this squealing piece of manflesh rattling his puny shield with his tiny knife. Though man and orc did not speak the same language, understanding between them was absolute. Throwing back his head, the greenskin chieftain emitted an ululating cry that drove the warriors from its path.

Challenge accepted.

Stahler fought to quell his fear. The battle around him appeared to lull. The world slowed, but it was as if the orc chieftain were moving outside of time as it came on inexorably and at speed. The captain's longsword was no ordinary weapon. Myrmidian priests had blessed it and a single rune was forged into the blade. Despite the keenness of its edge, the magical sharpness parted mail links like they were parchment, Stahler balked at the thickness of the orc's armour, its flesh and brawn.

'Sigmar protect me...' he whispered, making the sign of the hammer with his shield arm then bringing it up to meet the charge of the beast.

More Empire army novels

REIKSGUARD
by Richard Williams

IRON COMPANY
by Chris Wraight

CALL TO ARMS
by Mitchel Scanlon

More from Nick Kyme

· TOME OF FIRE TRILOGY ·

SALAMANDER
FIREBORN (audio drama)

ASSAULT ON BLACK REACH

· DWARFS ·

HONOURKEEPER
OATHBREAKER

A WARHAMMER NOVEL

GRIMBLADES

NICK KYME

For Kev Platts and Wednesday mornings listening to Jethro Tull's 'Broadsword'.

A BLACK LIBRARY PUBLICATION

First published in Great Britain in 2010 by
The Black Library,
Games Workshop Ltd.,
Willow Road, Nottingham,
NG7 2WS, UK

10 9 8 7 6 5 4 3 2 1

Cover illustration by Clint Langley.

Map by Nuala Kinrade.

A CIP record for this book is available from the British Library.

UK ISBN: 978 1 84416 864 4
US ISBN: 978 1 84416 865 1

Printed and bound in the UK.

THIS IS A dark age, a bloody age, an age of daemons and of sorcery. It is an age of battle and death, and of the world's ending. Amidst all of the fire, flame and fury it is a time, too, of mighty heroes, of bold deeds and great courage.

AT THE HEART of the Old World sprawls the Empire, the largest and most powerful of the human realms. Known for its engineers, sorcerers, traders and soldiers, it is a land of great mountains, mighty rivers, dark forests and vast cities. And from his throne in Altdorf reigns the Emperor Karl Franz, sacred descendant of the founder of these lands, Sigmar, and wielder of his magical warhammer.

BUT THESE ARE far from civilised times. Across the length and breadth of the Old World, from the knightly palaces of Bretonnia to ice-bound Kislev in the far north, come rumblings of war. In the towering Worlds Edge Mountains, the orc tribes are gathering for another assault. Bandits and renegades harry the wild southern lands of the Border Princes. There are rumours of rat-things, the skaven, emerging from the sewers and swamps across the land. And from the northern wildernesses there is the ever-present threat of Chaos, of daemons and beastmen corrupted by the foul powers of the Dark Gods. As the time of battle draws ever nearer, the Empire needs heroes like never before.

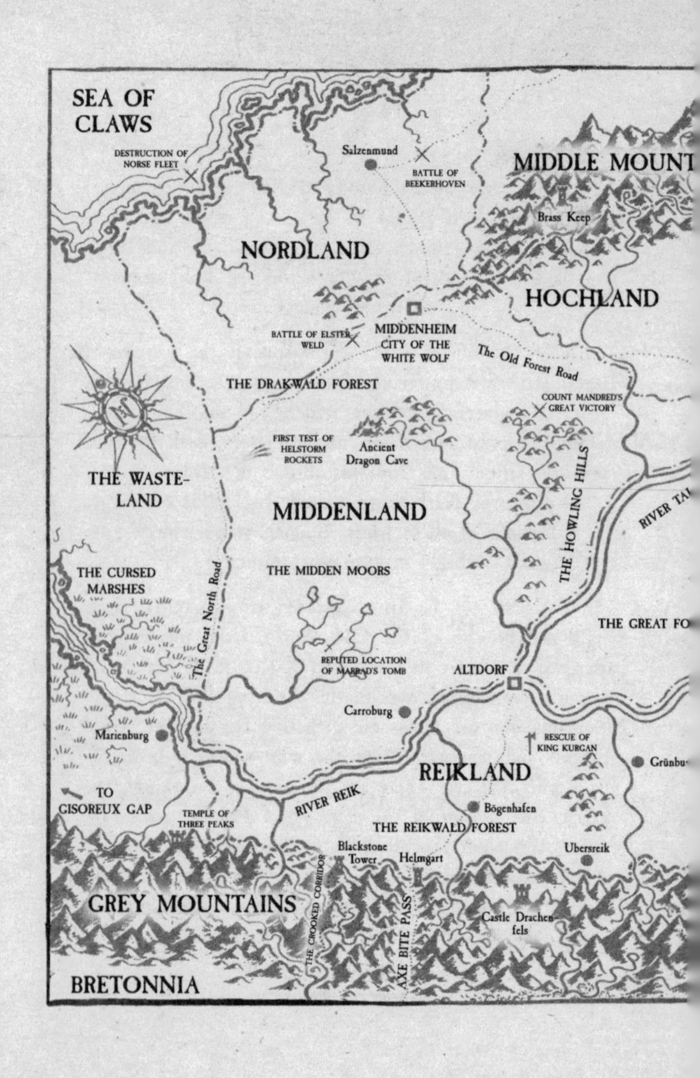
SEA OF
CLAWS
DESTRUCTION OF
NORSE FLEET
Salzenmund
BATTLE OF
BEEKERHOVEN
Brass Keep
NORDLAND
HOCHLAND
BATTLE OF ELSTER
WELD
MIDDENHEIM
CITY OF THE
WHITE WOLF
The Old Forest Road
THE DRAKWALD FOREST
COUNT MANDRED'S
GREAT VICTORY
FIRST TEST OF
HELSTORM
ROCKETS
Ancient
Dragon Cave
THE WASTE-
LAND
MIDDENLAND
THE HOWLING HILLS
THE CURSED
MARSHES
THE MIDDEN MOORS
The Great North Road
REPUTED LOCATION
OF MARBAD'S TOMB
ALTDORF
Carroburg
Marienburg
RESCUE OF
KING KURGAN
REIKLAND
TO
GISOREUX GAP
TEMPLE OF
THREE PEAKS
RIVER REIK
Bögenhafen
THE REIKWALD FOREST
Blackstone
Tower
Helmgart
Ubersreik
GREY MOUNTAINS
THE CROOKED CORRIDOR
AXE BITE PASS
Castle Drachen-
fels
BRETONNIA

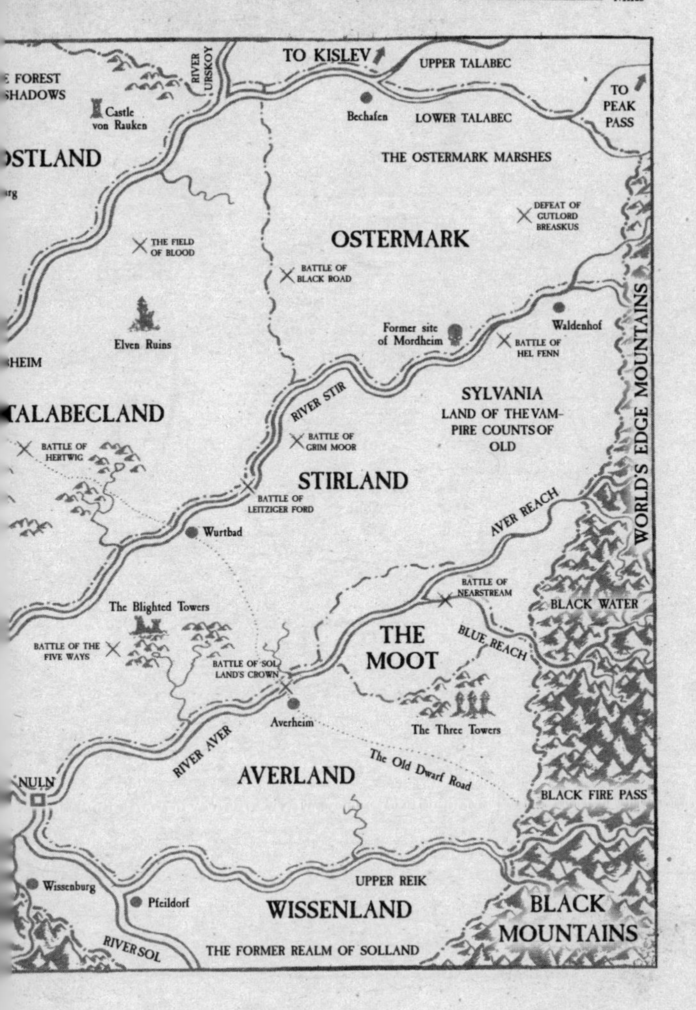

0
50
100
150
200
Miles
TO KISLEV
UPPER TALABEC
RIVER URSKOY
FOREST
SHADOWS
Castle von Rauken
Bechafen
LOWER TALABEC
TO PEAK PASS
STLAND
THE OSTERMARK MARSHES
DEFEAT OF GUTLORD BREASKUS
THE FIELD OF BLOOD
OSTERMARK
BATTLE OF BLACK ROAD
Elven Ruins
Former site of Mordheim
Waldenhof
BATTLE OF HEL FENN
HEIM
WORLD'S EDGE MOUNTAINS
TALABECLAND
RIVER STIR
SYLVANIA
LAND OF THE VAMPIRE COUNTS OF OLD
BATTLE OF HERTWIG
BATTLE OF GRIM MOOR
STIRLAND
BATTLE OF LEITZIGER FORD
AVER REACH
Wurtbad
BATTLE OF NEARSTREAM
The Blighted Towers
BLACK WATER
THE MOOT
BLUE REACH
BATTLE OF THE FIVE WAYS
BATTLE OF SOL LAND'S CROWN
Averheim
The Three Towers
RIVER AVER
The Old Dwarf Road
NULN
AVERLAND
BLACK FIRE PASS
UPPER REIK
Wissenburg
Pfeildorf
WISSENLAND
BLACK MOUNTAINS
RIVER SOL
THE FORMER REALM OF SOLLAND

PROLOGUE

Iron Gate, dwarf-held bastion of Black Fire Pass,
690 miles from Altdorf

THEY CAME FROM the east. The green tide that swept across the Worlds Edge Mountains went through its southern causeways with the pounding of drums and the call of beasts. They burned and sacked as they went. The sky blackened with the smoke of their charnel fires. Horns and bestial roars announced them. Tribes upon tribes heard the call to arms: the waaagh! One by one the orcs and goblins emerged from their caves, bringing cleavers and spears and a brute desire to kill. This was the greenskin way, and with each fresh warband the horde swelled and its belligerence grew.

Black Fire Pass – the name was legendary. Orcs had come here before, and would again. Over two thousand years ago, they fought the nascent man-god and were defeated. Now, a goblin led them. An apparent lesser cousin of the orc was the goblin, but not this beast. This beast was different. It was driven. It was ruthless. It was deadly. And neither dwarf nor man who guarded the gates of this ancestral battleground would oppose it.

'Name the dead!' King Bragarik boomed above the battle. He could barely think, such was the thunder coming from the orc drums. His skull throbbed with it, and their debased chanting.

'Thord Helhand, slain by an urk's blade; Norgan Stonefinger, crushed under a grobi chariot; Baldin Grit-tooth, bard of the halls, eaten by a troll...' The dwarf king's grudgemaster reeled off the names of the fallen as if he were inventorying weapons from the hold's armouries.

There was no time for remorse, or for grief. Dwarfs were pragmatic, especially about death. Retribution was all that mattered, and a levelling of the scales made in blood.

Life was balance. A death for a death. Blood for blood. The grudgekeeper's way.

Grudgemaster Drengk scribed perfunctorily, in the same manner as his declarations. There might be no time later. If he died, who then would remember the fallen? Who then would scribe his name in the book? The 'book' was a massive, hide-bound tome which hung around his neck as heavy as a millstone. But dwarfs were stout and strong: they worked and lived underground, digging, mining, hauling rock and ore. Drengk wore his discomfort, as all dwarfs did, with a stoic scowl.

In front of king and grudgemaster were Iron Gate's hearthguard, its hammerers. These redoubtable warriors were the king's own and they stood in file with shields locked. Hammers rose and fell like pistons and oaths were hurled like spears into the greenskin hordes trying to punch through them. King Bragarik was at their centre, his grudgemaster just behind him.

The hammerers' gromril armour was dented and stained from hard fighting. Each suit was an heirloom, worth as much as a human town. More than one hammerer had lost his battle helm. Dark, hateful eyes were revealed underneath, where before they'd been occluded by a mass of beard and metal. The elite of the dwarf hold brought low by cleavers and clubs.

King Bragarik hadn't escaped without injury. His mail gorget was split and the links spilled down his armoured chest. A cut just above his brow drooled blood, gumming his left eye and making it dark and rheumy. Bragarik had discarded his own shield. A troll's mace had shattered it. The beast was destroyed – the dwarf king had burned it with his rune axe – but so too was his shield.

Even Loki and Kazûm, his bearers, laboured underneath him with injuries. A long hard fight. One the dwarfs were losing.

For a moment, the line bowed as a renewed thrust came from the rear of the orcs and rippled forward to the fighting ranks. A hammerer screamed and fell with a black haft protruding from his neck, only to be lost from view in a red haze.

'Close ranks,' bellowed the king. A blaring warhorn answered above the rumble of drums. Blood laced his gilded gromril armour, painting its runes black as he severed an orc's neck. He crushed the skull of another with his gauntleted fist. Below him, his shieldbearers hacked furiously with their axes.

When the killing abated for a moment and the line was strong once more, King Bragarik scowled back at Drengk.

'Godrin Stoutbellow,' the grudgemaster concluded, 'killed by an urk spear.'

'Let it be known,' proclaimed the king, 'that on this day they did fall and were revenged.' His eye traced the line of battle, too long and too thin for his liking, strung out across the width of Black Fire Pass, its valley sides teeming with greenskins. Bragarik saw his hammerers, a cliff of gromril breakers against a green and turbulent tide. To their right were the 'Venerable', silver-haired long-beards that had lived for centuries but whose place by the eternal hearth was calling. Most were older than the king, and twice as cantankerous. Every one of their dead was not only the loss of a dwarf, but an end to a piece of living history. The warrior clans followed them: metalsmiths, fletchers, candlemakers and rockshapers all – the craftsdwarfs of the hold arrayed in battle and fighting alongside their brothers.

Quarrellers regimented upon a shallow mound filled the air with shafts from their crossbows, exacting a heavy toll. Thunderers boomed just below, between their volleys, spewing smoke and fire. More greenskins fell to their fusillades too, but it wasn't enough; not nearly enough.

Rodi Coalthumb's miners were overrun. Bragarik saw the thane laying his oathstone as he prepared a final stand.

Drongi's rangers had long been lost to the greenskin swell, swept up like sticks before a rushing river.

The king's own son, Orig, lay on a bier of shields in a cold room, silently reposed. It had been a bitter blow.

Yes, only retribution was left to the dwarfs now as Black Fire Pass filled with orcs and goblins, just as it had done in recent years when man and dwarf first stood together.

'Is there sign of–'

A blast of cannons behind him smothered even Bragarik's imposing voice.

'Their chieftain,' he tried again. 'Is there sign of him?'

Skane, the hold's banner bearer, was standing on top of a small hillock and gazed across the field beyond the rolling gun smoke.

'I see him, thane-king.' He pointed to the east, his grubby finger encrusted with rings.

Bragarik's eyes narrowed when he saw the Paunch.

The bloated goblin king spewed curses with every breath as he hacked and hewed with a double-bladed axe.

Bragarik hawked and spat, before despatching another orc with his rune axe. He'd dearly love to vent his wrath on the fat goblin swine.

A shadow crept across a lightning cracked sky. Fell voices churned the air, deep and animalistic – the Paunch's shaman was abroad.

The voice of Hungni, runesmith of the hold, rose up to challenge it. Orcish sorcery met dwarf tenacity and the heavens burned with green fire.

Emboldened by their shaman's magic, the greenskins pushed and the dwarfs gave. Just one step, but Bragarik felt it all the way down the line as his shieldbearers retreated.

'At this rate, the walls of Iron Gate will be at our backs,' snapped the king, to no one in particular.

And then there would be no more ground to give.

He turned again to Skane.

'To the north, does he come?'

The hammerer line rippled with another greenskin assault, bringing shouts, death cries and more naming of the dead from Drengk.

Rodi Coalthumb was gone. Laments from slayers weighted the air, doleful and fatalistic.

Skane shielded his eyes against a pellucid light above that was far from natural. Hungni was losing to the shaman. The beat of a wyvern's wings was drawing nearer...

Unmoving as a rock, Skane did not waver. He looked northward. A speck was growing there, like a piece of grit at first. It became larger as a grim wind began to build. The edges of Skane's cloth banner shivered.

The dwarf line withdrew another step.

'Skane!'

The banner bearer let his hand fall. 'He comes, my king! He comes!'

Cresting the mountain crags around Iron Gate, a figure ran slowly but steadily towards the king. The dwarf's cheeks were puffed, his armour split. A cudgel blow dented his helm.

Six messengers the king had sent and only one returned. He had a scroll tucked in his belt. Bragarik's eyes were keen and he saw a wax seal upon it, wearing the Imperial crest of Emperor Dieter IV.

'Let him through!' he bellowed. More horns conveyed the order, and the dwarf rearguards parted like a metal sea to admit the messenger.

As the dwarf approached, he was still catching his breath. Bragarik's attention was half elsewhere, looking askance at the eastern flank crumbling as a force of orc boar riders rolled over it.

Drengk's voice was hoarse by now. It vied with the heavy report of drums and the shouts of thanes as they fought to shore up the broken flank.

Heavily-armoured ironbreakers were already moving in to intercede against the boar's riders and they planted their banner firmly.

'Speak quickly,' snapped the king.

The messenger proffered the scroll to him.

Leaning down to snatch it from the messenger's grip, Bragarik split the seal, unfurled it and read swiftly. Hope faded as vitriol clouded the king's granite features. He crushed the scroll in his fist and let it fall.

The king looked at Skane. 'Signal the retreat.'

'Thane-king?'

Bragarik's beard quivered with rage, setting the torcs and ingots bound there jangling.

'Do as you're bidden!'

He turned back towards the line and looked over the wall of hammerer shields defending him.

'The day is lost...' he growled to himself, and then in a smaller, hate-filled voice. 'Old oaths are sundered.'

Skane raised the hold banner and gave the signal to retreat. All across the killing field, horns sounded and drums crashed. The line narrowed, its long haft becoming a hammer's head as the stoutest dwarf armour put itself between its retreating brothers and the greenskins. They withdrew by steps, slow and reluctant. King Bragarik was amongst the last to leave.

Bodies of dead dwarfs were revealed in their wake amidst a mire of broken blades and shattered hafts. Snapped shields stuck out of red-rimed earth like partly excised teeth. Fallen battle helms served as paltry gravemarkers. Greenskins littered the field, too, together with the carcasses of slain beasts. Already, they had begun to stink and a pall of decay hung over the air.

Bragarik's nose rankled as he surveyed the dead.

Drengk had lost his voice and scribed silently in his tome of remembering, the hold's book of grudges, its *dammaz kron*, where all the ills done to its many clans were recorded.

Bragarik wagered that several dark chapters would be writ by the grudgemaster's hand before the day was out.

Bitterly, the dwarfs left the field of battle. Their hammerers and ironbreakers guarded the retreat, but the greenskins did not pursue. The Paunch had not come here to taste dwarf flesh, nor did he want to fight a siege against an intractable foe. As the dwarfs fell back, so too did the way into the lands beyond the pass open. Here was the Empire, the heartlands of the greatest realm of men.

Iron Gate shut its hold tight with a forbidding clang and as the last of King Bragarik's warriors came to stand with their brothers, darkness reigned in the outer hall.

'Keep 'em doused,' the dwarf king snapped at his lamplighters. They could see well enough without light.

'Think of brothers lost,' he said, his voice sounding louder in the gloom. 'Remember the dead. And remember aid asked for but not given. Men have no honour this day. They break old pacts sworn by High King Kurgan. They bring dishonour to his name too.' King Bragarik was breathing hard and fast, his anger only just contained. 'Let the grobi go, and the urk and the troll. No rangers will oppose them, no watchtowers will warn of their approach. *Umgi*-men are alone in this,' he swore in a voice that held enough canker to scour iron. 'Let them look to themselves against the greenskins. For the dawi will not come. We will not come.'

CHAPTER ONE

ROUSTING IN REIKWALD FOREST

Reikland border, domain of Prince Wilhelm III,
185 miles from Altdorf

CROUCHED IN THE lee of a gnarled oak, Eber adjusted his sallet helm for the fifth time. Unlike the rest of his Reikland uniform, it was too big. It kept slipping over his eyes and obscuring his view of the shadowed boughs of the Reikwald. His grey-white tunic and red-slitted hose stretched to contain his bulk, but the buttonholes still gaped with the tension from his muscles.

Eber was his family name. His first name was Brutan, given to him by his father. A cruel joke as it turned out. Even as a boy, it summed up his intimidating physique. 'Dumb ox', 'clumsy oaf' and 'fat brute' were some of the less flattering appellations his father had also chosen when the mood took him or when he had no more coin to stay in the tavern.

Those nights were the worst for Brutan and his waif-like mother. Violent, drunken, red nights; they were filled with accusation, ridicule and resentment. Brutan was tough, like a slab of butcher's meat, and his father had turned to his frailer wife when he'd been frustrated at the tenderiser's block. Brutan still remembered her pleas, her screams. Sometimes they went on into the night even now, years later. Brutan had clenched his thick, ham-like fists, but had done nothing. By the time he grew out of adolescence he was twice his father's size, but years of indoctrinated fear had left him scared of the man. Not a father; more a monster, like those he hunted in the forest at this very moment.

No, Brutan had lacked the courage to act then. Instead he had simply balled his fists impotently by his sides and stared at his feet, his large, ungainly feet, and done nothing.

'Hsst!'

The sound came from Eber's left and broke his unhappy reverie.

'Eber, advance!'

It was old Varveiter, glaring at Eber out of his good eye, giving him his parchment-cracked voice. The other eye was misted over with cataracts, but old Varveiter often claimed that he'd lost the sight in it fighting orcs in the Middle Mountains.

The veteran soldier had seen greener years. His beard was wiry and thin, with more grey in it than brown. The leather hauberk he wore under his plate cuirass was a similar texture to his skin, only not as cured, and black instead of tan. But he was strong and held his halberd haft with a soldier's purpose.

Varveiter nodded ahead as the line began to move: Eber, Rechts, Lenkmann and Varveiter with Sergeant Karlich at the centre keeping them spread out and steady. Masbrecht and Keller ranged on the extreme left and right, each guarding a flank.

About fifty feet ahead were the scouts, Volker and Brand, their advance low and silent. Heinrich Volker had a hunter's gait, a trapper's poise. He went without a helmet and his short, black hair was bound with a band of crimson cloth. He led the way towards the beastman encampment. Whilst scouting, Volker eschewed his halberd for a long dirk. Markus Brand was no poacher, but he moved with silent menace. He wore a tan leather cap with a short, protruding feather over his helmet. A long vambrace up his left arm supported three small knives. Brand was a killer, a quiet man but with violent urges that he sated on the battlefield. He too carried a long dagger, but its blade was serrated and the metal dark from use.

Together, they were the front rankers of the Reikland 16th Halberdiers, also known as the Grimblades. The rest of the forty-strong regiment waited several hundred feet back in a partial clearing. Surprise, according to Sergeant Karlich, was best effected in smaller numbers.

The foul stench that had polluted the shallow breeze wafting through the forest for the last hour abruptly intensified and Volker raised a hand for the halberdiers to stop.

Karlich didn't need to relay the order to his men. A low clanking of metal breastplates and tassets sounded in response to Volker's warning. It lasted just a few seconds as each man in the rank became still and watchful.

Hunched silhouettes cavorted in the gloom ahead. Karlich saw the suggestion of horned heads and shaggy-hided bodies in those shapes that parodied men. Hooting and braying carried on the charged silence around the Grimblades. Wood smoke and something else... burning meat, supplemented the rank odour of the beastmen. Somewhere in the Reikwald depths a fire cracked. There were no animals here, no deer, no birds. Beastmen were unnatural creatures, their very presence was repellent to the native denizens of the forest.

Volker was moving again. Karlich could only just make out his route through the undergrowth by the faintest tremble of bracken or a carefully parted branch. Brand matched the scout's step exactly. Karlich saw him pull a knife from his vambrace before he too was lost from sight. He ordered the rest of the front rankers forward.

Masbrecht and Keller closed in on the flanks. Rechts and Lenkmann kept close to their sergeant. Varveiter just about kept pace, sweating profusely under the weight of his armour and his years. Eber stayed close to the old soldier. They were only fifty feet or so away, close enough to taste the corruption emanating from the beasts, when Eber set off a poacher's trap with the haft of his halberd. The trap sprang shut with a loud clang, disturbing a flock of ragged carrion crows. Kindred of the beastmen, the wretched birds cawed loudly as they pierced the forest canopy overhead.

The cavorting stopped abruptly, and the beastmen snarled and brayed at the men in their camp. Once Volker had established the likely spot of the beasts, Karlich had chosen to approach downwind of them. Like most animals, natural or otherwise, beastmen had a strong sense of smell and Karlich wisely didn't want to alert the creatures to the halberdiers' presence by their scent. That mattered little now. The beasts had seen them and bayed for the taste of man-flesh. Snatching up crude spears and bone clubs, the beasts charged straight at the Grimblades.

Volker and Brand were the first to be discovered. The Reikland hunter rose from the foliage to stab a beast in the arm. The creature howled and made to strike back when Volker cut it again, this time across the belly, spilling its rancid guts. They were ungor, the smallest of the beastmen broods, but no less vicious or bloodthirsty. Brand took one in the throat, ramming his dagger in all the way to the hilt before yanking it free and releasing a long spurt of blood. The ungor crumpled with a burbled rasp. He killed a second with a throwing knife, the beast's head snapping back with a jerk as the blade filled its left eye socket.

The element of surprise lasted seconds. After their initial kills, Volker and Brand were on the defensive, ungors chasing them as they ran.

Karlich swore. Abandoning his initial plan, he turned to Rechts and Lenkmann.

'Sound the attack, signal the rest of the regiment!' He drew his sword. 'Grimblades! Forward!'

Rechts beat out a battle rhythm on the small drum lashed over his shoulder for his brother soldiers to follow. Lenkmann found a clear spot and unfurled the banner that had been on his back. Swinging it back and forth, he signalled their position to the other Grimblades.

Cursing his own stupidity, Eber snapped the end of his halberd haft with his foot to free the weapon from the trap, and stormed at the beastmen.

From either flank came the growling of hounds, the ungors' whelp creatures, too muscled and hairy to be mere dogs. Out the corner of his eye, Eber saw Masbrecht and Keller move to intercept the hounds. A tract of heavy scrub and bracken stood between him and his fellow halberdiers.

Volker had given up the fight now. He was simply running for his life. Brand lingered, stopping occasionally to gut an ungor. One that had got ahead of the fleeing halberdiers raised its club to stave in Volker's skull before Brand used the last of his throwing knives to kill it. The hunter flinched as the blade whipped past his face, but nodded a hasty thanks to Brand.

'Move, Grimblades, move!' Karlich raged. He held the line with Lenkmann but could have overtaken Varveiter who was finding the pace hard to match. Eber outstripped the old soldier by many yards, spurred on by guilt.

Rather than negotiate the foliage, Eber just barrelled through it. He met Volker first and kept on going, smacking straight into a chasing ungor with all the force of a bull. Eber used his shoulder like a battering ram. He felt the crunch of bone as he met the beast, the impact throwing it off its feet. Another came at him from the shadows, shrieking like some mutant swine. Eber swept his halberd in a high arc and cut off the ungor's head. He impaled a third with a thrust. He cried as a club smashed against his shoulder guard and dented the metal. Numbness spread up his arm like ice, and he nearly dropped his weapon. To be disarmed was to die, so Eber held on.

A slew of blood arced from the ungor's neck and it fell, Varveiter's halberd following it.

'Eager for the killing, eh, Eber?' Varveiter said between breaths.

Eber nodded as a deeper cry tore from the forest depths. Ungor corpses littered the floor, but more were coming and something else, something larger.

A muscled gor, a much bigger beastman kindred, emerged out of the gloom. A coiled goat's horn hung from a ragged belt attached around its thick waist, and it clutched a rusty cleaver in its massive hand.

Tilting its head back, the gor released a ululating bellow that resonated around the Reikwald, setting a tremor off in Karlich's spine. The remaining ungor gathered to the stronger beast, acknowledging its superiority. More whelp hounds stalked at the periphery of the group.

'Hold, lad,' gasped Varveiter. 'We need to wait for the others and form rank.'

But Eber was already plunging forward to meet the gor's challenge.

'Wait!'

Eber wasn't listening. He was determined to make up for his earlier mistake and if that meant fighting the gor, then so be it.

With the gor easily a foot taller, even the mighty Reiklander appeared puny next to the brawny beastman. The lesser creatures seemed to sense the challenge unfolding between their herd-leader and the man-skin and didn't interfere. Instead, they sped forward on reverse-jointed limbs to fight the others.

'Eber!' Varveiter cried out as the gor loomed over his Reikland brother. But his attention was quickly forced elsewhere as the ungor came at him. He blocked a knife slash with his haft then punched the creature in its snout to daze it. Ignoring the pain in his fist, Varveiter swept his halberd around to cut the goat-like legs from under another creature whilst the first ungor staggered. A thrust to the belly did for that one too.

'Eber!' he cried again, only able to take a few steps before another ungor blocked his path. Its spear thrust was deflected by Varveiter's tasset, but it deadened his leg and he half-collapsed. Seizing its advantage, the beastman dropped its weapon and tried to rip Varveiter's throat out instead. The old soldier turned just in time, putting his armoured forearm into the creature's mouth. He roared when the ungor bit into the leather of his vambrace. Though small, the beast had a jaw like a blacksmith's vice and kept on pressing.

Its foul breath assailed Varveiter, redolent of rotten meat and dung. Just when he thought he'd pass out from the pain, the ungor's eyes widened and it let go.

Brand was revealed behind it, wiping the flat of his dagger on his tunic. His cold, dead eyes regarded Varveiter for a moment before he offered the old soldier a hand up.

'Thank you, son,' he said as he was being hauled to his feet.

Brand gave a curt nod.

'Are you hurt, Siegen?' It was a voice like a blade being drawn from a scabbard, but it held a note of familial concern. Brand was not Varveiter's son but the killer regarded him like a father figure nonetheless, and was the only Grimblade left who used his first name.

'I'm fine. Go help Eber.'

The brutish Reiklander was holding his own against the gor. Trained to use polearms in the Grünburg barracks, Eber made the most of those lessons now and kept the beastman at bay with sharp thrusts from his halberd. But the tactic also served another purpose. The gor was getting more and more frustrated, and increasingly reckless. It stomped and snorted, aiming savage swipes that sliced only air or clanged against Eber's blade. One attack overstretched it, bringing its head forward. Seeing his chance, Eber lashed out and cut off one of its ram-like horns. Howling, the gor backed off a step and the Empire soldier came forwards. Eber jabbed his halberd into the beast's thigh and drew blood. But it wasn't enough to slow the creature, let alone kill it, and the gor came on with renewed fury.

Varveiter looked on as Brand ploughed into the forest after Eber. He could barely move, the pain in his leg was so bad. The bruised flesh pressed against his tasset as it swelled and drove hot pins of agony in the old soldier's thigh. Despite the danger, he bent down to loosen the buckle and strap. A shadow passed across him as Varveiter came back up and was face to face with a snarling ungor. He scrabbled for his halberd, ramming the tip of its haft into the ground like a defensive stake. The charging ungor impaled itself, spit through like a boar, but left Varveiter defenceless as a pair of whelp hounds scrambled through the brush to savage him.

The old soldier licked his lips before balling his fists.

'Come on then, you ugly bastards.'

One of the hounds leapt at him, as the second rounded on Varveiter's blind side to come at his unprotected flank.

He grimaced, but the expected impact didn't come. There was a loud *thunk* of flesh on metal as Sergeant Karlich put his shield between Varveiter and the leaping hound. A yelp came from the second as Keller stuck it with his halberd's point. Masbrecht, also returning from the flanks, staved in the creature's skull with a hammer.

'Sigmar's breath, they do stink!' he spat.

'No worse than Eber,' laughed Keller, a cruel smile splitting his hawkish features.

'Aye, and he'll be worse still dead,' said Karlich. 'Now shut your mouths and follow me.'

The sergeant led them the rest of the way to Eber, forcing back the ungors and what was left of the hounds. More were coming though, summoned by the death cries of their herd and the reek of blood.

'Form rank!' shouted Karlich when Rechts and Lenkmann had joined them.

'The rest of the regiment is just behind us,' Lenkmann reported, planting the banner and drawing his sword.

Rechts beat out the order to form up with his drum. The others fell in dutifully.

When it saw the gathering of men the gor backed away, recognising a threat. Eber was content to let it go. His muscles burned from the effort of fighting it, but he still took up his post in the fighting rank.

'They're regrouping for another charge,' said Varveiter. He'd freed his halberd and levelled it forward at the same angle as the others. Volker too had his familiar polearm, as did Brand, both collected from Rechts who'd strapped the weapons to his back before the engagement.

'Hold this line!' hollered Sergeant Karlich. The beasts outnumbered them, but they were a rabble. The front rankers only needed to keep them back until the rest of the regiment arrived. Already, he could hear soldiers crashing through the undergrowth behind them.

The gor herd-leader roared, snarling and lashing at the ungor trammelling the foliage to close with the man-skins.

'Brace and meet them!' bellowed Karlich. In response, the angle of the halberds lowered again by just a fraction. Each man put his foot behind the base of the haft. Maddened by bloodlust, the ungors and whelp hounds struck the thicket of steel and were scattered. Some were shredded, others impaled. Any that got through were cut down by Karlich's sword or brained by Masbrecht's hammer.

'Thrust!' came the sergeant's next order and each man drove his halberd forward to strike a second wave of ungor. Rechts cried out when a rusty blade pierced his shoulder. Karlich battered the creature senseless with a blow from his shield before it could follow up, then Lenkmann stabbed it in the throat whilst it was prone.

'Stay together.'

At least a dozen more dead and injured ungor littered the ground, but with the gor at their backs the rest dare not falter.

'Taal's mercy, how many more of these swine are there?' asked Volker.

'Come on, come on...' Karlich muttered under his breath. The sound of reinforcements was close, but was it close enough?

The battle was fierce, and Karlich dare not avert his attention from it for even a second. In the end, it was the ungors that gave him his answer. The vigour drained out of them like air from a pig's bladder and they retreated. Even the brutish gor lost its nerve. The scent of so much man-flesh and Empire-forged steel spooked rather than emboldened it. Bringing the coiled horn to its bovine mouth, it blew a long discordant note.

Like cattle fearing the drover's whip, the beasts took flight. Some reverted to all fours, galloping awkwardly alongside the hounds; others jerked with two-legged strides.

Karlich felt the rest of his regiment at his back and found his confidence renewed.

'All Grimblades,' he rallied, 'advance!'

Rechts drummed the pace as Lenkmann raised the banner. The forest was thinning and the beastmen headed to a clearing.

Forty men drove nigh-on seventy beasts, broken by their good order and stolid defence.

About twenty feet from the forest's edge, Karlich called a halt. He could see through the trees and scrub to the broad clearing beyond. Caught up in a fleeing frenzy, the beasts didn't stop until they burst through to the other side.

Captain Leorich Stahler waited for them there with a block of fifty Bögenhafen spear and two lines of twenty handguns from Grünburg.

An explosion erupted in the previously peaceful clearing as all forty handgunners discharged musket and shot. Smoke billowed in a vast cloud, swathing the field and drenching it with the acrid stench of blackpowder. Those beasts that survived the fusillade wandered from the grey smoke pall dazed and confused. A clipped command from Stahler sent the spearmen forward to mop them up. Some of the ungor at the rear of the herd had the sense to turn and flee but were swept up by Karlich's Grimblades in short order.

It was all over in a few bloody minutes and by the end all seventy-six beastman corpses were accounted for. Stahler killed the gor himself, when the two balls of shot embedded in its chest didn't stop it. His sword flashed once with military efficiency and the herd-leader's head was parted from its shoulders.

'No trophies,' warned the captain calmly, as Karlich's halberdiers emerged from the tree line. 'Burn them all, every one.'

Stahler was a tall, stocky man with a thick moustache and a dark beard. His lacquered armour was black and etched with Imperial motifs, amongst them the blazing comet and the rampant griffon. His longsword carried a laurel emblem just above the hilt and the pommel flashed as its embedded ruby caught the sun. A hat and helm sat snug in the crook of his arm, and his black hair was lathered in sweat from where he'd taken the headgear off.

'Well met, Feder,' he said warmly, using Karlich's first name and seizing his hand in an iron grip. 'Any casualties?'

'Mercifully none, though it was close.'

Stahler raised an eyebrow, but the sergeant shook his head.

'Nothing that troubled us unduly, sir.'

'Good. We're making camp in the next clearing. This one will stink to high heaven by the time we're done with the pyres.' Stahler's nose wrinkled as if he could already smell them. 'The Reikwald is our pitch for the night. Come the morrow, we cross the Reikland border into Averland.'

Karlich nodded.

'Shall I have my men help with the building of the pyres, sir?'

Stahler clapped him on the shoulder and leaned in. 'You've done enough for one day, Feder. Head for the clearing and break camp. Your men have earned a rest.'

'Thank you, sir.'

'Rousting's over, Feder,' Stahler continued, staring into the middle distance. 'Prince Wilhelm is on the march and all musterings are to meet up with him on the Steinig Road, four days' march from Averheim.'

Several days ago, word had reached the western provinces of an incursion from the east through Black Fire Pass. Though it was impossible to substantiate any of the reports, the news from roadwardens and outriders that had made it across the Averland and Stirland borders was that a huge greenskin army was on the move, sacking towns and burning villages. The Emperor's response to the threat was, as of yet, unknown, at least to the likes of Stahler and Karlich. By contrast, Prince Wilhelm III of Reikland had raised what regiments he possessed, as well as a good number of citizen militias from his provincial villages and hamlets, and ordered them to march forth in defence of their eastern brothers.

'Any news from the other provinces?' Karlich asked. 'Are we to ally with their forces on the border or at some other strongpoint?'

Stahler laughed. It was a hollow sound, without mirth, and did nothing for Karlich's confidence.

'You know as much as I do. Though you'd think an orc and goblin invasion through Black Fire Pass would get some attention, wouldn't you?'

'Aye. But I'm surprised we're not marching for the pass itself in that case. Couldn't the dwarfs hold them?'

Stahler's gaze narrowed and he turned to Karlich again.

'By all accounts, the dwarfs stepped aside.'

'Why?'

'I don't know,' Stahler admitted darkly. 'We follow orders, Feder, you and I both. As soldiers that's all we can really do. Prince Wilhelm marches, so do we.' He allowed a long pause as if deciding whether or not that made sense to him too, then added, 'Faith in Sigmar.'

'Faith in Sigmar, sir.'

Eber watched from a short distance as Captain Stahler departed. He was overseeing the other regiments in the muster, making sure every single beast was hauled onto the pyres erected by the village militias and then set on fire.

Sergeant Karlich walked past him, but didn't meet Eber's gaze at first.

'You've earned a reprieve from pyre duty,' he said without smiling. 'Volker, we're setting up in the next clearing. Go on ahead and lead us through.'

The Reikland hunter nodded and peeled off into the forest. Nearer to the Reikwald's edge, the dangers within lessened. The Grimblades had driven the beasts some distance in the end, and the next clearing took them even farther from the forest's arboreal depths. A stream could be heard, babbling through the trees. There was a village nearby too, Hobsklein it was called. Some of the militia had come from here. They, like the rest of the village's inhabitants, were grateful to the Empire soldiers for rousting out and destroying the beastmen, and were only too happy for them to share a patch within sight of their stockade walls.

'The rest of you, stay in formation until you're on the other side,' the sergeant continued. 'Then you can break ranks.'

Karlich let them go on alone, turning his back and pulling a stubby pipe from his tunic pocket. One of the village militia came past with a torch and Karlich stopped him so he could stir some embers to life in the cup and light his pipeweed.

When the militiaman was gone, he took a long draw to steady his nerves. It was closer than he'd let on to Stahler. A bloody miracle, in fact, that no man had died in the forest. The bones scattered around the beasts' squalid encampment could quite easily have been theirs.

'You have your orders,' he said to thin air.

Eber shuffled into his sergeant's eye-line.

'Sir...'

Karlich's face was hard at first. They'd been lucky and no thanks to Eber's lack of concentration, but the halberdier had fought well in the end.

'It's all right, Eber. Any of us could have sprung that trap.'

The big Reiklander's expression suggested he thought differently.

Karlich sighed and his face softened. 'Go on, join the others.'

Eber nodded, hurrying to catch the rest and take his place in the front rank.

'SAW THE WAY you faced off against that gor, Eber,' said Rechts from down the line, smiling through his ruddy beard.

'He cut off its bloody horn!' added Volker, alongside him.

Varveiter chuckled but was robbed of his humour by the pain in his leg and grimaced.

Eber felt a little lighter, but he still knew he could have cost them all their lives.

They emerged through to the next clearing – there was only a relatively short tract of sparse forest between it and the last one – and Rechts drummed for them to break ranks. Baggage train camp followers were already pitching tents and lighting fires before night crawled in. The watchtower torches of Hobsklein were visible a few hundred feet distant. Some of the Grimblades shook hands, patted one another's backs or expressed other gestures of camaraderie as they wandered off into smaller groups.

The clearing was a broad expanse, mainly flat ground of soft grass and loamy soil. Had the villagers dared to, so close to the forest, they might have planted seeds in the patch of ground and a very different group of rank and file could've held sway in it.

The Grimblade front rankers stayed together and made for the nearest pitch. Other regimental troops were slowly making their way through in dribs and drabs. Volker would return soon, hopefully with game, but the others were content to wait.

Eber was about to follow when Keller crept up alongside him and leant near his ear.

'Fat oaf,' he snarled. 'Get yourself killed next time and spare us all your idiocy.'

Like a shadow passing over the sun, Keller drifted away, calling and joking out loud to the others.

Eber stopped. An ache was building inside him. He hated Keller, hated him for saying what he'd just said; hated him for making Eber hate himself. He wanted to lash out, to strike Keller and wipe away his cocky smirk. Instead he merely clenched his fists and looked down at his feet.

CHAPTER TWO

CAMPFIRES

Village of Hobsklein, on the Reikland border,
190 miles from Altdorf

EVENING HAD DRAWN in, but the sky above was dark and clear. Stars shimmered in the firmament and the moon was full and bright.

By now, the campfire was burning well and gave off the succulent aroma of cooking guinea fowl. Volker had caught the birds an hour earlier, plucked the feathers and spitted them over the hot flames. Fatty juices dripped from the birds' carcasses, six in all, and made the fire below spit and crackle.

'Smells good,' said Keller, licking his lips.

'Better than trail rations at any rate,' added Rechts, taking another pull on the bottle of Middenland hooch. The drummer was a resourceful alcoholic and had procured the liquor from a peddler he'd met on the road to the Reikland border.

'Nothing wrong with salt-pork and grits,' said Varveiter, stretching out his injured leg and hissing through his teeth as he eased it into position.

'Aye, if you've got a stomach like a warhorse or your tongue is so old and leathery that you're past caring about taste.' Keller laughed, and the others laughed with him. All except for Brand, who kept a yard or two away from the rest. He stayed to the shadows, sharpening his blades on a whetstone. Occasionally, the light caught in his eyes and they flashed with captured fire.

Varveiter grumbled something derogatory about Keller's mother under his breath and went back to massaging the stiffness from his leg.

There were several separate campfires set around the clearing. The sounds of good-natured jostling, tawdry songs and the clatter of knives on plates emanated from them. Smoke from slowly-burning kindling and pipe-weed scented the cloudy air. Tents stood in ranks or half circles, blades and polearms racked outside or leaning against trees. With the destruction of the beastmen, the mood was relaxed. Even the sentries stationed at all the cardinal points of the encampment looked undisturbed. It was a good time, and those came very rarely on campaign.

'By Taal, you're a good hunter, Volker,' said Rechts when he was given his first strip of guinea fowl. He devoured it whole, wiping the juices from his bearded chin and sucking at the heat baking his tongue. 'Why did you end up joining the army as a halberdier and not a huntsman?'

'State troopers' pay is better,' Volker answered simply. 'Even if the company's not,' he added with a wry smile.

Now it was Rechts's turn to laugh out loud, so hard that he jarred the shoulder wound from the ungor's blade. He winced and clutched at the bloodstained bandage.

'I could see to that for you, brother,' offered Masbrecht. As well as something of a Sigmarite puritan, Masbrecht also had some skill as a chirurgeon. His father had done it as his profession, and passed some of his skills onto his son before he died of pox nearly ten years ago. The death of the man he had idolised had hit Masbrecht hard and the youth fell into bad ways for a time until he found religion and the cult of Sigmar.

'It's fine,' snapped Rechts, as the mood abruptly soured, 'and I'm no brother of yours.'

'We're all brothers of Sigmar, Torsten.'

Rechts stood, leaving the rest of his guinea fowl but taking his half-empty bottle. 'Piss off, Masbrecht, and leave your sermonising for someone else. Don't call me that, either. My friends call me Torsten. You're just another soldier I happen to serve with.' He turned, stumbling a little with the grog, and stalked off.

Silence descended for a while before Keller let out a long, high-pitched whistle.

'What crawled up his arse and died?'

Masbrecht paled and kept his mouth shut.

'I heard he was victimised by zealous preachers when he was young,' said Brand, so grim the air seemed to get colder with his voice. 'Executed his family, left him for dead.'

More silence. Brand had as much of a knack for killing the mood as he did for killing in general.

'Ah, don't worry about that miserable whoreson,' said Keller, trying to lighten the atmosphere. 'Come and bless me instead, Masbrecht. Sigmar knows, I need it!'

He laughed again and drew some humour back out of the night.

Volker chuckled, though it felt forced.

'What about you, Eber?' Lenkmann piped up, his opening a little awkward. He was better accustomed to polishing his tunic's buttons or pressing the creases from his hose than conversing with his comrades. 'Why did you join up?'

The big Reiklander had been quiet until then, content to fade into the background. His guilt still felt heavy, like a lead ball in his gut, and he was hoping the night would pass without any further attention. The others were of the same mind, only poor old Lenkmann was about as intuitive as a rock.

'I, er... used to be with a band of travelling carnival folk–'

'A bumbling klown, no doubt,' quipped Keller, keeping his malice hidden from everyone except Eber and, unbeknownst to him, Brand too.

'Strongman,' Eber corrected.

To Keller's annoyance, the others appeared interested in Eber's secret life.

'What did you lift?' asked Volker.

'Ale barrels, anvils, that kind of thing,' said Eber. 'Once, I lifted a cart mule.'

Lenkmann was impressed. 'What, over your head?' He mimed the feat as he imagined it.

'Aye, just so.'

'Sounds likely...' Keller's sarcasm was biting.

'It's true,' said Eber, quietly. Evidently, the carnival was not a place of happy memories for him either.

'I believe him,' said Volker.

Keller sniffed impatiently, shaking his head. 'Aw, why are you even talking to the lout? He almost got us all killed today,' he said, adding under his breath. 'Dumb ox.'

Eber heard him, and it made him angry. 'Don't call me that.'

'What? Dumb or ox?'

'Leave him alone, Krieger,' Volker pleaded. He had been looking forward to a quiet evening of simple pleasures, of good food and reasonable company, when they could leave the horrors of the Reikwald behind them, if just for a night. Everyone else on the patch was getting on, why not them?

Keller turned on the huntsman.

'Why? But for Karlich's quick thinking, the oaf's stupidity could have seen us all dead.'

'Everyone makes mistakes, Keller,' offered Lenkmann, distinctly uncomfortable at the sudden turn.

'Mistakes that'll get us all killed, one day,' Keller replied, focusing back on Eber. 'Should've stayed at the circus, klown.'

Socially awkward as he was, the banner bearer could think of no way to defuse the rising tension. Volker had said his bit. Masbrecht was content to stay out of it, after Rechts's earlier outburst. He looked to Brand for support, but all he got was cold, hollow eyes, narrowed like knife slashes in the campfire gloom. In the end, it was old Varveiter that had the answer.

'He showed more bravery than some.' The old man was staring into the dark, picking at his guinea fowl idly.

Keller bared his teeth.

'What's that supposed to mean?'

'It means that I saw you, more than once, skulking in the shadows on the flank, keeping your head down and your blade unsullied.'

'I'm no coward, Varveiter.' Keller was on his feet. Brand made to move, too, his hand disappearing into the dark folds of his tunic before the old soldier warned him off with a look.

Varveiter fixed the other halberdier with a stony glare. 'Well, let's just say all of your enemies usually have their wounds in the back.'

'I *outmanoeuvre*, you bast–'

Varveiter cut him off.

'No need to sour the evening. And in my day,' he added, 'that kind of... *outmanoeuvring* was called cowardice.'

Keller snorted, backing down a little when he realised the old soldier was actually spoiling for a fight.

Lenkmann caught onto the ploy late: Varveiter was baiting Keller, just like Keller had been baiting Eber. It took the attention off the big Reiklander who didn't have the wit to match him and was already torn up with guilt so as not to be thinking that straight.

'In your day, our troops wore loin cloths and tattoos.'

'That so? I must be ancient, then. Well you should have no trouble besting me, should you?' Varveiter got up with a grunt and a grimace. Unbuckling his breastplate, he let it fall to the ground.

'Now, come on...' Lenkmann began, half an eye on the nearest campfires, but was far, far too late. The wheels had been long in motion by the time the danger presented itself to him.

Varveiter raised a hand. 'It's all right, Lenkmann. Keller wants to show us his skill. I'm happy to let him. Don't tell me you've never brawled with comrades before? Good for camaraderie, or so we *old* campaigners say...' He glanced at Keller, who suddenly looked less sure of himself.

'What are you doing, old man?'

'Readying for a fight,' he answered, rolling up his sleeves and rotating his shoulders. 'Come on, son, don't disappoint me.'

Keller caught another twinge as Varveiter moved. The old soldier betrayed the weakness in his bruised leg and stood awkwardly.

Fair enough, he'd dump the geriatric on his arse and then see what he had to say about 'cowardice'.

'You should've hung up your blade a long time ago, Varveiter. And now I'm going to show you wh–'

Varveiter lunged forward and punched Keller hard in the gut. The mouthy halberdier doubled over and heaved up his guinea fowl.

Backing up, he raised a hand.

'Bastard!' he managed through hard breaths. 'I wasn't ready.'

'I was,' replied Varveiter, and swung again. This time the move was slow, and Keller saw it coming. Dropping his shoulder, he took the punch on his back, most of the force lost through the extra distance the blow had to travel. Varveiter wasn't done, though, and threw in a left hook that Keller had to step back from to avoid.

The old man was breathing in short, sharp gasps. That last combination had taken something out of him. Keller smiled thinly, like a snake sizing up a mouse, and leant in with a quick jab. He struck Varveiter on his upper torso then he rained in another blow that clipped the side of the old man's head. It was like striking iron.

Much to Keller's delight, Varveiter was backing up. A space had cleared around the campfire, Masbrecht, Volker and Lenkmann moving from the 'arena' to avoid getting hit by a stray blow or a falling body. Eber was on the other side of the flames and well out of it. Brand just kept his seat and watched. If Karlich had been there, he'd have put a stop to it. Lenkmann, however, had lost the reins of the situation long ago, before he'd even realised it was brewing.

'Not so bullish, now, eh?' Keller goaded.

Krieger Keller was a small man. Not physically, but mentally and morally. And he *was* a coward, just like Varveiter had said. It was the truth of his remarks that set Keller off in the first place. He didn't like feeling small, and any chance to vent his wrath, his sense of inadequacy on something smaller, frailer, he took it. Eber was an easy target. A big man but a dumb man, without the resolve to fight back. Keller had heard his wailings in the night, about his mother and his abusive father. Eber was easy meat. And now he'd prove his superiority over Varveiter, too.

The old man didn't reply, just kept his guard up and spat out a gobbet of blood from where Keller had caught him in the mouth. He beckoned the younger man on scornfully.

Filled with over-confidence, Keller came forward again. He feinted with a punch to Varveiter's strong side then aimed a kick at his bad leg when the old soldier's guard was down.

Varveiter cried out, and the pain was there on his face for all to see. Lenkmann went to intercede but something in the old soldier's eyes told him not to. It had gone beyond a brawl. This was personal. Even Brand kept his seat, but his gaze never left the two pugilists.

'Aiming for a weak spot...' gasped Varveiter. 'Good tactic...'

'With you, your whole body is a weakness,' Keller snarled and threw an overhand meant to finish the old man off.

Varveiter was ready for it. He ducked beneath the punch, sending an uppercut into Keller's stomach at the end of the move.

'Yours is your pride, lad,' he hissed.

He followed the uppercut with a heavy jab to the man's ribs, not so hard as to break one, but hard enough to bruise and hurt like hell. The air was blasted from Keller's lungs as if he'd been hit with a hammer. The hammer came next.

As Keller bent over again, spewing up his empty guts, Varveiter smashed his elbow against the younger man's back, flooring him. By the end, it was Keller that was gasping for breath, puking bile and crumpled in a heap. Varveiter stood over him, all of his feigned fatigue abruptly gone.

When he leant down to pick up his breastplate, he whispered in Keller's ear.

'Don't let's you and me have this talk again, you little shit, or I will break something next time. Permanently.'

Keller scowled through his agony, having finished dry heaving, and nodded meekly.

'See?' said Varveiter out loud as he yanked Keller to his feet. 'Good for camaraderie.' He slapped the other halberdier hard on his back, a little harder than he really needed to.

Keller smiled thinly. His eyes conveyed all of his shame and impotent rage. They said something else too, a message just for Varveiter.

This isn't over between us.

Varveiter stared back, as stoic as stone. He'd had more than one run in with a fellow soldier in his career, men much tougher than the one before him now. Keller was just a jumped up little snot who needed taking down a peg. He wasn't even slightly worried. Other concerns were on his mind right now.

'I reckon that's enough excitement for me for one night,' the old man said. 'I'll bid you all a fair evening. You too, Krieger,' he added with a final glance in the seething halberdier's direction. Varveiter walked away in the night, heading for one of the tents.

After Volker had bid the old man good night, and Masbrecht had muttered a benediction to Sigmar for him, the familiar silence returned.

Keller decided he couldn't take it and, clutching his stomach and snarling, stomped away in the opposite direction to Varveiter.

'An eventful evening,' Lenkmann began after a minute or so, trying ineptly to leaven the heavy silence.

Volker chewed on his guinea fowl, but set the strip down after a few bites. He'd suddenly lost his appetite. Eber looked as sullen as ever, his brawny arms and legs tucked tight into his body despite the fact it wasn't a cold night. Masbrecht nodded to Lenkmann, just as awkward as the banner bearer, before his eyes dropped and he fumbled at the Sigmarite talisman hung around his neck.

Another silent minute passed before Brand got to his feet and went off without a word. Before he left the fireside, he leant down to put a dagger in Volker's guinea fowl, pausing to look at the hunter with the blade barely an inch away.

'Eat up,' invited Volker. 'No sense in it going to waste.'

Brand took the meat, devoured a strip off the blade, and walked on.

'Just we four then,' Lenkmann said optimistically after a few more seconds.

No one answered him.

THE SMALL STREAM babbled along with the placid night sounds of the forest. With the taint of the beastmen scoured from its boughs, at least the small tract of trees within sight of Hobsklein, the sinister pall that had lingered there had gone. In its place was life; good, wholesome, natural creation.

Varveiter liked listening to the nocturnal movements of the Reikland. It brought a small measure of peace, especially in a land that saw so little. If the coming war was as bad as he suspected it would be, he would likely not experience peace for some time after. He made the most of it and drank in the atmosphere of the night.

He'd come to the stream deliberately, picking out a secluded spot safe from prying eyes. After the fight with Keller, he'd only loosely strapped his breastplate back up. Now, by the water's edge, he shrugged it off his body. Fresh spikes of agony, worse than those he'd felt at the fireside, clawed at him. The injury he'd feigned in front of Keller hadn't been feigned at all, it was the outward strength he'd been lying about.

Next came the leg, and here Varveiter was afraid to even look. Easing himself into the stream, feet first once he'd struggled off his boots, he allowed the cool water to numb his thigh before he rolled up his hose. Varveiter hissed with pain as he did, forced to keep his tongue behind a cage of his own teeth lest he cry out. An ugly, black bruise showed itself as he peeled the garment back. There was some crimson too, where the blood vessels had burst painfully below the surface of his skin. Feeling daggers of fire with every step, Varveiter shuffled a little deeper and bent down as far as he could to splash the bruised leg. It was scant relief, but it was something.

When he was done, he clawed his way back out of the stream – he couldn't remember how – redressed and collapsed on the bank next to his discarded armour.

'Siegen?'

Varveiter was only semi-conscious. He'd slipped into a sort of fugue state, his body's reaction to the pain. Shadowed images of green trees and golden fields of corn filled his mind. Wood smoke carried on the breeze and somewhere a woman was singing.

'Siegen?'

Her voice was like warm fires on a cold day and cooling wind in the summer heat. She lifted him with her siren-like song. The sun was streaming through her auburn hair, and in his vision it blazed with the flames of her passion and spirit.

'Siegen?'

A hand was shaking him, it felt firm but tender. Varveiter opened his eyes and saw Brand looking down on him.

'Sigmar's arse!' he swore, and would have flinched had he been able.

'I brought some meat,' said Brand, offering the last strip of guinea fowl he'd taken from Volker's plate.

'Thank you, lad,' Varveiter said, pushing himself up into a seated position.

'Are you all right, Siegen?' Brand asked when he saw the discomfort in the old soldier's face.

'Fine, lad. You just disturbed a pleasant dream, that's all.'

'I don't dream,' said Brand flatly. The coldness returned to his eyes like hard steel. 'As long as you're all right,' he added, before heading off deeper into the night.

Varveiter watched him go and thought again of the enigma that was Brand. Whenever encamped, he would often wander out into the dark and only return again come morning. No one ever asked him about it. Karlich didn't care enough to bother, and Varveiter thought a man's business was a man's business and the others were too scared.

Still, it did perplex him.

As rested as he could be, Varveiter was pulling on his boots when he got his second visitor of the evening. When he heard the crunch of grass nearby, he thought of Keller at first and went to grab his dirk.

'As bad as that, was it?'

Varveiter realised it was Karlich and he moved his hand away again.

'Sir?'

'Don't play coy with me, you sly goat,' said Karlich, as he stepped into view. 'And don't call me "sir". You'll make me feel as old as you are.'

The burn scar on the left side of the sergeant's face looked livid in the moonlight, and he'd taken off his hat and helm to reveal the shaven scalp beneath it. Karlich still wore his breastplate, though, and had a long dagger strapped to his left leg.

'A lesson was needed, is all,' Varveiter explained, getting to his feet and stretching out the fresh aches.

'Long as that's all it was.' Karlich cracked his knuckles. He wore leather gloves. In all the years under his command, Varveiter could never remember seeing the sergeant without them. 'Keller's a whoreson bastard,' he went on, 'but he's our bastard and I like to keep him on a tight leash. Last thing I need is you stirring the hornet's nest.'

'It won't happen again, si– *Karlich*.'

'Good, now share some of that meat with me. I'm bloody starving.'

'Volker left a place for you by the fire,' Varveiter returned, passing a piece of now cold guinea fowl to his sergeant.

'Needed some time by myself,' said Karlich. His gaze was on the distant village of Hobsklein. The stream ran right up to its stockade walls. As they'd been talking, a Taalite priest had emerged from behind the gates, ushering out a small group of villagers bringing barrels of ale, sacks of grain for the horses and raw vegetables. One youth even dragged a sow by a rope, such was the Hobskleiner's gratitude at ridding their patch of forest of beastmen. They'd obviously waited until all the tents were pitched, the men settled and sentries posted before coming out. They probably wanted to be sure all of the beastmen were dead, too.

'I *feel* old,' Varveiter confessed out of nowhere.

'Eh? What are you talking about? You're a warhorse, Siegen, proud and strong.' Karlich clapped him on the back.

'Am I? I don't feel it. It's like my muscles are ropes that have been stretched too tautly and left to sag. And the bruises linger, and the blood. I can't remember the last time I didn't go through a day without tasting blood in my mouth.'

'You're just tired,' Karlich replied. 'We all are. It was a hard fight in the forest. In any case, I need you to help me keep the rest in line,' he laughed, though it failed to convey much mirth.

Varveiter faced him, a terrible sadness coming over his face.

'If I could no longer soldier, Karlich, I don't know what else I would do.' His voice cracked a little with emotion.

'You've many good years left in you, yet, warhorse,' Karlich said, doing well to hide the lie in his words. 'Go back to camp and get some sleep,' he ordered. 'I'll be along in a while. We march at first light.'

Varveiter nodded, before saluting his sergeant and heading back to camp.

When he was alone, Karlich looked back at the procession of villagers. He'd seen another figure abroad in the night, but moving away from him and towards the village itself. He rode an armoured steed and wore a black, wide-brimmed hat. As he stooped to address the village priest, the figure's coal-dark cloak drooped downwards, revealing a studded hauberk the colour of burnt umber and a brace of pistols cinched at his belt. An icon hung from his neck, too. It was of a silver hammer, the sigil of Sigmar and the holy seal of his templars, the witch hunters.

Karlich's eyes shadowed as he saw him. Rubbing his gloved hands reflexively, he shivered at first, before a hot line of anger came to quash his fear.

CHAPTER THREE

THE EMPEROR'S NEW COURT

Along the River Reik, near the Bögenhafen road,
7 miles from Altdorf

THEY STUCK TO the banks of the Reik, keeping the river in sight at all times and watching the boats, skiffs and trawlers as they plied the waterways in packs. It was a light evening, but the mood was heavy. The prince wore a severe expression, as impenetrable as a mask, and rode his steed intently. The other riders with him, plate-armoured Griffonkorps whose own faces were hidden behind shining war helms, were as cold and impassive as statues. It was not their lot to question or to challenge; they obeyed, protected without pause. It was the job of others to probe the prince's mind.

'We could have taken a river barge, you know,' said Ledner. He rasped when he spoke, an old neck wound covered by a Reikland-red scarf affecting his voice. Riding at the front of the retinue with the prince, Ledner was able to turn and look at his patron directly.

Prince Wilhelm, the third Wilhelm after his father and grandfather, glanced askance at his captain.

'And be caught behind Dieter's gilded barges from Nuln? I think not.'

The captain looked again at the mighty river. Even this late, the Reik was thronged with waterborne traffic, bearing the many trappings and fineries of their glorious Emperor Dieter IV. The 'Golden Emperor' some called him, on account of his gilded palace in the capital at Nuln. Perhaps 'Yellow Emperor' would have have been more apt given the current state of affairs.

'War brews in the east and Black Fire is broken through, and what does he do?' continued Wilhelm. 'He moves his court farther west to Altdorf.' The prince knew he spoke out of turn to discuss his lord Emperor so disparagingly and in open company, but he was exasperated at Dieter's reaction. Lines of barely restrained anger marred his handsome features, a noble bearing born of pure Reikland stock. He wore his gilded breastplate with its lion rampant proudly. The colours of his state, the red and white of the Reikmark, were entwined in his elegant riding tunic and leggings. Even his black, leather boots carried an eagle icon. It represented Myrmidia, patron deity of the art of war and one Reiklanders held in great reverence, second only to their progenitor, Sigmar.

As he rode with greater impatience, his crimson cloak billowed behind him. Ledner found it hard to keep up.

'Altdorf will still be there if we tarry a little, my prince.'

Ledner wore a breastplate, too, but it was unlike those worn by the rest of Wilhelm's charges. He was no Grifonkorps, no warrior-knight. Ostensibly, Ledner's rank was that of captain, but his influence and importance to the prince went much deeper than that.

'It's not Altdorf that concerns me,' returned the prince, casting a weary eye on the vessels ferrying chests, barrels and even servants down the wide, black ribbon of the Reik. 'It's what my cousin is doing to the rest of the Empire.'

Prince Wilhelm spurred his horse to a gallop. Over the next rise, the great city of Altdorf loomed. It had been some time since he'd last entered the capital. At least that's how it felt to him. When news had drifted west that a huge army of greenskins had broken through Black Fire Pass and were invading the Empire, bound for its heartlands, two things happened almost simultaneously: Emperor Dieter moved his court west, away from the battles; and Wilhelm relocated his princely lodgings east to the town of Kemperbad, where he could keep a better eye on Reikland's border. Given all of his letters and petitions had fallen on deaf ears, and his messengers had been ousted back to Kemperbad, Wilhelm had had little choice but to return. It was hardly a chore. Altdorf was a city he loved dearly, warts and all. The only thing that might mar his homecoming was the man who sat upon its palatial throne.

Late into the evening, the smoke from tavern fires and smiths still plumed into the night air, settling over the city in a grubby pall. Towers reached up like clawing fingers, trying to scratch out the moon. Tenements and warehouses, revealed on the higher contoured islands above the wall, squatted on top of one another. In the distance, the shadow of one of the Colleges of Magic could be seen. Eldritch lightning crackled in the clouds around its borders, evidence of the wizards and magisters at work within its clandestine halls. Rising proudly above the squalor of the lower, lesser districts was the University of Altdorf, a seat of learning and enlightenment like no other in the entire Old World. There were other landmarks, too: the recently commissioned Imperial Zoo, the austere and forbidding Temple of Sigmar and the many marvellous bridges fashioned by the School of Engineers at Nuln, spanning the numerous waterways flowing through Altdorf from a confluence of the Talabec and the Reik upon which the city sat. Wilhelm felt its presence as surely as his own thumb or finger.

'First city of the Empire…' he breathed reverently as the shadow cast by a white wall passed over them, 'with a Stirlander sullying your glorious throne.' Reikland was in his blood in more ways than one.

The walls were high, watch lanterns lit, crossbowmen patrolled Altdorf's ramparts and a great gate bearing the icon of a griffon barred passage into the aspect of the city that Wilhelm and his entourage now approached.

'Welcome home, my prince,' uttered Ledner as the gates parted with a cry from one of the watchmen. The Prince of Reikland's banner was upraised for all to see, his knights a formidable talisman of his heritage and identity.

'Aye, let us see what kind of a welcome Dieter has for us.'

Galloping under the great triumphal arch, Wilhelm led the way up the Reikland road, north to the palace where the Emperor had made his court. He didn't slow, not for the peddlers, or the ranks of soldiers marching three abreast – for Dieter had moved troops as well as trappings to the city – not even for the nobles as they entered the Rich Quarter and closed on the palace. Griffonkorps bellowed for the way to be cleared, a preceptor lifting his face mask to shout through his long, curled moustaches. There was no time to waste, no time at all.

THE AUDIENCE CHAMBER was filled with tension. Wilhelm felt it emanating between the Lord Protector of Stirland and the Count of Talabecland in particular. The antipathy of these two closely bordered states was well known. Their enmity stretched back to the Time of Three Emperors, before Magnus the Pious had united the land and the Empire was engaged in a bitter power struggle that led to bloody civil war. Some wounds went deeper than a blade cut or an arrow gouge; they lingered through time and hereditary, passing on to scions and then their sons in a destructive, feuding circle. Neder von Krieglitz of Stirland and Hans Feuerbach of Talabecland epitomised this.

Strange that the Emperor Dieter, also a son of Stirland, did not regard Feuerbach sourly. Perhaps this was the reason why Krieglitz, Dieter's cousin, was similarly disaffected towards his provincial lord and Emperor, though he would never voice it in open company. Such were the vagaries and conundrums of Imperial politics.

By contrast, Markus Todbringer, Count of Middenland, remained stoically silent as he stood in the ostentatiously appointed room. It had once been Wilhelm's audience chamber, but the prince didn't remember the gilding and ornamentation lavished on it. Portraits of the Emperor bedecked the walls of the long hall, and there were additional tapestries, statues and other artistic luxuries on show. He suspected that

Dieter was making himself at home. There were chairs, finely upholstered and opulently decorated, but no one sat. Stately ritual demanded that they wait for their potentate and sit only after he was first seated. The Emperor, though, had kept them standing for longer than was reasonable.

Tempers were beginning to fray.

'Wissenland hides behind his towers and fortifications. What other explanation is there for his absence?' said the Lord Protector of Stirland. Though not an elected official, in the same way as the counts, he watched over Stirland in the Emperor's stead, whose business kept him in the capital and now Altdorf. 'No surprise, really,' he continued. 'It would be just like Pfeifraucher to shut the gate to his province. He has the mountains at his back after all, and need only defend one open border. Not like us at Stirland. We face foes in every direction.'

'You whine like a maiden, Krieglitz,' sneered Feuerbach, the Count of Talabecland. 'Show some stomach like your ancestors.'

Feuerbach referred to Martin von Krieglitz, Neder's grandfather, who had famously slain the undead fiend Mannfred von Carstein and ended the so-called Vampire Wars that had plagued Stirland in particular for generations.

'You speak of stomach, yet it was your antecedents that declared Ottilia Empress despite our own claimant's Imperially sanctioned ascension to the throne. That is the calibre of Talabecland.'

Feuerbach laughed derisorily.

'Over a thousand years passes and still the backward-looking folk of the Stir cannot let old grievances go. No wonder you're all mentally-stunted peasants.'

'We have long memories,' growled Krieglitz. 'And I'll see you on the duelling field for insulting my people.'

'With what? Your pitchfork and hoe?'

Krieglitz went for his runefang, one of the twelve dwarf-forged blades given unto Sigmar and his barbarian chieftains.

'Nobles,' Wilhelm's voice broke in, 'hold your anger for the foe banging on our gates. Old rivalries mean nothing compared to the greenskin horde from the east.' He scowled at both men. 'And act like your station, not like tavern brawlers drunk on ale and bravado.'

Chastened, Krieglitz let it go. He muttered something in Feuerbach's direction but the count either ignored it or didn't hear.

Feuerbach looked about to send a final parting shot to end the debate on when the huge double doors at the back of the audience hall opened and Emperor Dieter stepped through.

The doors were thick oak, inlaid with silver filigree that depicted a griffon rampant on either smoothly carved face. They were lacquered black and reflected the refulgent gleam of the Emperor's own finery. Dieter wore a long velvet gown, traced with gold and studded with amber. A thick cloak sat upon the already voluminous gown, again velvet but of a darker, less verdant green. Upon his brow, he carried a crown. This too was encrusted with jewels. The rings on his fingers *clacked* as he drummed them idly against the hilt of an ornamental dagger at his waist. His boots were deerskin, pale and pristine in the glow of the lamps ensconced on the walls. Dieter walked between the pools of light they cast in a processional fashion, his lackeys and fawners in tow like a clutch of parasitic birds, flapping this way and that, eager for a crumb of the Emperor's attention.

Salted pork and grain had been all Wilhelm needed to sustain him on the long journey from Kemperbad. It was at risk of being shown again to all present, such was his disgust at Dieter's brazen opulence. The toadies were artisans and craftsmen; a tailor examined the fit of his latest creation upon his Imperial master. In relation to its provincial brothers, Stirland was a poor state but one of solid men with strong characters and hardy hearts. Dieter, as its elector count and now Emperor, had risen high and yet, at the same time, fallen far.

The four nobles acknowledged the Emperor immediately as he approached, bowing as one.

'My lord–' Wilhelm began, stepping forward, before Dieter gestured for him to be silent. He held up his finger, glaring through small, widely spaced eyes that glittered with some private amusement. An inane smile rippled across a face fattened by decadence and largesse. His aquiline nose appeared to point upwards as if he was always sneering down at those beneath him. Clean-shaven to the point of pre-adolescent smoothness and with blond curls spilling down from his head to rest upon his shoulders, Dieter had the look of an overweight child about him. In many ways, he was exactly that.

Dieter shushed his obsequious entourage with an angry hiss, and then sent them scurrying away into numerous anterooms flanking the audience hall with a flick of his other wrist. His finger was still upraised as if he were remonstrating a naughty child, and Wilhelm reddened with anger.

As soon as the doors to the anterooms closed and the toadies were all gone, fresh footsteps filled the brief silence that followed their departure. Looking over Dieter's shoulder, Wilhelm saw four burly men, strapped in arms and armour bearing the red and blue state colours of Altdorf. Between them they hefted a large, ornate throne, carved from Hochland cedar, lacquered and furnished with gold. It could not have been an easy burden, and the men sweated and heaved as they carried it across the length of the hall. Dieter never even glanced at his retainers as they set the throne down. They merely bowed and left again as the Emperor took his seat.

After a bout of shuffling to get his corpulent behind in just the right position, Dieter let his hand fall and looked up.

'Be seated,' he beckoned with a mirthless smile.

All four of the nobles sat down.

'My lord,' Wilhelm began again, unable to conceal his frustration. 'War comes from the east and yet our combined armies remain listless and profligate behind city walls, in barrack houses and bastions. We must act against this threat,' he implored.

'I know of no threat, cousin,' said Dieter. His mood was idle as he rubbed the rings on his fingers with his thumb. 'I hear... *talk*. Rumours of a rabble come through Black Fire. A pass, I'd like to note, that is supposedly guarded by the dwarfs, our sworn allies since the time of Sigmar.'

All except Todbringer muttered a small prayer at the mention of the man-god's name.

'It is worse than that, Emperor,' Wilhelm persisted. Despite the fact they were related, the Prince of Reikland observed due deference. 'I've sent numerous letters and petitions to your court here in Altdorf, and all were either ignored or rebutted. You've forced me to ride over three hundred miles from Kemperbad–'

'Well you needn't have come so far, dear Wilhelm,' Dieter interjected, his tone innocent and benevolent. 'I told you a place was set for you here. Simply because I have moved west, does not mean you need move east. Altdorf is large enough to accommodate both its Emperor and its prince.'

'I moved to Kemperbad to better watch the border, but that isn't the point. Why did you ignore my petitions?'

'We are constantly at war, cousin. If the Emperor were to leap up and rally his armies at every drawn sword, every razed village, his armies would be quickly exhausted and his elector counts as dependent as a newborn calf. I saw no need to reply.'

Exasperated, Wilhelm got to his feet. As he did, he noticed one of the statues shift at the side of the room. It was then he realised that the penumbral shadows between the lamps held more than carved effigies. Armoured knights were poised in the half dark too. And was that movement he heard from the balconied gallery above them, and the suggestion of a crossbow cradled by a marksmen's silhouette? Dieter was as paranoid as he was decadent it seemed.

'If you won't acknowledge the severity of the threat facing us, then at least commit some troops,' he said, easing down again. 'The few state levies and Griffonkorps at my disposal aren't enough. Altdorf and Nuln have the largest and best-trained standing armies in the Empire – they must march east to the aid of their beleaguered brothers.'

Dieter looked unimpressed. 'Have you seen this greenskin horde for yourself? Do you know first hand what threat they truly possess, Wilhelm?'

The prince had to bite his tongue for a moment before he replied. 'No, I have not. But there are reports–'

'Not worth the tongues that gabbled them or the muddy parchment on which they are writ.' Dieter flapped his hand in a lazy, dismissive gesture. 'The orcs and goblins will turn to squabbling soon enough and this whole crisis will blow itself out.'

'When? At the point where our villages and towns are ash and ruins? The Empire is burning, my lord! If you don't believe me, then listen to the testimony of your other nobles.' He gestured to Krieglitz, who cleared his throat before speaking.

'It's true, my liege. The river patrols have seen orc and goblin warbands marching uncontested. Averland is under almost perpetual siege, Wissenland cannot be reached and has shut all lines of communication behind border walls and watchtowers, and more greenskins pass through my borders daily. Only Sylvania is untouched, but then no sane creature would ever wander there without good reason,' he added gravely.

'Refugees dog the edges of Talabecland,' Feuerbach said. 'I have no wish to see Stir folk flooding my hinterlands, poaching and begging. I have enough peasants.' He glanced daggers in Krieglitz's direction. The Lord Protector of Stirland clenched his fists and looked about to draw his weapon again. Were it not for the crossbowmen above, he might have.

Instead he stood.

'My lord,' he said to the Emperor. 'I apologise, but there is urgent business that requires my attention in Stirland. It cannot wait and I beg your leave.' A hot vein of fury laced Krieglitz's forehead, directed at the slightly smirking Feuerbach.

Dieter waved a hand impassively, acceding to the lord protector's request.

'I'm sorry, Wilhelm,' said Krieglitz in an angry whisper as he turned to leave the chamber, 'but there can be no alliance with Talabecland. None at all.'

Krieglitz left and Wilhelm sighed in his wake. His case was growing thinner with each passing moment. Even if he could convince Dieter to act, there was nothing to say his provincial brothers would take up arms together. Right now it seemed just as likely they would kill one another before marching under the same standard. In spite of it, he went on.

'So far, the greenskins are at large in most of the east and north-east provinces,' he said. 'If we unite our armies now and march to the orcs, they will get no further westward. They cannot simply go unchallenged. I beseech you, Emperor, unleash your armies and ally this nation under a banner of war.'

Dieter appeared not to notice the prince's urgency and instead gazed around the room. 'Do you like what I've done with your audience chamber, cousin? I thought it too stark and utilitarian before, not fit for royal habitation.'

Wilhelm shook his head incredulously. Even Todbringer exchanged a curious glance with Feuerbach.

'What possible bearing does my opinion of your decorations have on the war that will soon be at our borders?'

The mood changed abruptly. Dieter exchanged languor for anger. 'It will endure,' he said darkly. 'When the war is done and all the dead are accounted for, all of this,' he spread his arms to encompass the room, 'will still be here. *I* will still be here. There are deeper matters of state for me to consider. This greenskin rabble does not warrant Imperial attention. What's more, I tire of this conversation.' He glared at Wilhelm intently. 'Your request for troops is denied. The provinces must look to their own borders. I cannot rescue them at every calamity.' He turned and showed his cheek. 'Now go.'

Exhaling his anger, Wilhelm rose without another word. His jaw was gritted so hard he thought he might snap a tooth. Feuerbach was the next to leave, bowing swiftly and getting on his way. Perhaps he hoped to catch Krieglitz and continue their feud on the duelling field after all. Todbringer followed, utterly unmoved and unconcerned.

As Wilhelm turned to go, he was stopped by a final few words from his Emperor.

'This matter is concluded,' he said. 'Don't return to Altdorf, *Prince* Wilhelm. Her gates will be barred to you.'

'As you wish,' Wilhelm said through clenched teeth. Just as he was passing back through the entrance way, he heard the double doors at the back of the audience hall open again. Out of the corner of his eye he saw three men enter, nobles by the look of their lavish attire. There were enough gemstones and gilding upon their vestments alone to buy a small town, lock, stock and barrel.

'My lords...' He heard Dieter declare with false bonhomie, before the door was closed and the rest of the meeting left a mystery.

He met Todbringer on the other side, talking quietly with one of his aides.

'Markus...'

The Count of Middenland turned at the sound of Wilhelm's voice. They shook hands, favouring the warrior's grip.

'I had hoped for more support from you,' said Wilhelm honestly.

Todbringer released his grasp.

'I've already committed all the troops I can afford to your army, Wilhelm,' he answered. His voice was cold and gravelly, as if it had been hewn from the rocky steppes of the Fauschlag itself. 'Averland and those other peasant provinces are far from Middenland. When the City of the White Wolf is in danger, then I'll act and bring the fury of Ulric down on the greenskins' heads.'

'You sound no better than Feuerbach, full of provincial rivalry and bad blood,' Wilhelm accused.

'Had the Emperor agreed to go to war, I would have backed you brother, but the fact is we *are* divided and noble as your spirit is, you cannot bring us together. If the greenskins rampage through the east and north-west, so be it. By the time they reach Middenland, my army will be ready and they will be worn down from fighting the other states.'

'So you'll wait in Middenheim until the enemy is at your gates and crush them after they've spent their wrath killing your Imperial kin.' Wilhelm shook his head in disappointment. 'I had thought better of you, Markus.'

'I'm a pragmatist, just like you, Wilhelm,' said Todbringer, starting to turn away. 'You do what you feel you must to protect the Reikland, it is no different for me and Middenland.'

'I assume your troops will be feeding your generals regular reports of the greenskins' martial strength and advance.'

'You know they will.'

With that, Markus Todbringer showed his back and walked away with his aide in tow. 'Good luck, Wilhelm,' he called.

Wilhelm sagged, feeling the weight of his armour and his runefang as never before. He couldn't let the Empire burn, nor his brothers struggle. The campaign would go ahead as planned.

His thoughts were interrupted by Ledner, the captain approaching silently despite his armour and other trappings.

'We must join our forces, Ledner. Victory can come no other way,' said Wilhelm without looking at him. 'But it cannot work like this.'

'Then what must be done?' asked Ledner in his rasping voice.

Wilhelm looked around. There were Altdorf soldiers and Dieter's lackeys everywhere.

'Walk with me.'

After passing through a number of corridors that led them back out of the palace and into the wide esplanade of a courtyard, Wilhelm spoke again.

'Dieter was meeting with more nobles after we left,' he said. 'Marienburgers, I think. He's up to something. The rest of the Empire is slowly being crippled by the greenskins, yet funds are coming into Altdorf from somewhere to gild his rooms and furnishings.'

'I saw no less than five mercenary companies pass through the palace gate whilst you were gone,' offered

Ledner in a shadowy tone. 'High price too, by the looks of them. No rabble or criminal sell-swords, they were professional soldiers. Some from Tilea, and with Marienburgers in their ranks to boot.'

'What is he planning?' Wilhelm asked as they reached the stable yard and their horses. Word had reached the Griffonkorps that their prince was ready to depart and they were already mounted and vigilant.

'I don't yet know, my lord,' admitted Ledner, helping Wilhelm into his saddle.

'Find out for me. Do whatever is necessary.'

Ledner nodded slowly. 'As you wish, my prince.'

CHAPTER FOUR

FIRST BLOODING

Captain Stahler's encampment, Reikland border,
190 miles from Altdorf

RECHTS WOKE TO a murderous hangover. After leaving the campfire, he'd found two more bottles of Middenland hooch in his belongings and drunk them both. Masbrecht's presence, his predilection towards religion, had stirred up some uncomfortable memories for him. Crackling thatch, plaintive screams and the stench of burning flesh had come to him in his drunken dreams. His tunic and hose were sodden, and not just from alcohol sweats.

'Walk it off, Rechts,' growled a deep voice.

The Grimblades' drummer looked up. Through bleared vision he saw Karlich, sitting on the hewn stump of a tree, pipe in hand. The sergeant looked as grey and ragged as he felt.

'Yes, sir,' Rechts replied, surprised to find his voice so hoarse, adding, 'Karlich?'

Blowing a long plume of smoke, the sergeant regarded him.

'Have you even slept, sir?'

'Worry about yourself, soldier. Walk it off. Go on.'

Rechts did as ordered, aiming himself in the vague direction of cooking smells emanating from the camp. He suspected Volker was up already and preparing breakfast before they marched. Dawn was still a couple of hours off, or just a little less. Rechts would eat and sober up as much as he could.

Karlich watched him go, taking a long draw from his pipe to still his nerves. He'd watched the witch hunter until he'd finished talking with the priest and entered the village through its stockade wall. After that, he'd found the tree stump, taken a seat and waited the night out. He'd seen daemons in the darkness, heard them whispering to him on the breeze as the boughs of the Reikwald shifted. They were not real, of course, just apparitions from his past, coming back to taunt him, as they always did, when the world was still and peace within his grasp.

No peace for you, Feder. Peace must be earned and you have yet to pay its price.

He waited there for another hour, until the camp followers came to pack up tents and clear the pitch for the baggage trains. Stiff from staying in one place for too long, Karlich stretched his unyielding bones and rubbed his legs to get the circulation going again. Wiping the tiredness from his eyes and running a hand through his mousy hair, he started walking to the Grimblades' pitch.

On the way, he saw the encampment was busier than before. Several regiments had joined them in the night from the north. Their banners could be seen hanging low, stirred by the faint pre-dawn breeze. Karlich recognised the red and black of Carroburg, their famed greatswords no less, and the deep blue of Middenland. He heard the latter northerners before he saw them, boasting and pushing their weight around.

'Swordsmen...' he said beneath his breath, noticing their swagger and arrogant nonchalance as they barracked a group of militia huntsmen for some cooked pheasant.

'You'd be doing a service for the Empire, lad,' a brawny-looking Middenlander was saying to a huntsman with downy hair instead of thick stubble around his chin. The boy must have been all of sixteen and was obviously terrified of the bearded northerner. To the youth's credit, he was steadfast.

'Get your own meat,' said another boy brave enough to speak up. 'This is ours, we caught it.'

'Ask yourself one question,' invited a different Middenlander, a grey-haired veteran with a bare chin and long moustaches. He was the regiment's sergeant. 'When we meet the orc on the road to Averheim, who will be doing most of the fighting?'

The youth shook his head and pulled the meat close to his chest as a third Middenlander, blond-bearded with a shaven scalp, spoke up.

'Hand it over, boy,' he warned in a deep voice. When the youth protested still, blond-beard cuffed him hard around the ear and took the meat anyway.

'Now we'll take all of it,' declared the grey-haired sergeant in a low voice.

'Stay seated,' ordered the brawny Middenlander as one of the huntsmen made to stand. Four more northerners stomped over their camp, taking the cooked pheasant, together with what the huntsmen had flensed onto their clay plates, with them. One raised his voice in anger, pulling a dirk halfway from its sheath only to stop when he felt the touch of cold, Middenland steel at his neck.

'Don't make me blood you, peasant,' said blond-beard.

Karlich was almost to the camp and about to intervene when someone else beat him to the punch.

'Give it back,' said Volker. He had Rechts and Eber with him.

'It's only vittels for the Empire's *fighting* men,' explained grey-hair coolly. Karlich saw the Middenlander's hand had strayed to his pommel. 'What need have scouts and peasants for food?' he added. 'Let them eat when battle's begun.'

'Don't make me ask you again.' Volker patted the dirk at his belt.

Grey-hair laughed. 'What are you going to do with that? Cut my thumb?'

'No, your throat,' hissed a voice in his ear.

'Oh sh–' Karlich began, hurrying over. Brand had crept up on the Middenland sergeant. His serrated dagger was pressed against the northerner's neck.

'Grimblades!' yelled Karlich. 'Men of the Reik, stand down.'

The Middenlanders had drawn swords as soon as they'd seen the blade at their sergeant's throat. Some were shouting. Blond-beard merely glared at Brand, his eyes conveying murderous intent. More were coming, too: Grimblades and Middenlanders. A few more minutes and a regiment against regiment brawl would be in prospect. Stahler would hang those responsible if he found out.

Only the Carroburgers looked unmoved by the whole affair, sitting just a few feet away in their own private encampment, supping pipes and talking quietly over cups of steaming broth. They could have interceded at any time, and likely broken up the impending brawl before it had escalated – none with any sense would challenge a soldier of the greatswords – but they chose to keep to their own.

'Brand!' Karlich bawled. 'Put up your blade or face charges.' The threat of charges was moot. Karlich knew that Brand cared little about facing military discipline, but the sergeant hoped he respected him enough to do as he'd told him.

Reluctantly, Brand edged his blade away from grey-hair's throat and backed off a step with hands raised.

'And the rest of you,' Karlich added. 'Back to your pitch. Get your arses ready to march. I want you all armoured with halberds by the time I get there.'

Volker looked reluctant to go. Brand merely waited impassively for the rest, watching blond-beard. He'd do whatever his brother halberdiers did.

'Do it!'

Volker acceded, and they sloped off, casting dark looks at the Middenlanders as they went.

Freed from Brand's blade, the grey-haired northerner walked up to Karlich, still rubbing his throat at an imagined wound.

'If he'd meant to cut you, he would have,' the Reiklander told him.

The Middenlander smiled, and left it alone. 'Well met,' he said, offering his hand. 'Vankar Sturnbled.'

Karlich declined his handshake.

'Feder Karlich,' he answered curtly. 'Do you mind telling me what you and your men were doing, sergeant?'

Sturnbled let his hand fall. His comradely mood went with it.

'Just sport, sergeant, is all it was. Surely, as a fellow warrior, you can appreciate that. Or do they not have sport in Reikland?'

'Aye, we have sport, and we have bastards like you and your men too, so I shan't judge your entire state on the example you've set,' Karlich replied. 'Give the huntsmen back their meat. Take a strip each to save face, but leave the rest.'

Sturnbled's face darkened and he lowered his voice so only Karlich could hear him.

'We've never met before, Reiklander, and I'm a forgiving man, so I'll consider this a mistake,' he said. 'But address me or my men like this again and you'll see just how inhospitable the north can be to soft southerners like yourself.'

Karlich kept his silence and looked Sturnbled in the eye. With his men gone, he was surrounded by Middenlanders.

Sturnbled held his gaze for a few moments more, and when it became obvious that Karlich wasn't about to look away, turned to his men.

'Steel Swords! One strip each and back to camp,' he snarled. 'Give 'em back the rest.'

Blond-beard's face was sour enough to scorch steel, as the other swordsmen sheathed blades and went back towards their camp amidst disgruntled mutterings.

'You too, Torveld.'

The stern-faced Middenlander put away his sword and stalked off.

'He doesn't like backing down,' explained Sturnbled as he turned to Karlich again. 'None of us do.'

Karlich was still deciding if it was meant as a promise or a threat, when Sturnbled took his leave.

One of the huntsmen nodded curt thanks in the Reikland sergeant's direction, which he reciprocated.

Bad enough that there were orcs abroad, now the Grimblades faced an enemy within as well. As he went on his way, Karlich wondered if Rechts had any more hooch. He needed a strong drink right about now.

As he passed the greatswords on his way to the encampment, Karlich caught the eye of their leader.

'Why didn't you stop it?' he asked. 'None of them would dare challenge a greatsworder. You could've ended it before it had begun. Blood could have been shed and men lost their lives to a fellow soldier's blade or the noose.'

The greatsworder straightened. In his black plate-mail he looked massive and imposing. His shaven head was grey with stubble and his silver moustaches immaculate. A leather eye patch gave him a grizzled appearance that suggested he was a campaign veteran. 'Not our fight,' he answered simply.

Karlich scowled, continuing on his way.

'Bloody Carroburgers...' he muttered.

SMOKE MARRED THE Averland horizon, too thick and black to be cook fires. Somewhere up ahead, over the grassy rise, a village was burning.

Stahler's army had crossed the border into Averland at dawn, just as the captain had predicted. The camp had broken up, all tents and trappings secured on the modest baggage train and the troops, except the militia levies, organised into marching order by their sergeants.

A small stone bridge over a stream had conveyed them into the province, a wide and open plain known for its horses. Much of Averland was flat with little undulation. It made for perfect equine breeding terrain. So far, they had seen no horses save for a forlorn pair of dead horses, rotting and alive with flies, across the width of the Aver. The mighty river, almost as thick as the Reik and just as impressive, barred the way into Averland proper. Most of the byways and ferry crossings were burned or abandoned. Some supposed the Averlanders had done it after fleeing their borders to prevent pursuit or to stop enemies from crossing the river on the Stirland side. For Stahler and his men, it made life difficult. The few fords and crossings they had encountered were unsuitable for the baggage train, so the order had gone down the line to follow the river until a more substantial bridge could be found.

It wasn't only dead horses that they'd passed on the other side. Trains of refugees spilling from undefended villages trudged vacantly along the river's course, heading for the border, clutching their meagre possessions. One little girl, her face blackened by smoke, clung to a wooden toy. It was hard to tell what it was supposed to be, so bad was the fire damage. The Middenlanders had ignored them, treating the miserable wretches with the same disdain as the grass under their feet or the hot sun on the backs of their necks.

Masbrecht and Lenkmann had wanted to go and help the Averlanders, but Karlich had forbidden it. He did allow Rechts to break ranks and holler directions to the border at them. The drummer had an excellent singing voice and could project loudly. Even still, the refugees looked not to notice his words and trudged on indifferently.

The soldiers saw other Averlanders huddled around roadside shrines. A priestess of Shallya tended to one ragged mob, leading them in a prayer for succour from her goddess. So far, it appeared that Shallya's mercy was absent from these lands. The devastation was a shock to all. No one in the army, even Stahler, had suspected the greenskins had advanced this far into the Empire, and so quickly. It showed a determination and purpose the beasts were not known for. It was reasoned to be a vanguard, for they would have seen the greenskins had they been it a full army.

A short while after this the Reikwald huntsmen had spotted the smoke. Another mile and they could all see it, heavy and dark like a storm cloud but promising death instead of rain.

'So, I heard you had a run in with the northerners,' Varveiter said quietly to Brand. The old soldier had been sleeping when the ruckus had broken out, but Lenkmann had told him everything that happened. 'That you put a blade to one of their necks.'

'Sergeant,' Brand replied without emotion. 'I put a blade to their sergeant's neck.'

'Ah yes, their sergeant…'

Brand gave Varveiter a side glance, expecting to be chastised.

'Sorry I missed it,' the old soldier admitted with a chuckle.

Brand allowed himself a mouth twitch that for him approximated a smile, before his sergeant's voice interrupted.

'Can you smell that?' Karlich asked Lenkmann.

The banner bearer marched doggedly at the head of the group, he and Rechts on either side of their sergeant in a rank of three. He sniffed loudly.

'Whatever it is, it reeks like old boots left out in the sun,' offered Rechts as he too detected the stench. Lenkmann nodded as he wrinkled his nose. It was coming from up ahead, from the same direction as the smoke. As far as the Grimblades knew, it *was* the smoke.

'Are you saying it's worse than Eber's feet?' chimed Volker, from two ranks behind.

Karlich cast a look over his shoulder. 'Or your breath.'

The smile vanished off Volker's face and he was silent. Eber jabbed him playfully in the ribs as he marched alongside him, which drew harsh mutterings from the scout. Unusually for him, Keller stayed quiet. He was in the second rank with Varveiter and Brand. That left Masbrecht in the third rank next to Volker, and the other Grimblades behind them, marching in time to Rechts's drumming.

The halberdiers were third in the line of march. Ahead of them were the handgunners from Grünburg. The Middenlanders – the Steel Swords – took the lead with Captain Stahler. Behind the Grimblades marched fifty Bögenhafen spearmen, their spear tips pointed towards the smoke-stained sky. The greatsworders kept the rearguard, arguably the most dangerous part of the column. Karlich had learned their champion's name was Reiter von Rauken and his men the so-called 'Carroburg Few'. It was an apt way to describe them; aside from the militia levies that ranged either side of the column or with the dawdling baggage train as bodyguards, the Carroburgers were the smallest regiment in the army at only eighteen heads. It didn't make them any less fearsome, or Karlich like them any more or less than he already did. Rauken and his men could have stopped the fight that was brewing between his men and the other northerners, but they didn't. That was a black mark in the Reiklander's book, and he didn't strike them out easily.

'It doesn't smell like any meat I've ever tasted,' said Eber. The stench was really noisome now, and infected the breeze like a miasma. The Grimblades were just cresting the grassy rise after the handgunners. Karlich noticed that some of the Grünburg men had stopped to gag. He heard another retch up his trail rations shortly afterwards.

'That's because it's not any meat a man would ever feed himself with...' Varveiter's expression was grave as he came over the hill and saw what had upset the Grünburgers.

Eight wooden stakes lined the road ahead, fashioned from charred timbers. At first it was hard to tell just what was fastened to each because it moved in the sunlight.

'Carrion,' uttered Brand, as if that explained everything. The marching column had ground to a halt and several of the rear rankers, including the Bögenhafen spearmen, had started to complain about the hold up.

'Quiet your men!' Karlich snapped to the Bögenhafen sergeant, calling down the line. Something in the other Reiklander's eyes told the leader of the spearmen that he should do as asked.

Feathers. It was feathers that were moving on the wooden stakes, crows mainly and the odd raven. Carrion birds, just as Brand had said.

When Lenkmann realised what they concealed, he retched too and only just held on to his breakfast. In the valley below the rise, Captain Stahler stepped out from the Middenlanders and fired his pistol into the air.

The birds scattered, a living carpet of darkness sent fleeing by the report of blackpowder, to reveal the corpses of eight roadwardens. The men were obviously dead and horrifically picked at by the carrion crows. Every one had red-rimed sockets where their eyes should be. The eyes were always the first to go: easy meat, full of nourishment and quick to reach for snapping beaks. The dark cavities that remained seemed to go on forever as if the manner of such a death had condemned these poor men to eternal torture in limbo. A wooden crossbar bisected the upright stake, and the roadwardens' arms had been hung over them to look like gruesome scarecrows. The irony of their appearance was not lost on Karlich. If anything, the corpses had enticed the hungry birds.

Thick, crude iron spikes had been hammered into the men's torsos, some even in the groin; the wrists and ankles too. Their skin was flayed in places, their bodies opened up by a ragged blade just below the stomach so that their entrails spilled out like so much offal. Karlich hoped that this last torture had been done after death, and heard Masbrecht mutter a prayer to Sigmar at the sight of such degradation.

'Bring axes!' A weary-looking Captain Stahler called from the base of the valley. 'Cut them down… cut them all down.'

Militiamen came with axes, and together with volunteers from both the Reikland and Middenland regiments, the dead roadwardens were cut down. Baggage train trenchers and sappers dug shallow graves alongside the Aver, just deep enough to keep casual predators away, and the men were laid to rest. Masbrecht said a few words over the corpses, as the army possessed no priest. Rechts was absent from the short ceremony.

After that, the Empire army carried on their way. On the flat Averland plain the village was still visible, despite the smoke wreathing it like a funeral veil. The same stench that had emanated off the poor roadwardens was coming from there too.

THE VILLAGE'S NAME was Blösstadt. At least that's what the fire-blackened sign lying before the broken gate and shattered stockade wall said. Furriers, smiths, farmers and muleskinners had all lived here once, venturing out to ply their trades and wares on market days in the nearby towns. No anvil sound rang upon a breeze, foetid and rank with decay; no horses whinnied, nor did their hooves clack against the cobbled village square as they were led to market; no voices came at all as the Grimblades passed through the gate and into a scene of utter destruction.

It was as quiet as his father's mortuary, or so Masbrecht thought, levelling his halberd warily at every shadow. The quietude was unsettling, almost unnatural, and he was glad he wasn't alone. Eber and Volker had joined him as he walked towards the village square, a gravel road to guide them. A strange drone pricked at his left ear and he waggled a finger in it experimentally to see if he could shift it. Then he saw the first of the bodies and realised the drone came from the flies buzzing around it, feeding off death.

'Parasites!' he raged, rushing over to the bloodied body of a farmhand and trying to shoo the flies away.

Volker gripped Masbrecht's arm firmly before he got too far.

'Keep it quiet,' he hissed. 'No telling what we'll find here and I'd rather find it before it finds me. Understand?'

Masbrecht nodded, and Volker let him go. The scout patted his arm where he'd seized it. 'Sorry, Pruder,' he said, calling the other soldier by the name his mother had given him. 'Just be mindful.'

After that they continued their slow advance into the village, the flies returned to their putrid feast.

On the other side of the village, losing sight of Volker's group each time they passed one of the large stable yards that Blösstadt had used for its horses, Varveiter led Brand and Rechts along the inner side of the stockade wall. They too found bodies, human and mutilated cattle. So far, they had also seen no sign of life.

'Quiet, but not peaceful,' muttered Rechts. He had his drum slung to one side and a drawn short sword in his fist.

'Aye,' hissed Varveiter in reply. The old soldier had seen villages ravaged before, by bandits, beastmen and orcs as well, but this looked different somehow. 'It's the stillness of the dead, a feeling the living, at least the right-minded of them, can't abide.'

He let Brand move ahead. The other halberdier was silent too. He knew the feeling Varveiter was talking about, he'd known it many times, and here in Blösstadt it put him on edge.

Karlich was approaching the lookout post, a small hill near the middle of the village. There were the remains of a watchtower at the crest of the rise. The corpse of a milkmaid hung slackly over its damaged palisades, doubtless seeking refuge when the greenskins came or trying to bring a warning to her kith and kin. She'd probably known it was a lost cause, but she'd done it anyway. Karlich wondered if she was pretty under all that blood and matted hair.

The watchtower was unsafe to climb, but the hill itself offered a reasonable vantage point from which to view the rest of Blösstadt. The huntsmen Captain Stahler had sent in ahead, while he remained outside the village with the rest of the army, had reached the inn and hovels at the village's southern end. They moved through the narrow lanes with their bows held low but nocked and ready. Nearby there were several hay barns, locked and shuttered. Farther still, Karlich made out a small mill, a waterwheel just dipping into a shallow stream that bisected Blösstadt into two uneven portions. The Grimblades took the larger east section, whilst the smaller regiment of Middenlander Steel Swords took the west.

Karlich caught Sturnbled's eye as he led one patrol. The northerner returned his gaze without expression and then looked away. The Reiklander was glad that the stream kept the two regiments apart. The bad feeling between them had surfaced quickly but would be slow to submerge again, if at all. Where the stream broke the village in two, the Reikland and Middenland patrols did overlap, however.

Somewhere in the distance a dog was yelping. In the abject silence, its presence startled Volker before he realised what it was. He followed the noise to an outdoor privy, the handle tied shut to the doorframe with a length of fraying rope. The poor mutt's wailing awoke something in Volker and he made for the privy at once, crossing the stream and wetting his boots to do so.

'Volker, where are you going?' asked Masbrecht. 'What happened to keeping quiet?'

'A creature is in distress, maybe hurt,' Volker replied, not looking back but forging on instead, 'and I intend to rescue it *quietly*.'

Masbrecht turned to Eber for support, but the big Reiklander merely shrugged and went after Volker.

A few feet from the privy and the blond-bearded Torveld came into view, together with another Middenlander called Wode and Sergeant Sturnbled just behind them.

'What have we here…' said Torveld, slashing open the privy with his dagger. The door flew open almost at once as the burly Middenlander was pitched off his feet by a sudden rush of fur and fangs. The dog was a brutish and well-muscled mastiff. It had black fur and a tan leather eye patch over its right eye with a single stud in lieu of an iris. The beast growled and took a nip at Torveld but did very little damage, before bounding off the Middenlander and growling a warning at the strange-smelling men in its village.

'Little bastard…' snarled Torveld, his pride more wounded than his skin. He bundled to his feet, retrieving the dagger he'd dropped when the mastiff had sprung out at him. 'I'll gut you!'

'Leave the dog alone,' warned Volker calmly. 'It's just scared.' He approached the mastiff, which was now shivering with anger and fear, and when he was only a few feet away, crouched down to his knees.

The crack of a pistol's flintlock arrested his attention from the dog. Sturnbled had drawn and was levelling the weapon at the mastiff.

'It's rabid,' declared the Middenlander sergeant, his arm arrow-straight as he aimed down a small, round sighter at the end of his pistol's barrel. Froth was spilling from the mastiff's jaws, and ran off its chin to pool on the ground.

'The poor beast has dry-mouth, it's not rabid, you idiot,' replied Volker. Ignoring Sturnbled, he cupped his hands to draw water from the stream and offered it to the mastiff. Wary at first with the rest of the soldiers looking on, the beast padded up to Volker, sniffed at the air around him and then started lapping at the stream water. It was thirsty and went back several more times as Volker fetched more. By the third time, the Reikland hunter was patting the mastiff's forehead and stroking its muzzle. After he'd smoothed down its flanks and given it a strip of salted pork from his trail rations, Volker stood up.

'See. Not rabid, just hungry and thirsty. As you would be if you'd been locked up in there for days.'

'More like hours,' snarled Torveld, gesturing towards the nearby corpse of a blacksmith. Volker wondered briefly if it had been the man's dog. 'The blood here is still fresh.'

'How fresh?' asked Masbrecht, a note of concern in his voice.

Torveld rounded on him. 'Like I said, Reikland sop, a few hours.'

Masbrecht still pressed. 'How fresh *exactly*?'

A foul stink pervaded the air suddenly like corpse gas escaping from the recently dead.

'Draw your swords...' Sturnbled told his men, then looked directly at Wode. 'Find Hallar, have him signal the others.'

'What's happening?' asked Eber, scanning the middle distance.

'We didn't meet the greenskins on the road...' answered Volker, the mastiff at heel beside him but growling.

'And? So what? I thought that was a good thing.'

'We didn't meet them on the road because they are still here. Look!'

Now Eber saw them, two orcs attempting to creep up on them, using a narrow tethering pole to hide behind despite their obvious bulk. It was ludicrous, but then they *were* greenskins. They weren't alone.

A garbled scream came from up ahead. It was one of the huntsmen.

VARVEITER HAD LOST Brand when he'd disappeared into the ruined shack. A few minutes earlier, they'd heard something coming from the ramshackle abode a few feet ahead of them, one of a small clutch of three arranged in a half circle. The laconic Reiklander had glanced at Varveiter, signalling his intent to investigate, before jogging ahead and then into the shack.

Rechts had wanted to go after him, but Varveiter had made him stall.

'Let him check it first,' the old soldier had told him.

Rechts looked nonplussed.

'He's quieter than you or me,' Varveiter explained. 'If there's danger he'll find it, and if he can't kill it he'll come running.'

They were both standing at the threshold to the shack. The door was off its hinges with more than one axe hole in the wood. Less a door and more a shattered window now.

'Easy...' whispered Varveiter, using his polearm to ease the door remnants open a fraction. Cold, harsh light spilled in from the outside reluctantly as if afraid to enter. Bare wood and bloodstains were revealed. Varveiter looked back at Rechts. The drummer's eyes were wide and his knuckles white where he gripped his short sword too tightly. His attention back on the door, Varveiter blew out a calming breath and took a step inside.

Slowly scanning the shadows, he found Brand crouched motionless in the corner of the shack's single room. A small pottery cauldron was upturned in the centre; spilled broth washed the floor like vomit, mingling with the blood. There were two beds, the thin sheets and sacking mattress dark with vital stains. Bodies lay unmoving in both. Varveiter counted five in total but couldn't tell if they were male or female because of the darkness and the blood. Another body was strewn on the floor, a cleaver blade still wedged in its back. From the build, it looked like a man. A woodcutting axe lay a few inches from his grasping fingers. He too was dead. The woman mewling quietly before Brand was not.

Varveiter went to his fellow Grimblade whilst Rechts watched the door nervously. His hands were shaking a little, and not just from delirium tremens.

'Merciful Sigmar...' Varveiter breathed as he took a knee beside Brand. He grimaced from the pain in his thigh but took care not to let it show.

Brand was holding the woman's hand. It looked limp and pale like a dying fish. She appeared incoherent, on the verge of death. Doubtless, she'd seen her family butchered by the greenskins and it had deranged her.

'They stood no chance,' uttered Brand without emotion.

'Poor bastards.'

The woman opened her eyes, a jerk of nervous energy impelling her. Whether she'd snapped into lucidity briefly or Varveiter's words had brought her around, it was impossible to tell. Her mouth started moving, but she could form no words because she had no tongue. Blood trickled down the edges of her mouth and Brand dabbed it carefully with his tunic sleeve. The dying woman's eyes widened and she appeared desperate to speak. A waft of something unpleasant drifted through the doorway, like spoiled meat and dung.

'Shit...' hissed Varveiter, recognising the signs and getting to his feet. 'Out of the house,' he said, then louder. 'Get out of the house!'

Placing his hands almost lovingly upon the woman's cheeks, her slowly nodding as he did it, Brand broke her neck with a savage twist to end her suffering. Varveiter was limping for the door, calling to Rechts. Brand followed them out into the gloomy day and saw the greenskins that he already knew were there.

IT ALL HAPPENED terrifyingly fast. One moment they were scouting through the village, picking past corpses and the ruins of burnt buildings, the next the greenskins were upon them. Karlich saw the ambush unfold from the summit of the lookout point. In truth, it was poorly executed. Several orcs sought to hide by lying down under paltry scraps of hay. Others merely stood still, buckets over their heads. The goblins showed more cunning. They at least stayed out of sight, closing off escape routes when bands of scouts spotted the orcs easily. The poor huntsmen were the first to die. Three made it from the area around the inn but didn't get far.

As they emerged into the street, goblin archers put several arrows in each Reiklander's back. The charging orcs that followed, trussed in chainmail and wielding cleavers, cut down the injured. Karlich saw one man, the brave youth who'd spoken out against the Middenlanders at the camp, crawling for some cover before a blade struck him in the back and he was still. His murderer snarled and roared in exultation of its kill before barrelling on after its rampant kin.

Throughout the entire village, orcs and goblins were emerging from concealed positions, out of hovels, from hay bales, even underneath piles of corpses. The stench of the dead had masked their scent, but now it drenched the air like a contagion. The Empire troops had sprung the ambush early, thanks mainly to the stupidity of the orcs. It gave the soldiers precious minutes to prepare.

Brutish and wild, their porcine faces studded with rings and nuggets of iron, the orcs were a fearsome sight. Karlich had fought the beasts before. Easily the equal of a man, he knew orcs to have tough skin like leather and almost unbreakable skulls. He had even seen one studded with arrows, its left arm severed at the shoulder, still fight on and kill two more men before it was brought down. Orcs lived to fight and as a consequence were very good at it.

Goblins followed in their wake. Smaller and weaker, goblins possessed a low cunning and if anything were more malicious than orcs. It was not unknown for goblins to torture the victims of their raids, exacting the cruelty they suffered at the hands of their orcish brethren upon the poor humans at their mercy. Essentially, they were cowardly creatures, but revelled in hurting anything smaller or weaker than themselves.

'Lenkmann, raise the banner and rally the rest of the men to this point,' said Karlich, heading for the watchtower.

'Some of the others on the east side of the village may not see it,' offered Keller quickly. 'Should I go and warn them, sergeant?'

Karlich paused to think: Brand, Varveiter and Rechts were on the eastern side. 'Do it,' he said quickly, 'but be careful. The greenskins are everywhere.'

Keller nodded and sped off.

Lenkmann looked to his sergeant as he threw open the door to the watchtower. 'And what will you be doing, sir?'

'Signalling reinforcements. If Stahler doesn't get in here quick, we are all dead men,' Karlich said and raced inside, the door banging shut behind him.

Karlich had his shield strapped on his back and was able to take the watchtower steps two at a time with his sword drawn. He reasoned the villagers had made them close together so children or women could also 'garrison' the tower as required. There was no blood on the steps and they were largely intact despite the damage.

The wood creaked ominously with his every footfall though, magnified by the silence inside the tower. By the time Karlich neared the top, the tremors of battle sounded on the breeze: the clash of steel, the shouts of men and the roar of beasts. He knew he had to gather the regiment quickly. His men were spread too thin around Blösstadt. Without regimental coherency, the greenskins would pick them off without a fight, but he needed Stahler and the rest of the army even more.

His mind was racing as he burst through the trapdoor that led to the tower's parapet, so much so that he didn't see the goblin lurking in the shadows waiting for him. Hot agony seared Karlich as a ragged blade stabbed into his breastplate, glanced off and scraped rib bone at his side. The wound quickly became wet with blood, but the armour had saved his life. Not expecting its prey to survive, the goblin was on the back foot when Karlich stabbed it in the throat. The greenskin died, gurgling blood. Kicking it from his path, Karlich moved further onto the parapet. He spared a glance for the slain milkmaid hanging over the palisade like a red, rag doll and was tempted to pull her down for the sake of her dignity but knew there wasn't time. Instead, he went straight for the watchtower's warning bell. Sheathing his sword, Karlich yanked on the clapper so hard he almost pulled the bell from its yoke. A warning ring pealed over Blösstadt, carrying to every part of the village and beyond.

CHAPTER FIVE
AMBUSHED

Blösstadt village, Averland,
319 miles from Altdorf

THE REPORT OF Sturnbled's pistol was smothered by a series of loud clangs as Blösstadt's watchtower bell pealed its warning. Powder smoke discharged silently into the air like a gust of grey breath. The Middenlander's shot was true and struck the charging orc in the forehead. Blood, brain and bone fragments blew from the back of the greenskin's skull in a ruddy plume. The beast staggered a few more steps, slumped down and was still.

Another trampled over it as if it was just another obstacle to be trammelled in the pursuit of violence. A further two orcs followed: one carried a long spear with a barbed tip, the other a rusty sword and a shield. Goblins had joined the greenskin vanguard too, and rushed ahead of the burly orcs. One came at Sturnbled. With no time to reload, the Middenlander twisted his pistol around so he could use its weighted butt like a club. In his other hand, he'd drawn his sword. Parrying the wild slash of the goblin's blade, Sturnbled brained it with the pistol. A second died to Torveld's expert sword thrust, before the orcs caught up and the fight was on.

Despite bracing himself, Volker was barrelled off his feet by a charging orc. It was the beast bearing the shield. The orc had used it like a battering ram and now had the Reiklander at its mercy, until the mastiff pounced, wrapping its frothing jaws around the greenskin's forearm and biting down hard. Shaking its sword arm fervently, the orc took several seconds to shrug the hound off. The mastiff went scrambling off into the dirt but had clung on long enough for Masbrecht and Eber to end the greenskin with their halberds. Undeterred, the mastiff bounced to its paws and launched itself at another goblin. The greenskin squealed in pain and shock as the vicious dog tore its throat out. Volker was back on his feet by then.

'Good dog!' he praised, weighing in against another orc fighting Masbrecht. The sounds of battle had drawn more Reiklanders and Middenlanders from the surrounding streets and they came with weapons bared. It was hectic and blurred, filled with blood, grunting and metal clashing against metal. Sweat stung Eber's eyes and orc stink rankled in his nose, but he kept on swinging until there was nothing left to kill.

Sturnbled reloaded his pistol, the greenskins kept at bay by Torveld and his other men, and another blast filled the air, this time without the ringing of the warning bell to silence it. Two goblins took flight at the noise and the smell. One was dragged to heel by Volker's mastiff, the dog's master finishing what it had begun with the point of his halberd; the other Torveld killed with a flung dagger.

It was over in minutes, but each man was heaving for breath and red-faced with effort. A soldier wearing a Reikland uniform was lying face down on the ground, blood seeping from a wound to his head. Masbrecht knelt by his side and whispered a few words of prayer, but didn't turn the poor wretch over.

'It's Gethin,' announced the other Grimblade that had come with him to join the fight. 'Fourth ranker.'

Volker knew the speaker to be a man called Lodde, and laid a reassuring hand on his shoulder. Eber looked on grimly at the morbid scene. He hoped he would not die face down in the dirt like that.

The Middenlanders weren't spared from grief, either. One had been decapitated by an orc's blade, so Torveld took the deceased's cloak and shawled it over the body. In lieu of a funeral, it was the best he could do.

'Ulric will keep them to his breast,' said Sturnbled solemnly, casting a glance in Masbrecht's direction as he performed the benediction. 'Aye, and Sigmar too,' the Middenlander concluded.

By the end of it, four orcs and six goblins were dead, compared to the one each of the Reiklanders and Middenlanders. But it wasn't over, not nearly done. More greenskins were coming, many more. Another horde erupted from the opposite direction in a running battle with some more of Sturnbled's men.

'Get them to the hill,' the sergeant told Torveld, recognising the sense in Karlich's plan to rally there. It was painfully clear the Empire men were outnumbered and the only way they'd survive long enough for reinforcements was to stage a dogged defence. For that they needed a strongpoint, and in a village like Blösstadt the lookout hill with its watchtower was as good a place as any.

Torveld started bellowing at the retreating men, seeing Wode amongst them and pointing him to the hill where the Reiklanders were already gathering. He tried not to balk at the sheer number of greenskins in pursuit, nor the horde that had now emerged from the same direction as the initial vanguard they'd just despatched.

VARVEITER HEARD THE tolling bell as he came out of the shack. Another three Grimblades had been drawn to the woman's soft pleas and were outside in the small square of dirt before the hovels. One was already dead, his helmet split in two by an orc's cleaver. It could have been Mensk. Varveiter had seen death on the battlefield many times, he was no stranger to it, but even so he tried not to look at the slain Reiklander. The other two, Prünst and Otto, were fighting hard against a pair of orcs. Brand went into the fray, just as another orc and a pair of goblins rushed into the lane facing the hovels, bellowing war cries.

Gutting the first orc, but not quick enough to save Prünst, Brand then moved on to the second with Rechts in support. The three halberdiers overwhelmed the beast with sheer weight of numbers. As it died, Otto went to give Brand his thanks but the words died on his lips with a gurgle of blood. His legs twisted beneath him and he crumpled, a black-feathered shaft protruding from his neck. The goblins were carrying short bows.

'Shields!' cried Varveiter, bringing up his own shield to protect him. While the others had been fighting, he'd moved ahead to waylay the second group of greenskins. The arrow hitting his shield made him slow a little, enough for Brand to catch up. Rechts was on his heels. Together, Brand and Varveiter presented a wall of halberd points for the orc to career into, which it did with bloodthirsty abandon.

Though impaled, the beast still swung wildly at them with a rusty axe. It caught Rechts on his shoulder as he tried to stab the greenskin with his short sword. The tunic ripped and blood welled in a narrow gash, making the drummer cry out with pain as the old spear wound from the ungor opened up again.

'Die you dirty, green swine,' spat Varveiter, shoving the halberd deeper into the orc's gut. Arrows *thunked* into the creature's broad back as the Grimblades put the orc between them and the goblin archers. Brand twisted his blade then secured the haft in the dirt with his foot as the orc squirmed. Rechts had backed off, pressing at the gash in his shoulder and trying to staunch the blood flow. It left only two of them to hold off the beast.

Pinioned to both halberds, the orc had little movement save to slash madly with its axe. Ducking one swing that tainted the air with the reek of old blood, Brand went around the creature's blindside. He idly killed one of the goblins with a throwing knife – the other had run out of arrows – before pulling out his dirk and ramming it straight into the back of the orc's skull. He needed to use both hands to make it penetrate. Varveiter grimaced in disgust as the blade point punched through the greenskin's eye on the other side, rupturing it like a red grape. At last, he yanked out his halberd but the dead orc stayed upright affixed to Brand's weapon. Together, all three men rolled the creature over and onto the ground.

When Brand had retrieved his weapons, he turned to Varveiter who was leaning on a horse trough and breathing heavily.

'You all right, Siegen?'

'Fine, lad. Go get that little bastard, before it fetches more of its kin.'

After loosing all of its shafts and seeing its fellows slain, the last goblin had fled further north into Blösstadt. The way ahead looked clear for now, most of the fighting sounded like it was happening across the stream on the other side of the village.

Brand nodded and started to jog in that direction. He was of the killing mind now; Varveiter saw the feral spark in his cold eyes. Rechts was about to go after him, when he decided to lag behind for the old soldier, who was gasping for breath.

Varveiter waved him on.

'Go! Make sure he doesn't get himself killed.'

Rechts looked at Varveiter then around the hovels at the bodies of man and greenskin. There were no enemies nearby.

'Be right behind us, old man.'

Varveiter scowled as only the curmudgeonly can but caught the note of concern. 'Get gone!'

And he did, short sword in hand, after Brand.

As soon as the drummer was out of sight, Varveiter staggered and nearly fell. The pain in his leg was bad. Much worse than he'd let on to Rechts or Brand.

Just wait a while, and I'll be fine, he told himself. *Can't let them see me like this. I need to fight, I need to be a soldier, I–*

A dizzy spell came and went. Varveiter sorely wanted to take off his helmet and breastplate, the tasset that felt as if it was cutting off the blood to his leg, but knew that was foolish. So he gritted his teeth and bore it.

To be duped into an ambush was one thing, but for it to be perpetrated by orcs was just galling. Even as badly executed as it was, even with the corpses masking their stench as well as concealing the greenskins physically, it should not have got to this. It was rare cunning, and Varveiter suspected a goblin's nous. Orcs had no aptitude for anything except violence. A man will recoil from an effigy representing his own mortality. He will not look too closely at the dead. They are repugnant, tragic; a cautionary tale that there but for the grace of Sigmar goes he. Yes, the goblins were wise and now with their larger brethren they were upon them.

Gauging their position by concentration of stench, and the likely sites for an ambush, Varveiter reckoned on the bulk of the greenskin horde being across the stream in amongst the more densely-packed buildings. It would be too risky for the creatures to try and stay concealed any closer. No orc could pull it off, for sure. They wouldn't stray too close to the lookout post, either. Maybe just the odd lurking sentry, looking for a quick and dirty kill. It was largely open ground and with few places to hide, save the watchtower. Put too many greenskins in there and they'd be dead within minutes as the Empire men burned it to the ground. The situation was grim. Orcs would be flooding the village and Karlich would no doubt send a warning to Captain Stahler, hence the tower bell, and rally the rest to the lookout.

Varveiter only hoped he had the strength and will to join them.

Agony flared up his side again, the focus of which started at his thigh where the beastman had stabbed him. Vomit regurgitated into his mouth, and he tasted the acrid sting of bile at the back of his throat. The dizziness came back with a vengeance as Varveiter took a tentative step from the horse trough he was using as a crutch. He stood upright in spite of it. Blood pulsed in his ears, louder than Rechts's drum at full marching beat, and black fog billowed threateningly at the edge of his vision. He was close to passing out, so bit his lip hard. He drew blood, the copper taste of it filling his mouth, but the fresh pain kept him from falling. Then he heard him.

'Warhorse...'

A shadow clouded over Varveiter, smothering the old soldier in shade. When he realised it wasn't his failing eyesight, he turned and saw Keller.

'What'd you want?' he snapped with more conviction than he truly felt.

Perplexity turned to horror when Varveiter discovered he'd been stabbed in the side through a gap in his armour. Funny, he couldn't remember Keller getting so close to him. Maybe he'd blacked out for a second. Survival instinct took over now. Keller was close, but that also meant he was in reach of the old soldier's hands. He'd killed men with those bare hands before; men he'd had no grudge against. This was different. Varveiter seized the wiry Keller around the neck and squeezed. The younger man's weasel face contorted as he struggled to breathe, but Varveiter kept up the pressure. Something warm was running down his side, dampening his leg and collecting in his boot. It sloshed as he adjusted his footing to get a better grip and take the weight off his ailing thigh.

Panicked, Keller dropped the knife now slick with Varveiter's blood and pawed at the old man's leathery fingers. They were like petrified oak: unyielding and rigid. Desperation crept into his movements now, as the life was slowly being choked out of him by a vengeful veteran with an aptitude for pugilism: an aptitude that had seen him humiliated and stoked an ember of resentment and bitterness into flaming rage within Keller's core. He lashed out, striking the old soldier's wounded thigh.

Varveiter screamed as lightning tore through his lower body, shocking him with tiny forks of pain. His leg crumpled and he lost his grip. Keller heaved in a relieved breath. The world was fading around Varveiter. Keller was saying something to him but it was as if his voice was too far away to make out the words, as if he was at the top of a long well and Varveiter was at its bottom. He fell, a cynical punch to his jaw putting the old soldier on his rump. Keller kicked and the lightning flared again, building to a thunderhead of agony. He couldn't feel his leg at all now, and looked dumbfounded at his red palm and fingers as he brought them up to his face. He'd lost a lot of blood. It was pooling under him in a sticky morass.

Suddenly, Keller was gone. A strange silence descended, an eerie peace. Shadows were moving in the narrow lanes of Blösstadt. It took a while for Varveiter to realise they weren't phantoms at the fringes of his clouding sight. The goblins had returned, or perhaps they were different creatures – Varveiter could no longer tell. He reached for his halberd. He didn't remember dropping it, but there it sat in the dirt. Even as his fingers closed on the haft, he knew he couldn't grasp it. He was too weak from blood loss.

You bastard, Keller, he thought, his mind the only faculty left to him he could rely on in his final moments. *Didn't even have the guts to do it yourself...*

Blood pulsing from his side, slumped in the dirt without his weapon in his hand, it wasn't the way Varveiter had wanted to die. The last thing he saw as his vision faded was the goblins stowing their cudgels as they approached him. Instead, they drew daggers and Siegen Varveiter realised then his death would not be quick...

KARLICH EMERGED FROM the watchtower pale and out of breath. The wound in his side was still bloody, despite the rag of tunic he'd tied off to stymie it.

'Found more than a dead milkmaid up there, eh, Reiklander?'

The Grimblade sergeant gave Sturnbled a dirty look as he reached the summit of the hill and approached him.

'How many men do you have left?' asked Karlich, ignoring the jibe.

'Just over twenty. What's your plan?'

Karlich trudged a few feet down the hill to where his men were gathering. In the distance, he saw the greenskins hustling towards them in a mass, coming from all four compass directions. The last few halberdiers were just ahead of them, emerging from Blösstadt's eastern side. They slogged the final steps across the partially forded river, one man losing his footing and then his head to a flung axe as he went to rise. The stream ran red with his blood.

'Form ranks!' bellowed Karlich, half in answer to Sturnbled's question. He regarded the Middenlander over his shoulder, who was priming his duelling pistol. 'We need to cover every aspect of this hill,' Karlich told him. 'Make two half-circles – my men to the north and east, yours to the south and west. We make our stand as low as we can, while maintaining the advantage of height and retreat by steps as necessary.'

'You want to hold out for Stahler to save us, then,' Sturnbled replied, as if unaccustomed to the concept of being saved and not being the one doing the saving.

'Yes.'

Sturnbled didn't like it, but knew enough to realise they were out of options. He hastily organised his men and ordered them to lock shields. Just over twenty Middenland Steel Swords and maybe thirty-five Reikland Grimblades opposed the greenskin hordes swarming Blösstadt – less than sixty men against twice that number or more in orcs and goblins.

Keller returned to the ranks and hurriedly found his position alongside Rechts. They were strung out in a long file of twelve men, just three ranks deep with some stragglers. It meant Keller was pushed up to the front.

'Where's Varveiter?' asked Lenkmann, starting to raise the banner.

Keller's face darkened. He couldn't help but glance in Brand's direction, who was also in the front rank but on the opposite side of the command section.

'He's dead then,' said Karlich bitterly, not feeling patient enough to wait for Keller to find the courage to spit out his words.

'I was looking for Rechts and Brand when I found him,' Keller said. His gaze went involuntarily to Brand again.

The other Reiklander gave away nothing – the whitening in his knuckles could just be tension before battle. Brand's expression was cold, but he saw what the others did not. He saw the finger marks around Keller's throat where someone had tried to throttle him; too large for goblins, too thin for orcs. He knew the truth and if they survived this, knew what he was going to do to Keller.

'The old man was bound to get himself killed someday,' muttered Volker, wiping away a tear. Behind him, Masbrecht intoned a quiet litany that made Rechts stiffen in anger despite its intent. Eber was dumbstruck and hung his head a little, as a dog might when it loses its master.

'Did he die with a weapon in his hand, Keller?' asked Karlich, fighting hard not to show emotion. Varveiter had been a father to them all of sorts by the end.

Keller nodded meekly, afraid his voice would give away the lie.

'Then it's as he'd have wanted.'

'Likely we'll all die in this Sigmar-forsaken place anyway,' said Volker, grabbing the mastiff by its scruff and dragging it close. The beast had bonded with the Reikland hunter and snarled at the approaching orc horde.

'Shut up, Volker,' snapped Karlich. 'Speak like that again and you'll be lashed when this is over. Stahler will come,' he said. 'We just have to hold out long enough for it to matter when he does.'

There was no more time for talk or grief, only time for fighting. The greenskins had arrived.

CHAPTER SIX
A CAPTAIN'S DUTY

Blösstadt village, Averland,
319 miles from Altdorf

THE WARNING BELL pealed long and loud beyond the stockade wall of Blösstadt and fed all the way to Stahler's position a few hundred feet from the gate. The captain recognised its urgency and shouted the order to march. Von Rauken's Carroburg Few took the lead, the greatsworders keen to face danger but still highly disciplined as they advanced. A block of handgunners followed them, then the spearmen and finally the second regiment of gunners. Stahler joined the spearmen to better view the entire line and not be too far from any one element of it. Besides, he knew that Von Rauken was a capable leader and didn't need the morale-boosting presence of a captain. The militia units, a few scattered free companies and archers, ran alongside and to the rear of the column. Most stayed with the baggage train and camp followers a few yards behind the professional soldiers.

They were only fifty feet or so from the looming stockade wall when the air was split with the sound of battle cries. The harsh and ululating timbre of those cries told Stahler that the greenskins had planned more than one ambush. Shading his eyes from the sun that was beginning to dip behind some cloud, Stahler made out a patch of dust billowing on the horizon. From a shallow valley, large enough to hide a cavalry force, a horde of orc boar riders barrelled forth. The greenskins hooted and brayed, banging shields with their crude weapons, whilst their shaggy mounts snorted through ringed snouts. Another cry echoed across the flat land – a hidden dip on the opposite side of the column concealed further riders. As the orcs crested a small, grassy rise, Stahler raised his sword aloft.

'All troops to the village! Run for the stockade wall!'

Out in the open, surrounded by the greenskins' shock cavalry, the Empire troops were severely outmatched. At least in Blösstadt there were buildings and lanes to defend, walls to impede an otherwise devastating boar charge.

Armour plates clanked and scabbards slapped, regimental sergeants bellowed frantic orders and the column began to move. For a time the Empire force lost its coherency in the mad dash for the walls. The gaping gatehouse offered salvation, a promise of possible survival within the confines of the stockade that surrounded Blösstadt. That promise was shattered abruptly when a fully laden lumber cart rolled into the gap, blocking off the gate, and burst into flames.

Arrows whickered through the fire, the silhouettes of goblins just visible through the haze and smoke. One of the greatsworders was struck in the armpit and cried out; others took the crudely-feathered shafts against their full plate armour and marched into the arrows stoically.

They were trapped with the orc boar riders bearing down on them, and had only a few minutes to do something about it. As Stahler marshalled his thoughts and tried to devise a plan that wouldn't end with them all dead on a bloody plain outside Blösstadt, a discordant war horn reverberated in his ears. He winced at the noise, a whining and tuneless clamour, and saw more riders. This time they were goblins, clinging maniacally to giant, slavering wolves. One of the diminutive greenskins was so fervid that it fell, and several wolves broke from their loose formation to feed on it. The act of wanton savagery barely slowed them. They were heading for the baggage train.

'Signal the militia to surround the carts, archers behind free company men,' he snapped to the spearmen's standard bearer, a soldier named Heiflig. The banner went up and in concordance with the regimental horn blower conveyed the message. Stahler didn't wait to see if they'd respond. He couldn't do any more for them. If they failed, they were dead – it was that simple. Instead he yelled loudly.

'Break column and form square!'

The spearman musician blew again, this time accompanied by the beating of drums from the Grünburg gunner regiments. Cavalry were deadly to long lines or unguarded flanks. They could reap right through them, cutting men asunder with no reply, come about and then charge all over again. Blocks of infantry facing every aspect were a much tougher prospect, where weight of numbers and the reassuring presence of rear ranks would count for something. Stahler knew it, as did every Empire captain worth his salt, and watched with grim satisfaction as the units in his command reformed.

Only the greatswords differed in their formation, making a tight circle of blades, every man three feet apart. The gaps in the line were risky, but necessary as they provided clearance for the swings of the Carroburg Few's mighty double-handed blades. It also made the most of the greatsworders' prodigious fighting strength – every one of Von Rauken's men would face an enemy.

With the appearance of the greenskin riders, the greatswords had allowed the handgunners to pass them and close on the gate. It meant Von Rauken was close enough to Stahler to be heard as he shouted.

'We need to get inside. We'll be slaughtered out here, in squares or not!'

Stahler knew he was right, and was about to shout back when a percussive bark erupted from the handgunners closest the gate. The goblin archers disappeared from view. No more arrows whickered from the flaming cart.

Deciding he didn't wish to debate strategy across their regiments, Stahler broke off from the Bögenhafen spearmen and jogged quickly over to the greatsworders. He kept low and behind the regiments. Some of the wolf riders carried short bows and he couldn't risk being killed by a lucky arrow. He needed to make it fast. The greenskins had started far off, using distance as well as terrain to hide their ambush, but now they were closing.

'I agree,' said Stahler, a little breathlessly. He had one eye on the advancing greenskins and one on Von Rauken who glowered at him like an armour-plated juggernaut. The greatsworder was easily a head taller than Stahler and his eye-patch and thick moustaches made him look imperious. But Stahler wasn't intimidated; he'd faced off against lords and counts before now. 'Hit and run tactics will decimate us,' he added. 'But we aren't getting into the village until that obstruction is out of the way.'

Von Rauken nodded and gestured to a pair of handgunners who had joined them whilst Stahler was talking.

'Sergeant Isaak and his best marksman, Utz,' said Von Rauken by way of introduction. The two Grünburgers nodded curtly. 'Tell the captain what you told me,' he invited, fixing them with his iron-hard glare.

To his credit, Sergeant Isaak didn't wilt, but his marksman looked a little peaked.

'My lord,' Isaak began, thumbs tucked into a thick weapons belt off which hung two large pistols, 'Utz here,' – he nodded towards the marksman, who had his harquebus slung over his shoulder and was wringing a leather cap in his hands – 'believes he has a way we can breach the gate.'

Stahler regarded the man at once, as did they all.

'Then speak, Utz, the enemy will be upon us in short order.'

'Grenades, m-milord,' Utz stammered in a thick accent, reminiscent of the Grünburg boatyards.

Stahler raised a questioning eyebrow at Isaak.

'His father is an engineer,' the sergeant explained. 'Lad's picked up a thing or two. There's nothing he doesn't know about blackpowder, sir.'

The hooting cries of the orcs and the bray of their boars was coming closer. Peeling off from the main horde, the wolf riders had already engaged the militia, circling the baggage train like predators circling their prey. Out of the corner of his eye, Stahler saw three men were dead with black-shafted arrows sticking out of their bodies.

'How quickly can you do it?' he put to Utz.

'We'll need socks and caps for the powder, more than just the bags we carry,' Utz replied. 'Then twine. It shouldn't take more than a few minutes, my lord.'

'Get to it then.'

Utz and Isaak hurried off to the regiment, the sergeant already calling for every man to relinquish his socks or cap if he had them.

Left with the burly greatsworder, Stahler had one thing left to say before he ran back to the Grünburg spearmen, who were looking anxious in his absence.

'Keep them safe, Von Rauken. If we don't break though that barricade–'

'Then you and I will be dining in Sigmar's longhouse before the day is out,' the greatsworder replied.

As Stahler nodded and then went to his men, Von Rauken rejoined his own.

'Carroburg Few…' he called, taking his place between standard and drum, 'we bloody few. Steep your blades this day. Steep them in the red of your tunics. Steep them in greenskin blood. Let all remember the Siege of Carroburg and how our courage was measured and made.'

A clash of blades, the slip of steel on leather greeted Von Rauken's proclamation as the Carroburg Few drew swords and prepared to meet the enemy.

* * *

THICK, BLACK SMOKE was visible from his vantage point on the hill. Karlich was familiar enough with Blösstadt's layout to realise it was coming from the gate. He'd also heard the faint echo of horns – not the trumpets and clarions of the Empire, but the throaty, strident blaring of greenskin pipes – and knew that Stahler was cut off. It changed nothing, only his resolve to dig in harder and make the orcs pay for every inch they took.

'Hold together!' Karlich shouted, blocking the swipe of a rusty cleaver before stunning the orc he faced with a stiff punch to the nose. It was like striking granite but the beast felt it too and backed off just enough for Karlich to finish it with his sword. Respite was brief, more of the porcine brutes were clamouring to the battle.

The sheer swell of it was incredible, like the pitch and yaw of a ship in a stormy sea. With the initial charge, the halberdiers' line bent, but then reasserted itself like steel flexing back after being tested. They braced hafts into the hill soil and levelled blades outwards in a dull, grey metal palisade. Orcs were skewered, goblins kicked and split by swords but still the greenskins came. Gazing through the gaps in the fighting, Karlich dared not make a headcount – beyond the Grimblades' front rank, there appeared to be no end to the orcs.

Backing up the slope with the massive press of the horde, Keller slipped. Brand was beside him immediately and kept the soldier on his feet. Keller only had time to flash a brief glance in his direction. It was met with icy cold and if it wasn't for the greenskins to his front, he'd have been reluctant to turn away.

'It won't be in your back,' he heard Brand whisper, before he was lost from view in the melee.

Lenkmann and Rechts fought doggedly by Karlich's side, protecting his flanks and hacking furiously with their blades. The drummer closed his ears to the sound of Masbrecht's vocal devotions, concentrating on the scrape of metal, the grunts of the embattled and the cries of the dying.

Volker felt the line thinning. The front rank was dug in hard, a core of strong men, he knew, that had fought many battles together and lived to tell of it. No doubt they missed Varveiter, the old soldier was the source of much inspiration, but they were holding. Volker's keen eyes picked out goblins creeping through the orcish wall of muscle and fury. He'd slain two already, the corpses had rolled down the hill to be crushed underfoot. Another pair had dragged a Grimblade, Jorgs, to his death by first stabbing him in the legs when his attention was on the orcs. Once Jorgs was down the malicious creatures had gone to work with their knives. Volker had seen the man collapse and heard him screaming as the goblins took him. Keeping his eyes low and high at the same time was impossible, but the mastiff guarded his master's legs, tearing out goblin throats and keeping them at bay with its frothing bark and bite.

THE EDGES OF the line were being hit hard. Eber felt it like a physical blow. Several men had lost their lives on the flanks as the greenskins levelled most of their strength at the 'hinges' between the regiments. Though Eber couldn't really see that well, he realised the Middenlanders were struggling to hold off the beasts just as they were. Cutting down another orc, splitting its skull with a roar, he vowed to make the greenskins fight for every step. Eber was strong and his harsh upbringing, first at his father's hand and then as part of the circus troupe, had made him tough but the orcs were testing his limits. He buried his halberd into the face of one, imagining it was his abusive father and the killing came easier.

'Retreat two steps,' hollered Karlich. 'In good order, Grimblades.'

Eber moved with the rest of the line. He could feel the summit of the hill getting closer.

A RAKING DISCHARGE from the Grünburg guns filled the air with a flurry of smoke. Another crack of flintlocks immediately followed it as the second of the handgunner regiments fired its weapons. This was a much lesser discharge, as a quarter of its number was preparing grenades under the tutelage of marksman Utz. Sergeant Isaak stayed with the greater regiment, unleashing his pistols one at a time to maintain a steady rate of fire.

The orcs bore the brunt of the fusillades on their shields. Powder and shot left wood chips and dented plate in its wake. Despite the heavy barrage – a fact made possible by firing in ranks, whereby rear rankers replaced front rankers with fuses primed in a constant cycle of powder, shot, ram, fire – the greenskins had lost few riders and fewer boars. They circled the Empire infantry squares like carrion choosing the tastiest morsels to descend upon. Several of the handgunners were dead already, slumped in the dirt with axe and spear wounds. Every death meant one less ball of shot to unleash at the orcs.

'Stay together!' shouted Stahler, as an orc bounced off his shield and nearly felled him as it careened past. 'Maintain square,' he urged, once he'd righted himself.

Boar stink and foetid orc spore had turned the air around them into a febrile soup. Several spearmen gagged, but kept their polearms steady under the gaze of the captain.

Stahler wiped away the sweat streaking his face, sparing a glance towards the Carroburgers and Utz's forlorn hope. The greatsworders were fighting hard and had yet to lose a man. Through the melee, the Empire captain couldn't tell if the grenades were ready yet or not. He hoped it would be soon. They were holding right enough – even the militia were doing a satisfactory job of protecting the wagons – but holding was not enough. His instincts told him the orcs were merely toying with them and that a concerted push was coming.

It arrived sooner than Stahler thought.

From out of the boar riders' ranks, which until then had been a blur of snorting, dark-furred hide and metal, emerged a massive creature too large and imposing to ever be called a mere boar. It was more like a hairy bull, thickly muscled and armoured like the caparisoned steed of a knight, albeit with crude plates and belts of chainmail. Its tiny eyes shimmered red and it snorted a long drizzle of mucus. It might have been a challenge, Stahler was unsure. The deep bellow from the dark-skinned orc upon the boar-beast's back could be nothing other.

Digging its spiked heels into the boar's flank, the greenskin chieftain drove at the greatsworders and Stahler saw the orc in its full terrifying aspect. Curled rams' horns extended from a black iron helmet; chainmail draped its obscenely muscular body like a second skin; fists the size of circus dumbbells gripped a pair of axes, notched from the kills it had made and dark with old blood. It was a monster, a thing of nightmares and it was coming for Von Rauken.

Stahler knew the strength and courage of the greatsworders, and Carroburgers were tough men. But their thin line could not stand against this beast and his entourage. They would stand but shatter soon after, driven under hooves or before rusty blades and then there would be nothing between Utz's men and certain death. The death of Utz meant the death of them all, and the orcish chieftain was cunning enough to realise this.

There was little time to act, and Stahler knew if he thought too hard about what he was going to do he might falter and it would be too late. So instead, he roared.

'Charge!'

Galvanised by the presence of their captain, the Bögenhafeners went from a steady jog to a run. They barrelled into the path of the boar riders, bellowing war cries to stump up their courage.

'Forward in the name of Prince Wilhelm,' shouted Stahler, 'and for the glory of the Reik!'

In the path of the charging boars, there was little time to set themselves and level spears. The men of Bögenhafen did what they could before a thundering wall of fur, fangs and tusks exploded into them. It was like being struck by a battering ram full in the chest, the earth trembling underfoot.

Stahler lost his helmet and very nearly his shield. He clung to it, this lifeline on a thread of leather, by sheer will alone. Spearmen were tossed into the air like dolls, limbs flailing. Others were ground under hoof or gored by tusks and blades. One man had his neck cleaved in twain, and the decapitated head bounced amongst his brethren like a grisly ball. Blood and screaming, the hoot of beasts and the desperate reek of combat filled the air around them. The standard almost fell, poor Heiflig gutted by an orc's cleaver, before one of the rear rankers came forward to seize it. The war horn was forgotten, in favour of the grunts and cries of desperate battle. In the initial boar charge, the Bögenhafen spears had lost almost their entire front rank – only Stahler and the musician remained. And yet they held.

'Spears!' shouted Stahler, though he hardly needed to as the second rank thrust their polearms over the first who went down on bent knee to let the steel tips pass over their shoulders. Several orcs and boars were pinioned, two even fell to mortal wounds but the greenskins were not done.

After hacking off an orc's hand at the wrist then ramming his shield into its boar's snout, Stahler saw the chieftain a few paces down the line. Its axe blades were a crimson blur, reaping heads and limbs like a farmer reaps corn during harvest. Except this was a visceral, bloody yield.

'Fight me, pig-face!' shouted Stahler. He didn't relish taking on the beast. It was almost twice his height without the mount; with it, the orc was utterly monstrous. Yet he couldn't let it attack the spearmen. They would simply be butchered, and any hopes of survival with them.

'Come on, you stinking scum!' he roared, stabbing a boar rider in the gut as it leaned to strike at him and very nearly losing his head as it swung back.

A line of blood laced Stahler's face, still warm on the orc's blade, and he fought not to gag. A spear to the beast's throat ended its life, but he couldn't see who'd done it. It was impossible to discern anything in the madness. Stahler's focus was just on the orc chieftain.

'To me, you spineless bastard!'

At last the orc took notice, this squealing piece of manflesh rattling his puny shield with his tiny knife. Though man and orc did not speak the same language, understanding between them was absolute. Throwing back his head, the greenskin chieftain emitted an ululating cry that drove the warriors from its path.

Challenge accepted.

Stahler fought to quell his fear. The battle around him appeared to lull. The world slowed, but it was as if the orc chieftain were moving outside of time as it came on inexorably and at speed. The captain's longsword was no ordinary weapon. Myrmidian priests had blessed it and a single rune was forged into the blade. Despite the keenness of its edge, the magical sharpness parted mail links like they were parchment, Stahler balked at the thickness of the orc's armour, its flesh and brawn.

'Sigmar protect me...' he whispered, making the sign of the hammer with his shield arm then bringing it up to meet the charge of the beast.

'LAST STEP!' CRIED Karlich as they reached the summit of the hill. Through the fog of battle, the Grimblade sergeant vaguely made out Sturnbled issuing a similar warning to his men. The Middenlander had given up on his pistol and fought with sword and buckler instead. Torveld fought beside him and, despite his disliking of the northerners, Karlich had to admit they were ferocious fighters.

Twenty minutes is a long time on the battlefield where seconds can stretch to lifetimes and every swing of your sword or sweep of your halberd feels like lifting a tree. Proud of them as he was, Karlich knew his men were flagging. Another of the Grimblades – Helmut? – was struck down, and the line thinned again. It had been some time since they'd had two full rear ranks and the gaps were telling. Three times Karlich had narrowed the formation already, the small circle of soldiers around the hill tightening as they ascended its rise, as if pulling their own noose. Occasional peals of Rechts's drum relayed the command to close ranks, whilst Lenkmann hollered and cajoled them to maintain good order when they did.

Smoke was still rising from the gatehouse. If Stahler didn't make it through soon, this would be one of the shortest Imperial campaigns in history.

THE WORLD WAS drenched red before Stahler's eyes as the blow against his shield forced him back. He staggered with the sheer strength behind the attack. Putting his weight on his back foot, he lashed out wildly with his blade. Laughing – a deep, throaty noise full of malice – the orc chieftain merely swatted the sword aside with the flat of its axe. It sported long cuts, the odd gouge in its skin and armour, but these small blows Stahler had inflicted only enraged and empowered the beast.

Blood was leaking into Stahler's eyes from a cut on his forehead that he couldn't see or feel. A deep throbbing in his head dulled the battle noise, but he thought he heard the final pulses of his heart in this world as the orc came again.

Stahler lunged in an effort to maybe put the orc off balance, salvage a little more time for Utz, but the beast swatted the weapon away again. Leaning down from its mount, the chieftain seized Stahler by his tunic. Snarling stinking spittle into the man's face, the orc butted him hard.

The red world turned black. It was like being hit by granite. Stahler felt his nose break. He became vaguely aware of being spun around, his shield fleeing from his grasp, sword slipping from his nerveless fingers.

'Wilhelm…'

The words brushed past his lips like a death rattle as the long well came for him. It was cool in its shadowy depths and the water was dank. Old things lingered in it: old unquiet things that he would soon be joining. Earth came up to meet him, the bloody mire embracing Stahler's body like he was a babe in arms. For he was a child of war and she, the battlefield, was his dark mother.

Thunder boomed above, and with the last of his fading sight Stahler saw dead, bloody faces staring back at him, welcoming him.

Join us…

An almighty crack announced the destruction of the gates. Karlich saw it happen as surely as he felt the greenskins falter. Flaming debris and smoke plumed fifty feet high in an orange, grey bloom that expanded into the orcs around the gates. The greenskins were engulfed, riddled by wood splinters the size of swords, burned to death in the booming conflagration.

Some of the orcs and goblins fighting the Grimblades were looking over their shoulders. Confidence that had been so abundant moments ago ebbed like water in a punctured skin.

Something else was happening too. There was thunder, only not from the heavens. This thunder shook the earth and sent it trembling all the way up to the summit of the hill.

'Wilhelm…' breathed Karlich, in revered thanks for their deliverance. Having planned to join his armies on the road to Averheim, the Prince of Reikland had come. He had come and they were saved, but only if they were still willing to save themselves.

Karlich saw his chance.

'Grimblades! Push them back!'

As one the halberdiers thrust forward, leading with spikes and cleaving with blades as they surged down the hill, scattering the greenskins before them. There came the sound of powder cracks from a fusillade as beautiful and welcome as an orchestral chorus. Smoke plumed the air like grey pennants billowing on the breeze, announcing the arrival of salvation.

No longer pressed from all sides, greatsworders, handgunners and spearmen spilling into Blösstadt to leaven the intense pressure, Grimblades and Steel Swords reforming their ranks in a thick, narrow fighting block. Shields and blades went deep, as deep as they could. The greenskins were broken, all sense of purpose and coherency lost in a moment. The men of the Empire were merciless as they routed them.

Outside it was a similar glorious story. Karlich and the others would not get to see the magnificent charge of Prince Wilhelm and his knights, nor would they witness the efforts of the regiments from Kemperbad, Auerswald and Ubersreik. There were scores of militia soldiers too, drawn from the surrounding Reikland villages, all impassioned by a prince's cause and a desire to protect their borders and the borders of their neighbours. If they did not look to the defence of their Empire, then who would? It was a rare moment of solidarity in a land rife with internal strife and politicking, but then Wilhelm was an inspirational man and ruler. He spoke to men's hearts, not their heads or their coffers.

The goblin wolf riders broke first. The sight of such enemy numbers bearing down on them from the west – the serried ranks of pikes, halberds and swords all eager for blood – was enough to put them to flight. The militia regiments protecting the wagons cheered and jeered at the fleeing greenskins but knew, deep down, how close they had come to being food for the worms.

Prince Wilhelm was at the tip of a gleaming lance head, driving his knights forward from the back of a barded steed. Captain Ledner was at his right hand, Preceptor Kogswald at his left. With their banner unfurled and a blazing clarion call bursting from a silver bugle, the Griffonkorps rode onto the bloodied field like avenging warrior angels laying waste to the foul and the wicked.

Trapped between the doughty spearmen of Bögenhafen and the irresistible charge of Wilhelm and his knights, the orc boar riders were split apart like rotten kindling and scattered to the wind. Only the chieftain and his loyal bodyguard cadre stayed, recognising the prospect of a good fight and unafraid of death.

Griffonkorps lances skewered the first, splintering shields, piercing armour and flesh. Orcs were flung from their mounts as if punched by a cannon ball and those boars not kicked to death by the knights' armoured horses, were stabbed with longswords.

Even after penetrating the first greenskin line, the impetus of Wilhelm's charge was not spent. It rolled on, gathering momentum like a tidal wave. As its apex, the Prince of Reikland met the orc chieftain in single combat. Storm clouds were billowing across the heavens, as if the elements heralded the battle about to unfold, and dry lightning raked the sky in jagged forks.

'In the name of the Empire and Reikland!' shouted Wilhelm, his gleaming runefang held aloft as the thunder answered.

He struck just as the lightning cracked, a close heat drenching the field in a feverish sweat. Haze flickered in the distance and the air thickened. The ancient runefang descended like a comet and cut the chieftain down. Axe hafts splintered, armour parted, flesh and bone were cleaved – nothing could stop it. The chieftain died, split in two, both halves of his body spilling gore and viscera onto the earth.

It proved the end for the greenskins. Fear ran through them. In that moment, the heat broke and the clouds, as if they had been holding their breath, let go and the rains came. Wilhelm rode into Blösstadt like a warrior-king of old. Orc blood ran down off his armour, washed away and purified by the rain.

'Victory to the Empire!' he cried, as the fires around him died and the last death throes of the battle with the greenskins played out. 'For the Reik!'

'For Prince Wilhelm!' the men of the Empire replied, and Wilhelm knew then that his people loved him.

Perhaps they could win this war and send the Paunch back over the mountains to the east.

Little could Wilhelm have known the futility of that dream and the dark days that lay ahead.

CHAPTER SEVEN
GOOD COUNSEL

Prince Wilhelm's encampment, Averland,
324 miles from Altdorf

IT WAS CLAUSTROPHOBIC in the war tent, and the air was thick with pipe smoke. Sergeant Karlich didn't mind the latter, but he found the presence of the great and good a little hard to bear. He was not a politic man; he was a soldier, plain and simple. He knew how to fight, how to command men and get the best from them. He understood tactics and he feared death – any man that didn't was not to be trusted – but here, in this war tent, before his lords and masters, he felt profoundly out of his depth.

'You are all known to me, so I'll speak plainly,' Wilhelm began. The Prince of Reikland was still wearing his golden breastplate but had removed his greaves and tassets. The vambraces on his wrists carried the symbol of a rampant griffon. His blond hair, slightly damp and unkempt from wearing his helmet, shone like fresh straw in the lamplight, and his blue eyes flashed like sapphires. Noble blood was obvious in his features and bearing.

'No aid comes from Altdorf.' The prince's conclusion landed like a hammer blow.

Preceptor Kogswald bore this statement with knightly stoicism and gave nothing away, but the others present, Captains Vogen of Kemperbad and Hornstchaft of Auerswald, Engineer Meinstadt and Father Untervash of the Holy Order of Sigmar, balked at this news. All had thought Altdorf would respond to the threat, that its vast armies would march in support of the prince. If Altdorf had closed its gates, then Nuln had too and that meant the Emperor was content to hole up behind the walls of Prince Wilhelm's former domain.

'What of the other states? What of Talabecland and Stirland? Does Wissenland answer the call to arms? Its borders are under threat too,' asked Vogen, a portly man with thick plate armour, and a feathered helmet sat in the crook on his arm. He sported a dark brown beard to hide his jowls and double chin.

'None are coming. Middenland, too, has sent what troops it is willing to commit,' said Wilhelm before his expression darkened. 'We are alone in this.'

'Ha!' scoffed Hornstchaft. 'So Middenland waits for the storm to vent its wrath against our bulwarks, only to then see it dashed upon its own when it rolls over the eastern Empire and the Reik. I'm surprised the northerners sent men at all.'

Where Vogen was all bulk and flab, Hornstchaft was hawkish and slim. Slightly taller than his counterpart, he held himself straight like a rod, and wore light chain armour. A small breastplate, emblazoned with a laurel and skull, finished the ensemble. He preferred a wide-brimmed hat over a helm. His had three griffon feathers sticking out of it.

'If our brothers do not come, then why are we marching out to Averheim? Why aren't we looking to our own borders? Tell me that,' said Meinstadt. The engineer was a fastidious man, his buttons and buckles polished and pristine. His face was pale and narrow from too much time spent in his workshops, and his hands bore powder stains like faded lesions. He wore a monocle with what appeared to be a targeting reticule placed over it in thin strips of brass. Leather, part smock, part armour, covered his upper body and carried an icon of the College of Engineers, a sideways image of a cannon. Evidently, Meinstadt was a gunnery captain. Karlich had seen no artillery in the camp, though.

'By marching to Averheim, we *are* defending our borders,' countered Wilhelm. The frustration of the prince was obvious, but he had encouraged his officers to speak plainly. He reminded himself of the fact that he already knew this news and that he had asked the very same questions himself during the long ride from Altdorf.

Another figure stepped forward from the shadows. This man, Karlich knew, was Adolphus Ledner. He held the nominal rank of captain, but most who knew him were aware of other *services* he provided for the prince and the Empire. Ledner was a scary bastard. Thin-faced like a blade, with hooded eyes that could pierce a man's soul and an aura of inscrutable intensity that made his mood impossible to gauge. Whenever Karlich had seen him, Ledner had always been wearing a red scarf around his neck. Some in the army suggested it was to cover a neck wound from where one of his many enemies had tried to slit his throat. Karlich could believe that. Exploitation, assassination and intimidation were Ledner's forte. He was as secretive as a witch hunter, and twice as resourceful. He traded in information, lies and half-truths and Wilhelm, for the good of the Reik, was content to turn a blind eye to most of it.

'Uncontested, it will not be long before the orcs drive westward,' he said. Ledner's voice reminded Karlich of a snake. It was harsh and rasping, but when he spoke all in the tent listened. 'And as they rampage, burning villages and murdering as they go, other tribes will gather to their banner.' He leaned forward on the table in the middle of the tent that was covered in maps and hastily written reports, and shadows pooled in his face from the lamps, making him appear ghoulish. 'This "Grom the Paunch" is like no other greenskin we have fought in recent times. It has an army large enough to sack Altdorf and if we do not meet it now and stop it, then that is exactly what it will do. Irrespective of whether the Emperor can see the danger or not, we must preserve our greatest cities. Nuln too, is under threat and we cannot allow the capital to fall without a fight. This goblin king must not cross the Averland border. It must not reach the Reikmark.'

Meinstadt's jaw clamped shut like a trap. Ledner, and therefore Prince Wilhelm, had spoken – it would not be wise to contest further.

Karlich cleared his throat, breaking the sudden silence. 'So what must we do?'

All eyes turned to him, and he felt suddenly very small and insignificant.

Wilhelm's was the first face to soften. 'I am glad there are some soldiers in our midst,' said the prince. 'How is your captain, Sergeant Karlich?'

Taken aback that Wilhelm even knew his name, Karlich faltered before replying.

'Fighting for his life in the chirurgeon's tent, your majesty,' he said at last, unsure if he should bow and instead producing a sort of half nod.

Stahler had been dragged off the battlefield by what was left of the Bögenhafen spearmen. His bravura had saved many of their lives, but left the captain badly wounded. Most of the blood that soaked his clothes had been his.

'Then we should all pray to Sigmar that he recovers to fight again.' Wilhelm half glanced at Father Untervash as he said it. The bald-headed warrior priest, who was even thicker set than Eber, gave a barely perceptible nod and touched the hammer icon hanging by a chain over his breast.

'Sigmar does not abandon his fighting sons,' he intoned, his voice full of sepulchral import. 'Your captain will take up his blade again. It is the will of the Hammer.'

Somewhere in the shadows, Karlich thought he heard someone cough, though he couldn't see who made the sound and realised there was another present whom he had yet to meet.

Wilhelm made the sign of the hammer before addressing the room. 'Averheim is under siege and we go to lift it if we can.' He gestured to some of the reports written by his scribes from the findings of the army's scouts. 'Greenskins push north, south and west. Stirland's borders are breached in a dozen or more places, entire tribes move on Wissenland despite its watchtowers and walls. None are untouched. But Averland is overrun and needs the aid of its brother states. We march on to the state capital and will meet with whatever provincial forces remain outside the city.'

At this remark, Preceptor Kogswald stepped forward.

'A local baron has marshalled a small army and moves westward,' said the knight commander, his tone as hard and haughty as his bearing. 'There are other temple knights with him and a small portion of state troops. We will intercept them, gather what information we can of Averheim's plight and march to the capital.' He brushed aside a clutch of scattered reports to get to the provincial map underneath. Kogswald's gauntleted finger pressed down on a dark blue band running along Averland's north-east border. 'The river Aver,' he said. 'We are currently on its north-east side. If we are to enter Averheim, we must find a large enough crossing to get us to the south-east side. That is our first obstacle, for the greenskins will be guarding the bridges, most likely destroying all but the few they require to move up from Averland and into Stirland.'

'Do we know how our military assets compare to that of the orcs?' asked Vogen, striking up his pipe.

'We are fewer by at least ten to one,' Ledner answered flatly, causing Vogen to almost choke.

'Breath of Myrmidia...' uttered Hornschaft. He failed to notice the raised eyebrow from Father Untervash at the invoking of a lesser deity's name. 'How can we prevail against that?'

'With faith in *Sigmar*, captain,' said Untervash.

Hornschaft turned on the man. 'We will need more than that, priest. I hear the Paunch's forces are not merely restricted to greenskins,' he added. 'That there are trolls and other beasts amongst the horde. I even hear tell of a shaman, one that rides a flying lizard!'

'A wyvern,' said a deep voice. It rumbled low and steady like an undercurrent of thunder. Karlich looked again to the shadows from where the voice had come and saw a cerulean flash light up the darkness, which came from a man's eyes. He was hooded and wore dark robes, but Karlich sensed they merely hid some grander attire underneath. Though the mysterious man was illuminated only briefly, Karlich saw he carried a jagged silver staff with a comet symbol at its tip. He had a forked beard that jutted impossibly from his chin, and there was the suggestion of a skullcap beneath his voluminous cowl. When he spoke again, Karlich felt a charge in the air and was put in mind of tempestuous storms and raging winds.

'The goblin's pet sorcerer rides a wyvern,' he confirmed. 'Do not fear it, though...' he added, opening his palm flat. Within, a tiny ball of lightning coruscated and forked, 'we are not without magic of our own.'

Karlich swallowed audibly. Truly, he was rubbing shoulders with gods and giants. When the council of war was finally over, he couldn't wait to get back to his men.

EBER SHOVELLED THE last of the earth onto the grave and wiped his brow with the back of his forearm. His back was sore from all the digging, but he had insisted on doing it alone. Varveiter's final rest was upon a grassy hill, radiated by shafts of sunlight. Eber had made it deep and buried the old soldier face down. He'd wept as he'd dug, the other Grimblades who knew Varveiter best looking on silently.

Rechts had left before Masbrecht could utter a benediction, walking away from the site with a bottle in hand and a scowl on his face. Keller had followed soon after, a dark mood over him that veiled his ordinary good humour. The other mourners thought it was grief. Only Brand, as still and lifeless as stone, knew it was actually guilt. When it was done and the others had started to walk away, Brand remained. None questioned it, or intervened in any way. They knew better.

Lenkmann did look back though and saw the man kneel and mouth a silent vow to the dead. Before he turned away, he watched Brand pull out his knife and cut his palm. He didn't know the ritual. To him it looked barbaric, but each of them would have to deal with Siegen Varveiter's death in a different way.

The old soldier was not alone, of course. Others joined him in death. A way outside Blösstadt tiny mounds littered the grassy knolls and plains. They were marked by blade hilts, broken helms or shields. Father Untervash blessed every single one to ward away necromantic interference. The village itself was no more. Greenskin spore blighted it. Fire had ravaged many of its buildings and destroyed large sections of the gate and stockade wall. Blood soaked its lanes and violence tainted its memory and spirit. Its people were dead. All of them. Wilhelm had ordered it burned down and razed from existence. Nothing good could come of its lingering ruins. Dark creatures, carrion and bandits would be drawn to its rotting shell as parasites are to a corpse. There were enough shadowed places in the Empire already without adding to them.

* * *

'LOOKS LIKE THE WAR council is over,' said Masbrecht, nodding towards the distant figures emerging from Wilhelm's tent. The encampment had been erected hastily, a few miles from Blösstadt and upwind so the smell of burning flesh from the pyres didn't infect it. The village was just an orange smudge on the horizon that no one cared to look at for the dark memories it held.

'So, does this mean Karlich will be leading the foot-sloggers in Captain Stahler's absence?' asked Volker. He'd knelt down to pet the mastiff, his newfound companion that he had named 'Dog'. The creature licked his face eagerly.

Lenkmann opened his mouth to answer when another spoke in his stead.

'The beast likely has pox or worms.' It was Torveld, passing by the Grimblades' pitch with two other Middenlanders. 'You'd do well not to let it lap at you, southerner. Better still, let me slit its throat so it can't spread disease.'

Volker stood and drew his dirk. 'Try it,' he warned. Dog knew its enemies, and growled.

Torveld had stopped to level his threat and laughed out loud at the Reiklander. 'Still have the stomach to fight, eh?'

Eber stepped forward, balling his fists.

'Move on,' he said in a low voice. Varveiter was dead. His comrades in arms were dead. But *they* had fought and lived. That meant something. He would be cowed by bullies no longer. His strength was not just in his arm, it was in his heart too. Varveiter had taught him that. To do anything less than stand up would besmirch his memory. Eber took another step forward but kept his weapons sheathed. For the honour of his regiment and the memory of the dead, he would crush the Middenlander's skull with his bare hands if he had to.

'Hold your bear back, southerner,' Torveld warned Volker, all the sarcasm and cruel mirth disappearing from his face.

'Please, we are all allies here,' said Lenkmann, hands raised plaintively. 'We fought alongside one another. There is no need for this. We are all at war together, on the same side.'

Torveld snarled. 'It is not *our* war, though, is it Reiklander?'

Lenkmann was slightly dumbfounded. 'It will come to us all if we do not act now and together. We are all sons of Sig–'

'We are not,' Torveld cut him off. '*We* are winter wolves and our borders are far from here to the north. Don't forget that.' The Middenlander looked like he wanted more, that he wanted to vent his wrath against the southerners. His fists clenched. There were only a few feet between the two groups and now more swordsmen had joined Torveld and his companions.

'Bury your dead,' came Brand's voice from Torveld's left. The swordsmen turned to see him walking slowly towards them. 'Before they start to rot,' the Reiklander added.

Torveld paused. He could sense the danger, the potential violence of this man. It made even his northern blood run a little colder.

'Torveld,' said the gruff voice of Sturnbled from behind him. The grey-haired sergeant looked as grim as ever. He needn't say anything further. Muttering beneath his breath, Torveld turned and walked away taking the other Steel Swords with him.

'They are belligerent bastards,' said Lenkmann when they were gone. The others looked around at him. The standard bearer rarely swore, but he was clearly shaken and angry at what he saw as a breach of the soldier's code. Men who had fought side-by-side, shed blood together for the same cause, should have respect for one another. It offended his sense of honour and propriety that the Middenlanders did not.

'What did you expect,' said Karlich, stepping in amongst his men. 'They are northerners.'

Lenkmann saluted crisply at the sudden return of his sergeant. The others mainly nodded. Brand just looked him in the eye. Rechts lazily waved a hand.

'So what now, sergeant,' asked Volker, 'or should we call you "captain"?'

The corner of Karlich's mouth twitched in what could have been a grin. 'You sorry lot aren't shut of me yet,' he replied. 'I'm still a Grimblade, thank Sigmar.'

'When will Altdorf and Nuln join us?' asked Lenkmann.

'They won't,' Karlich answered flatly, not waiting for questions or protests. 'We march on to Averheim to death or glory, by the grace of Sigmar.'

CHAPTER EIGHT
ON THE ROAD TO AVERHEIM

Near the town of Streissen, Averland,
378 miles from Altdorf

THE WAY TO Averheim was paved with misery and hopelessness. The closer they got to the capital, the more frequently they came across bedraggled regiments in Averland black and yellow. In truth, they were scraps of soldiers. Most were deserters or utterly routed troops. Encountered at a distance on the opposite side of the Aver, the broken merely trudged onwards, aimless and despairing. Those on the same side of the river fled like scared rabbits when they saw the column of Reikland troops. They wanted neither succour nor aid, instead fearing to be pressed into service by another lord. Many were wounded. Some carried dead and injured comrades over their shoulders, ignoring the stench of gangrene and decomposition.

There were human refugees too, alone and alongside the broken Averland troops, much like the ones the foot regiments had met earlier when Stahler was still in command. Dour priests of Morr walked with them, ministering to the dead and dying, flocks of ravens shadowing their every step.

Amongst a copse of trees, the army's scouts found a trio of hanged soldiers. From the scattered rocks beneath their dangling, bootless feet, it appeared they had committed suicide. Two more Averlanders were found slumped against the bole of the hanging tree. Their wrists were slit and bloodied daggers lay in their dead hands. Evidently, the desperate men had run out of rope for all five of them and didn't want to cut down the others to reuse what they had.

Mercifully the army did not meet any more orcs, nor did it stop at any other villages, empty or not. Deserters, refugees and suicides were not their only encounters, however. Late into the evening, just before the captains announced they would break camp, a single rider and a ragged band of followers on foot joined them, having come from the west.

Karlich shuddered inwardly when he recognised the same witch hunter from Hobsklein. The man had almost forty degenerates in tow. Around half were armoured to the hilt and carried an assortment of weapons. An eclectic mix, including a pair of dwarfs and several dark-skinned men foreign to the Empire, they could be nothing other than mercenaries. The rest were made up of flagellants and seekers, the latter being the homeless, pitiless wretches who had lost everything to the dark creatures that predated on the innocent and weak, and who longed only for vengeance or death. Dangerous men all, but nothing compared to their mounted leader.

'In search of gold and retribution,' remarked Volker from the second rank when he noticed Karlich looking at them. The Grimblades marched in column, three files wide, like the rest of the foot regiments. They were midway down the order of march, unfortunately, right behind the Steel Swords.

'Aye,' Karlich replied, keeping his feelings hidden from his men. 'Not a good combination.'

'Parasites and degenerates,' muttered Rechts to the sergeant's right, spitting out a gobbet of phlegm.

'Undesirable allies, indeed,' noted Lenkmann.

'All faithful men are soldiers of Sigmar,' said Masbrecht. 'We should not judge them harshly for that.'

Rechts glared over his shoulder at the man. 'Shut up, Masbrecht! No one cares what you think.'

'Both of you be quiet,' snapped Karlich, quickly nipping the situation in the bud before it could develop. 'Silence until we break camp,' he added afterwards.

The witch hunter and his 'soldiers of faith' joined the rear of the column, happiest with the militia companies and baggage train. Runners informed the prince of their presence. Encouraged by Father Untervash, Wilhelm tolerated them. He needed every man he could get if he was to lift the siege over Averheim.

Once they were out of sight, the rest of the army almost forgot about them. All except Karlich that is. The image of the witch hunter, attired in black and carrying his silver talisman like a death warrant, was burned into his mind. He could no more forget the man's presence than he could his own name. Was it just war and suffering that had drawn him to them, or did the Templar of Sigmar ride the plains of Averland for another reason? Was he, in fact, looking for someone?

Karlich did not consider himself to be a paranoid man. He met fate head on and didn't look over his shoulder for shadows in the night. The appearance of the witch hunter from Hobsklein had changed all that though.

BARON ERNST BLASELOCKER lolled in his saddle like an overweight klown. His steed, a stubby-legged mare, was as bulky as her master. Its bright yellow caparison hurt the eyes if looked at too long. Rings filled the baron's fat fingers and a great golden amulet rested on his breastplate which stuck out on account of his girth. A peppering of stubble swathed his triple chins but made him look neither swarthy nor rugged. All it actually did was to reinforce the baron's gluttonous image. His yellow and black tunic, echoed by the tiny pennant banner affixed to the back of his cuirass, affirmed his allegiance to Averland. A helmet, its visor raised, sat upon his head and failed to hide his thinning ginger hair. A broadsword sat in a scabbard at his waist which slapped against the man's bulging thigh in time with his wobbling jowls.

'Prince Wilhelm!' exclaimed the baron, throwing out an arm in over-enthusiastic greeting. 'It does my heart good to see that Reikland has not abandoned its brothers.'

The prince rode ahead of the army with Ledner, Preceptor Kogswald and a small contingent of Griffonkorps.

'Ernst,' the prince replied. The man was known to Wilhelm. They had attended Imperial functions together at the Emperor's Palace in Nuln. Baron Blaselocker was a toady, a lower ranked noble who sought to improve his station by association. More than once he had tried to court the prince's favour with offers of banquets or rides through his lands around the town of Streissen. Wilhelm had refused every one. Politely, of course. Emperor Dieter's functions were a trial he had no choice but to bear; Blaselocker's company was not.

Had he been able to choose his allies, Wilhelm would have placed the baron near the bottom of a long list. But such luxuries were not available to him. Every sword was welcomed to the cause, even Blaselocker's. To his credit, the baron had brought a decent-sized force with him. True to Preceptor Kogswald's word, there were a number of temple knights alongside the footslogging state troops. Wilhelm didn't recognise the order but judged them to be Sigmarite given the blazing comet device on their shields and banner. The rest of the army comprised spearmen and crossbows, with a few free companies. It was about a third the size of Wilhelm's force.

'A large army to escort a noble of my mere stature,' said the baron when he saw the marching column of men behind the prince's small entourage.

Wilhelm's brow furrowed. 'You misunderstand, Ernst. We aren't here to escort you anywhere. We march to Averheim to try and lift the siege.'

The baron's ruddy face paled at once.

'W-what? I thought...' The good humour vanished and his hands started to tremble a little.

'We march to Averheim, and so do you,' asserted Wilhelm. 'Now tell me, how bad are things at the capital? What forces do we face?'

The baron swallowed deeply and started to shake his head. 'N-no, no, no,' he blathered. 'You don't want to go there. We should head west to Reikland. I'm sure the Emperor will grant us protection in Nuln.'

'The Emperor has moved west himself already and resides at Altdorf,' snapped Ledner, 'you'll find no protection there. Now, do as your prince bids before I smack you off that horse, you fat oaf!'

As quickly as it came, Ledner's anger subsided, leaving Blaselocker dumbstruck.

'Speak to me, Ernst,' said the prince. 'Tell me what you know, and do it now.'

KELLER SHOOK THE dirt and stones from his boot, sitting by the side of the road and trying not to lift his gaze from the ground. He'd been seeing things in the shadows, in the lee of trees, at the crest of hills, in the cool quiet of valleys. During the march from Blösstadt, he'd noticed a shape flitting occasionally at the edge of his vision. But when he went to catch it the shape had gone, evaporated like mist before the hot sun. He knew what it was and begged for it to stop, before telling himself to get a grip on his senses. The shadow didn't listen. It dogged him every step he took. It haunted his every waking thought and came again, as a much more grisly apparition, not merely a shadow at all, in his nightmares. Even now, basking in the glory of the midday sun, whilst the regiments from Averland were integrated into the order of march, he felt it. There at his shoulder, he perched like a harbinger of Keller's own inexorable fate. His penance. Thankfully, none of the other Grimblades had noticed. At least not yet.

They rested briefly in a grassy plain with a few dotted trees and near a shallow stream. It was a minor tributary of the mighty Aver, which was visible as a glittering silver-blue band in the distance.

Almost as long and wide as the Reik, the river was an impressive sight. Ordinarily, skiffs and boats would ply its depths for trade and passage across. The Aver was strangely empty this day, and had been for several days before it. Even the river birds, the fishermen and water-borne creatures were few and far between. It was as if life had ceased to be along its banks, as if the river were abandoned in the face of the greenskin invasion, its own refugee columns passing unheeded in the night.

Rechts stretched his legs, and rubbed at the fading wound in his shoulder. He winced, but the pain was not nearly as bad as it had been. It had been a long march from Reikland and now, closing on Averheim and the enemy, the soldiers of the Empire were starting to feel it. Even Volker, a seasoned ranger and hunter used to trekking the wilds, rubbed at his back and grimaced.

'How much farther to Averheim?' said Rechts.

Though he'd asked no one in particular, Lenkmann took it upon himself to answer.

'Another thirty miles or so, just over that next rise,' – he pointed to the distant horizon – 'and we should see it. From there, I'd guess a day's march, maybe two.'

'Are you keen for a fight or something, Torsten?' asked Volker of the drummer.

'Not especially, but anything is preferable to this.'

'Maybe Eber could carry you,' laughed the Reikland hunter, one eye on Dog who was scurrying around the long grasses chasing imagined prey.

'Strap a cart onto his back and we could all travel in relative comfort,' scoffed Rechts, before leaping onto Eber's broad back. 'To Averheim, beast of burden!' he cried.

The big halberdier laughed loudly, seizing Rechts's ankles and then dumping him to the ground. 'This beast is not for riding,' said Eber, helping the drummer back to his feet, who was rubbing his sore rump.

By now, most of the Grimblades were laughing. Even Lenkmann managed to snigger. It was a welcome relief after the sombreness of Varveiter's death. Brand was nowhere to be seen, having wandered off. Likely he was sharpening his blades by the edge of the stream where a good number of soldiers were dunking their heads and washing their filthy pits, or refilling skins. The latter seemingly unbothered by what the former were doing in their future drinking water.

'Keller...' Masbrecht began, noticing the down-turned face of his comrade, 'are you all right? Not in the mood for banter? If you wish, I can bless you with–'

'*Go away!*' hissed Keller, risking a glance at a lonely tree a little way in the distance. Its limbs were swaying as if beckoning and a leaf cascaded forlornly from one of its branches. '*Leave me alone... please.*'

'Sorry, brother. I didn't mean to cause offence,' said Masbrecht and walked away to join the rest.

When he was gone, Keller looked up.

'What?' he asked of Masbrecht's departing back, only just realising he hadn't been alone.

KARLICH HAD A sour look on his face as he returned to the regiment and his men. He'd been listening to one of Prince Wilhelm's messengers, who related some change in orders directly from a scroll. The sergeant had neglected to even look at the parchment, let alone keep it, and instead nodded curtly to the runner before showing him his back and walking away.

'News doesn't look good,' whispered Rechts.

Even from behind him, Masbrecht could smell the alcohol on the drummer's breath but chose to hold his tongue. It awakened something in him, an old dependency and desire he thought was long buried. Clenching his jaw, Masbrecht pushed it back down into the deep places of his soul where it belonged. Lenkmann, standing rod-straight alongside the Grimblade drummer, failed to notice Rechts's booze breath. His gaze was fixed on Karlich.

'It will be what it will be,' he replied. 'We'll perform our duty all the same.'

'Definitely not good,' hissed Volker.

They were back in formation and arrayed in column with the Averland regiments. A few of the officers had received messages from the prince and the army was awaiting their return to the ranks before marching on to Averheim.

'Who is that overstuffed peacock riding behind him?' asked Keller. His voice was a little hoarse; he'd barely spoken at all in days.

They all saw the corpulent noble atop his stubby-legged steed swaying behind Karlich. Even mounted, the man was slower than the Grimblade sergeant by a good two strides. Karlich reached the men first as the noble slowed and then came to a stop a few regiments ahead of them, next to Von Rauken's Carroburg Few. The stern greatsworder champion looked about as pleased as Karlich to be in the mounted noble's presence, but then his mood was perpetually dour.

'Sergeant,' said Lenkmann, addressing Karlich with a clipped salute.

'You're probably wondering who that is,' began Karlich, not deigning to wait for questions. 'It's Baron Ernst Blaselocker of Streissen. His Averland regiments are the reason for our swelled forces.'

'Why is he riding with us?' asked Volker.

'He has replaced Captain Stahler,' Brand replied, prompting a glance over the shoulder from Karlich.

'Is he leading us now then?' asked Rechts, failing to keep the disappointment out of his voice.

Karlich was stoic in response. 'The baron has command of the Reik and Averland foot, until such time as Captain Stahler is fit to retake the field.'

'And how long will that be?' asked Masbrecht.

'How am I to know!' snapped Karlich. 'I have yet to visit the chirurgeon's tent and enquire after the captain. His screams suggest it will not be before we reach Averheim, if at all.'

'Let's hope it's soon...' mumbled Volker.

'I heard that!'

Volker bowed his head contritely at the sergeant's reprimand.

'Tender mercies of Shallya, can he even fight?' hissed Lenkmann, as surprised as anyone at his own impropriety.

Karlich knew something of the noble who now led them. He'd heard talk in the Averland camp and knew that some called him the 'Yellow Baron' and not on account of his allegiance to the province either. Together with the appearance of the witch hunter, Stahler's injury and now this, it was turning into an arduous campaign.

Karlich sighed. It was a question to which he suspected he knew the answer already but, for the sake of morale, chose not to voice. Instead he replied with as much tact as he could muster.

'We'll find out soon enough.'

CHAPTER NINE

RIVERS OF BLOOD

Brigund Bridge, Averland,
409 miles from Altdorf

THOUGH NOT AS long or wide as the Reik, the River Aver was still a formidable waterway. Its silvery expanse hugged the northern border of Averland and was as much a defensive barrier as it was a route for trade and commerce coming out of the east. Beyond the capital Averheim and along the edges of the Moot, the land of the halflings, it divided into two large tributaries, the Aver Reach and Blue Reach. Crossing it was a simple matter of securing passage upon a barge or finding a bridge or a ford near one of its narrower junctions. For a large force of men, together with baggage and beasts of burden, it was a more difficult prospect. The fact of the greenskin invasion made that prospect doubly problematic.

Out of tactical acuity or simple wanton destruction, the orcs and goblins in the Paunch's horde had destroyed most of the major crossing points over the Aver. Bridges were left fire-blackened ruins, ferrymen and their barges slain and burned, fords clogged with rotting corpses and the wreckage of the greenskins' violent rampages.

The search for a suitable crossing, large enough to accommodate his army, drove Wilhelm north-east. They shadowed the mighty river all the way. Every step closer to Averheim brought increased atrocities visited upon its people by the orcs. Isolated greenskin warbands were spotted across the far side of the Aver. Many of the men, particularly the Averlanders, wanted to engage them but Wilhelm forbade it – they had to reach the capital. Every moment wasted was time for another nail to be driven into Averheim's coffin. If the city was nought but a smoking ruin when they arrived then everything they'd endured so far would have been for nothing. The greenskins hooted and jeered at the passing army, loosing arrows ineffectually to land in the river's midst or break on the rocks of its bank. Angered, but maintaining discipline, the army of the Empire ignored them and marched on.

'Our fight will come soon enough,' Wilhelm had told them. 'Save your blades and your fury for that.'

It was to come soon, upon the Brigund Bridge, and the river below would run red with the blood of both man and orc.

A CHUNK OF Averland stone barrelled through the air, twisting slowly like a leaf caught in the wind. Empire men watched it as it turned. They looked with morbid fascination, wondering bleakly if they would be struck or spared. Reaching the end of its parabola, the rock crashed into the ground with a shower of earth, chalk dust and grit. A regiment of Averland pike was crumpled by it, their shields and their screams doing nothing to prevent the rock trammelling their ranks. Men were crushed to paste. Some became tangled around the rock as it rolled onwards, using its momentum to furrow the earth and churn up soldiers like they were dolls.

'Drive on, Grimblades!' bellowed Karlich, ducking instinctively as another chunk of masonry spiralled into the sky. Beyond the waves of orcs and goblins holding the bridge, he made out distant batteries of catapults. The launching arm of one snapped, sending three of its goblin crew into the air instead of its stone cargo, which was dumped onto its orc overseer instead. He smiled grimly at the greenskins' misfortune, but knew it meant little. The Paunch had not only burned and ravaged on his bloody way through the Empire, he had constructed and fortified too. Much of the material, including its ammunition used to build the catapults, had been taken from barns, homesteads and watchtowers. Crude, certainly, but effective and deadly too, and in abundance. Through glimpses between the ducking and rallying, Karlich counted at least ten onager and mangonel-like war machines. The barrage was almost unceasing. It was making a real mess of the foot troops.

Blaselocker had no answer, even though his objective was a simple one: take and hold the bridge, and do not yield it until Wilhelm and his knights arrive. Karlich had seen the tactic used by the Empire many times. The foot regiments drive the army's centre, claiming a strategic position by sheer weight of numbers. Once taken, they must then keep it until a smaller, but more powerful, force attacked from the flank. The idea was to frustrate an enemy into throwing everything at the defenders to try and break them. Whilst he vented his strength and his wrath to his front, he would be vulnerable to his flank and rear. The flanking force would tear into that weakness and rip out the enemy's heart. A determined push from the hitherto static foot soldiers would press the enemy to his front aspect and thusly surrounded would result in the enemy being broken and routed.

Military theory was one thing. Textbooks and scrolls relayed the tactic in impersonal terms, with the added benefit of strategic maps. They did not tell would-be generals of the reek of blood, the stench of men as they piss and shit themselves before the first push, the deafening clamour of steel or the wailing of the dead. They did not reveal how your heart beat louder than a drum in your chest, so violent it felt like it would burst right out of your ribcage. Nor did it make reference to the enemy launching chunks of rock the size of cattle at you, or of air so thick with arrows and powder smoke it was as if the sun had been permanently eclipsed. It told of none of these things, because to do so would stop any young officer from taking to the field and likely have them seek out a softer profession as a merchant or craftsman.

So it was that Karlich and the Grimblades, together with the rest of the foot regiments, were to be the rock around which Wilhelm's plan depended, holding long enough for the prince to launch his crippling counter punch at the head of an armoured wedge of charging steel. Only before they could hold the bridge, they had to first take it. In the way of that were the orc war machines. Two waves comprised the assault: the Grimblades were in the first. Smash a hole through the greenskin ranks, drive on to the machineries and destroy them. A simple enough plan with one subtle flaw, how can you fight back against a chunk of hurtling stone?

Yet another rock thudded into the ground just to the Grimblades' right. It sank down into the earth and didn't roll, but still spread a clutch of charging militia across the ground like crimson butter. Chips of broken stone spat out from the impact like pistol shots. One hit Gruber in the shoulder, making the Grimblade from the back ranks cry out and fall; another scythed Brand across the cheek, but he merely grunted and took the pain without slowing down.

A slow jog built to a flat out run from the Empire foot troops as the greenskins came within charging distance. The soldiers roared until their lungs burned, dredging courage from within. The war machines had to be destroyed. Wilhelm and his knights could not flank attack until they were gone, for even the formidable armour of the Griffonkorps and the Order of the Fiery Comet was as linen against several tons of falling masonry.

To his right, Karlich saw the shadow of a great flying beast passing across the smothered light of the sun. The air around it crackled, promoting the gathering of storm clouds tinged an ugly dark green. Fell voices filled the air. Their bestial words were indiscernible to the sergeant but their meaning was clear.

Bring war and death to men.

As quickly as he had seen it, the shadow of the beast was gone, lost beyond Karlich's peripheral vision, taking its master with it towards where he knew Wilhelm and his knights were riding. Karlich mouthed a silent prayer to Sigmar for the prince's triumph and forged on.

Regiments closed on either side of the Grimblades, the anchors to their flanks. On the immediate left, Averland swordsmen began to raise shields; on the right the remnants of the Bögenhafen spearmen, who had overrun the broken militia unit formerly attached to them, now levelled their polearms. On the extremes of the formation were the Steel Swords and Carroburg Few, to the left and right respectively. Blaselocker led from the rear, urging his men to charge behind a solid wall of shields and blades.

Overhead, arrows and crossbow bolts soared like flocks of barbed-beaked birds. Powder cracks came and went like thunder, accompanied by smoke and the reek of fire and soot. Karlich saw a distant line of greenskins fall to the wave of missiles. Goblins span on their heels, choking with arrows in their throats or clutching stomachs where iron shot had torn them away. Several fell with bolts to the brain, transfixed through the eye as if sprouting a black-fletched whisker.

The orcs were more resilient. Their armour was thicker, they wore helmets and carried shields – many tore out the shafts sticking from their bodies or barrelled on with them still embedded in their flesh like spines. Goblin short-bows were loosed sporadically in reply, but failed to have much of an impact. It didn't really matter. The horde was huge. Hand-to-hand was where it excelled, where the strength and brutality of orcs found domination.

The greenskins were coming up fast. A wall of rampant orcs and goblins was held together in ragged formations, clutching crude spears, clubs and axes. The beasts were daubed in blood and war paint, their round wooden shields smeared with orcish icons and tribal symbols. Their banners were fashioned from flesh and hide, baked black in the sun, and carried further sigils. They reminded Karlich of totems; skulls and other trophies rammed on their spiked tips in grisly stacks. Horns blared and drums beat, vying against the Empire's own, order meeting discord in a cacophony.

'In the name of Prince Wilhelm!' shouted Karlich, and his cry was echoed by the other sergeants down the line. The clash was just seconds away. The edge of the bridge was so close, just a few feet, but swamped with greenskins. He felt his heart beating, so loud it deafened the noise around him. Gripping his sword, the earth pounding by beneath his feet, the pull of the wind and the stench of greenskins swirling, he raised his shield and met the foe.

Several died in the initial rush, impaled on blades and spears, smothered in the crush, battered senseless against shields and unyielding bodies. It was over in moments. Then came the drive and the real killing began.

Karlich cut to his right, severing an orc's jugular. A fine spray of dark blood painted his breastplate. Turning towards a flash of green to his left, he impaled another orc through the neck, nearly ripping off its head as he withdrew the blade in a welter of gore. Something smashed against his shield and he would have fallen if not for the man behind him pushing him upright.

'In Sigmar's name, sergeant!' shouted Masbrecht from the second rank, thrusting his halberd over Karlich's shoulder to pierce an orc's torso. When the halberd spike was ripped free it released a gushet of blood and greenskin innards, spilling them like offal onto the ground.

'Aye, for Sigmar,' breathed Karlich, thrusting his shield forward to smash a goblin's nose and committing back to the fight.

At the end of the front rank, Eber grunted and blew, his halberd rising and falling like a pendulum in his thick-fingered grasp. He cut off a goblin's head, the wretched creature was still snarling even after it was decapitated, then lunged into another orc's body. Eber held the beast as it flailed at him, before Brand finished it with a downward cut that split its skull.

'Push forward!' the voice of Karlich was muted by the sheer madness of the battle around them. They saw Lenkmann raise the banner and heard the beat of Rechts's drum, conveying the order to press.

A tangible swell came from behind them as the rear rankers heaved. On either side, the flanking regiments of swords and spearmen did the same. The entire Empire battle line was making a concerted push against the greenskins. The orcs and goblins on the near side of the Brigund Bridge were only a vanguard, the bulk of the greenskins were on the other side. Still, all the Grimblades needed to do was punch a hole through the centre, surge through to the other side and assault the war machines.

Volker was breathing hard. The greenskins were everywhere, but he tried to keep focused on those in front of him, trying to kill him. Like they had at Blösstadt, goblins sneaked through the orcish ranks, aiming for legs and ankles with their knives as they emerged amongst the enemy. The tactic was less effective this time. The

Empire men had learned to look below as well as in front. Dog patrolled his master's legs, savaging any goblins that came close, ripping out their throats and keeping pace with the push.

The orc vanguard was breaking. Keller felt it from the second rank as surely as the wood of the Brigund Bridge beneath his boots. Blaselocker's determined push up the centre was actually working. Panicked, huge swathes of orcs and goblins fled backwards through their own ranks. Too slow to turn and join the flood, some were crushed underfoot. Others tumbled over the sides of the bridge to a watery doom in the Aver below. Suddenly an ever-widening streak of daylight began to emerge between the Empire forces and the retreating greenskins.

'Tighten formation!' The order reverberated down the line to the tune of trumpets and drums. As they gained the bridge, running past its midpoint in pursuit of the greenskins, Keller felt the files narrow and the ranks thicken. To his right and left, men withdrew to make additional ranks and deepen the Grimblades' formation. The spears and swords on either side did the same. Von Rauken's Carroburg Few and the Middenland Steel Swords closed in and the entire Empire battle line became a giant stopper, plugging up the bridge along its width.

'Advance!' shouted Karlich, screaming to be heard above the din of the battle. The greenskin vanguard was in full retreat. Other regiments on the far side of the Brigund Bridge were closing fast to seal the gap but were slow and unruly to respond. Bickering had broken out amongst several mobs, so all that stood between the Grimblades and the greenskin catapults was a thin line of goblins wielding short bows.

'Forward now! Charge you whoresons, charge!'

It was like breaking the surface of the sea having been submerged below its watery depths as the Grimblades burst from the battle line and headed straight for the goblin archers. Arrows whickered into them from the goblins' vantage point on the lowest step of a shallow hill. At the summit, the war machine crews looked on helplessly, the Empire men too close to target with the catapults. The Grimblades' momentum had carried them a long way across the short tract of plains that led up to the hill. Behind them, the other regiments had closed the gap, effectively 'shutting the gate' back onto the bridge for the other greenskins.

Eber felt an arrow glance his arm. He grimaced as it tore his tunic and opened a wet, red line in his skin. Another Grimblade fell somewhere behind him, gurgling blood from a neck wound, trampled to death in the maddened dash for the hill, but this was the only casualty. Seeing their arrows were ineffective, the goblin archers balked and some even started to run as the Grimblades charged them.

Ascending the hill in long strides, the Empire soldiers fell upon the hapless goblins in a hacking, lunging wave. The entire front rank of the greenskin archers was butchered in seconds. The few that remained squealed and ran. Some were swept up by the triumphant halberdiers as they drove on to attack the catapults; others were sent sprawling down the hillsides, breaking their necks and limbs. Fewer still just kept on running, abandoning the field and Averland for good.

The war machines were no greater challenge. Mainly crewed by goblins with the occasional orc overseer, the ones that didn't flee on sight of the massacred archers soon fell beneath the halberdiers' blades. The fight had lasted only minutes, but the catapults were silenced and as they took stock of the carnage around them, the Grimblades realised just how far from the battle at the bridge they had come.

Marshalling some order at last, huge mobs of orcs and goblins had started to converge on the bridge, determined to take it back. Massive brutes wielding double-bladed axes and feral beasts with bones through their noses, wearing furs and carrying stone clubs, roamed amongst the throng. Trolls lolled between the mobs, goblin overseers prodding them enthusiastically with long, barbed tridents. One of the witless creatures took offence at being goaded and ate one of its tormentors in a single bite. An armoured orc with a spiked whip took the dead goblin's place and the troll was driven forward again. Other, smaller beasts scurried between the unruly ranks. Reddish-orange, bulbous and festooned with warts, Karlich recognised them as squigs. Little more than fangs on legs, squigs were vicious creatures, the absurdity of their appearance belying their ferocity.

Von Rauken and the others faced a stern challenge to hold the bridge, but at least the war machines had been silenced. At least Prince Wilhelm and the knights were not far off, now the way was open.

Karlich looked to the east. A storm raged there, cerulean lighting clashing with green fire in the heavens. Clouds boiled up in anger, summoned by their masters as an unseen magical duel took place. Wilhelm and his entourage would be in its eye.

'They've met them...' said Lenkmann, proudly holding the banner aloft.

All eyes went to the Brigund Bridge where the greenskin mobs had finally clashed with the Empire defenders attempting to hold it.

'Madness,' breathed Masbrecht upon witnessing the carnage. 'Sigmar protect them.' He made the sign of the hammer.

'We fought in something similar,' Rechts shot back, but realised Von Rauken and the others were in a fight for their lives.

'Where is Prince Wilhelm?' asked Volker, looking to where the magical storm cracked and thundered.

Karlich had his eyes on the battle for the bridge. 'Waylaid,' he muttered. He looked around him. The orcs and goblins were leaving them alone for now, a wide gulf of open ground churned by booted feet but empty of foes, encircled them.

'We should hold the hill, sergeant,' said Lenkmann, guessing what Karlich was thinking. 'Those are our orders.'

Karlich grit his teeth. 'I know.' His gaze went eastward again. There were no trumpets, no calls to arms, only sorcerous thunder. All the while, more and more greenskins poured into the forces at the Brigund Bridge. It was impossible to see anything in the chaos. Did the orc mobs advance a step? Karlich couldn't be sure.

'What shall we do?' asked Brand. Several other Grimblades around him looked eager to hear the sergeant's answer.

Again, Karlich looked to the east.

'What if he doesn't come?' asked Eber, frowning at the thought of what might happen if Wilhelm didn't arrive.

'Something's happening!' said Lenkmann, pointing his sword towards the bridge.

Karlich went a few steps down the hill. 'What's he doing?' His eyes narrowed as he tried to see.

Masbrecht saw it before the rest. His voice was cold and distant.

'He's ordering a retreat...'

Scowling, Karlich turned to face him. 'What?' He looked back. Masbrecht was right. The troops in the rear ranks were pulling back. Blaselocker had taken his fill of bloodshed and death and decided he didn't like it.

'Von Rauken won't give up the bridge,' said Keller, blinking hard as if trying to shake off the sight. 'Have you ever known a Carroburger to relinquish anything?'

'Then he'll die,' said Rechts. 'They're fatalists, as well as stubborn bastards.'

'Aye, and for nothing!' snapped Karlich, then muttered, 'Blaselocker you spineless cur...' He strode back up the hill to address his men.

'We're going down there, aren't we?' said Lenkmann, his tone resigned.

'We are,' said Karlich. 'Into formation!' he cried to the regiment.

Rechts beat out the order on his drum.

'Tight ranks, narrow frontage,' hollered Karlich. 'We'll punch through like a lance.'

'Not wishing to speak out of turn,' muttered Rechts, 'but this is suicidal, sergeant.'

'Have some *faith*,' Karlich replied, deliberately bitter. 'Prince Wilhelm will come. Succour isn't only found at the bottom of a bottle, Torsten.'

The drummer shut his mouth and waited for the order.

Karlich gave it swiftly.

'Forward, in the name of the Reik and Prince Wilhelm!'

UNIMPEDED BY THE open terrain, the Grimblades marched quickly to the battle site. Karlich steered them on an oblique route that would see them hit the weakest flank of the greenskin line, using the river itself as a natural anchor to their own flank.

A ragged band of goblins were the first enemies to oppose them. Karlich and his men fell upon the smaller greenskins with fury. The Grimblades cut the goblins down ruthlessly, the greenskins' bloodied-eye banner soon crushed underfoot by the rampant halberdiers. Karlich finished the goblins' champion himself, severing the creature's neck and head. It proved too much for the greenskins, who turned and fled into the packed ranks before they'd barely struck a blow in reply. The large mob of orcs behind them, swathed in metal scale and carrying broad wooden shields and spears, were a different foe altogether. They killed their cowardly goblin cousins as they ran into the unmoveable line of their shields. It only set off the orcs' bloodlust. They whooped and hollered at the prospect of a real fight presented by the overrunning Grimblades.

'Into them!' Karlich was hoarse from battle, but made his voice heard above the clash of steel and the grunt of beasts.

Hitting the orcs was like driving at a stone wall; hard and unyielding. They had the greenskins in the flank, robbing them of much of their fighting strength and stopping their chieftain from bringing his axe to bear, but still they fought ferociously. So intent were the greenskins on getting to the bridge that their ranks were utterly rammed, like forcing an apple through the eye of a needle. The smaller beasts were crushed by the bigger ones. Karlich saw trolls, slime-skinned monsters with manes of lank seaweed-like hair and scales like fish, looming head and shoulders above the brawling mobs. Occasionally one would reach down and pluck a greenskin from the mob, biting off its head or swallowing it whole before it was brought to heel again by spears and whips. Patches of animosity broke out amidst the clamouring horde, so in the end it was hard to tell who was fighting who.

Through the carnage, Karlich could see Von Rauken and his men fighting like heroes to hold the bridge. He saw too that the greatsworders noticed the allies in their midst and redoubled their efforts. The Carroburgers were not alone, either, and it sent a shiver of fear down Karlich's spine when he recognised the mercenary rabble of the witch hunter. Whether to hold the bridge or simply to bring death to the enemies of Sigmar, or even for the templar's promised coin, the sellswords, flagellants and seekers stuck doggedly to the task when everyone but the greatsworders had already fled.

Madmen... thought Karlich, *but perhaps the templar would be slain?*

He dared to hope, then felt a heavy blow against his shield. Karlich was battered back but stuck out his sword and was rewarded with a porcine squeal of pain. He then righted himself, parrying a cut that would have cleaved his own head, and jabbed again. Steel met flesh and the orc assailing him, seen only in flashes from behind Karlich's shield, before it crumpled to the ground with its throat slashed open. After that, Karlich forgot about the witch hunter and put his mind wholly on staying alive.

With their brutish kin around them, the orcs were not giving an inch. The Grimblades had killed several and, fighting the beasts to their unprepared flank, had taken few casualties in reply, but the orcs were digging in and more were coming.

Rear rankers, impatient to get into battle, had now seen the flank attack by the Empire soldiers. Horns brayed and hooted and drums pounded out the order to reform and manoeuvre around the flank. Locked in combat, Karlich realised with rising horror that the Grimblades were exposed.

'Push them back, break through!' he urged, but it was like telling the wind not to blow or the mountains to part ways – the orcs were implacable.

Glory was not something that had ever concerned Karlich. He was a soldier, content with a soldier's lot. But throwing away the lives of his men because of a rash decision did not sit well with him. Suddenly, he wished they had stayed on the hill and the bridge be damned.

Blaselocker, you bastard, he thought. You've doomed us all with your cowardice.

Eber anchored the end of the line with Brand behind him, then Leffe and Gans in the rear ranks. His halberd was slick with greenskin blood and his muscles burned from the killing. Corpses littered the ground at his feet but for a moment there was respite as the orc back ranks had been despatched and others were still struggling over the dead to fill the gaps. Out of the corner of his eye he noticed another mob approaching. They were the biggest greenskins he had ever seen, as broad as oak trees with skin twice as thick as bark but just as gnarled. Huge black metal plates covered their bodies, dripping with swathes of chainmail. Horned helmets rose up in exultation to their heinous gods, a challenge and an invocation in one. Gauntleted fists, as large as a horse's head and studded with spikes, wrapped around thick-hafted glaives that glinted dully in the half-light. Graven totems, tiny skulls and rings of brass and copper, jangled against the metal like cruel laughter.

'Monsters...' Eber breathed, and for the first time in his life found something that frightened him more than his father. 'Brand!' he cried.

'I see them,' said Brand, levelling his halberd at the onrushing greenskins. They were like charging bulls, and lowered their horned helms as they closed.

'Do you believe in the power of Sigmar, Brand?' asked Eber. The other two Grimblades, Leffe and Gans, had swung around too but kept quiet.

The bull-like orcs were just twenty feet away.

'I believe a man must save himself if he wants to live. Sigmar protects the strong.'

Eber muttered, 'I wish Masbrecht were here beside me...'

The Empire men roared, prepared to meet their enemy defiantly, when a blinding flash lit up the gloom. Thunder, loud and percussive as cannon fire, erupted a split-second afterwards. Eber blinked back the after flare of lightning, the reek of ozone heavy in his nostrils, and saw a row of charred corpses where the monstrous orcs had been.

Brand noticed the hairs on his hands were standing up. His teeth ached.

'Maybe I was wro–'

Another flash... this time they saw it come from the heavens, splitting the darkness like sun pierces cloud.

Brand managed to keep his eyes open long enough to see the orcs struck, to see the lightning arc race through all that metal, burning and shocking as it went.

The storm came again, several bolts coursing from above like spears of righteous anger. They weaved and raked, splitting and coruscating through the greenskin mobs like hot, angry fingers. Wherever they touched, death followed. The stink of smouldering orc flesh was soon heavy on the breeze.

Eber was laughing, loud and booming in concert with the thunder.

Brand laughed too. It was a wicked sound, full of malice and sadistic joy.

'Burn you bastards, burn!'

Some of the greenskins were running. Karlich felt the rout before he saw it, a sudden shifting of weight to their embattled front. He'd lost sight of the flank by then, so buried was he in blood and bodies. Something lit up the battle, too stark and short-lived to be sunlight.

Did I just hear laughter?

The tide had swung again and he didn't need to see the banner of Altdorf snapping on the breeze to know the self-same saviour had delivered them again.

Thunder came from the east. It wracked the heavens above and shook the earth below. Hooves pounded the dirt, clarions announced a glorious charge. A sudden rush of movement came upon the greenskins as if an unseen wind was propelling them west, away from the storm of steeds and lances. They panicked as one, some flailing into the Aver to be drowned in its unforgiving depths. Others were crushed in the relentless press from the Brigund Bridge now that Blaselocker, with victory in sight, had re-committed the troops. Despite the fact they'd been fighting longer than any other regiment, the Carroburg Few led the rampant pursuers.

For his part, Karlich ordered his Grimblades to hold. The bridge was won and they would keep it that way. He contented himself with watching the enemy flee, safe in the knowledge that no more of his men would die, for the moment at least. A blur of silver, gold and red sped past them, so long that he had time to strike up his pipe and stand in awe of it.

Karlich could only glance at Wilhelm riding at the head of the Griffonkorps, the horses were moving too swiftly for a longer look. The gold-armoured Order of the Fiery Comet drove alongside them, their flanged maces spitting arcs of greenskin blood when they rose and fell. The prince was majestic, his runefang like a streak of captured fire in his hand. On his left, Preceptor Kogswald, his own blade etched in enchanted sigils; on his right, the wizard Karlich had seen in the command tent, no longer wearing a dowdy cloak and cowl. Stars and comets decorated his robes of deep, cerulean blue. Silver edged the cuffs and trims. Constellations stitched into the fabric appeared to shimmer and shift. Lightning bolts and other heavenly symbols hung from chains on his belt and around his neck. Even the skullcap the wizard wore carried the image of celestial phenomena.

Hope sparked within the sergeant, kindled by the lightning that had raged from above and so decimated the greenskins. Perhaps victory at Averheim was possible after all.

'Quite a sight, isn't it?' Von Rauken's voice brought Karlich around.

The greatsworder champion was walking towards him with some of his men. The lacquered black plate of his cuirass was dented and smeared with blood. He'd removed his helmet, revealing a few strands of hair covering an otherwise bald head.

'Comes from living in Carroburg,' he said. Von Rauken grinned, showing a missing tooth. Evidently, the greatsworders had hung back after all and had merely moved aside to allow the fresher regiments to pass.

'Aye, I hear you're a serious people. A little levity and you might have some hair to warm that pate of yours.'

Von Rauken smiled and held out a gauntleted hand. It looked massive and the leather palm was well worn from sword wielding.

'Your service to Carroburg, and to the Few, will not be forgotten, Sergeant Karlich.'

Karlich gripped the greatsworder's hand firmly and nodded.

'Call me Feder.'

Von Rauken clapped him on the shoulder. 'Very well, Feder. I am still Von Rauken.'

At that the two men laughed loudly. There was palpable relief in it, of a battle over and won, of having survived to tell of it and endure the nightmares later. It passed to the men around them and soon Grimblade and Carroburg Few were exchanging names and stories in the way that Lenkmann had expected of the Steel Swords.

For their part, the Middenlanders were livid. Glory had been denied them, supplanted by ignominy at being part of Blaselocker's retreating force. They strode across the bridge wearing scowls like masks, not meeting any other soldier in the eye. Sturnbled looked ashamed, but used his pride to conceal it. Torveld was looking for someone to blame for this smear on their honour. His gaze fell upon the Grimblades and was then lost again to the middle distance.

The battle was done, the greenskin army in full rout. Most of the Empire regiments had given up pursuit and were consolidating at the bridge. Even as they spoke, Karlich and Von Rauken were being joined by troops from the north side of the river. The wagons, too, were now starting to move across. Priests of Morr went with them, leather-bound 'death-books' clutched in their bony fingers, ledgers for the prince's quartermasters when they had to reorganise the army in the face of casualties.

Blaselocker trotted over last of all, his bodyguards surrounding him, glad their faces were obscured by battle-helms. The baron would have to answer to Prince Wilhelm now.

'A pity he did not die in the battle,' spat Von Rauken, his mood souring at the sight of the pompous Averland noble.

Karlich was a little taken aback by the blatant outburst, even though he felt the same. He supped on his pipe to cover his surprise, but found himself liking the outspoken greatsworder more and more.

'He'll wish he did if Ledner is allowed at him,' he replied.

Von Rauken smiled again, but this time humourlessly. 'Then let us hope for that.'

CHAPTER TEN
LICKING WOUNDS

The town of Mannsgard, Averland,
383 miles from Altdorf

LEDNER CLOSED THE tavern door and turned to face an almost empty room. An iron tub sat in the middle of it where Prince Wilhelm was taking a hot bath.

'How is it?' asked the prince, whilst a local priestess of Shallya rubbed healing salts into his heavily-bruised shoulder. The charge by the prince and his knights might have been glorious, but the battle to fend off Grom's shaman and his 'flying lizard' was not. The beast had raked Wilhelm's pauldron before he'd nicked its snout with his runefang and sent it fleeing for the sky.

'Quiet,' said Ledner. His gaze went to the armour and clothing slumped on a chair near the tub. Wilhelm's runefang rested on top of it, inside its scabbard. The captain noticed his liege kept the blade within reach. A sensible move. Perhaps the young prince was learning to be cautious after all. 'Mannsgard might as well be a tomb,' he went on. 'The townsfolk that haven't fled or been killed cower behind locked doors carrying picks and cudgels. The few people we have encountered offer limited services and don't indulge in much talk.'

Wilhelm frowned at the annoyance in Ledner's voice.

'And this bothers you?' he asked.

'Yes, it bothers me. Where are the peddlers and the whores, the illicit traders and profiteers? War brings death, my liege, but it also brings opportunity for those who have a will and a way to make coin.'

Wincing with the pain in his back and shoulder, Wilhelm sat up in the bath.

'They're mostly dead, Ledner. That or they've run westward with the refugees,' he explained needlessly. 'We are less than ten miles from Averheim. I can almost hear the greenskin chanting on the breeze and smell their spore tainting it. Is it really any wonder that the land, this town, is abandoned, even by its human carrion?'

Ledner's face darkened.

'No, my liege.'

'So, how do we fare?' asked the prince, glancing at the death-books piled in one corner of the room.

They were in the tavern's taproom. The floors were timber, the wood stained but worn. A simple bar sat to the left at the back. Most of the alcohol was gone. A stairway curled up to an upper floor. The iron tub had been moved from one of the upper rooms – 'guest quarters' a placard read – and brought down to the prince. It looked almost ludicrous in the expansive room, the many tables and chairs that might once have stood there having been either looted or used as barricades.

Though the day's march from the Brigund Bridge to the town had proven uneventful, Mannsgard had suffered many attacks since the invasion. The town's walls were thick, hewn from rough stone taken from the mountains, and overlooked by watchtowers. Its militia regiments had been many, several bands of soldiers seeking refuge had also added to its garrison, but still they had suffered. The cemeteries and mortuaries were full. Even the temples of Shallya, Sigmar and Verena could hold no more bodies. So much corpse traffic had been foisted upon the gardens of Morr that the old prefect had died himself, of a heart attack. Ledner heard talk of a town watchmen finding the poor old bastard, his withering body food for the crows.

Morr giveth, Morr taketh away...

A black mood pervaded here, the final rest before the march on Averheim. It was like a funeral veil, only no one had said when they could stop mourning. At least, the presence of the army meant that greenskin raiders would think twice before attacking again. Not that there'd been any sign for several days, not according to Mannsgard's gate sentries anyway. Ledner supposed the orcs and goblins had been drawn to the Brigund Bridge instead and the army of 'humies', as they called men in their crude speech, gathering there. A black stain was upon this place. It was no different to Blösstadt, only unlike the village they'd been forced to put to the torch, Mannsgard didn't realise it was already dead. Old men and withered women mainly populated the town now, its youth having been cut down in its prime, an end to its legacy and future.

'Adolphus?' Wilhelm pressed.

Ledner blinked, recognising his first name, and realising he hadn't answered the prince's question.

Sometimes the dark moods came when he least expected it. Usually he could master them, the baggage of too many years of war and blood. Occasionally they got the better of him.

'We lost a lot of men at Brigund Bridge. More than we could comfortably spare.'

'Any loss like that is uncomfortable to me, Ledner,' chided the prince, standing and accepting a towel from the Shallyan priestess.

'I meant no offence, but it's simple numbers my lord. We can't hope to prevail at Averheim with the forces we have left. At best our chances are slim and bloody.'

Stepping from the tub, Wilhelm's brow furrowed. He looked heavy, as if he still wore his armour. Ledner continued.

'Of course, our dear ally the baron was somewhat instrumental in that debacle.'

'I heard Karlich's men helped hold the bridge with the Carroburgers.'

'Stubborn bastards,' muttered Ledner, before a stern look from Wilhelm forced an apology. 'They are certainly resourceful, and brave, these halberdiers. True sons of the Reik,' he added, cracking his knuckles, just another of his idiosyncratic traits. 'Vanhans and his rabble earned their keep, too.'

'The witch hunter?'

'Yes, my lord. They are camped outside the town walls. The templar claims there is only "debauchery and unholy art" to be found within.'

'I'm surprised he hasn't come in to burn and stake it all then. Watch him,' said Wilhelm, finishing up drying off. He handed the towel back to the priestess, who bowed and took her leave.

'Like a hawk, my lord.'

A pregnant pause invited Ledner's next question. He waited to ask it until they were alone. 'Would you like me to remonstrate with Blaselocker?'

Wilhelm pulled on his undergarments and hose. 'If I wanted to find him hanging by his medallion from the rafters or drowned in his own drink, then yes. I'll deal with him,' the prince asserted. 'The Averlanders need a figurehead, even one as craven as he. What of Sirrius?'

'Weak from his exertions. It doesn't take an augur to know he won't be fighting again for a few days. Even if we wanted to move on Averheim tomorrow, I wouldn't advise it, not without the wizard.'

Wilhelm considered that for a moment before his mind went elsewhere. 'Any word from the other provinces?'

'Messengers were sent as requested, but none, as of yet, have returned. The scouting parties have come back though, some of them. They report Stirland is under almost perpetual siege and that greenskin armies are as far north as Talabecland.'

'So we are alone in this, after all, just as the Emperor predicted.' Wilhelm couldn't hide his bitterness. After buttoning his tunic, he sat down heavily in the chair, his sword and armour now resting against the leg. 'I love the Empire, Ledner…'

'As do we all, my liege.'

'But I love the Reik more. What are we doing here, old friend? Is this really our war? Was Markus right? Should I be back at Kemperbad, strengthening our border for the inevitable tide?'

'Someone must stand for the Empire when its emperor does not,' Ledner answered plainly. 'I am not a righteous man. I have killed and bribed, extorted and committed larceny to keep my province safe. I do it knowing I must live a life of compromise, because that is who I am and my lot. You, my lord, *are* a righteous man.' Ledner paused to look outside, an old habit, to make sure no one was within earshot. He looked back at Wilhelm. 'Dieter is a fatuous emperor. His time is ending. Whatever business he is brokering with Marienburg will undo him, and when he falls the Empire will have need of a decent man, a strong lineage to guide it.'

'I don't make war five hundred miles from home as part of a bid for succession, Ledner,' said the prince, slightly perturbed.

'I know, my liege,' the captain replied, 'and that is what makes you just.'

Wilhelm tugged on his boots and strapped on his breastplate. He cinched his runefang to his belt with care. What the sword stood for had faded in the current time, yet the prince still believed. 'Perhaps, but it'll all be for nothing if I cannot bring allies to my banner, Ledner. The only Empire left to govern might be a tattered ruin by the end.'

'So you still plan to ride to Wissenland. It's several days' journey from Mannsgard. Are you sure that's wise?' said Ledner. 'Send me in your stead.'

'I must go. If Pfeifraucher can be convinced to fight, then it will only be done by my intervention. I'll have the Griffonkorps to protect me.' Wilhelm smiled, hooking his cloak to his pauldrons and picking up his helmet. 'In any event, I need you here to be my eyes and maintain order in the ranks.'

Ledner bowed. 'As I knew you would, my liege. As I also knew you would not rest at Mannsgard, either.'

'The soak has eased my bones. How can I rest when my land is in danger? If I am the just and noble heir apparent you say I am, then I must act.'

'Send the count my greetings,' said Ledner as Wilhelm was making for the door.

Outside the tavern, a small band of Griffonkorps were already gathering. The prince's empty steed was with them.

'I want Pfeifraucher to join us, Ledner,' Wilhelm replied as he was leaving, 'not lock his gates even tighter.'

Both men laughed, but their humour was fleeting. A dark road lay ahead for Wilhelm, darker than he realised.

When the prince had gone, Ledner's face fell. If they could not unite their provincial brothers beneath one banner, this war would very likely be the death of them both.

ALL OF THE regiments in Prince Wilhelm's army, together with their officers, were billeted in Mannsgard. Foreign soldiers outnumbered Averland citizens now. They would need to make the most of their respite. Word had already reached the masses that the prince rode with all haste to Wissenland, at least a three-day journey there and back. After that, irrespective of Count Pfeifraucher's decision, they would march on Averheim and try to lift the siege. Some of the soldiers went carousing in the towns in what many had started to call 'the last days'. Though most of Mannsgard was empty or simply waiting for death, there were still pleasures to be found, booze to be drunk if you knew where to look. Others sought out notaries and scribes, eager to make their last will and testament before the march. Many went to the temples, to pray for their loved ones or make peace with Sigmar or Morr.

Keller was not a praying man, though he had given some thought to it recently. Instead, he had found a different vice to assuage his guilt. The One-Eyed Dwarf was one of the few taverns left in Mannsgard that still carried alcohol. Most of the others had already been drunk dry by the nervous townsfolk or their stock carried away in the refugee wagons. It wasn't a wise move. Orcs and goblins ranked ale and spirits a close second to brawling and rampaging.

Rechts was asleep in one corner of the small establishment. He'd kicked off his boots and propped up his bare feet with a stool. The drummer's drunken snoring echoed around the almost empty bar. Across the room was the tavern's only other patron, a dwarf with an eye patch, a tramp by the look of his festering clothes. Keller wondered if it was coincidence or whether the dwarf had been there since the tavern existed, hence the name above the door outside. The dwarf held a dead fish in one gnarled hand and piped up when he saw Keller looking.

'Dead fish!' he raved, in thickly-accented Reikspiel. Obviously he was an ex-patriot, an exile from the Vaults or Black Mountains. 'Keeps ogling me,' he added. With a shout he slammed the fish against the table where he was sitting. Judging by the stains and fish scales in the wood, it wasn't the first time he'd done it. 'Not natural when it's dead.'

Keller moved on, ignoring the dwarf. There was no barkeep, so he poured himself a drink. The liquor was hot and abrasive when it hit his throat. Coughing, he poured another and then a third. He kept the bottle next to him like an old friend and had drained half of it when someone whispered in his ear.

'Drowning your sorrows or trying to take the edge off?'

Keller swallowed hard but could no longer taste the alcohol.

'Thought you said you wouldn't do it in the back,' he said. His voice came out in a rasp.

'That's why you're going to turn around.'

So he did, and came face-to-face with Brand. Keller gave a half glance at Rechts.

'He won't help you,' said Brand, his icy stare chilling Keller to the bone. 'Shout out and I'll do it here, now. It'll be messy, painful.'

Keller nodded. Tears welled in his eyes.

'Drinking with a friend?' asked Brand, when he saw the two glasses on the bar. One of them looked untouched and had two shots of grain whisky in it.

'S-something like that...'

'He wouldn't have drunk with you anyway.'

'Probably not.'

Silence fell in the tavern as Brand stared. His gaze was more piercing than steel.

'Are you sorry for what you've done?' he asked. 'I am,' he added, without waiting for an answer. It was the most and the longest Keller had ever heard Brand speak, but he still wasn't done. 'I've killed men, lots of them. Innocent and guilty. It's why I joined the army. I could tell you my upbringing was violent or some trauma made me this way, but it isn't true. I've always *needed* to kill. I'm trying to make up for it, now,' Brand said, looking over at the empty glass and the empty seat before it.

'Their faces come in the night, the ones I've killed.' He looked back at Keller. 'Like you're seeing a face right now, aren't you, Krieger?'

Keller nodded meekly. Warm piss trickled down his leg, staining his hose.

'I scream for them. In the night, I find a quiet place and inside I scream,' Brand said. 'War is one thing, but it takes a lot to kill a man in cold blood. A part of it clings to you, like their phantom unwilling to let go. It'll drag you down, Krieger, if you don't master it. You're not like me…'

Krieger was shaking his head. He was crying. When he realised, he wiped at his face.

'You can't keep the guilt,' Brand continued. 'Bloody hands lead to retribution in the end. Mine will come one day. Yours has already found you.'

Keller pointed feebly at Brand. The other Reiklander nodded slowly.

'I won't do it when your back is turned, you're right. You'll die with a weapon in your hand, but you will die. Varveiter's honour demands it. Now,' said Brand finally, 'take your dagger and come with me.'

Keller was already standing up, legs shaking, when Eber and Volker came in. The huntsman knew something was up at once.

'Too late for a drink, or are you moving on?' he asked.

Eber's forehead wrinkled, as if he knew something wasn't quite right but couldn't put his finger on it.

Keller sat back down gratefully, trying to obscure the wet patch in his hose.

'I'll take another.' He sounded a little breathless.

'Some other time,' said Brand, though it wasn't clear if he was talking to Keller or Volker. He was heading for the door, about to leave, when more would-be patrons joined them.

Torveld, Wode and three other Steel Swords stood in Brand's path.

'Popular place,' said Torveld, smiling thinly.

Brand backed up. So did the other Reiklanders. They moved farther into the room, pushing aside the few chairs and tables as they went.

The Middenlanders stepped after them slowly, Torveld taking the lead. A few feet of open floor stood between them.

'A good day for you at the Brigund Bridge,' said Torveld. He was armed. So were his compatriots. The Grimblades just carried dirks. Their halberds were stocked at an armoury in the town. Sturnbled must have dished out the blades to his men.

'What do you want, northerner?' Volker got straight to the point. Dog was with him and growled at the Middenlanders.

'Him,' Torveld snarled, pointing at Rechts.

Eber gave his slumbering comrade a shove. Unfortunately, the big Reiklander didn't always know his own strength and Rechts was dumped off the chair and onto the ground.

'Whoreson! Wha–' he began, scrambling to his feet and reaching for his dagger before he saw Eber. Then he noticed the others, and Torveld glaring at him. Indignation became mockery on the drummer's face. 'Ah, the Yellow Baron's lackeys have come to schlow their courage, have they?'

Wode balled his fists, prompting Eber to step forward, but Torveld kept the Middenlander back.

Rechts was steaming drunk. He slurred his words and belched loudly. Three empty bottles of hooch rolled around his feet as he stumbled a little before standing straight.

'What have you been saying, Rechts?' hissed Volker, one eye on the belligerent Middenlanders.

The drummer looked offended. 'Jusht the truth,' he said, licking his lips. 'They schwagger about, arrogant bashtards,' – he imitated the movement by swaying his shoulders and putting on a disdainful sneer – 'but when push comes to shove, they run like milkmaids.'

'Shut up, Rechts,' Volker warned him.

Torveld was shaking his head. He and his countrymen had heard enough.

Eber made fists. Keller looked relieved that the attention was no longer on him. He wrapped his hand around the half empty whisky bottle. Brand just stood with his hands by his sides, taking it all in, planning to kill Torveld first.

'I'm going to gut you like a pig, southerner.' Torveld was looking at Rechts.

'Shure, you are...' he replied, before promptly passing out and crashing to the floor.

The Middenlanders had half drawn their blades when the tavern door opened again. Everyone turned to see who it was. Captain Stahler stood in the doorway, ashen-faced and looking far from pleased. Von Rauken and several of his greatsworders accompanied him.

'Put up your blades,' he said calmly to the Middenlanders.

'This is a matter of honour, they've–' Torveld began.

'Put 'em up! Do it now!'

The Middenlanders obeyed, stepping aside as Stahler stalked into the room appraising all present with a filthy look.

'Get to your billet,' he said to the Steel Swords, 'and tell Sergeant Sturnbled I want words. Go on, get out!'

Torveld was livid, but he held on to his temper. He nodded with a last look in the Grimblades' direction before storming out with his men.

'Now you lot…' said Stahler, once the Middenlanders were gone. The captain wore his breastplate, but had yet to don his helmet. He walked with a limp and the effort clearly pained him, but he was still formidable. The greatsworders stood behind him like plate-clad sentinels. Von Rauken was doing his best to keep the smirk off his face. Concealed behind his beard, no one could see it anyway.

The Grimblades were downcast, suddenly ambivalent about their captain's return. Volker was about to speak when Stahler cut him off.

'Not a damn word!' He looked over his shoulder. 'Karlich, get in here.'

A stern-faced Sergeant Karlich entered the tavern, Lenkmann and Masbrecht in tow. He was shaking his head and scowling. He looked more annoyed than Stahler. 'It appears my return was timely,' said Stahler. 'Blaselocker is gone,' he added flatly. 'I'm back and this kind of behaviour in my regiments won't be tolerated. If we weren't so short of bodies you'd be flogged. Some of you would swing. Do your killing on the battlefield. Don't worry, you'll get your chance, we all bloody will.' He glared for a few moments, regarding each man in turn before facing Karlich.

'I'll leave this rabble to you.'

Karlich saluted, waiting for Stahler and the greatsworders to leave, before turning his attention on the Grimblades.

'Captain Stahler has recovered well enough to fight, praise Sigmar,' he recounted deadpan. 'We are heading out. On patrol. Now.' Karlich punctuated the last word firmly.

'Those northern scum–'

Karlich cut Volker off.

'Are out for blood, I know. But it'll be Stahler who has it if you carry on like this. All of you, with me, right now,' he said. As Karlich was leaving, he added, 'Eber, get him up and make sure he's sober by the time we reach the gate.'

Eber nodded and hauled Rechts onto his back, carrying him like a sack of grain. The big Reiklander remembered seeing a horse trough a little way from Mannsgard's gate. Rechts would either be sober or drowned by the time he was done.

CHAPTER ELEVEN

A DARK DISCOVERY

Outside Mannsgard, Averland,
386 miles from Altdorf

SEVERAL MILES OUTSIDE Mannsgard, the land grew wilder. Though still largely flat and open, the Averland forests were thicker here. Men had not come with fire and axes to clear them. There were no other towns. Even villages were sparse, just smoking shadows on a distant horizon.

Volker noticed an isolated farm up ahead, not reported by the other patrols. The eight Reiklanders had met the last party on the way out, a tired-looking band of Averland pike. They had nodded and exchanged muted greetings as they'd passed one another, but that was all. The Averlanders had been south-east but found nothing. Volker had brought them westward and to the farm. He stopped a few hundred feet from it, waiting for the others.

'Looks deserted,' said Masbrecht as he joined the huntsmen.

The farm was ramshackle, comprising a small stone house, a barn and some stables. There were wooden fences and several fields could also have been part of the farmer's land, but no animals grazed in them and there weren't any crops either. A stream ran through the land, its banks coloured by blood. Volker had followed the watercourse all the way to the farm.

'Best be sure,' said Karlich. The sergeant's mood hadn't improved. He had other things on his mind, too. Like the witch hunter's encampment they'd passed when leaving Mannsgard. Of the templar, there'd been no sign. Small mercies. He looked at Rechts. 'You first, soldier.'

Hung-over and red-eyed, but sober thanks to the liberal dunkings in the horse trough by Eber, Rechts nodded and headed up to the farm. The regimental drum and banner were back in Mannsgard, so at least he didn't have anything to weigh him down. As Rechts came within the farm's boundary line, he drew his short sword.

Volker looked nervously at his sergeant.

Karlich sighed. 'Try and make sure he doesn't get himself killed.'

The huntsman saluted and jogged after Rechts.

'The rest of you, come on,' added Karlich, and continued tramping through the high grass after the scouts.

UP CLOSE, THE farm and its buildings looked even more wrecked than at a distance. Much of the wood from the barn was rotten. Several of the stones that made up the house had slipped or were cracked. After Rechts and Volker had scouted out the land around the buildings to check for ambushers, Karlich had divided them into three groups to take the house, barn and stables respectively. A shallow wind howled across the plains. As it passed through the open buildings, it took on an unnatural sound. It disturbed Lenkmann greatly, who paused as he was about to enter the stables.

'Do we really need to go in?' he asked.

Brand shook his head and walked right past him.

'Orcs or goblins, more likely, could be hiding inside,' said Masbrecht. 'Part of a vanguard or a splinter from the horde besieging Averheim. Either way, we have to know. How would Prince Wilhelm react if his troops allowed the greenskins to sneak up on us, waking up to find the walls of Mannsgard surrounded, as well as those of Averheim?'

'The prince is in Wissenland, or on his way at least.'

As they'd left the town behind, they'd seen Prince Wilhelm and his Griffonkorps riding hard for the provincial border. They needed to move swiftly. Not only were greenskins abroad, but with every day that went by Averheim was squeezed further by Grom the Paunch. If Wilhelm's army didn't march soon, the goblin king might have crushed the Averland capital to rubble by the time they arrived.

'Come on,' Brand called from inside. He lingered just beyond the stable threshold, not willing to commit himself in case he found a goblin dagger in his back.

Lenkmann gave the skeletal structure a sour look. The wasted timbers reminded him of bones. Shadows loomed within the stable's creaking confines and he could hear the buzzing of flies against the wind. Lenkmann was not a cowardly man. He'd do his duty to the Empire, fighting greenskins or beastmen. Even marauders from the north held no true terror for him.

But the unquiet, the revenant scratching at its coffin lid, digging through its earthy grave, that did unsettle him.

'Masbrecht...' he said.

The other Reiklander smiled and made the sign of the hammer.

'I always feel better when you do it,' Lenkmann admitted.

'There's nothing to fear, brother. Sigmar is always with us.'

'I'm not afraid,' snapped the banner bearer. 'Just being careful,' he added, striding into the stables with unnecessary gusto.

THE FARMHOUSE WAS quiet except for the creaking of its only door on broken hinges. Karlich was the first inside, pushing the door with his sword tip so it was wide enough to enter.

The stench in the room had faded, but Eber still wrinkled his nose.

'That's a foul reek,' he said, peering over Karlich's shoulder to get a better look.

'Don't blame me,' snapped Keller. He held his arm low instinctively, trying to conceal the stain on his hose. The tang of it still lingered in his nostrils, even though it had long since gone. Like Karlich, his mind was also on other things. He kept his gaze ahead, not wanting to look at the lonely cart dumped next to the house with no mule to pull it. Something else was standing by it. Keller had glimpsed its presence in his peripheral vision before looking away. He didn't want to see it directly. It had... *changed* in the last few days. To look upon it now... Keller feared he'd cry out in spite of himself.

Though he'd secured the door, Karlich still heard creaking. It got louder as he went inside. The house had one room. There was a simple bed, table and chair. A wool rug, dirty from use, covered a small patch on the stone floor. A thatch roof overhead filtered the sun in thin, grainy beams. Though gloomy, there was enough light to see the farmer hanging two feet from the ground.

'Sacred Morr,' breathed Eber when he noticed the corpse.

Keller made the sign of the hammer, determined to make the penitent streak stick.

'How long?' he asked.

'A while,' said Karlich, approaching the body. Its sunken flesh was grey and ghoulish. Empty sockets remained where the eyes had been. Rigor mortis curled the farmer's toes and fingers into claws. Rough clothes hung off the body like flaying skin.

There was no sign of greenskins, none at all. Karlich supposed the farmer had heard of the invasion while in town for market day, returned to his farm and decided it was better to take his own life than face possible torture and certain death by the orcs. How could he have known the greenskins would miss him? At least the house was clear. It was bitter compensation.

'Shallya's mercy,' Karlich muttered. He sounded weary. 'Cut him down.'

RECHTS WAS STILL dizzy. The open air was doing nothing for him. About to enter the barn, he staggered and would have fallen if not for Volker catching his arm.

'Easy does it,' said the huntsman in a low voice. 'Let me go first.'

Rechts gladly moved aside and followed Volker in through the half-open barn door.

Despite the shafts of sunlight lancing the cracks in its roof, it was dark inside the barn. The air was stale and smelled of hay and dung. Bales were bound up with string in the two far corners. Stacked on top of one another, they stretched halfway to the door. Vertical beams supported the roof, hung with chains, sickles and scythes. It didn't look like they'd been used for a long time. A loft loomed above. It was the perfect place for an ambush, so Volker kept his eyes on it.

'Something's off,' he said to Rechts, who had just sidled through the door.

'Hot in here.' The drummer looked nauseous.

'Quiet!' hissed Volker. The huntsman had moved under the trapdoor that led up to the hayloft. A length of rope dangled to the ground from it. Volker wrapped the rope around his fist and pulled. The trapdoor doubled up as a ramp, and an entire section of the loft floor came down to rest on the ground. Standing near the foot of the ramp, Volker secured the rope on a hook attached to a wooden beam and waited.

Now Rechts could smell it too. Something was definitely off in the barn, and it was coming from the hayloft. Hangover forgotten, he edged closer to Volker. They needed to be careful. Karlich had split them up to search all three structures at the same time. Help, if they needed it, would be a little way off.

Volker whistled sharply. A few seconds later, Dog trotted into the barn from where it had been told to wait outside. After a gesture from its master, the mutt ran up the ramp and into the hayloft.

'Now we wait,' said Volker, the sound of snuffling and rooting coming from above them. Then Dog barked, low at first but building in pitch with each successive sound.

Volker moved up the ramp, keeping low.

Rechts followed, amazed at his comrade's stealth. Volker barely made a sound.

The hayloft was almost full. A pitchfork stuck out of the loose stacks like a marker, but Dog wasn't interested in this. It was scratting at the far end of the loft, pushing its muzzle eagerly into the piled hay. It was a gloomy spot. The loft's open window was on the opposite side. Glancing at it only seemed to make the patch where Dog stood even darker.

'Come!' said Volker, and the mastiff stopped rooting to rejoin its master.

Crossing the loft to the site of Dog's interest felt farther than it actually was. Volker kept his eyes on the stack the entire time, his dirk held low and close to his body. A faint crunch of hay assured the huntsman that Rechts was right behind him.

'Grab that,' he said, indicating the pitchfork.

Rechts went over and took the implement. He then passed it to Volker, who hadn't moved and was waiting for him. Stalking the last few feet to the haystack, Volker prodded carefully with the fork. The first attempt went straight through, the second hit something. He lunged harder and the pitchfork came back with blood on it. Using the pitchfork in a scraping motion, Volker dragged away some of the hay. There was a body lying beneath, dead a few days but no more. The seal on its tunic was familiar. It was the griffon rampant of the Emperor.

'Go find Sergeant Karlich,' Volker said, stepping away. His hands were shaking, but he couldn't explain why. 'Right now!' he snapped, when Rechts didn't move straight away.

Stumbling a little at first, and not from the hangover, Rechts ran out of the hayloft and across the barn. Only when he reached Karlich at the house, did he stop to puke. An already long day was about to get much longer.

THE DEAD MESSENGER lay on the floor of the hayloft in full view. After Rechts had gone to get the others, Volker had carefully cleared away the hay concealing the body.

'Altdorf colours,' said Karlich, under his breath. Under a long tan cloak, the dead messenger's tunic was red and blue. His garments looked fine and unroughed. His boots were expensive and polished. One of them lay on the floor alongside the body. Even the man's stockings were clean and white. He looked lean and healthy, except for the dagger sticking out of his chest.

'From the royal house,' said Masbrecht. He noted the dead messenger's hands: they were clean, his nails manicured. 'An aide, perhaps?'

'This is how you found him?' asked Karlich, weighing up Masbrecht's theory with some of his own.

Volker was crouching next to the body, examining the wound, and nodded.

Except for Brand, who knew something about dagger wounds himself, the rest of the Grimblades were down in the barn. Rechts was sitting on a hay bale, nursing his head and stomach. Keller kept to himself, his eyes on the ground, whilst Lenkmann and Eber watched the door.

'That's no orc blade; it's Empire,' said Karlich, stooping to get a better look at the dagger.

'Greenskins didn't kill him,' said Brand, lurking in the shadows. 'The cut is too precise, one thrust right into the heart.'

Karlich turned, suddenly feeling a little colder. 'And?'

'It's assassination work.'

And you would know, I suppose, thought Karlich. Sometimes he wondered how they all slept at night with Brand around, then he remembered the man was on their side and that was how. Since Varveiter's death, Brand had retreated further into himself. They all missed the old warhorse, Karlich especially. But for Brand, Varveiter had been the one stable element in his life. Now he was gone, bloodily, and that bothered Karlich, more than he wanted to admit.

'You search him?' he asked Volker.

'Found this.' The huntsman gave Karlich a scroll of parchment. 'Hidden in his boot.'

'What's on it?' Karlich asked, noting the broken seal as he unfurled it. The scroll was actually a map that showed Averland and Wissenland. Several landmarks were detailed, including Mannsgard and Pfeildorf, the capital of Wissenland and Prince Wilhelm's destination. A route was marked out between the two locations with a line that ended in an arrow leading back to Mannsgard. A small red 'X' fell about halfway along it where some hills were also sketched.

'What does it mean?' asked Volker.

Karlich looked back down at the body, then at the Reikland dagger plunged into its dead heart. Brand was already heading down again. He knew they were going back.

'I don't know,' Karlich lied. He had some ideas. 'We should return to Mannsgard and report it. We go now.'

CHAPTER TWELVE

TO SAVE A PRINCE

Outside Mannsgard, Averland,
386 miles from Altdorf

THE GRIMBLADES RAN the five miles back to camp. The high grass made hard work of it and all except for Brand were gasping for breath by the time they reached Mannsgard's gates.

Old Varveiter would have been complaining, the last to come in. Eber missed it. They all did. Or at least, that's how it appeared. Keller had said nothing since the barn. He was finding it increasingly difficult to lift his eyes off the ground lately. Masbrecht had asked him about it, but Keller just mumbled something and walked away. Masbrecht dropped it after that.

Karlich had said nothing to those who were down in the barn when the body was being examined. Rechts knew of it, of course, and they knew what he knew, but only Volker, Brand and Masbrecht were privy to the map and the dagger. Karlich had worried at it all the way to Mannsgard, trying not to jump to conclusions. Captain

Stahler would know what to do. He was billeted in an old counting house close to the gate. At least they wouldn't have to slog through the streets to reach him.

'You three, come with me,' said Karlich, upon entering the town. 'The rest of you will wait at The One-Eyed Dwarf until I come and get you. Understood?'

Brand, Masbrecht and Volker stayed with the sergeant. As the others were moving off, Karlich added, 'And stay out of trouble.'

Lenkmann saluted, and assured the sergeant that wouldn't be a problem.

When they were out of earshot, Masbrecht asked in a low voice, 'Why meet so close to Mannsgard? The messenger and his would-be killer, I mean.'

'Closeness to his mark,' said Brand. 'He can observe and predict, gather information first hand if he needs to. The messenger obviously came from the prince's camp. He served his purpose and was silenced.'

'Perhaps Templar Vanhans or one of his faithful saw something,' offered Masbrecht.

Karlich stiffened at the mention of the witch hunter's name. He tried not to react and focused on getting to the counting house.

'Scouts and patrols are leaving the town all the time,' said Brand. 'A lone rider would be lost with the rest.'

'Shut up, both of you.' Disturbed also by Brand's knowledge of contract killing, Karlich had finally listened to all he could take. Bad enough that they'd found the dead messenger at all, they didn't need someone overhearing them on the street. Things were complicated as it was. When they reached Stahler's billet, the matter became tangled even further.

* * *

THE COUNTING HOUSE was a dusty place with grey walls, full of wooden furniture. It had two floors, the upper one had an archive and vault but was boarded over; the lower had a hallway leading to a small office with a writing desk and was full of old ledgers. A side room contained a bed and chair. It was close to the Temple of Shallya, so Stahler was in reach of ministration if he needed it.

The shutters were drawn and the counting house was dark when the four Grimblades entered. Smoke hung in the air, obscuring the view further.

Karlich went in first, his men a few paces behind. Their steps sounded loud and echoing as they walked down the hallway. Upon reaching the office, Karlich saw a silhouette sitting at the writing desk. Stahler was smoking a pipe, though it didn't smell like his usual tobacco. Perhaps the priestesses had provided a curative leaf. Karlich had heard of such things, though didn't place much stock in them.

'Sir,' he ventured. 'We've made a disturbing discovery.' Stahler was little more than a black outline against a dark-grey canvas, but he sat up when Karlich spoke. The sergeant took it as an invitation to speak further.

'There's an old farmstead about five miles west of Mannsgard. The farmer was dead. There was also another body,' Karlich paused, choosing his next words carefully. 'It was hidden in a hay loft and wore the trap pings of an Altdorf messenger, one from Prince Wilhelm's camp.'

As his sight adjusted, Karlich began to see Stahler's eyes in the gloom. They narrowed at the mention of the prince and suddenly the sergeant felt that something was wrong.

'You're not Captain Stahler,' he said flatly, straightening his back to show his annoyance. Karlich didn't like being fooled. He liked liars and charlatans even less. 'Who are you?'

The silhouette struck a match, lighting up a nearby lamp. Ledner was revealed in its wan glow. Shadows pooled the crevices of his thin face, making him appear gaunter than he actually was. Ledner kept the light behind him, blinding his visitors but enabling him to see them clearly.

'You were saying, sergeant?'

'I thought I was speaking to my captain. I'm sorry, sir. There's been a mistake.' Karlich went to go, not sure what Ledner would make of what he had heard so far, when the voice of the prince's spymaster stopped him.

'The only mistake would be to leave this room,' Ledner said calmly. 'Please go on. Captain Stahler is with the sisters of mercy having his wounds redressed.'

Karlich wished he had had the temerity to ask what then Ledner was doing in his captain's billet with his aide obviously elsewhere. In the circumstances, he didn't think it wise. He took the map scroll from where he'd secured it in his belt and unfurled it on the desk.

'And what is this?' Ledner asked.

'A map of Averland and Wissenland,' said Volker, nonplussed. Karlich glared at him and the huntsman shut his mouth like a trap.

Ledner smiled thinly. His eyes were predatory as he regarded Volker.

'What is its meaning?'

'The messenger was carrying it when he died,' said Karlich.

Ledner began to study the map. He traced a thin finger down the line describing Wilhelm's route.

'How was he killed?'

Karlich cleared his throat, making Ledner look up.

'We think he was assassinated. An Empire dagger had pierced his heart.'

Ledner sighed, rolling up the parchment. 'Well, that would do it I suppose.'

When the spymaster permitted a long silence to descend, Karlich told him, 'Something must be done.'

Ledner fixed the sergeant with a cold stare that bled all heat from the lamp. Karlich felt a shiver but suppressed it.

'About what? What is it you think is happening here, sergeant?' Ledner was enjoying the inquisition and suddenly Karlich could imagine many men who had fallen under the spymaster's scrutiny. He thought those 'conversations' would be markedly less pleasant than this one. That they would end with hot steel and fire, maybe the noose or rack. Ledner was famed for his strong stomach and his sociopathic nature. A keen combination in a torturer and confessor.

Karlich drew off his courage, speaking aloud what he had believed since finding the body and seeing the map.

'Prince Wilhelm is in danger, my lord. I think someone's planning to kill him.'

Ledner smiled again. There was no warmth in it. It was a gesture as far from humour as it was possible to get.

'You were wise to come to me, sergeant. Even if it was by accident,' said Ledner. 'You are certain this messenger was slain by an assassin, the same man you think is after the prince?'

'It may already be too late,' said Karlich. 'If the prince's would-be killer attacked him on the way to Pfeildorf... My lord, I must speak to my captain at once. Something must be done.'

'No you won't,' Ledner replied, standing.

'I beg your par–'

'You won't, because the fewer people who know about this the better.' Ledner opened up the lamp's shutter, exposing the flame within. 'Who else was with you?' he asked. 'Just these three?'

'No. There were four others, all men of my regiment.'

'Where are these men now?'

Karlich's brow furrowed. 'At a tavern in the town. What does it matter?'

Ledner opened the oil valve on the lamp so the flame burned at its fiercest. He took the map and poked one corner in through the shutter.

'What are you doing?' Karlich reached out for the parchment, which was already burning, but Ledner seized his wrist in a grip as strong as a serpent's jaws.

'You remember the location on the map, the low hills, the mid-point between Prince Wilhelm's route?' He sniffed scornfully. 'Of course you do. A man like you, sergeant, would have seared it into his mind. Am I right?'

Karlich backed down. He nodded slowly and Ledner released him so he could continue burning the map. The flames seemed to fill his eyes, revealing a dark glint in the pupils. When he was done reducing the parchment to charred fragments, he turned his gaze back on Karlich.

'A plot against the prince that comes from within his very camp,' said Ledner. 'No one is to be trusted, sergeant. You shouldn't even have trusted me but then you had little choice in the matter since you had to do *something*. No one else can know of this – *no one*. If word slipped out of an assassination plot against the prince, by his own court no less, two things would certainly happen. Our killer would realise his plan was compromised and change it, thus denying us the opportunity to stop him. Furthermore, this campaign, the Empire itself, would be thrown into even greater turmoil. We are divided enough as it is without talk of assassination within our own ranks.

'What do you think would happen next? Electors, barons, earls, they'd be even more paranoid than they are now. Instead of one assassin, you would have hundreds.' Ledner breathed deeply, as if making up his mind. 'Stahler cannot know,' he said. 'But here is what you'll do. Fetch your men, the other four who saw the body, and bring them here to me.'

'Why? What do you plan to do?' asked Karlich, forgetting his place for a moment.

'Other than finding out who ordered the contract on the prince, *I* am not going to do anything. *You* however will be responsible for stopping this assassin.'

Karlich was already shaking his head when Ledner interrupted him.

'This must not get out. Be very clear on this. So far, the only ones who know of it are you, your men and I. Keep it that way or risk far more than the death of a beloved prince.' Ledner waved a finger at him. The glint in his eye returned. 'Civil war, sergeant, just like in the old days.'

Karlich still wasn't convinced.

'There must be those better equipped than us to deal with this matter.'

'Yes, of course there are,' said Ledner, 'but we've been over this. The fewer people who know, remember?'

'Sigmar be damned,' muttered Karlich, and knew they had no choice. A trained killer against him and seven of his men. Were it not for Brand, he wouldn't have liked the odds.

'Halberds are hardly made for stealth,' Karlich added.

'Get your men, bring them here. I will have weapons waiting,' Ledner told him. 'You can use a pistol?' he asked.

Karlich nodded.

'Anyone else?'

Volker raised a hand, as Masbrecht shook his head.

Ledner's eyes went to Brand, who had watched the whole affair intently from the darkness.

'Oh, I bet you can use one. I bet you're no stranger to having blood on your hands, are you?' The spymaster's smile was almost venomous.

Brand never moved.

Ledner looked as if he was about to say something else to him, but he turned his attention back on Karlich.

'The prince will make his return in just over a day. You need to be in those hills and root out the killer before the prince reaches them.' He doused the lantern, plunging the room back into darkness. 'Go,' he added, sitting down again. 'Weapons will be waiting for you.'

Karlich didn't know what else to say. He turned on his heel, glad to be leaving the counting house and Ledner behind.

* * *

EIGHT GRIMBLADES LEFT the town of Mannsgard just before dusk, armed with short swords and bucklers. Three men also carried pistols. Ledner had met them at the counting house and told them to wait until night was approaching to make their way out. Patrols were not that uncommon at the end of the day and their presence would barely raise an eyebrow amongst the watchmen and gate guards. By way of a parting gift, Ledner provided fur-lined cloaks for them all. Without the sun to warm them and few trees and valleys to shield against the wind, the plains would be bitterly cold after dark.

They were to travel on foot, a journey that would take the entire night and most of the next morning. Ledner reasoned that the prince and his Griffonkorps would likely ride from Pfeildorf at dawn, bringing them to the assassination site – the hilly valley denoted at the map – no earlier than late morning. The Grimblades had to find the assassin and kill him before then. They'd be cutting it fine.

WITHOUT THE CRACKLE of a fire for company, it felt eerie on the grassy heath. Some of the Grimblades huddled together against a harsh wind, as it tossed their cloaks about, trying to work them free with its chill fingers. The fur lining might as well be soaked through for all the protection it offered; blowing from the east, the wind was like daggers shearing through their clothes. It brought the smell of burning meat with it from the huge ritual pyres erected by the orcs. It wasn't animal in origin; the stench was human.

'If I imagine a fire, will that warm me?' said Rechts. He was shivering more than the others, a grey pallor affecting his face.

'Aye, and draw fewer greenskins and other beasts to our camp than a real fire,' Karlich replied with a scowl. He nursed a pipe in his hands, taking care to shelter the small flame.

'Wish I was still drunk,' Rechts muttered.

'Perhaps if you'd stayed sober you wouldn't feel the cold so much,' snapped the sergeant. He was starting to lose his patience. They all were.

Since leaving Mannsgard that evening, the men had said little to one another. Each had his mind on his thoughts and the awful truth that someone within the Empire, within their camp, was plotting to kill Prince Wilhelm. Worse still, they were the ones supposed to prevent it. Karlich, for one, didn't appreciate the burden. He'd noticed something cruel in Ledner's eyes when he'd sent them off. The spymaster didn't expect them all to return.

What are men like us to men like him, he thought bitterly? Just fodder for his schemes and lies.

A low howl from the distant hills to the south startled them. Volker turned quickly, soothing Dog who had been lying beside him but was now on his feet and growling. He made out a silhouette on the far away hills, of a beast prowling the moors near the Wissenland border. All men of the Aver had heard tales of the balewolf. It was a legend spun by housewives and bored soldiers. The Grimblades had listened to a veteran piker tell it in Mannsgard. Now it came back to haunt them with the shadows, real or imagined, on the wind-tossed grasslands of the wild.

'Easy boy,' he murmured, using the tone of his voice to quieten the mastiff. Volker blinked and the silhouette was gone, like a wisp of smoke carried off by the breeze.

'Good dog...' said Lenkmann, reaching over to pat the mutt's head. He snatched his hand away when Dog snapped at him, fangs bared.

'Not really,' Volker replied with a smile. The moon was high overhead, revealed through scudding cloud, and it cast his face in a sinister light. 'It means no offence. Just knows its master.'

Lenkmann mumbled something before planting his hands firmly back inside his cloak.

Volker tickled Dog under the chin and the savage beast growled appreciatively before licking the salt off his fingers.

'It scents evil,' said Brand. He was sitting a little way back from the circle of men, who turned suddenly at the sound of his voice. 'Can't you smell it, too?'

Masbrecht made the sign of Sigmar and watched the darkness where the beast had been with fearful eyes.

'Smell what?' asked Eber. Of all the Grimblades, the big Reiklander appeared least troubled by the cold. The layers of muscle obviously made for good insulation.

'Orc spore. It's thick.'

Now they all smelled it, coming from the east on the same breeze that brought the reek of burning meat. Orange smudges blighted that part of the horizon from the villages and towns still ablaze. Men and women would be burning. Some might have fled if they were lucky. Perhaps the fell beasts of the wild had easier prey that night than the Grimblades.

Overhead, there came the flapping of wings and a shadow passed over them like a curse. Every man, even Brand, flattened to the ground and didn't look up again until the shadow was gone.

'We all saw that, right?' asked Volker, wanting to be convinced he wasn't just hallucinating.

Keller nodded meekly. Like in the barn, he'd kept his eyes on the ground for most of the journey, using whoever was in front of him as a guide. No one questioned him about it. They all knew something had happened to him since Blösstadt. Only he and Brand knew the truth.

'It was the shaman and his wyvern,' said Karlich, trying to slow his racing heartbeat.

Keller's teeth were chattering, and not from the cold. Masbrecht was muttering a prayer of warding under his breath. The others just huddled, trying to look as small as possible. Even Brand was shaken. If this was the effect that the creature caused hundreds of feet away, up in the air, then how could men face it on the battlefield? It only made Wilhelm's victory at the Brigund Bridge, when he had driven the beast and its master off, all the more impressive. It also convinced Karlich that they had to save this man, that without him they would surely fail. He'd been right in the tent all those days ago: men like Wilhelm were greater than he, capable of doing great things.

Several minutes passed before they felt comfortable enough to return to the circle. No one spoke of the wyvern again, nor did they look in the direction of its heading if they could help it. In the end, it was Rechts who broke the fearful silence.

'What are we doing out here, sergeant?'

It was a valid question, one Karlich had asked himself several times already. But it wasn't what Rechts really meant. What he really meant was: why us? Karlich's answer, as he'd already told himself, was simple.

'Our duty to prince and province,' he said.

'To Ledner, you mean. That bastard doesn't care if we live or die. He probably hopes we don't survive.' Rechts was emboldened by his anger, grateful to it for smothering his fear. 'And if we succeed? What then? What recompense will we get?'

Karlich was tiring of the drummer's belligerence. He knew he was only scared, just like the rest of them. But this wasn't helping.

'Nothing! We get nothing, save the knowledge that we prevented the murder of our liege-lord and prince,' he snapped. 'Is that not enough? It should be enough.'

Rechts bowed his head, shamed.

'Aye, I thought so,' muttered Karlich and instantly regretted it.

After that the rest of the night without incident, but it was long and uncomfortable, filled with the shadows of monsters and the howl of wolves.

CHAPTER THIRTEEN
GHOSTS

Averland plains,
411 miles from Altdorf

THE DAWN BROUGHT little comfort for the Grimblades, despite the rising sun. It had yet to warm the plains or their aching bones. Breath still ghosted the air. It came out in white gusts as Karlich had coughed and wheezed. They'd slept sitting up, and there was nothing to pack, though Lenkmann had leaned over onto Eber's shoulder and was profoundly embarrassed when he woke.

'Didn't even buy him a drink!' Rechts had chortled with uncommon good humour. He'd obviously slept off the booze at last.

Brand had stayed awake all night. Volker, who'd been the first up, would later say how he rose to find the cold eyes of the man regarding him through the twilit mist. Volker didn't stay to chat. In minutes he was gone, scouting off into the distance with Dog.

Few words were exchanged when the others stirred and began to move. No one felt like talking after a harrowing night. It was a while trudging through the long grasses before the grim silence was lifted.

'Who would want to kill the prince?' asked Eber, unaware of the sour mood and more out of exasperation than any desire to actually know. 'I can't understand it.'

'All political figures have enemies, Brutan,' Lenkmann replied. 'Wilhelm is no different. It could be one of a hundred or more men.'

'It's poor timing,' muttered Keller, his displeasure at the mission currently outweighing his other 'concerns'.

'So there's a good time to try and kill a prince of Altdorf?' asked Karlich. He looked towards the sun, gauging its position and therefore the time. By his reckoning, they had maybe three hours before the prince could arrive at the valley. The pace suddenly didn't feel fast enough. 'Hurry it up,' he said, eyes front, hoping to see Volker. The huntsman was still ranging ahead with the mutt, keeping them away from any greenskins that might be roaming nearby, and leading them to the hills. His last report had been some time ago.

'When his back is turned and his guard is down,' said Brand to the sergeant's first comment.

Karlich scowled at the dry humour, finding it inappropriate.

'I wish Varveiter were here,' said Lenkmann, to Karlich's right. 'We could use his wisdom now.'

'Aye, he might've been canny enough for us to get us out of this shitheap we currently find ourselves in,' said Rechts, his humour fleeting.

Masbrecht looked affronted. 'Saving a prince is an *honour*, brother. It is Sigmar's work we go to do this day.'

Rechts was livid. 'He calls me "brother" one more time and it won't be Wilhelm's assassin you'll be stopping.'

'Shut up, Rechts,' snapped Karlich. 'Whatever it is between the two of you, deal with it. This is the most important deed you'll ever do in your entire life, don't wreck it,' he warned, before turning his anger on Masbrecht. 'And you. Save the sermons. You know he doesn't like it. Not all of us are willing converts.' He wanted to say more, but saw Volker running back towards them.

'Just beyond the next rise,' he said. 'The land slopes downward and lifts again to a set of hills. That must be the place.'

'You sure?' asked Karlich.

'As I can be. The map was quite well detailed and there are few hills in Averland, especially so close to the road.'

'Makes you wonder why the prince came this way at all,' said Lenkmann. 'A valley is a good place for an ambush.'

'The road is the most direct route, I suppose,' said Karlich, 'but who's to say the prince even chose it.'

None of it really mattered. The morning sun was high and its rays were creeping steadily across the plains. Time was running out.

CRESTING THE RISE, the Grimblades had the sloping plain laid out below them. A short distance and the flat land rose up again, the road bending with it, and there were the hills. Strewn with rocks, hollows and wild bracken, it was a rugged place full of shadows.

'Lots of places to hide,' observed Volker.

They came at the hills from an oblique angle, ever watchful for movement, keeping the sun behind them all the way.

'He'll be up high,' added Brand, 'probably with a bow or harquebus. He'll want to kill the prince from a distance, so he doesn't have to fight his Griffonkorps.'

'So we're looking for a marksman, then,' said Karlich. 'Perhaps we'll be able to stop him, after all.'

'A marksman, yes,' said Brand. 'And a swordsman and a knife-wielder, and a pugilist. Assassins are killers. They're trained well in the art. Don't make the mistake of thinking just because he wants to shoot the prince that he can't execute him, or us, in ten or more other ways.'

Yet again, Karlich felt a cold shiver but couldn't deny the sense in what Brand was saying. He decided to change tack.

'He could be anywhere, behind any rock, hunkered down in any hollow, hidden in the long grasses or crouched upon any ridge, as still as the earth,' said Karlich. 'We root him out before the prince gets here. He cannot know of it. To do so would mean this whole dirty business gets out and, alive or dead, the prince and his cohorts can't ignore it. You heard Ledner – the Empire would fracture under the strain. We'd have civil war.'

Karlich eyed his men and felt a surge of pride, even for Keller who he considered a bastard of the highest order.

'We're not assassins or spies; we're just men, soldiers of the Empire who face a difficult duty. This is an enemy like any other. At Blösstadt you gave me your resolve, at the Brigund Bridge your courage. Now I ask for cunning. Find this whoreson, stop him and stay alive into the bargain.'

He allowed a short pause to think, how in Sigmar's name did we ever get here? and then deferred to Volker, who knew the ways of hunting better than any of them.

'We split into pairs, four groups, one compass direction each. Start wide and move in slowly. Stay low and keep your eyes open. Chances are, he's already in there, waiting.'

'Sobering thought,' muttered Rechts.

'Just as well, where you're concerned,' said Karlich, before addressing his men. 'No heroics,' he said, looking at Brand in particular. 'Find him, signal your comrades and we'll silence this cur together without our blood being spilled to do it. Faith in Sigmar,' he added.

The Grimblades echoed him, all except for Rechts.

'And Morr be damned,' said Karlich to himself, trudging down towards the road where the hills loomed with quiet menace.

Eight against one. So, why did it feel like they were the prey?

UP CLOSE THE hills were vast, easily sprawling a half mile either side and along the road. They dipped, rose and undulated as if in a pact with the assassin to frustrate the Grimblades' search. Patches of scree and loose rocks made the ground treacherous. There were small ravines and caves. Crags and sheltered gullies were everywhere. Each and every nook had to be searched. Other creatures might lurk along the hillsides. It wasn't unknown for trolls or even larger beasts to make their lairs in such places. Keller, for one, hoped that wouldn't be the case.

Maintaining his concentration was hard, what with the *other* looking on and dogging his every step.

'Leave me be,' he hissed. A side glance revealed his plea had gone unheeded. *'Plague me no more!'* he said louder, prompting an angry look from Volker who he was paired with. Even Dog looked annoyed, but then that little bastard always did.

Keller allowed himself a smirk, the first for some time – Volker loved that mutt more than he did his own family. Back in Mannsgard, he'd seen the beast lick the huntsman's feet. Volker slept in his boots. He was not one to take them off regularly. Keller assumed the affection between mutt and man was probably mutual.

The sliver of his old self passed, like a flash of sun on metal, as the *other* reasserted its presence again. Still no sign of the assassin. The two men carried on.

LENKMANN STUMBLED AND cursed through his teeth. He'd jarred his ankle. It was painful as he felt down at it, but he could still move well enough. The sun was high now, and he had to squint when he looked up. Morning was nearly done. Brand was leaving him behind, hurrying through the hills like a wolf hunting deer, or maybe another wolf.

There was something of the bloodhound in the man, so driven to find the assassin was he. Lenkmann noticed he'd left his pistol unloaded. Brand wanted to face his adversary up close, push steel into his flesh, so the assassin knew who had killed him, who was his better. It was as if *need* compelled him. Lenkmann had seen Brand in battle before, the man was frightening, but this was different. This was a whole other side to him. And as he struggled to catch Brand, so intent on his prey, so utterly possessed with scarcely restrained violence, Lenkmann thought this was the truest side of the man. Brand had been a mystery until then. Now Lenkmann saw him for what he really was and it scared him more than the wyvern.

A GREEN OCEAN stretched before them and the hills were its waves, and the rocks its shore. Here they trawled for a single fish, one with hollow eyes, black and lifeless as a doll's. Karlich felt those eyes upon him. Ever since entering the hills, he'd not been able to shake the feeling of being watched. Paranoia was becoming an unwelcome bedfellow for the sergeant.

The sun was rising and though it warmed his face, it also sent the shadows fleeing into the deeper crevices of the land, filling them with darkness. Karlich began to imagine enemies lurking there: a masked assassin, wraith-like and undefeatable; Vanhans the witch hunter, armed with murderer's noose and a traitor's brand.

Karlich gasped when he felt Rechts's hand on his arm.

'Sergeant, you all right?'

He found his composure quickly, hiding his surprise behind annoyance.

'Fine! Never mind me, Rechts. Keep your eyes on the hills He's here, I can feel it.'

They forged off together in silence.

Karlich was annoyed at himself for allowing his mind to wander. If the assassin had been watching then he would have loosed an arrow or shot in the sergeant's back and ended him then and there.

Idiot!

He didn't mean to take his anger out on Rechts, either. At least the drummer was sober and alert. It was more than could be said for him. Rechts needed watching closely. If nothing else, he needed keeping apart from Masbrecht. He'd developed a passive loathing for the man, taking umbrage at his piety. Karlich had no desire to see that become more than angry words. Honestly, he wasn't sure what Rechts was capable of. He knew something of the man's past. He'd spoken of it once after their first battle together. Rechts wasn't a drummer back then and Karlich only just a sergeant. The Reikland border was under attack by beastmen out of the Reikwald. It had been a tough fight and many good men had not seen the sunrise. Perhaps being faced with mortality, so close and immediate it could be felt as a shiver in the bones, Rechts had decided to talk of his troubles. It had just been the two of them, huddled over mugs of strong spirits in a booth in some tavern, the name of which Karlich could no longer remember.

Through slurred whispers, Rechts had told of the day a mutant was discovered in his village. A boy back then, he'd been fishing in a stream nearby his village when a girl had cried out. A sullen child, who kept to himself, was being bullied by the edge of the stream. He scuffled with his attackers: a blacksmith's son, his head full of soot, and a farrier's lad who'd been hit on the head with too many horseshoes. There was low cunning in these boys, who pulled at the sullen child's clothes, intent on first stripping him then dumping him naked into the stream. They'd succeeded in removing his boots and leggings when the girl, skimming stones on the bank, had noticed something terrible. The sullen child had fleshy webs between his toes and a small tail of bone protruded from the base of his spine.

Cries of *'Mutant! Unclean!'* echoed across the stream and down to the village. Men with hooks and staves came running with the local priest in tow.

The sullen boy was crying, tugging on his leggings and reaching for his boots when the village men seized him at the priest's orders. So disturbed was he by what he'd seen, the old cleric sent messengers to the nearest town and the chapter house of the Order of Sigmar there.

Everything changed when the witch hunters arrived. Their leader was a brutal man on a crusade that was anything but righteous. Rechts never saw the sullen boy again, but he knew what happened to him. The 'purging' didn't end there. In a fit of pious rage, the witch hunter declared the entire village spoiled by Chaos. He found signs of taint where there were none and condemned innocents to the pyre and noose. When some of the villagers resisted, it only enflamed him further. Rechts's mother could see to the end of what was happening. She took her son away from the village square where a mob was baying for blood, little realising that soon their own flesh would crispen on the pyre.

For the witch hunters brought men with them, hard men who served the order in a grim, unspoken role. At the points of their swords, they herded the villagers one-by-one into the flames. Only the priest was spared, baying for blood and retribution, transformed by fear into a madman. From his hiding place under the floorboards of his house, Rechts could hear their screams. He covered his ears against the terrible noise and screwed his eyes shut. By the time he opened them again, the village was quiet. Smoke and the smell of cooked meat lingered on the air. The stench aroused no hunger in him; he retched and fetched up an empty stomach in the street. Rechts emerged to find his village was gone, just a burnt out skeleton of wood and scorched stone. Piles of ash and charred bones were all that remained of his kith and kin. Though he searched on his knees, tears streaking his soot-stained face, he never found his mother amongst the remains. A part of him hoped she had escaped, but knew deep down that his fingers might have brushed the ash of what she had become in the pyre's flame.

Desolated and alone, Rechts had wandered down the road leading from his village wishing for death. Against the odds, he reached Grünburg and lived on the streets until he was old enough to take a piece of silver and join the Emperor's armies.

Even as a boy, Rechts had been a survivor. It was no different when he became a soldier but he bore the mark of that day in the village deeper than any physical scar. He never trusted priests again and hated witch hunters with a passion. In that, he and Karlich had an accord. Karlich had listened to the tale quietly and consoled him at the end. It was like talking to stone for all the emotion Rechts had shown him. Neither man could have known that Karlich would meet that self same witch hunter many years later, and that the zealot would not live to torture another innocent. The man was gone, but his legacy remained, and like a shadow creeping over the face of a setting sun, it was getting closer to Karlich.

A flash of light caught Karlich's attention. Something glinted in the morning sun.

Metal?

He followed a second flash south-east and what he saw turned his blood cold.

Prince Wilhelm and his knights were on the road and heading towards them. Still several miles distant, there could be no mistaking the Griffonkorps banner and the troop of armoured men on horseback. Karlich surveyed the hills quickly out of instinct, as if the murderer would present himself now the moment drew near, but he saw nothing. Just rocks and rugged earth, patches of gorse and bracken, a hundred places where the shadows could hide Wilhelm's would-be slayer.

The flash of light came again. Soon it would be a flash of blackpowder and a prince's blood would be sullied on the ground.

EBER SQUINTED AND scowled. He rubbed at his eyes as he was momentarily blinded by something shining into them. Shielding the sun overhead with one meaty hand, he tried to blink away the after flare but it came again. He tried to follow its origin. Too late he saw the mirror being used to blind him. Too late he realised the blurry shadow figure was coming for him. Eber heard Masbrecht cry out a warning. The burly Reiklander wasn't fast enough as he brought his shortsword up to guard.

'Fat pig, you're so slow!' said his father's voice, echoing in his head from beyond the grave.

Then he felt the knife enter his body. The first few stabs were hot and sharp, but the ones that followed grew cold and numb. Even Eber with all his strength couldn't stop the blood flowing from his body. As when his father used to beat him, his arms fell to his sides, his head went down to his boots and he could do nothing.

CHAPTER FOURTEEN
AN UNEXPECTED MURDERER

Averland plains,
413 miles from Altdorf

THE FIRST MOMENT Karlich knew something was wrong, Masbrecht was shouting.

'Eber's dead! He killed him! He's here!'

That couldn't be right. He'd seen Eber but a half hour ago, he was fine. A strong ox of a man was Eber. No, he couldn't be dead. There must be a mistake.

Then came the running, Karlich and Rechts together, Karlich's legs working in advance of his mind, his fingers tugging the pistol from his belt before his brain had told them to.

Eber *was* dead. The assassin had killed him.

A sound like thunder echoed throughout the hills, the natural depression within the valley rebounding and intensifying it so it was loud and difficult to pinpoint. A rock just above Karlich's head exploded a half-second later.

Karlich cried out as stony shrapnel embedded in his cheek like hot needles. He went down behind some scattered boulders lodged in the hillside – so did Rechts – and not from the injury. The next shot could be his skull instead of a rock.

'Grimblades!' he roared, trying to staunch the blood flooding down his face and neck, spilling through his fingers and soaking his shoulder. Karlich searched the hills. His head was down but he saw his men moving through the gaps in the rocks. The sun was in his eye-line, partially blinding him.

The bastard had been waiting all along, waiting for the perfect moment.

Grimacing with the pain in his cheek, Karlich cursed and stepped out from behind the boulders. He had to join the hunt. He just hoped the assassin had switched aim or the next iron ball would indeed be in his head.

BRAND KEPT HIS anger like a caged thing, deep inside him. Now it was threatening to spill over, so annoyed was he about being on the wrong side of the hills. He bolted like a maniac across the road, leaving Lenkmann behind. Intent to the point of recklessness, he powered up the opposite hillside in long, rangy strides. He met Eber a short distance up, ashen-faced and lying on his side in a pool of his own blood. The red rivulets coming from his body were like thick veins threading the grass. Brand barely glanced down as he raced past him.

Masbrecht was knelt beside him. 'I didn't see, I didn't see...'

Brand wasn't listening.

Not far now.

He ran harder.

* * *

VOLKER DREW HIS pistol when he saw Eber go down. It was so quick. A snatch of movement, the fading memory of a lithe figure in dark-brown and green felling an oak in the time it should take to cut down a sapling. Then the assassin was gone and Volker lowered his pistol with a curse.

'He's here. Come on!' he urged Keller, who looked like his wits had deserted him.

'Get away! Get out of my head!' he murmured, staggering after Volker and Dog. The mutt was barking loudly, drawing the others to the fight.

'Good boy, good boy,' said Volker, bounding across the hillside, his words coming out in a breathless rush. He ducked through tight ravines, hooked around boulders, leapt over mounds of earth. Just the flicker of his enemy, the waft of something incongruous on the breeze, kept him on the assassin's tail.

As a huntsman on his native lands, during all the years he'd been in the Reikland army, Volker had never tracked a prey so elusive. The assassin left foils and false signs everywhere he went. He had just seconds to do it, and Volker had even less time to decipher them. He went on a winding path, first down and then up again, across the length and breadth of the hillside.

Volker lost concentration for a split-second when he saw Brand barrelling up to meet him. In the corner of his eye, he noticed Karlich and Rechts too. In that moment, he lost his prey. Volker paused, annoyed at himself and felt a slight shift in the air nearby. Ducking out of instinct, he heard something whip over his head that ended in a dissonant *clang* against the rocks beside him. Volker was swinging the pistol around when he saw the assassin. Lithe and tall, he wore a tight leather bodice tied off down the middle. Their leggings and boots were of a dark animal hide. No skin was visible, hidden as it was behind long sleeves, gloves and a mask to cover the face. Something flashed between the eye-slits. It looked like enjoyment. The assassin had blades up his arms, daggers at his belt, a short sword down one leg and some kind of rifle, like no harquebus Volker had ever seen, on a strap slung over his shoulder.

The huntsman's skill at observation had always been keen, and all this he discerned in the moment it took for the assassin to loose another throwing dagger and end Volker's life.

Fate intervened in the huntsman's favour, a burly mass of fur and fangs smashing into the assassin and spoiling his aim. The dagger clattered harmlessly to one side and Volker was on his feet a moment later. Dog was fastened to the assassin's arm, biting down and growling. It elicited a screech of pain from the masked killer, a lot higher in pitch than Volker was expecting. Before he could get there, the assassin threw Dog off. The mastiff rolled and leapt again, but faltered in mid-flight. Volker thought he'd seen the killer raise a hand in warding, a natural reaction to a savage beast coming at him, but as Dog yelped and crumpled to the ground, he suspected something else. Horror built in Volker's gut, all thought of stopping the assassin momentarily forgotten in his concern for Dog. The mastiff wasn't moving. Something bubbled from its maw amidst the foaming saliva.

Frantic, Volker searched Dog's cooling body for sign of injury. Under its chin, he found a tiny dart. So innocuous-looking, yet so deadly. He went to tear it out before realising the barb was poisoned. Dog was dead. There was nothing Volker could do.

BRAND GOT THE assassin's attention simply by running towards her at speed. He redoubled his efforts when he saw the mastiff fall to the dart. Unless the assassin's attention was elsewhere, she'd gut Volker next while his grief made him defenceless. No such weakness from Brand. He knew her, this killer, because he knew himself.

Karlich and Rechts were coming from below. Even Keller was catching up to where Volker cradled his beast's lifeless head. The others were not far, either. They were herding her. She knew it. But Brand knew that an animal was deadliest when cornered. He followed her as she raced up the hillside. She was trying to reach higher ground and find an escape route. Perhaps, with Wilhelm closing by the moment, she merely wished to stall her attackers and execute her mission and the prince with a kill shot from the summit of the hill. The rifle she wore on her back looked like it was up to the task.

With Volker incapacitated, Brand easily outstripped the others for pace. Powering up the rugged slope, he had the assassin exactly where he wanted her – to himself.

Weaving around a rocky outcrop, Brand saw the flash of steel just in time. He parried with his blade, sparks and metal slivers shearing off in the air like falling stars. The second thrust came just as swiftly and he was forced to deflect low to avoid having a knife in his abdomen. The assassin, surprised her victim had lasted this long, drew a second dagger. Brand stepped back, pulling a throwing knife from his vambrace and using it like a foil. Her attack exploded against him in a rain of blows. High and low thrusts, wide slashes and overhand cuts prodded and probed the Reiklander's defences, seeking an opening.

She was good, faster than him. Brand knew he couldn't beat her while she had the upper hand. But all he had to do was hold her off and wait for the others. He'd wanted the assassin for himself, but was pragmatic enough to accept help when he needed it. A flurry of blade strokes pushed Brand back. A hot line of pain seared his arm as she opened up a bloody gash in his wrist. A well-aimed kick punched the air from Brand's lungs and sent him sprawling down the slope. Winded, but with anger fuelling his body in lieu of air, Brand scrambled back after her.

'Bitch…' he muttered in a rare moment of pique.

Then he saw the rifle levelled almost point blank at his chest and knew he'd made a mistake. Closing his eyes, Brand accepted the inevitable. He heard horses in the distance and men shouting from the valley below. But when the shot rang out, he felt no pain. He didn't fall with an iron bullet in his heart.

Brand opened his eyes.

She was dead, the left eye-slit of her mask exploded outwards in a bloom of bloodstained leather. Volker was revealed behind her, an empty look on his face, a smoking pistol in his hand.

EBER FELT COLD and clammy to the touch as Karlich stooped beside him. Masbrecht was crouched next to the sergeant, tearing strips from his cloak and jerkin, and pressing them against Eber's flowing wounds.

'I was wrong. He's alive,' said Masbrecht.

Below, the prince's entourage could be heard charging past. It was likely they'd heard the shot, but impossible to know what they made of it. Bandits and rogues of all stripes were common in the wild and often attacked travellers on the road. In truth, it seemed most of these reprobates had abandoned ambushing the Imperial byways in the wake of Grom's invasion, but Wilhelm and his Griffonkorps couldn't be certain of that. At least it was easier to countenance than an assassin hired to slay him from the shadows.

Karlich had seen the assassin fall to Volker's bullet. At least they'd managed that. It would all be for nothing if the prince discovered the truth, though. The Grimblades kept down, staying out of sight to add weight to the lie that errant bandits were lurking on the hillside. Rechts threatened to shatter the deceit with what he said next.

'We should hail them. Eber's alive and he needs help,' he pleaded to Karlich. 'A horse will get him back to Mannsgard faster than we can.'

Masbrecht replied before Karlich could answer. 'I can help him.' He felt Eber's trunk-like neck. 'His pulse is weak, but he's a strong one. I can help him,' he repeated.

Rechts balled his fists as his jaw set in a firm, unyielding line. 'If you say you'll pray for him...'

Masbrecht turned to him, stony-faced. 'My father was a physician. I learned some of his trade.'

Rechts wasn't convinced. The horses were almost gone. He went to Karlich for a second opinion.

The sergeant considered hard.

'We can't risk it,' he decided in the end.

'Eber will probably die!' said Rechts.

'We can't risk it!' Karlich hissed, his eyes urging the drummer to be quiet and stay down like the rest of them. 'One life for the fate of the Empire. I won't do it, Rechts. Stay down.'

The clacking of hooves against the road slowly receded into the distance. Morning had passed, the prince and his knights were gone.

THE LEATHER MASK was almost black. It had two angular eye slits and bent outwards along the middle to accommodate the nose. It came off easily when Karlich pulled at it, sticking only slightly to the bloodied mess underneath.

Lenkmann had joined them and gave a sharp intake of breath as the assassin's identity was revealed.

Prince Wilhelm's would-be killer was a woman, a pretty one if not for the bullet hole ruining one side of her face. Only Brand had known it beforehand.

'Doesn't look Imperial,' said Rechts.

The dead assassin had olive skin with big, dark eyes and hair like sable to match.

'She's a hireling, a sell-sword,' said Brand. 'A dog of war.'

Karlich felt that same tremor of unease whenever Brand spoke of things that hinted at his old life. It had been a short while since Wilhelm had passed through the valley, alive and well. Together with his Griffonkorps, the prince was just a dust cloud on the horizon now, riding hard for Mannsgard. Karlich wondered idly if their entreaties to Wissenland had been successful. He suspected not. He winced when a bitter smile pulled at his injured cheek. Masbrecht had removed most of the stone shards but it was still painful. Dried blood covered one half of the sergeant's face like a mask. The shoulder of his jerkin was caked in it.

Four men surrounded the corpse. Volker was off somewhere, burying Dog. He'd not spoken a word since the mastiff's death. He didn't appear to be distraught or even angry, just null of feeling, as if he were made of marble. Masbrecht was still tending to Eber, fulfilling his promise to help the burly Reiklander if he could. With Eber's wounds bandaged, there was little more Masbrecht could do. Eber remained unconscious, his breathing laboured. The paleness of his skin suggested he'd lost a lot of blood. Some of it stained Masbrecht's sleeves and stuck between his fingers and under his nails. It wasn't a pleasant sensation.

Keller sat off to the side of the group of four around the assassin. He was downcast, lost in his thoughts.

'Looks like a tattoo,' remarked Rechts, noting the mark on the side of the assassin's neck. Brand had brushed aside her hair and revealed it.

'Do you know what it means?' asked Karlich.

'No,' said Brand. 'I don't recognise this one.'

This one... thought Karlich.

'But I know what this is,' Brand added. From a small pouch tied to the assassin's belt he produced a gold coin.

Karlich took it to examine it.

'Stamped with the burgers' seal,' he muttered. 'This is Marienburg gold. Freshly minted too, if the sheen is anything to go by.'

'I don't understand,' said Lenkmann.

Karlich's face darkened as the possibilities ran through his mind. This business was growing murkier by the minute.

'Neither do I,' he said.

'She was expensive,' Brand told them. 'Those blades, that rifle... Doesn't come cheap. And she was good. Really good.'

Karlich thought he heard a note of reluctant admiration in the other Reiklander's voice.

'Have you ever seen anything like that?' asked Lenkmann.

He was pointing at the rifle next to her. The lacquered wood stock was finely carved and it had a metal barrel and trigger. It was much longer than an ordinary harquebus with a deeper, narrower barrel. It was unadorned, though a gunsmith's mark was engraved in the wood of the butt. A small circlet of iron with a cross through it was hinged to the end of the barrel. A sighter of some description.

'It's Tilean, like her,' said Brand.

Karlich knew little of Tilea, save it was a country far south of the Empire renowned for thieves, sell-swords and adventurers. She certainly had a foreign cast to her features and Tilea had a prominent and powerful assassins' guild whose reach stretched through much of the Old World. He couldn't be sure, though. He wanted to know how Brand could be.

'How do you know?' Karlich asked.

'I've been there.'

Karlich was incredulous. He didn't know of any soldiers that had travelled beyond the Empire. 'When?'

'I was sixteen.'

Karlich waited but when it was obvious no further explanation was coming, he dropped the subject. Brand's past was as cloudy as the Reik during fog. Instead, he focused back on the rifle and the question of what to do with it.

'We have to destroy it,' he said.

Lenkmann made to protest. 'Such a masterpiece weapon, couldn't we–'

'How would you explain it when we return to Mannsgard? We can't just say we found it in the wild. Questions would be asked. The truth would come out.'

Lenkmann had no answer.

'Every trace of her must disappear,' Karlich concluded.

Rechts pulled off his cloak and rolled up his sleeves. 'Then we'd best get started.'

CHAPTER FIFTEEN
OLD WOUNDS

The roadwarden's rest, Averland woods,
408 miles from Altdorf

THEY BURIED THE assassin on the hillside in a shallow grave. There was no time to dig a deeper one and Karlich hoped that scavengers might unearth and then devour her. It was a gruesome thought, and no one voiced it out loud, but they'd been forced to compromise ever since discovering the Altdorf messenger's corpse and becoming Ledner's thugs. Brand dismantled the rifle, smashing its mechanical parts beyond repair with the butt of his pistol and setting fire to the wooden components.

Eber lived, for the moment. His breathing was still shallow and he hadn't regained consciousness yet. By the time they were able to move him – lifting his body with a pair of cloaks like a hammock and carried between two – evening was already drawing in.

It was Volker who found the roadwarden's rest, a small shack well hidden in the woods with a second outbuilding that served as a watchtower nearby. It was bare wood, but sturdy and well kept. Judging by the dust and the smell, it hadn't been occupied in weeks. As they entered the hut where the roadwarden would sleep and eat his meals, Karlich was reminded of the crucifixes they'd found on the way to Blösstadt. The fluttering of dark wings, the frenzied pecking and the excited caws of crows came back to him, unwelcome as bad eggs.

The hut was sparse with a small iron stove in one corner, an empty skillet perched on top. There was a bed. It had mildewed blankets and was stuffed with straw for comfort. This was where they laid Eber, his bearers grateful for not having to haul him around for a while. A stool sat by the bed – Karlich imagined the roadwarden tugging on his boots or sharpening his blade. A hook on the wall contained the empty echo of a crossbow, a darker patch in the wood where the light hadn't touched it. A small cupboard revealed salted meats and a barrel of warm ale. The Grimblades tucked in without thought, not realising how hungry they actually were until presented with food.

Small windows revealed a dingy view. The shack had a flat roof but angled at one end. It had started to rain, thunder in the east announcing a heavy downpour, and it teemed over the window in thick streaks. Through it there was the watchtower, a hundred feet or so from the hut and a small tethering pole where the roadwarden would have secured his horse. They'd found rope and spare iron horseshoes in the shack, but there was no animal in sight. The entire place was desolate and forlorn, as if missing the presence of its occupants.

'This is a cold house,' moaned Rechts, huddled in his cloak. His gaze went longingly to the empty iron hearth and the weeks-old soot coating it.

On Karlich's orders they'd kept the fire doused. Like much of the shack, it was well tended. Apart from the recent soot, the stones were swept and the iron grate that kept the logs in place was brushed. A small chimney poked from the canted roof. Smoke would be a certain signal that the shack was occupied. The roadwarden had picked his spot well. It was untouched because no one, save an expert tracker, would know it was there. Even Averland, with its abundance of plains, had its forests. Like all the places of the Empire, darkness lurked there too, out of sight in the shadows. With greenskins and other beasts abroad, Karlich had reason to be cautious.

As an added precaution, the sergeant had posted a watch. The small outhouse was a perfect location for sentry duty.

'These are cold times,' added Lenkmann, 'as bleak as winter.'

With the bed occupied by Eber, most of the Grimblades squatted on the floor. It *was* cold but warmer than the outdoors, and at least they had a roof over their heads. Masbrecht sat on the stool, keeping an eye on his patient. He'd redressed the bandages and cleaned the wounds with water from a well around the back of the hut, but there was little more he could do for poor Eber. While he lived, there was hope. He was a strong man. Masbrecht prayed silently for him to pull through.

'What do you make of the gold?' asked Rechts, trying to occupy his mind with something other than how chill his bones were. It was the first time anyone had said anything of it or the assassination plot since they'd left the hillside. With the few words he'd spoken, Volker reckoned they were well over halfway to Mannsgard, possibly another day's journey encumbered by Eber.

Prince Wilhelm would have returned already and by the time the Grimblades got back to town, preparations would be underway for the march to Averheim. Karlich hoped they wouldn't be missed. Ledner probably hoped they were all dead.

'Marienburg seal, clearly fresh,' said Karlich, bringing the coin to his mind's eye. Like her trappings, the coin had been buried with the dead assassin. 'I'm not sure what to think. Honestly, I don't really want to.'

'I cannot countenance a prince of Reikland would be the victim of a blade in his own camp,' added Masbrecht. 'We are not savages. Sigmar-fearing men are godly and honourable, they–'

'Stop your preaching,' snapped Rechts with the weary ire of a frustrated drunk.

Karlich intervened before it went further. 'First time was a warning, Rechts. Don't make me come over to you.'

Rechts scowled behind his cloak, but backed down.

'I only meant it is hard for me as a devout...' Masbrecht paused when he saw Rechts glaring at him '...for me to believe a Reiklander could wish harm upon his own prince. Have we fallen so far?'

'We are not on the Warrior's Hill, if that's what you mean,' said Karlich.

Warrior's Hill was where in ages past that Sigmar gathered his chieftains and had them swear allegiance to an ideal, to the birth of an Empire. It was an act of fealty, not just to an emperor, the first emperor in fact, but to each other and the realm of man as a whole.

'Dreams fade with the dawn, Masbrecht,' Karlich continued. 'Like a wisp of cloud, they are at once beautiful and lofty, but also unreachable, transient. At best, they're a memory. At worst, they're entirely forgotten.'

'Gods, but that's bleak,' said Lenkmann, shaking his head.

Karlich was impassive. 'I'm a realist, that's all. I've seen the dark things men do.' His eyes met with Rechts's out of reflex rather than design. He went on. 'What remains after idealism is gone is life.' Karlich was almost sanguine. 'It is the pledges we make to one another, on the field of battle, in this very room.' He spread his hands and looked at Masbrecht again. 'Not all men are as pure-hearted as you, Masbrecht. Even I have... *regrets*.'

For a moment, Karlich went to a place inside him, where he kept his own dark truths. Whenever he opened that door, he smelled smoke and felt again his hands burning in the pyre, tearing at the ropes that held *her*... then pushing *his* face into the mud when he knew it was too late and *they* were gone...

Masbrecht wasn't done. His voice brought Karlich back. 'We're expected to keep all knowledge of this to ourselves, of what we did,' he said. 'I'm not sure I can do that.'

Karlich looked serious now. 'Well you must. We all know what's at stake.'

'If we don't, yes I know. But what's at stake if we do keep our mouths shut?' He put it to all of them. 'One killer has failed, but who's to say others won't be sent for the prince. He must be told his life is in danger.'

'We've been through this already, *brother.*' Rechts's upper lip curled into a snarl.

Karlich sighed deeply. 'Yes, there may be others. Perhaps this is also an end to it, we can but hope. But I doubt they'll strike now Wilhelm is back in Mannsgard with the army. Assassination will be the least of his concerns. Greenskins await us at Averheim, a horde the likes of which we've never seen if the scouts are to be believed.

'There is much we don't know here, Masbrecht. Don't act before being certain of the facts at hand.'

Masbrecht wasn't happy about it, his moral code was a strict one, but he nodded his agreement all the same.

'Ledner knows more than he's saying,' said Volker, sticking to the shadows, a few feet from the rest of the group. Lenkmann offered him a strip of salted beef but he declined.

'You could hang princes on that man's secrets,' Karlich replied in a bitter voice. The irony of the statement was not lost on him. By using Wilhelm as bait to draw out the assassin, Ledner had almost done just that.

There were rumours that Marienburg desired independence from the Empire. Karlich had heard traders in Altdorf and on the Reik claiming as much. It was so far fetched an idea that it had become something of a joke, an idiosyncratic quirk of a people joined by land but divorced in ideology. A rich state wanting to get richer. Even the underclass were well heeled.

There are no peasants in Marienburg, so the popular myth went, *because they can't tend fields with all those rings on their fingers.*

'And what if he hangs *us*?' added Volker.

Lenkmann raised an eyebrow. 'A dour thought, Volker.'

'I have plenty to be dour about.'

Lenkmann was closest to him and reached over to pat his shoulder. The gesture was a little awkward, but his expression conveyed sadness. 'It was a brave animal.'

Something dark flashed across the huntsman's eyes as he looked back.

'It was a mean bastard.'

Karlich was looking around. 'Speaking of which, where is Brand?'

All eyes went to one corner of the room. Brand had been sitting there, almost invisibly in the deepest shadows. Now he was not.

'I could've sworn...' Lenkmann began.

Karlich was on his feet. His anxious mood passed to the others, a sudden sense of urgency charging the air. He asked a question to which he already knew the answer.

'Who is on watch?'

Masbrecht was the first to answer. 'Keller.'

Karlich left the door banging loudly in the wind as he bolted from the shack.

SLIPPING OUT WAS easy. It was gloomy in the shack and filled with shadows. A few candles had been scavenged from a drawer but they were stubby and weak. Karlich was wise to light only a few. Any more and the fiery glow would have attracted more than just moths. Just like smoke from a chimney, larger nocturnal predators would be drawn to a flame, drawn to the warmth it promised and that of the humans crowded round it.

A back door led out into a small yard where they'd found the well. Without a handle or any discerning marks, it was hard to see. Brand had found it easily enough, though. Easier still was disappearing when the debate about Wilhelm's would-be killers was going on.

No one noticed the slightest flutter of the candle flames or the faint draft of cold air, so fleeting it could have been imagined.

Brand was out in the rain. To some it would be a cleansing experience, but no amount of rain could purify the taint Brand felt on his body like a second skin. Rain reminded him of drowning, only by degrees, one drop at a time. He'd led a violent life, and associated everything with death. Brand circled around the back of the hut, staying low and moving steadily but calmly. Sudden movements, even out in the rain-drenched darkness, might attract the attention of his comrades, and they had no part in what he was about to do.

Brand knew his chance would come again. Keller was a slave to his guilt now. He couldn't stand to be in the presence of others for fear that the sickening lump behind his ribs would make him speak out and confess his sin. Blood, Brand knew, especially old blood, was heavier than it first appeared.

The outhouse was ahead, little more than a silhouette, like a piece of driftwood sticking up from a clinging sandbank. The earth around it, despite being sheltered by the canopy of the forest, was sodden like a quagmire. Brand trod lightly and swiftly once away from the shack and in the open.

He barely noticed the rain anymore as he approached the door. Somewhere behind him another door was banging. It was hard to hear, muffled by the weather. The door to the watchtower was unlatched. Easing it open with his foot, Brand drew his dagger. Inside, Keller was waiting.

* * *

NEARLY SLIPPING SEVERAL times on the mud, Karlich reached the watchtower a little out of breath. He drew his sword, vaguely aware of the others behind him. Throwing open the door, he rushed inside expecting to see Brand murdering Keller. It had taken him a few days, but he'd realised there was something between the two men. He didn't know what precisely, but suspected it had something to do with Varveiter's death. He'd watched Brand ever since, but had let him slip from his sight when his guard was down.

Keller *was* dead, but not from Brand's dagger. He swung by a rope tied around his neck. A stool lay on its side nearby. The tips of Keller's boots barely scraped the floor. By the pallor of his skin, he'd been dead for some time.

Brand was sitting on the floor, sobbing into his hands. For a moment Karlich was taken aback. He'd never seen the man cry. Ever.

The others were coming in from the outside.

Karlich slammed the door in their faces, locking it shut.

'Get out! Go back to the hut,' he said, shouting so they wouldn't question him. Someone tried the door. He heard Lenkmann's voice but the meaning of his words was lost in the rain. 'Do it now. That's an order.'

When he was sure the others had gone, Karlich turned back to Brand. His gaze drifted upwards to Keller's swinging body. The rope groaned with the weight. In that gruesome moment he realised what must have happened at Blösstadt.

Keller had murdered Varveiter in retribution for humiliating him at the camp, and the guilt of it had driven him to hang himself. Brand had known it too, much sooner than Karlich, and had planned revenge of his own. Only Keller had robbed him of it, too afraid to face the consequences of his actions.

'I would've done it,' sobbed Brand, as all of his grief flooded out. 'I wanted to do it.'

Karlich sheathed his sword and knelt down beside him.

'I know, brother.' He made to touch Brand's arm but stopped short, letting his hand fall to his side. *When soothing a wounded wolf, it's wise to keep your hands to yourself.* Karlich had heard that spoken in Middenheim once. 'It's all right.'

They sat like that in the silence and the dark for a while, until Brand stopped crying and Karlich decided to cut Keller down.

NO ONE WOULD ever know the truth, nor would they ask for it. The Grimblades had been through much together and knew when to leave things alone.

Keller was dead. Karlich had told them he thought the man simply couldn't take the pressures of the war and the burden placed upon them by Ledner, and it was left at that. All had noticed how withdrawn he'd become since their first engagement at the slaughtered village. It wasn't so beyond reason – men had taken their own lives for less.

An unmarked grave was Keller's only legacy. Volker had found a suitable spot in the forest that was shaded and the soil less like the sucking bog surrounding the watchtower. Masbrecht had delivered a short sermon, a soldier's prayer. Rechts had stayed, but made his discomfort obvious. It wasn't that the drummer didn't believe in Sigmar, far from it. His faith had been shaken, yes, but it was priests and dogma he had issue with. Karlich knew that, and recognised himself in that conviction. It was why he tolerated the outbursts and the drunkenness.

Even Brand had attended in the end. Karlich assumed he had his reasons.

When it was done, when Keller's bones were laid to rest, Rechts had sung a solemn lament. It was a marching song of Reikland, *My brother in our Land,* one that commemorated the fallen and asked their comrades to remember them. The rain had persisted until morning and framed a sullen scene around the grave.

There was no time to tarry. As soon as Rechts was done they left the roadwarden's rest and headed back to Mannsgard. The mood was grim, but Eber, at least, had shown some signs of life. Masbrecht had performed his task well. The burly Reiklander would live.

CHAPTER SIXTEEN
MARSHALLING FOR WAR

The town of Mannsgard, Averland,
383 miles from Altdorf

An army was growing outside the town by the time the Grimblades returned. Imperial banners caught on the wind, snapping against their poles as if fighting to be free. Soldiers in the colours of Averland, Middenland, Reikland and Carroburg gathered. There was a hubbub of voices and the dull *clang* of metal from breastplates and tassets as the soldiers slowly formed into regiments. The lines of men filing from the gates seemed endless. An entire town emptied, leaving only its graven citizens behind. Karlich would later remark that he couldn't tell if they were pleased or distraught to no longer be harbouring soldiers.

Pikemen, spear, swordsmen and halberdiers stood shoulder to shoulder with archers, crossbowmen and handgunners. Militiamen roved in loose bands until their sergeants bellowed for order. To their credit, the free companies made rank and file quickly. Mules dragged baggage caravans or hauled cannons and mortars, gunnery crews shadowing them like dutiful hounds. Engineers rode in the wagons themselves, together with their best journeymen. Karlich saw one muttering to his war machine and smoothing the barrel in the same way he'd stroke a beloved pet.

Madmen, he thought. Blackpowder was as dangerous as sorcery. Only the insanely brave or the bravely insane dallied with it. Exploding shrapnel could kill a man just as easy as a blade or bow and before an enemy had even deigned to launch its first attack. He remembered an incident a few years back when a gunner had lost his head to a spinning axle flung from his machine when it misfired. The irony of it was the battle was already won, and the guns were being fired to salute their victory. Since that day, Karlich had vowed to give war engines and their like a wide berth.

Mad they may be, but compared to the footsloggers the gunners looked positively sanguine. Most of the infantry were drawn and pale, moving with the uncertain purpose of condemned men. It wasn't so far from the truth.

Karlich had yet to see the cavalry as he and the others walked past the processional exodus from Mannsgard. He assumed they'd be last, after the foot soldiers were readied to march.

It was mid-morning, the sun was rising quickly and the last of the night patrols were returning. Karlich had blended his own troops in with them, so as not to arouse suspicion. Passing the last of the thronging soldiers on their way through the gate, he noticed Von Rauken and his 'Carroburg Few'. The hoary old veteran nodded with the slow certainty of iron. Karlich returned the gesture and tried to hide his nerves. Though he was the last man he wanted to see, he had to find Ledner and tell him what had happened.

Karlich found the spymaster at the counting house where they'd met in secret two nights ago, gathering up maps and charts from the desk.

It was still gloomy, though the window slats were open and allowed a little light in. Dust whirled about the air in thick, grey clumps. Karlich coughed, giving away his presence.

Ledner did well to mask his surprise when he looked up at him.

'It's done.' Karlich was in no mood for niceties. He wanted to get away from this man and this place as soon as possible. He was alone, having left the others to find the rest of the regiment. If Captain Stahler asked, Karlich was giving his report to one of Wilhelm's scriveners for the prince's perusal later.

'Fine work,' said Ledner. Something flashed behind his eyes. Karlich thought it was amusement, but the kind of emotion shown by a snake as it circled a plucky mouse.

'Not without cost.'

'Yes, I heard you lost a man. And the one who was injured?'

'He's with the chirurgeon. He'll live, but won't fight at Averheim.'

'You'll miss his blade.'

Karlich was downcast. 'Aye, I will.'

Ledner went into a drawer in the desk and tossed a heavy-looking bag in front of Karlich.

'What's this?' he asked, not bothering to keep the angry tone from his voice.

A few coins spilled out onto the desk, the weight of the pile inside the bag pulling it over.

'Your payment.' Ledner didn't look up as he sorted the last of the charts and scrolls. 'There's five crowns each in there. Two more for you as sergeant.'

Karlich dumped a large bundle on the desk. It struck the bag of coins and scattered them over the scarred wood.

'Your guns and blades,' he said.

Ledner barely glanced at the leather skin binding the weapons together.

'And the cloaks?' he asked, rolling up the last of his scrolls.

'We'll keep 'em, if it's all the same to you. Nights on the Averland plain can be cold. You can keep the blood money.'

If Ledner felt the barb, or even cared, he didn't show it. He ignored the scattered coins, too.

It would be just like the man to leave them out of spite or to demonstrate just how much higher in the Imperial hierarchy he was, thought Karlich. We are little more than insects to men like him. He suppressed the urge to punch Ledner in the face. Karlich fancied his dagger-like nose would break fairly easily.

'There's more?' asked the spymaster, when Karlich didn't leave.

'Don't you want to know about the assassin?'

The sergeant was genuinely nonplussed.

'You stopped him, that's all that really concerns me.'

'The assassin was female, a Tilean by her cast and features.'

Ledner kept silent, inviting more.

'She was a sell-sword hired with freshly-minted Marienburg gold but then I suppose that doesn't really surprise you, does it?' Karlich couldn't keep the sneer from his tone or his face.

Now Ledner looked up at him. 'And what makes you say that, sergeant?'

'Only that you know more than you're telling me.'

The spymaster laughed wryly. 'You knew what was needed,' said Ledner. 'A little information can be a dangerous thing, especially if it is heard out of context. I'm sure you're aware of that, sergeant.'

Karlich felt a sudden chill enter his spine. He swallowed hard. Did Ledner just allude to something in his past?

Does he know about Vanhans?

The look of playful humour vanished off Ledner's face, as if deciding he'd pushed far enough for now.

'You should get back to your regiment,' he said, returning to the scrolls. 'If you're late for mustering, questions might be asked.'

Recovering his composure, Karlich said, 'Well then, let me ask you one more thing.'

Ledner peered up at him from the table. 'Go on.'

'What was Count Pfeifraucher's answer?'

'You'd like to know your sacrifice wasn't in vain, that the prince's journey wasn't a needless waste of time and effort?'

'Just tell me.'

Ledner snorted at some private amusement. 'Have you looked around the town or at the army gathering outside? What do you see, sergeant?'

Answering questions with questions, how like a spymaster.

'I see nothing different, except perhaps a few more unhappy faces.'

Ledner collected the scrolls and charts under his arm. As he walked past Karlich on his way out, he said, 'Well then, there's your answer.'

Karlich *really* wanted to hit him now. He clenched his fists and it took all of his considerable willpower not to do it. He realised Ledner was trying to goad him. Execution was the punishment for striking a senior officer and Ledner knew it. So instead, Karlich kept his back to him and let the spymaster go.

'I'll send someone back for those pistols, unless you want to take them?' Ledner didn't wait for an answer, the sound of the door closing echoed in the man's wake.

'I have somewhere you can put them…' Karlich snarled at the gloom. He waited until he was sure Ledner was gone then left the counting house to go and find his regiment. Any longer away from the gathering army and Stahler might begin to miss him.

CAPTAIN STAHLER COULDN'T believe what he was hearing. Judging by the reaction of Prince Wilhelm's other officers, neither could they.

'So we'll return to Reikland then, fortify our borders,' said Captain Hornschaft, 'and consolidate our forces with the Averlanders,' he added when he caught a petrified look from Baron Blaselocker. The Yellow Baron, as he was now known around the camp, was really just an officer in name only. He had no troops to command, save his own retinue, and his position on the field would be at the rear, near the war machines where he could cause the least amount of trouble.

Prince Wilhelm had pointed it out on one of the maps before him only a few moments ago. It was a few moments after that when he idly let slip that Wissenland had refused all overtures of alliance with Reikland and Averland. Just as before, they were alone in the liberation of Averheim.

'Why do you think we are going over strategic plans of attack, Hornschaft?' asked Preceptor Kogswald. The Griffonkorps captain had a way of making even the simplest question sound like an impatient challenge. His mood was sour, and he flushed angrily behind his oiled moustaches – Kogswald had vehemently opposed the prince's diplomatic mission to Wissenland.

The captain from Auerswald balked a little before the knight's ire. He removed his wide-brimmed hat to mop his brow. 'Without Count Pfeifraucher, we are badly outnumbered.' He appealed to Wilhelm who was watching his officers keenly. A general could tell a lot about the men of his command when they were under pressure. Who would fight, who would rather flee to die another day. He was still undecided about Hornschaft.

'And yet, here we are,' said Vogen. The captain from Kemperbad stabbed a gauntleted finger down onto the map, which showed the lay of the land near the outskirts of Averheim, as if to suggest that battle was now a formality in his eyes.

Wilhelm smiled privately.

A fighter, that one.

'So, what's to be done?' asked Stahler, displaying the earthy pragmatism he was known for. Truth was, though, he agreed with Hornschaft. Marching on Averheim with an under-strength force was near enough suicide. The difference was, Stahler's pragmatic streak also manifested as a stoic adherence to duty.

At that moment Ledner entered, throwing a shaft of light into the darkened confines of the tavern. Wilhelm had hastily summoned all of his military officers to his temporary lodgings in Mannsgard. He'd hoped against hope that Wissenland would answer the call to arms and fight beside its brothers. But instead of solidarity in the face of a common enemy, all Pfeifraucher had offered was a provincial mindset that saw him shutting his borders for good. Well, at least until the orcs moved farther south-east and tore them down.

All of the captains were present, including Engineer Meinstadt who'd remained in pensive silence since the council began. Preceptor Kogswald of the Griffonkorps was seldom far from his prince's side if he could help it, and represented all of the templar knights in the army. Vanhans and his 'soldiers of faith' were, obviously, excluded.

Of the others, Father Untervash was outside the town leading his fellow priests and novitiates from regiment to regiment, offering blessings and instilling the courage of Sigmar where it was needed. The wizard had removed himself, meditating in solitude to consolidate his magical strength. Apparently, his powers were all but returned since the exhausting battle near the Brigund Bridge.

The light died quickly as Ledner shut the tavern door, as did the warmth in the room. Fear mongering and disinformation were the man's stock-in-trade, and rolled off him like a mist wherever he went.

'Apologies, my liege,' he said to Wilhelm in his familiar rasp, the other officers parting to allow him a place at the strategy table. 'A matter arose that required my attention. Also, I needed to gather the additional charts and scrolls for our quartermasters.'

The prince nodded once, in a gesture that all was well, before Kogswald outlined the plan of battle.

'There is an army within Averheim. Trapped behind its gates, there is little it can do but defend the walls,' he said, taking a nub of charcoal from a clay pot on the table. 'Our force is not insignificant,' he added, starting to draw. 'We bring the greenskins on to us with artillery fire, archers and shot…' Crosses represented the missile troops. Three arrows, arcing from where Averheim was depicted on the map to the crosses he had just drawn, represented the enemy's movements. 'Thus leavened, the wall guard can be thinned, its surplus used to form a large sortie in the courtyard.' Kogswald looked up and smiled. The expression was a grim rictus, framed by his moustache. Steel coloured the emotion in his eyes.

'No less than five knightly orders are holed up within Averheim. By pulling the greenskins towards us and using our cavalry to cut a path through to the gate, we can unleash them. Caught between a massed force of knights and the infantry, the greenskins will soon become disorganised. Rout, after that, is inevitable.'

Kogswald stood straight after leaning over the table for so long. He looked pleased with himself.

Prince Wilhelm waited patiently for the reaction.

The other captains were nodding. Vogen folded his arms to suggest it met with his approval. Even Hornschaft looked mollified by what he'd heard. Stahler had to admit it sounded like a winning strategy, but he also saw the burden it would place on the infantry. When the orcs came at them, goaded by the guns, it would fall to the foot soldiers to hold them off and prevent the line from being overrun. Despite his ardent loyalty to the cause, he was starting to find the role of punching bag a little wearisome.

'And what if the greenskins will not be baited or if they maintain their order?'

Kogswald swung his gaze over to Ledner. He shook his head. 'They are orcs,' he said, confused at what his fellow captain was implying. 'Ignorant beasts that are easily distracted and dissuaded. It is their nature. They can no more fight it than you or I could renounce our duty to the prince. It is what they are.'

Ledner's eyes never wavered. He met Kogswald's indignant steel with silken guile. 'And yet, the question remains…'

Kogswald laughed again, not bothering to hide his scorn and incredulity. He looked about to reply when he went to the prince, instead.

'My lord–' he said, half as a question, half exasperation. Kogswald opened his palms as if to say, *Are you going to listen to this snake's drivel?*

Wilhelm breathed deeply, his eyes blind with thought. Wrong-footing them all, he turned to Meinstadt.

'Master of the Guns, how much artillery do we have?'

The engineer adjusted his monocle, by way of nervous affectation. He loudly cleared his throat.

'Six great cannon, one volley gun, three mortar and ninety-six harquebus, my lord.'

Stahler was taken aback at Meinstadt's rapid inventory. He'd heard little and seen less of the war engines in the army's arsenal. True, there were wagons driving out of Mannsgard with machineries aboard but he had not known of the volley gun, nor had he appreciated the sheer numbers. Engineers were secretive bastards, and evidently Meinstadt believed in that clandestine code, but they were also notoriously eager for 'trialling' their weapons of mass destruction. Stahler assumed Prince Wilhelm had instructed most of the artillery be held back and saved for breaking the siege at Averheim.

'Keep a portion of the guns in reserve,' said the prince. 'I'll leave it up to you, Meinstadt, to decide what is appropriate.' Now he addressed the entire council. 'If our attack falters, or the orcs surprise us all and hold their ground, we'll cover our retreat with artillery. Nature or not, no mortal creature would gladly walk into a fusillade of shot if there are easier pickings elsewhere.'

The engineer was nodding at this wisdom when Wilhelm glanced at him. 'Do it now. Make your preparations.'

Meinstadt was already leaving when the prince spoke again.

'We are done, my captains. We march to Averheim, to glory or death.' He nodded with a knowing sort of fatalism. 'To blood, certainly. Fight for me,' he added. 'Fight for the Reikland and the Empire. Turn the tide.'

The gathered captains stood a little straighter, a little taller and saluted together. Hornschaft was nodding again. With all the feathers on his hat, it put Stahler in mind of a bird pecking at its feed. Vogen puffed up his chest with war-like pride. Kogswald was imperious as ever. Ledner gave away nothing.

These were the men that would deliver Averheim or see it fall, of this Stahler felt sure. The air felt cold. It was the touch of death closing, of Morr's heavy sword above all their heads. It only made Stahler more determined.

'Faith in Sigmar,' said the prince.

His captains answered as one.

'Faith in Sigmar!'

It would need to account for much in the hours to come.

As the officers departed to their regiments, Stahler made an excuse to linger behind. Ledner and the prince were still inside. With the others gone, he went around the side of the tavern. When Stahler was sure no one was watching he bent double, hands on his knees to hold himself up. Sweat cascaded off his forehead as he removed his hat and helm. It felt as if an anvil were lying on his chest.

'*Gods...*' Stahler was surprised at the breathless rasp that came out of him. At Blösstadt the orc's wound had gone deep – deeper than he'd realised. He clutched at his breastplate, it was like a vice seizing his body. When he drew away his hand it was dappled with blood.

When Karlich returned to the regiment, a surprise awaited him.

'Refugees from Averland,' Lenkmann explained after a crisp salute. Karlich eyed the new recruit in his ranks wearily.

'Just one? Doesn't seem worth it,' he chuntered to himself.

'Welcome back, sergeant,' Lenkmann added facilely. He stood forward of his comrades, as if distancing himself in the relative pecking order.

'I've hardly been away,' Karlich muttered and approached the fresh blood. He was young, that much was obvious, with the slight tan of a life lived on the Averland plains. The uniform was mismatched with yellow, black hose and a red tunic. The leather jerkin he wore over it had a crimson and white ribbon tied to one of its straps. He had one around his arm too. A metal gorget protected his neck and he had a peaked helmet.

Karlich beckoned the lad forwards. He came to stand beside Lenkmann.

'You a halberdier, son?'

'As sure as Siggurd!' the lad answered forcefully.

The perplexed look on Karlich's face made him go further.

'I mean, yes sir, I am. Gerrant Greiss, formerly of the Grenzstadt 5th,' he added.

Karlich sized him up. He scowled as if unimpressed. Behind them, Rechts and Volker were trying to keep a straight face.

'You've fought "the Paunch" many men are speaking of?'

'Not face-to-face, but our lord general did. At the Averland border, our army watched the western end of Black Fire Pass. We were amongst the first to resist the greenskins.'

'Your lord, where is he now?'

'His head is mounted on the goblin king's banner, sir.'

Averlanders were a straightforward, earthy people. Perhaps it was why they enjoyed such good relations with the dwarfs. Even still, Greiss's forthrightness caught Karlich unawares.

'I see,' he said, recovering. 'Rejoin your comrades. Welcome to the Grimblades, Greiss.'

Karlich looked around at the growing army. Blocks of troops were discernible now. An order of march, come through from the returning officers, was slowly being established. The Grimblades had yet to learn of their position in it. Stahler, much to Karlich's relief, still hadn't shown up.

He did see that other regiments, besides his own, had been swelled by refugee recruits too. Some, like Greiss, wore spare uniforms or elements thereof. Many looked incongruous amongst their new postings, however, wearing only a regimental ribbon on their arms to identify them.

'Reappropriated after Captain Ledner's instructions to the quartermasters,' Lenkmann said when he saw his sergeant surveying the army.

Karlich remembered the charts and scrolls in the counting house. He vaguely recalled a number of the so-called 'death-books' amongst them.

As his gaze continued uninterrupted, Karlich noticed further additions. He saw a large regiment of dwarfs, probably expatriates from the Grey Mountains given their obvious penchant for Imperial trappings such as feathered helms and slitted tunics. Karlich had met Worlds Edge Mountain dwarfs before, and they did not dress like that. He also saw halflings, likely travelled from the Moot. More diminutive than dwarfs, but not as stocky and without beards, halflings were regarded as something of a nuisance in the Empire. Still, they were braver than they looked and fairly stout on account of their well-fed bellies.

These halflings were an odd band, well-armed despite the shortness of their weapons and stature. They carried short bows and a variety of small daggers and dirks.

One wore a kettle for a helmet, another a pot with a ladle tucked in his belt. Karlich spotted forks and spoons too, even a frying pan. Satchels slung over the halflings' backs were stuffed with vittels. A chicken's foot poked from one, the stopper from a jug of mead from another.

'At least they've brought their own food,' said a familiar voice. Von Rauken blew a plume of smoke as he chewed on his pipe. He smiled when Karlich saw him.

'Are you jesting, greatsworder? That's just a morsel to those gluttons!'

Von Rauken laughed with a sound like grinding iron and the two men shook hands warmly. 'Aye, you're probably right,' he said.

'Once done with the supply wagons, they'll be on to the horses,' Karlich replied.

Von Rauken laughed louder. His humour was infectious and as far removed from the grim champion as Karlich had ever seen.

'Levity is good before battle,' he said, the dourness returning. Something unspoken passed between the two men, a shared desire that both should survive what was to come at Averheim.

Von Rauken clapped Karlich on the shoulder and nodded.

'We'll drink to it after.' With that, he turned away and went back to where his greatswords were waiting.

Karlich replied in a quiet voice, 'Aye, after.'

'The army grows, but why does it feel like the end of times, like our last battle?' Lenkmann asked after a moment of silence.

Around them the infantry was almost ready. Heavy horse could be heard above the muttered voices of the throng. The cavalry was leaving Mannsgard. They were about to begin marching to Averheim.

'Because it is, Lenkmann,' Karlich told him. His tone was slightly wistful. 'It probably is.'

Thunder trembled in the heavens. Lightning drew jagged arcs across a steel-grey sky a moment later. Karlich's eye was drawn to a desolate heath, a mile or so from the town. There he made out the wizard he had met in the war tent. He was channelling the storm in and out of his body, like a lightning rod. His hair stood on end, ablaze with celestial fury. A tempest was growing to the east. The faintest echoes of it whirled around the army and tore one of the banners free from its pole. Karlich watched some men reach for it, but it got caught up in the wind and gusted away. Ragged and forlorn, it sped back towards the Reikland.

The thunder came again with renewed vigour, filling Karlich's world with noise.

CHAPTER SEVENTEEN

BESIEGED

Outside Averheim, capital city of Averland,
483 miles from Altdorf

THE EARTH TREMBLED under the hooves of Wilhelm's horse. Loud and deafening, the guns reminded him of thunder.

The great cannons fired one after the other, each fresh report adding to the resonance of the ones before it. Smoke spewed from their iron barrels, the ends fashioned into the mouths of mythical beasts, and thronged the air with the stench of blackpowder. A second percussive blast provided a deeper chorus, just beneath the sound of the cannon. These were the mortars, their fat shells whining overhead to land in the packed greenskin ranks.

Wilhelm tried to follow the destructive course of the war machines but was too far away. Together with the cavalry, amounting to six lances of templars and a roving band of pistoliers, Prince Wilhelm occupied the far right flank of the battleline. He was nearly a hundred feet from what could be considered the war front. The *refused flank* was a well-known military theorem in the Empire. Here, on the killing fields before Averheim, it would be tested in practice.

Averland's capital looked like a broken silhouette in the distance. Like most large cities, it was surrounded by a wall. It had suffered badly under the attentions of the greenskins. Their crude catapults were too far advanced to be hit by the Imperial cannonade. Mangonels and onagers loosed relentlessly. Walls and towers, even sections of the heavily fortified gatehouse, resembled the nubs of broken teeth. Even at a distance, Wilhelm could tell that men hung dead in some of the ruins. The clouds of flies made it gruesomely obvious.

At other parts of the wall, the orcs launched continuous assaults with ladders, ropes and log rams. Through a spyglass, the prince made out an orc slavemaster urging a band of trolls to heave a battering ram against Averheim's main gate. The ornate carving that had once adorned it had been bludgeoned into oblivion. Dust and grit from the neighbouring gatehouse walls shook loose with every fresh blow. Wilhelm could already imagine it splintering. It was making the wait worse, so he lowered the spyglass.

To his left, he knew, was the rest of the army.

The rear was anchored by Meinstadt and his war machines. Two brace of cannon and a pair of mortars comprised the battery. The remaining engines were primed but left unfired.

Five regiments of handgunners stood sentinel before the larger guns above and behind them. Little did Wilhelm know, but Utz and his sergeant, Isaak, were amongst them as part of the Grünburg contingent. Due to their longer range, four regiments of Averland crossbowmen were stationed a step above them.

In order to accommodate the blackpowder troops and the gunnery crews, Imperial sappers had been forced to raise earth embankments. They did this by digging trenches and then heaping up the mud. It had to be packed hard so the weighty machineries didn't sink. It also needed shoring with timber along its sides. Palisades were erected at the base by way of a makeshift rampart to protect the handgunners. The trenches were filled with abatis as a final deterrent. It was backbreaking work and the labour gangs earned their bread and coin that day, but it was also necessary. The land around Averheim was very flat and Meinstadt needed elevation for his guns if the plan was to succeed.

Militia were interspersed between the blackpowder troops. Their ranks were much deeper, their frontage narrow by comparison. They were to act as foils should the greenskins break through to the guns.

In front of them came the infantry.

A huge wedge of Empire soldiery dominated one half of the plain beyond the ersatz embankment. Three lines, ten regiments each, made up the infantry throng. Swordsmen and halberdiers took the back line. The dwarfs from the Grey Mountains were deployed here too, together with large groups of militia. No regiment was less than six ranks deep.

A second line of halberdiers and swordsmen stood in front of the first. Here the Grimblades were stationed. Von Rauken's greatsworders were nearby, occupying a central position. His smaller regiment was in addition to the main body of troops but no less imposing for its smaller size.

The front line had the pike and spears. Vanhans's mercenaries and desperadoes pitched their banner here too. It would fall to all of these brave souls to bear the brunt of the greenskin attack and weather it if they could. Once battle was joined, they'd narrow their formations and allow the rear line to engage.

Roaming just in front of the formal infantry wedge were free companies, huntsmen and archers. The halflings were amongst them. It was the job of this skirmish line to frustrate and disorganise the orcs as much as possible before they charged. By pulling and dividing them, it was hoped the greenskins wouldn't attack as a cohesive mass, thusly making it easier to resist them.

Across the line, drums beat and horns blared. They were challenges, designed to goad the greenskins and bolster the Empire's fighting men.

They will need it, Wilhelm thought grimly, donning his helmet as the orcs began to turn.

The greenskin army was like a tide.

'HAVE YOU EVER seen such a horde?' Lenkmann uttered from the front rank. Even the banner he carried sagged in assumed defeat.

'I can feel Morr's breath on my neck,' said Volker, one rank behind him. His mood had turned maudlin ever since the death of Dog.

'Enough of that!' snapped Karlich. 'It doesn't matter if there is one orc or a hundred thousand. You can still only kill them one at a time.'

But even he had to admit the enemy was vast.

Unlike the precise and militaristic order of the Empire army, the greenskins were a densely packed rabble.

Through gaps in the Empire's own ranks Karlich made out tribal banners that appeared to unify certain mobs. To his dismay, several carried the desiccated remains of Imperial soldiers. Other greenskins could be identified by markings and tattoos. Brawling was mandatory. Smaller goblins bickered continuously, whilst their larger cousins engaged in more violent acts against their own kind. Rival clans fought tooth and nail in the rear masses.

Even as the cannon balls bounded through their ranks, chewing up bodies and ripping off limbs, they still brawled. Only when explosive mortar rounds blasted them apart, separating combatants, did the orcs stop fighting one another and turn to the 'humies on the hill'.

It was slow at first, like a boulder rolling down a lightly canted slope. It took time to build and spread like an angry flame through the greenskin ranks. But gradually, and with fearsome momentum, the orcs began to charge.

Bellows and war cries accompanied the shuffling gait of greenskin feet. The dark sea surrounding Averheim rippled. They thumped their chests and smashed cleavers against chipped wooden shields. Standard bearers rattled totems, cursing the weakling men who had chosen to pick a fight with them. Huge flesh-skinned drums beat. Raucous pipes screeched. The ocean of green was moving.

Amongst the bestial mob were larger beasts, creatures that shared the greenskins' desire for carnage and cruelty. Lumbering trolls, pugnacious ogres and gangling giants roamed alongside orcs and goblins of every tribe.

Hooded in black cowls and cloaks, festooned with bone charms, armoured with thick dark plate – the one known as 'the Paunch' had allied a massive and diverse horde together. With guile, intimidation, sheer strength or perhaps all three, this warlord, this 'Grom', had overcome the single greatest weakness of the greenskin race, the one thing that had, until now, prevented their wanton destruction of the Empire – animosity. Gathered in warbands, orcs were fearsome and tough enemies. Amassed in their tens of thousands, they were nigh on unstoppable.

The end of times, indeed, thought Karlich with a morbid smirk.

As the greenskins came on, surging full pelt at the waiting Empire infantry, riding beasts broke out from the ranks. Wolves and boars scurried and snorted in packs, but Karlich also caught flashes of other things bearing greenskins to battle. Hulking cave spiders carrying tattooed goblins scuttled hideously. Ovoid squigs, all fangs and rough, red hide bounded on two legs, their hooded riders hanging on by their claws. Karlich hadn't realised the monsters grew to be that big.

The roar of the guns intensified, as desperate as their firers. Cannons boomed, loud and dissonant behind the infantry. The sharp cracks of harquebus accompanied them in a ballistic symphony. Though they were far from the front, overlooking the battlefield on the embankment, the artillery batteries and their ranks of gunners could still hear the rage.

'*WAAAAGHHH!*'

It was like a primal invocation, bursting from greenskin mouths in a tumult of sound. Men fell, as if struck by a physical thing. A soldier in a sword regiment from

Streissen dropped dead from fright. Several others soiled themselves, unable to control their bowels. Behind the Grimblades, a militia band broke and fled.

Several others turned, thinking about desertion too. Karlich saw them out the corner of his eye. They held, for now.

'Merciful Sigmar, even the sky is turning...' Masbrecht pointed to the heavens where dark, myrtle-tinged clouds had begun to boil. Fell voices wreathed the air, now thick with unnatural heat. The sun was smothered, snuffed out like a candle and a gloom sullied the field of war, tainting everything green.

Shadows lingered in the firmament. Karlich saw the suggestion of a sloped brow, a jutting chin. Eyes like malevolent red stars burned in those clouds. There were two of them, two hulking figures so massive and terrible that he knew if he looked upon them any longer his mind would shatter.

Suddenly, Karlich felt a tremendous weight upon him. His arms and armour seemed heavier than before. He realised it was despair, sapping at his strength and resolve. The others felt it too. Volker had shut his eyes. Masbrecht was praying under his breath. Rechts licked his lips, in need of a drink. He'd never felt so dry. Even Brand twitched as he experienced the oppressive presence of the entities in the storm above.

'Faith in Sigmar...'

Karlich heard it distantly.

'Faith in Sigmar...'

Louder now, he recognised the voice of Father Untervash.

'Faith in Sigmar!' On the third time, Karlich shouted too. 'Give me your courage, men of the Reik!'

The shadows above chuckled at his defiance. It sounded like malicious thunder. A spit of green lightning threaded the clouds. Karlich bit his lip, drawing blood, and used the pain to shut it out.

'Grimblades!' He roared it like a call to arms.

Across the line, other regiments were refinding their purpose too. Empire men gripped their hafts a little tighter, brought their shoulders closer to one another. Together they were strong. Sigmar had taught them that. Banners that had dipped rose again. Drums and pipes struck up against the orcish din crashing into them like a disharmonious wave.

Above, the clouds began to recede. The shadows there grew fainter.

'*He* is with us...' Masbrecht was weeping. He clutched a talisman of a hammer in his left fist.

Even Rechts was moved.

A clarion sounded from somewhere near the army's centre. Other horns took up the call that spread slowly down the line. More than two dozen banners thrust into the darkling sky. Wilhelm's banner was proudest. It rose like a rallying cry. Eldritch wind buffeted it but it snapped and thrashed defiantly.

We shall not be bowed. We are Empire. Sigmar is with us.

Though the prince himself was not riding alongside the army banner, all who saw it recognised its authority and the order to march.

'We are to meet them then,' Volker hardly sounded pleased.

'You hoped to cower behind pikes and spears?' said Karlich.

'Stay together, brothers,' said Greiss. 'They can't break us if we keep to our bonds of soldiery.'

Nodding, Volker looked girded by the newcomer's words.

Karlich peered over his shoulder at Greiss, who was part of the second rank next to Volker. 'Well spoken,' he said. 'You sure you're not a Reiklander?'

They all laughed, even some of the rear rankers who were in earshot.

Levity was good before battle.

Captain Stahler bellowed above the throng. The din of over two thousand tassets and breastplates rattled into movement. The Empire began to march.

CHAPTER EIGHTEEN

BATTLE IS JOINED

Outside Averheim, capital city of Averland, 483 miles from Altdorf

WILHELM'S WARHORSE HAD caught the scent of battle and strained at the bit before the prince reined it in.

'Easy now…' he soothed, patting the beast's armoured flank.

They were all eager, not just the steeds, but the men too. The orcs had been goaded by Meinstadt's cannon and though mauled by guns and bows, they had engaged the infantry. The skirmishers were either fled or consumed. Only the plucky halflings and a few isolated groups of huntsmen remained. Even now, they were being harried by goblin scouts. Sensibly, the Mootlanders had found a rocky outcrop on which to stage a desperate defence. The huntsmen were in the open though. A large band of wolfriders swept over them. When they'd passed, the Empire men were dead.

At the battle line, the bloodshed was even worse.

Within seconds, ranks of spear and pike just disappeared, swallowed by the green tide. So furious was the melee between the Empire's front and the greenskin rear mobs, it was tough to discern anything of meaning. Already, the corpses had begun to pile up. Those orcs and goblins slain by the artillery barrage were lost from view, crushed underfoot by their own kin. The bodies of men, butchered and bloodied, joined them on the killing field. Heaps of them rose up like fleshy bulwarks on the churned earth.

Though at first Grom's green horde had appeared endless, gaps were emerging between the warbands. Prince Wilhelm had been cunning in his deployment of the army. They occupied an area of the battlefield at an oblique angle to the orcs. It meant when the beasts engaged them they would have to charge *away* from Averheim and the gathered knights. As the seconds passed and the greenskins pressed more and more tribes into the fray, the aspect facing the Empire cavalry thinned and presented its flank.

'We should ride now,' advised Kogswald, impatient to bloody his lance.

Wilhelm lowered his spyglass for the second time.

'Hold,' he warned. 'We wait until the way is almost open.'

'It may shut again if we don't act,' Kogswald replied.

'Just wait,' said the prince, about to look through the spyglass again but stopping himself.

He'd hoped to see some sign of Grom, but had failed to find the goblin king in the masses. Likely, the beast was closer to the gate. It would show itself soon enough.

'I've heard talk that the greenskin warlord cannot be killed,' uttered Ledner, as if reading his liege's thoughts.

'That it ate the flesh of a troll and has a girth to match. No less than three lords, a knight templar amongst them,' he added with a wry smile at Kogswald, 'have alleged inflicting a mortal blow and yet here we are before Averheim's ragged gates.'

'What do we do with trolls, preceptor?' Wilhelm asked.

Kogswald's indignation turned to spite. His moustache curled up in a feral grin. 'Burn them, my liege.'

'Just so...' He tapped the pommel of his runefang. *Dragon Tooth* it was called. Its inner fire raged with all the fury of its namesake. He slammed down the visor on his helmet. The green waves had parted. Wilhelm drew his sword and raised it high.

'We ride!'

THE SKY WAS boiling. Clouds tinged green billowed and twisted, occluding the sun. The presence of the orcish deities in the gloom had lessened but not abated. Like a looming threat they feasted on the greenskin rage swamping Averheim and the land around it. Their chanting voices bubbled on the air like a feverish sweat.

They were not alone.

Another accompanied them. Not a deity but a totem of its fell gods' power. Its shadow soared through the clouds on leathery wings, a dreaded silhouette once witnessed on a desolate plain at night.

'Wyvern!' yelled Rechts, gesturing to the sky as the Grimblades were driving forward. 'The greenskin shaman is abroad.'

'Eyes ahead,' said Karlich. The pikes in front were barely holding. Just a few feet separated the two regimental lines. The Grimblades and the second front could enter the fray at any moment. Their booted feet marched in unison, matching the pace of the halberdiers from Auerswald to their right and the Middenland swordsmen to their left. Mercifully, there'd been little time to mingle with the belligerent northerners, though they'd scowled and muttered amongst themselves upon seeing their neighbours in the line of deployment.

Nearby, Karlich heard Von Rauken urging on the Imperial soldiers nearby. He sounded impatient for blood. The warrior priest in his ranks was adding fervour to his steel.

'Sigmar is my shield, the hammer in my hand. I shall not fear darkness,' cried Father Untervash, hurling dogma as if it were a spear.

Beyond a mass of cluttered pikes, Karlich made out the greenskins. Shouts of men merged with the brays of orcs into a cacophony. Though only glimpsed through a press of bodies, he could tell the fighting was fierce.

It was but a piece of a much larger struggle.

From his vantage point mounted on a warhorse, Stahler watched the pikemen crumple and give. They'd held off the orcs as long as they could. Their defensive formations had done a lot to staunch the initial rush, but now they were shedding men like autumn leaves. Tattooed orcs, their shoulders like fat slabs of meat, hacked into them as they fled. Their snarling white faces were painted to resemble skulls and they wore no armour, save their beast-hide jerkins. The Imperial spear regiments were losing a similar war of attrition. In the end, they had to break and fall back or risk being annihilated beneath the greenskin tide.

Stahler held his sword aloft. Its single rune glowed defiantly, throwing light across the blade. He winced but tried not to let it show. His wound still ached like hot pins in his gut. It was why he rode a horse rather than went on foot. Stahler had always warred on foot. He preferred to be near his men, in the dirt and the mire. Soldiers respected a captain who was willing to bleed and stand with them. But he feared if he did, he might not stand at all. Perception was everything. He had to inspire and embolden. Stahler couldn't do that doubled up in pain or flagging in a fighting rank.

The left flank was buckling. Spears from Kemperbad and Bögenhafen, and four blocks of Averland pike, were in danger of being overrun. Three regiments of halberdiers including Karlich's Grimblades, of whom Stahler was fond but would never show it, and a pair of sword regiments out of Streissen and Middenland was ready to fill the gap soon to be created by the fleeing polearms. Thankfully, the infantry centre and its front line right flank were holding. Despite his loathing of the fanatics, Stahler had to admit that Vanhans's soldiers of faith were proving resilient. They'd moved to the centre and girded it with their reckless passion. It struck him as ironic that the witch hunter fought like a man possessed. To the right of the Grimblades Von Rauken's greatsworders moved up, eager for carnage.

'Second line...' Stahler roared, '...forward, in the name of Prince Wilhelm!'

Most of the pikes and spears retreated in good order, though they were still bloodied before the halberdiers and swordsmen could relieve them. There was the swift beat of drums to signal the charge then came the clash of steel and the grunting of men.

On the left flank, battle was joined with the second line.

Stahler rode up just behind them. His face was an ugly grimace. He prayed he could stay the course.

SCREAMING PIKE AND spearmen barrelled through the Grimblades and the halberdiers from Auerswald.

Karlich ordered his men to let them through and come together again once they'd passed. Panic must not spread. The broken could be allowed to flee but must not get swept up in their fear.

'Hold true,' he cried. 'Maintain rank and file!'

It was hard to think, let alone speak. The clatter of arms and armour was everywhere, growing louder by the second. Blood scent reeked on the air. Steel and leather, too.

They were beyond the fleeing spearmen, a frantic blur of yellow and black disappearing in the Grimblades' peripheral vision. A slab of orcs with bloody cleavers and studded-leather hauberks confronted them, eager for more.

Karlich roared without words. His heart pounded like a blacksmith's hammer. Then there was the rush and the carnage that followed. He took a blow on his shield, hard enough to jar his shoulder. Karlich ignored the pain and stabbed the snorting greenskin in the face. Dark blood gushed from the wound, threading from his withdrawn blade in an arc. A line of halberds slammed down in unison, splitting two orcs apart. Someone screamed. Karlich didn't recognise who. A rear ranker moved up to fill the gap.

Stabbing and thrusting now, the halberdiers fought hard to keep the greenskins at bay where their strength and brutality would count for less.

Karlich cut again, slashing an orc's thigh. He barely saw the beast. His enemies were a haze of snarling slab-browed faces and jutting jaws. Taking a punch to the side of the face, Karlich nearly fell. He almost lost his shield. Strong hands behind him held him up, while a halberd blade thrust overhead into the orc's neck. It died choking blood.

'As one we stand,' he heard the voice of Greiss saying. No one other than Brand could have applied the death-blow.

Back on his feet and fighting, Karlich felt the weight of his warrior brothers at his back and knew that Greiss was right.

The Grimblades held. The Auerswalders and the Steel Swords held. With Father Untervash, Von Rauken's greatsworders were reaping a heavy toll of greenskins. But the orcs refused to yield. Even the goblins were undaunted.

The bloody day was far from over.

KICKING ITS FLANKS, Stahler rode his warhorse in a loop around the back of his command. The second line was holding. In the gap between it and the third, a decent amount of pike and spear had rallied and were already reforming. Their drums and horns carried orders on the air, though some had lost their banners in the panicked rush to flee.

Captain Hornschaft was supposed to be leading the front line. Stahler had lost sight of him ever since the greenskins' initial charge. He hoped, a little forlornly, that he was still alive.

A cry echoed loudly from the far right, accompanied by the shrilling of silver trumpets. Stahler's pride soared when he saw Prince Wilhelm and his knights ride onto the field of war. Over a hundred templars and half as many pistoliers again charged with glorious voices. Break through the greenskin horde, reach the gate and free the army of Averheim. Stahler willed them on, his voice escaping as a breath.

'For Sigmar, noble prince...'

He averted his gaze when another, much less inspiring, sight seized his attention.

Trolls were lumbering through the greenskin rear ranks, swinging tree trunks and the bodies of dead Averheimers like clubs. Orcs and goblins were left bludgeoned in their wake. Others, battered aside in the beasts' eagerness to feed, flew like broken dolls over the heads of rival mobs much to their cackled amusement. Plucked from amongst its kin, a goblin squealed before being devoured, a quick morsel before the feast to come. An orc flayed by acidic bile collapsed into a pile of sticky bone. The troll responsible wiped its drooling maw with a meaty hand. Vomit hissed and burned against its craggy skin before evaporating. The beasts lived only to eat and to kill. Food was neither friend nor foe. Goaded by orc slavemasters, the trolls would reach the second line soon.

Stahler was about to spur his horse – he'd need to reach his men before the trolls – when he hesitated.

A black shadow drew over him and the Grimblades, eclipsing what little light shone on the battlefield. Evil lurked within that shadow.

Blacktooth...

The name was uttered like a curse into his mind, and the minds of those who saw it, in a guttural cadence. The breath snagged in Stahler's throat, as if too afraid to escape. Whinnying in terror, his steed caught the scent of the monster before seeing it.

A wyvern, an old beast from deep within the mountains, loomed over them. Mounted on its back in a crude saddle was the orc shaman. Blacktooth wanted a fight.

HUGE, BEATING WINGS funnelled the scent of the wyvern's rage and hate towards the puny men who could only cower. Akin to a giant winged lizard, the monster's hide was thickly scaled and shone with a gelid lustre. It put Karlich in mind of dank places, of ancient slime-skinned caves where men should never venture. A ribbed belly, thicker than a cannon's barrel, heaved and sucked with the effort of keeping it aloft and steady. Its barbed tail quivered, seeping poison. Fangs as long as swords, and broad as axe heads, were stained crimson. Trying to muster his courage, Karlich imagined the wyvern's appetite for flesh was not yet sated.

Men howled before the beast wrenched straight from the depths of their darkest nightmares. Scenting fear, the wyvern roared. An ululating, unnatural din resounded over the battlefield. Those who heard it felt their blood freeze and their bodies stiffen in fear.

A band of militia, a detachment of a much larger regiment of halberdiers from Streissen, panicked and fled. Blacktooth snarled his displeasure. As the shaman sat up in rusted-iron stirrups, Karlich got a better look at him.

Blacktooth was festooned with skull charms and totems. He clutched a strange wand in his right fist, some bizarre daemon-head charm hammered onto a stave of dark iron. A dirty, furred jerkin of many colours swathed his body. Blacktooth was barefoot. A horned hat, crested with a halfling's skull, covered his head. He held a notched cleaver in his other hand. One of the large fangs protruding over his upper lip was blighted with decay.

The fleeing men didn't get far. Blacktooth unleashed a blast of green lightning from his eyes. The militia never even had time to scream before they blackened and died.

'Sigmar preserve us!' someone shouted from down the line.

'Morr's shadow is upon us!' said another.

Masbrecht was praying in the front rank. His eyes were closed and he clasped the hammer icon around his neck as if it could make him invisible.

Karlich wanted to speak, to galvanise his men, but found his mouth was dry and his tongue leaden. The urge to run, to save himself, was strong. Burning meat was redolent on the breeze. He did not want that fate.

Blacktooth and his beast aimed their malign gaze at the Grimblades. There was a form of low intelligence there, capable of much cruelty.

'T-tur…' Karlich could barely speak.

Run, run! his mind pleaded.

Try as he might, he was fixated on the terrible wyvern and its master. Something else was moving behind the orc hordes too. A caustic stench came with it. Karlich thought he could smell sulphur.

Were all the creatures of the dark beneath the world coming for them?

A bright light surged into being to Karlich's right. He blinked, fighting the after flare. Dimly, he was aware of the greenskins squealing in pain. It took a supreme effort of will to tear his eyes off the wyvern and look past it but, with his vision returning, Karlich saw the greenskins in front of them were blinded. They scratched at their eyes, thumped their kin with clubs or hacked with cleavers. Enraged and afraid, the orcs were cutting themselves to pieces.

The cold dread he had felt was scoured away by a sensation of heat. Suddenly emboldened, Karlich followed the source of the light.

Father Untervash glowed with an inner glory. His every pore exuded stark and blazing fury. It filled his eyes and made them burn. The warrior priest's voice resonated with power as he stepped forward from the front rank of the greatsworders.

'Denizen of the deep, foul spawn, with the wrath of Sigmar I will smite thee!'

Holy fire coursed over the priest's warhammer, flickering along the haft and up Father Untervash's arms. He swung it three times in a wide arc then planted the head into the ground where a pulse of fire erupted. Orcs within its path were seared. Blacktooth and his wyvern were assailed by the backwash but didn't yield to it.

A horrible, bestial grunting came from the orc shaman when it was over. The sound was deep and abyssal, drunk with unfettered power. Blacktooth shucked up and down. It took Karlich a moment to realise the orc was laughing.

'In Sigmar's name, I denounce thee wret–'

With a serpent's reflexes, the wyvern snapped at Father Untervash and seized him in its jaws. Blood spewed from the warrior priest's lips, preventing him from finishing the holy diatribe. Gasps of shock echoed through the Imperial soldiery as their keeper of the faith slowly drowned in his own blood when his chest was crushed.

Defiant to the end, Father Untervash spat through red-rimed teeth and tried to lift his hammer. His pain and anger ended when the beast snapped its jaws and him in two.

'Morr protect my soul!' One soldier from Auerswald fell to his knees, awaiting the end. Several more from the same regiment ran, discarding their banner as all hope faded.

The light, in many ways, died with Untervash.

Ragged halves of his torso fell out either side of the wyvern's mouth, trailing ribbons of red meat and crumpling to the ground like scraps. Somewhere farther down the line another regiment fled. The gruesome display and the presence of the monster had unmanned them. Karlich felt the shift all the way to the front rank. Part of the second front was overrun, the pressure telling at their flank. They at least had to hold.

Without the priest to repel them, the orcs returned. Mercifully, Blacktooth took to the sky but Karlich sensed he was far from done with them. Guttural chanting infested the breeze as the shaman channelled a more powerful spell.

Remembered terror still numbing his bones, despite Untervash's holy aura, Karlich was fighting for his life again. The orcs were badly burned by the priest's holy fire, and they were angry. In the madness, it felt as if there was no end to them.

They'd barely begun to swing their halberds again when darkness loomed above the Grimblades. At first Karlich thought it was the wyvern returned to devour them but then he saw the giant orc foot manifesting in the clouds. One of the hulking orc deities laughed and snorted as it prepared to flatten them.

Even as he cut and hewed at the enemy to his front, wary of the devilry above, a feverish sweat overcame him. Karlich's hackles rose. His armour became hot to the touch. Glancing skyward between thrusts, he saw tendrils of green cloud spool off the giant foot as it plummeted with inexorable finality.

Ahead, the stench of sulphur got stronger as the trolls reached them.

'Helena, forgive me...' He used his dead wife's name like a blessing.

But the orcish foot did not fall. Winds billowed from the west, carrying a figure of silver and azure. Borne aloft on a wisp of cumulonimbus, Sirrius Cloudcaller stalled the wrath of gods with sorcerous will.

One hand halted the foot's descent, a gulf of turbulent air between them. The other hand spilled lightning from its fingertips. Forks of it lanced down and burned the trolls to charred meat. Even their incredible regenerative powers were unable to mend them.

Blacktooth bared his fangs, sweeping down to confront the Celestial wizard up close. The shaman growled and clenched his fist. The orcish foot descended again but crashed against a shimmering, azure shield. Sparks cascaded like dying comets as Sirrius Cloudcaller put all of his effort into resisting Blacktooth.

The magical shield glittered like a false firmament of stars. It cracked with the immense pressure, but held. Taking a deep breath, the Celestial wizard exhaled a blast of wind that forced the shaman back. Even his wyvern could not keep them from spiralling.

Sirrius soared into the storm-wracked heavens after him. Soon he was nothing more than a shadow chasing another, climbing, ever climbing into the sky above.

A patch of fiery amber began to glow in his wake. It tinted the clouds where the Celestial wizard had pierced it to pursue Blacktooth. The edges of the ragged hole slowly blackened and there rose a sound like the world cracking along its seams. Incredible, intense heat turned the clouds to steam as a flaming meteorite tore through the gloom with a blazing tail.

The fire-wreathed rock struck somewhere far behind the orcs. Hundreds died in the crater, their bodies reduced to cinder. A wave of fiery debris claimed hundreds more. The din of its impact was felt all the way to the Imperial line and brought the Grimblades and the rest of the soldiery to their knees. Mobs of orcs and goblins were destroyed utterly. Others were left decimated.

The tribe fighting Karlich's men lost three rear ranks in a single blow. The rest were seared by heat and left dazed and dying when the Grimblades charged. Karlich hadn't wanted to grant them mercy, but their deaths were swift.

A few hundred greenskin dead counted for little in the overall scheme of the battle, but it meant the way lay open for the infantry to advance.

The entire left flank butchered their way through the orc and goblin remnants at the edge of the meteor blast and marched onto the still smoking ground, slightly awestruck by what they'd just witnessed. Already, though, orcs and goblins were moving through the heat haze. Earth turned to glass crunched beneath their feet.

Wiping off his blade, Karlich cursed when he saw the Steel Swords advancing. Eager to chase down and slay a mob of shattered goblins, they had gone too far and left the Grimblades' flank exposed. The Middenlanders were heedless to the risk, ploughing on. A disingenuous part of Karlich believed the other regiment had endangered them deliberately.

'Sturnbled and that rabid dog Torveld would see us dead,' griped Rechts, beating the order to march on his drum.

'They may not have long to wait,' said Greiss, pointing from the second rank. A band of wolfriders was loping through the carnage. A manic goblin in the lead was cackling and pointing back. Its warriors did so too, sharing some unheard joke.

Karlich knew what it was. In moments they would be engaged by the vast goblin mob to their front, only to be charged a second later by the wolfriders. They'd be fighting towards two aspects at once.

'Wheel formation!' he shouted, causing Lenkmann to signal with the banner and Rechts to alter the tune of his drum. They'd try to face both enemies to the front. The Grimblades slowly pivoted on their right flank, the left shuffling forward using it like a fulcrum and angling their frontage.

A low explosion suddenly erupted behind them. It sounded distant, as if it came from the embankment. Leiter, who'd replaced Keller in the front rank, turned to look but a goblin arrow from the wolfriders pierced his neck. Gushing blood, he fell and Ensk took his place.

They braced halberds when the goblin mob struck but, to Karlich's dismay, the wolfriders arrested their charge at the last moment and skittered around them. The slight delay was hardly costly. They engaged the Grimblades' flank.

Pressured from two sides, the rear rankers found it hard to lend their support. Karlich felt the goblins pushing incessantly, even as he cut at them with his sword. It only got worse when the sergeant glanced to his left and saw Vanhans and his soldiers of faith. The witch hunter met his gaze and glared briefly before Karlich lost him in the ebb and flow of the melee.

Fatigue gnawed at him now, like an unwelcome guest who wouldn't leave. Karlich felt like giving in. They'd endured almost a half hour of unbroken fighting. Across the line, it was beginning to hurt. Troops that had regrouped from the original front were moving in support, plugging inevitable gaps, but they could only do so much. Every man was tiring. Karlich had hoped the enemy would be too. But they showed no sign of doing so; the greenskins' stamina seemed limitless.

CHAPTER NINETEEN
THE DEATH OF HONOUR

Outside Averheim, capital city of Averland,
483 miles from Altdorf

STAHLER KNEW WIZARDS had power, but until he'd seen Sirrius Cloudcaller summon the chunk of flaming rock, he'd not realised just how much. Deep down, it frightened him that some men could wield such a thing like he would wield a sword. He wondered at the price of it, at the sacrifice it must require.

His awe had banished his fear at least, and with the wyvern gone he could concentrate on the battle. It stuck in his craw that he couldn't commit to the fight. He had to lead, to guide tactically, so as many men as possible survived the next dawn, if there was one.

The left flank was beginning to push the orcs and goblins back. Though, to Stahler's chagrin, both the centre and right flank were making better progress. Buoyed by victory, the regiments commanded by Vogen were forging ahead. It meant the line angled awkwardly and Stahler wished he could haul them back, but he was too far away.

Behind him, smoke and fire billowed across the embankment. It was hard to make out but it looked like one of the great cannons had misfired and exploded, killing its crew. Meinstadt was still alive, labouring to free an iron ball stuck in the mouth of one of the mortars. Through the fog, Stahler discerned another of the cannons had slipped down the hill, part of the makeshift embankment crumbling beneath it. Gunnery crews pushed and heaved on ropes to bring it level again but were making little inroads.

The war machines had done their part. Meinstadt's reserves remained, but only in extremis. That left one cannon. It was up to the infantry now. They were fighting hard, gaining ground, but it was a ripple against an ocean.

Stahler had no illusions. Prince Wilhelm needed to break through and release the army inside Averheim very soon.

WILHELM AND HIS knights punched through a trailing warband of orcs, burst right through their flank and scattered them. Kogswald sang ancient war ballads as he slew, whereas Ledner was deathly silent and killed with brutal efficiency. Both such fine warriors, such contrasts in light and shade.

Dragontooth was well bloodied by now. The orc filth slipped off its blade like water, leaving it bright and unsullied as if newly forged. The Griffonkorps and the Order of the Fiery Comet hadn't lost a single rider. There was still some way to go, a field of orcs and goblins stretched ahead of them, but the Averheim gates were in sight.

Wilhelm's eyes narrowed, akin to when a hunter in the Reikwald spots prey. Free of the orcs, now either dead or fleeing, he was able to focus his attention on a figure standing out amidst the thronging battle for Averheim ahead.

It was distant, glimpsed through a clutch of swaying beasts and banners, horns and totems. Wilhelm could not believe the creature's size. The rumours, all he had heard and largely discounted, did not prepare him.

Grom the Goblin King was immense.

At first, the Prince of Reikland mistook him for an orc. No goblin had any right to be that big. Grom's girth was incredible, the paunch for which he was so famed. It spilled out from under dirty chainmail in a solid mass of flesh and muscle, pockmarked with warts. A helmet fashioned from a horned skull sat on his ugly, leering head. A necklace of claws and finger bones looped around his neck. The furry hide that served as a cloak was spattered with dried blood. Grom was in the killing mood, and Wilhelm need rely on rumour no more as he could now see the goblin's strength and prowess for himself.

A sortie of templar knights who'd possibly seen Wilhelm's gambit was trying to fight a route through to him and open up the way to Averheim. They had stalled upon hitting a vast swathe of miniscule greenskins. Though weak and diminutive, the creatures known in the Empire as snotlings were in such numbers that the brave knights were dragged down and engulfed. Vaguely, Wilhelm made out a mass of tiny jaws with teeth like pins gnawing at the stricken templars. The snotlings inveigled their way into armour plate, under chainmail, hungering for soft, yielding flesh they could feast upon.

Though they struggled, once off their horses the knights were as good as dead. Other, larger goblins armed with nets and barbed tridents hurried in stabbing and prodding at gaps in their armour.

Bravely, some had broken through and Grom was cutting them down. They barely made it twenty feet from the gate when the goblin king was amongst them, his double-headed axe cleaving limbs and reaping a bloody toll.

The knights didn't last long. None returned to Averheim.

Wilhelm was horrified. This menace had to be stopped. His determination to meet Grom in single combat and end the war grew.

The small tract of open ground they'd found upon smashing through the orc mob was coming to an end. A band of night goblins – hooded creatures that usually dwelt in caves and seldom fought in the day – scurried into the path of Wilhelm's knights. Ranting on behind the Paunch was his standard bearer. The nasty little creature spat and stuck his tongue out as he raved at the other goblins, urging them to charge.

Several mobs had allied together under a single banner, a jagged, bleeding eye. There were maybe eighty to a hundred of them. Wilhelm gauged they'd last less than half that number in seconds against his knights.

Just as he leaned in, lowering his body closer to his steed for the initial impact, he caught a final glimpse of Grom, looking at him over his shoulder, before he sidled away.

Was the goblin warlord grinning?

Seeing another opportunity to bloody his lance, easy pickings at that, Kogswald spurred his knights.

'Allow me, my lord,' he said, slamming down his visor and kicking his steed. *'H'yar!'*

He'd scythe the goblins down like chaff.

Moments from impact, the other lanceheads just a few seconds behind him, Kogswald's eyes widened and he tried to rein in his horse. The other knights followed suit but some were too slow and piled up behind those in front. A stray lance raked a horse's flank, tearing into its barding and eliciting a whinny of pain. Others crumpled against the armoured backs of the lead animals. Necks and limbs broke with an audible crack of bone. Men fell from their saddles and were crushed underhoof. But the carnage had only just begun.

Bursting out of the night goblin ranks came six greenskins each wielding a massive ball and chain. They swung the ridiculously huge weapons in an arc, slowly at first and then gradually gaining momentum until the displaced air from them whirling around created a low *whomp* with each successful circle. Frothing at the mouth like rabid dogs, the goblin fanatics were clearly insane. Their maddened voices were oddly distorted as they spun, like a reverberant howl growing and diminishing at rapidly increasing intervals.

One of the horses strayed into the whirlwind of iron and was instantly bludgeoned. Its rider raised his shield ineffectually. The desperate knight was battered into a greasy paste before he had time to scream. Unperturbed, the goblin fanatic carried on trammelling through the warriors behind. The other five inflicted similar devastation, their course unpredictable but deadly. One of the Griffonkorps tried to stab down at a greenskin with his longsword but succeeded in only snapping his blade and then losing his arm as it was dragged in to the goblin's killing arc and crushed.

In just a few seconds, Wilhelm's proud lancehead was in tatters. Almost half of his knights were dead or dying. The attack on the Averheim gate ground to a terrible halt.

Brand stabbed a goblin wolfrider in the neck, releasing a plume of gore just as the rain began to fall. It was light at first, a low *plink, plink* against their armour, but then it grew to a downpour. Tunics and hose were quickly sodden, leather stained dark like blood. It was so heavy it became hard to see much farther than a foot or so in front of their faces. Brand didn't mind. He only needed to see what he had to kill and that usually fell into those parameters. Disembowelling a giant wolf, he decided the rain had done nothing to cool the battlefield. In fact, the heat was more oppressive than ever. If anything, it made it more clammy and humid. As it died, the wolf upended the goblin on its back into a worsening swamp. Brand put his boot on the creature's head, holding it down while he fought another. A line of sweat was rekindled down his back and made him itch. He would have scratched were it not for all the greenskins on the flank trying to gut him.

Brand was at the 'hinge', where the front and rear ranks met. He protected Masbrecht's back, who was in the front rank fighting the horde of goblins on foot. Alongside him was Greiss, the recruit from Averland. The man was skilled and held his own. He had an aptitude for killing. His tally rivalled Brand's own.

At the front, Brand was dimly aware of Karlich shouting curses at the greenskins and encouragement to the men. Brand generally hated officers, but he respected Karlich. Not as much as Varveiter, but he held the sergeant in high regard. It was the only reason he hadn't killed him after he'd seen him break down in the watch-tower at the roadwarden's rest. That was a distant memory now, only Keller's face remained and the sense of his retribution being denied that Brand felt at the other soldier taking the coward's way out.

It was hard fighting, some of the toughest Brand had faced. The noise was intense and blended together into a hellish sort of din. Some men, if they survived, would not get over it. It would likely drive them mad. Brand had known soldiers, harder men than those around him, who had taken their own lives because of it.

Pressure could be felt on both sides, ever pressing. It was a task just to keep the goblins back, let alone defeat them. As he killed another wolfrider, Brand heard a man farther down the flank gurgle a death cry as one of the mounts ripped his throat out. Greiss still refused to yield. For Brand, it was like looking into a mirror, a cracked and slightly dirty mirror.

KARLICH DISLIKED THE Middenlanders almost as much as he hated the goblin hordes trying to kill them. After hacking apart a goblin's skull with his sword, he spared a glance at Vanhans's men. They were true butchers. The ruthless mercenaries and insane flagellants laid into a band of orcs with bloody abandon. Like madmen, they died in droves but fought without fear. The paid mercenaries were more careful but equally brutal. A promise of further coin was all that kept them in the fight, though. Karlich only glimpsed the witch hunter, a sliver of black, a flash of silver, but his voice was wholly apparent. Every cut came with a curse, a hateful catechism spat with phlegmy vitriol. If animus was a weapon then Vanhans's blade was sharper than the keenest diamond.

Ahead was no better. After plunging forward heedlessly, the Steel Swords had now stalled, forming a shieldwall against a mob of heavily-armoured orcs. Trying to stay alive and kill his enemies at the same time, meant Karlich couldn't see how they were faring. He cursed the Middenlanders all the same for having left his own regiment vulnerable, goaded by the promise of glory denied them at the Brigund Bridge. He only regretted he wouldn't get to pay them back for their dissension.

Just as Karlich was preparing to make a last stand, to be reunited with his wife and daughter in Morr's afterlife, the pressure on the flank lifted. Looking out the corner of his eye for as long as he dared, he saw the telltale black and red of Carroburg.

Sigmar bless his blade, Von Rauken had come to their aid.

With greatsworders cleaving into them mercilessly from behind and the halberdiers giving them hell from the front, the goblin wolfriders scattered and fled. The few that weren't slain in the retreat barrelled southward for the Black Mountains. Karlich fancied even Grom could not get them to turn, so badly had the Carroburg Few mauled them.

The goblin horde fighting to the Grimblades' front capitulated soon after. Worn down by Vanhans on one side, and the greatsworders on the other, Karlich and his men were at last able to overwhelm them and put the creatures to flight.

Several still lived, eighty or more goblins from the same tribe, but their will was broken. Their retreat left a short spurt of open ground before them. Karlich used the time marching into it to catch a breath and share a word with Von Rauken.

'A good time to repay a debt of honour,' he said.

The greatsworder champion merely grinned, showing a lost tooth.

'There's more blood to be shed still. Don't thank us yet,' growled the Carroburger.

Karlich's reply was arrested by the storm cracking above. He looked up and saw the Celestial wizard and the shaman duelling inside a massive thunderhead. Lit from behind by lightning, they appeared as frozen silhouettes. Every flash revealed a new vista, as if held in transparent amber, only for it to fade and reappear a moment later in a different duelling pose. Wizard and shaman were just ephemeral shadows painted on the underside of clouds, so high, so far away. It was impossible to tell who was winning.

Respite was brief. More orcs and goblins were coming.

Karlich cast a glance over his shoulder. Smoke was wreathing the embankment, spilling down onto the battlefield in a creeping, grey veil. Something was happening up there but he couldn't tell what. From the sound of the explosion he heard earlier, it couldn't be good. Peering through the smog he noticed that the back line had moved up and a good hundred feet or so now separated them. In the tight confines of the battlefield ahead, it felt like a gulf.

* * *

Gaps were forming in the battle. Whereas before it was clogged without room to manoeuvre, fleeing regiments and mobs had pulled at both armies. Formations and battle lines were breaking down. Together with the natural ebb and flow of combat, discrete masses were slowly emerging. A regiment from Grünburg and another from Streissen fought a savage orc mob and a horde of forest goblins. A stolid wedge of halberdiers struggled against a smaller band of trolls, their numbers dwindling. A force of pike and swordsmen clashed with a grunting tribe of orc boar riders, keeping the beasts at bay with a wall of shields and polearms. Each fought their own personal battle. Suddenly the wider war had become less important and immediate than merely living out the next minute.

Stahler knew how to read an engagement as easily as he discerned the palm of his own hand. The struggle for Averheim was reaching a crucial stage.

Between the fighting, patches of open ground strangled with the dead and dying were revealed. Like pulling back a dirty curtain, broken blades and shields, bloodied leather and mail was found cluttering the earth like scrap. From every struggle, fresh horrors emerged from underfoot as man and orc jostled for superiority.

The Imperial infantry was pressing ahead. Stahler knew it was important to maintain momentum, especially with such a large army arrayed against them, but he was weary about leaving the rear line and their support so far behind. Soon the men would tire too. Nothing could be worse than being stranded beyond help, surrounded by foes and with a heavy sword arm. They had to press on, though. If they could hold, even break through to Averheim, then the two armies would surely crush the greenskins. Perhaps the war could be won here after all.

Don't get ahead of yourself, old man. Damn fine way to get killed.

A wry smile turned to a grimace on Stahler's face when a jab of pain shot up his arm and side. Clutching his chest, he gasped. It was like breathing piping hot cinders. A clatter of metal announced he'd dropped his sword. Stahler watched it hit the ground. Sagging in the saddle, he almost followed it. Seizing the reins with his other hand, he tried to hold on.

Can't... see me... like this; even the voice in his head sounded agonised. He needed to get up. He thought about reaching for his blade.

Forget it, there's no way.

Stahler realised if he dismounted or leaned down to retrieve it, he might never get back up again.

'Merciful Shallya,' he rasped. The sound was wet and ragged. Stahler tasted copper in his mouth.

Darkness blinded him for a split second before he blinked it away. Tremors of mild panic went with it. The soldiers' backs were still hazy. It might have been because of the smoke. He wasn't sure.

Blackpowder smoke was creeping down the embankment. It swept the field in a dark grey fog from the constant discharge of harquebus, mortar and cannon. The rear echelons of the army were smothered and it was slowly layering the entire plain. Still groggy but mastering the pain, Stahler saw a scattered band of goblins approaching him through the murk. Some of the greenskin mobs had overshot or been left behind in the massive push by the Imperial infantry. Crossbowmen and handgunners were picking them off with isolated *clacks* of their weapons, but some were still getting through. Most of the greenskin remnants fled but some were prowling the dead and dying, stealing and murdering as they went. They wouldn't tackle a regiment, but a lone rider would be fair game.

Stahler realised abruptly that he was separated from the line, in a sort of grey no-man's land. Mist and gunsmoke coalesced into a dark fug that made it hard to see. The goblins were coming for him. He sneered, annoyed with himself.

Easy meat.

Stahler drew a pistol from his belt. He had already dropped his shield when he went for the reins. With both hands free, he wrenched a short sword from its scabbard on his steed's barded flank.

Something told him he was dying, that the wound he'd received at Blösstadt was mortal, only he hadn't known it. Until now.

By the gods, he'd take some more of the bastards with him before he fell.

Six against one.

The first of the goblins emerged from the smoke and mist, its pointy nose cutting through it like a knife.

Stahler levelled his pistol and fired.

Make that five.

KOGSWALD WAS DEAD. Bludgeoned by a huge iron ball, the spikes upon it had ripped his armour apart. The preceptor was lying on his slain horse with a chain wrapped around his crushed neck and torso. He hadn't even lifted his sword. It was an ignoble end for a noble warrior.

Several other knights, both Griffonkorps and Order of the Fiery Comet, joined him in grim repose. Their limbs were twisted, tangled together with one another and their horses, mashed beyond recognition by the deadly goblin weapons.

Cavalry killers. Wilhelm had heard of goblin fanatics before. Intoxicated on cave fungus, they were insane and utterly immune to fear and doubt. He had never fought against them, though.

'Ride through!' urged the prince. What was left of the knights charged on. Babbled hooting from the whirling goblins assailed them through their battle-helms as they thundered past.

In the frantic dash to escape, Wilhelm noticed one of the demented greenskins spin off wildly and into a patch of rock. It left a messy stain against the grey stone as it died. Another collided with one of its comrades and the two wrapped around each other in a fatal embrace. A fourth ran out of fervour and collapsed, its overworked heart giving out convulsively.

That left only two. The gauntlet was at least now runnable. Hot air whipped past the prince's face, displaced by a heavy ball and chain. Shards of debris carried along in its wake stung at his skin. He resisted the temptation to lash out. If he did, he'd lose his arm to one swing of the deadly weapon.

Despite the damage inflicted by the fanatics, Wilhelm and his charges cut through the night goblins that had harboured the fanatics with relative ease. Ploughing through the greenskin ranks was akin to butchery, not battle. By the time they'd reached the other side, the knights were less than half their original strength. Around fifty remained and even they were bruised and battered. Cracking flintlocks erupted from the few surviving pistoliers. Tiny plumes of blackpowder smoke erupted from their firearms before the last of the fanatics were shot and killed.

Relieved, Wilhelm turned to look at Kogswald. Lifting his visor, he gasped for breath. He'd known the man all of his life. He'd been his retainer and protector for almost thirty years. The sight of him so cruelly slain, bereft of glory, was almost too much.

'He's gone,' Ledner's snake-rasp banished the prince's nostalgia. Nothing could be done for the preceptor. Ledner's pragmatism outweighed sentiment every time. There was no love lost between the two men. Neither, to their credit, had pretended otherwise. But Ledner recognised the great shame in what had happened to his sparring partner.

Ledner was wounded too. He held his reins gingerly with one hand, the other clutching his sword. His arm was either twisted or broken, possibly at the shoulder. Ledner didn't let it show, despite his bloodied face. A cut above his right eye drooled gorily, but he was defiant as ever.

When the prince didn't reply, Ledner rode up alongside him and leaned in close so he could whisper. 'Marshal your knights!' he hissed between clenched teeth.

They'd stalled a little, the impetus of their charge faltering once free and clear of the night goblins. 'They need you to lead them. Do it!'

As if waking from a dream, Wilhelm came around. The knights were milling around, lacking in purpose. The prince reined his horse about, facing the enemy ahead. The briefest of nods in Ledner's direction acknowledged the service he'd just performed for his master.

'Onward,' cried Wilhelm, raising his sword. 'The gates of Averheim are close. We're nearly there. For Kogswald and our slain brothers!'

The knights cheered, though it was a dark and vengeful cry. Even in the face of death, their spirit was indomitable. It was what made them better than ordinary men.

Under fifty knights, just two and a half lances, to take the gate and release the Averheim army – Wilhelm had Sigmar's name upon his lips as they charged again.

His steed had saved his life, or at least prolonged it for another, perhaps more peaceful death. Unlike most soldiers, Stahler had no wish to die on the battlefield. It was a lonesome, depressing place. Death and death alone belonged there, not glory. He wanted to meet his end in the arms of a beautiful woman; or in a tavern, surrounded by friends and comrades; or old aged before a slow burning hearth, a smouldering pipe in his hand and a contented smile on his face that said: I'm ready now, I've lived.

Even as his warhorse had staved in the skull of the last goblin, the other four dispatched between them, Stahler knew that was not his fate. He'd die here in the mire, alone yet surrounded by his men. As if to punish him for his killing efforts, the pain in Stahler's arm and side returned. He stifled a cry. The tears in his eyes were from agony, not anguish.

Stay alive, he kept repeating to himself. Stay alive and make it count for something.

The rain brought him around. It *tinkled* against his armour. Rivulets inveigled their way down his back, chilling him. The effect was mildly reviving. It wasn't to last.

Only shortly after it had begun, the rainstorm stopped abruptly. The clouds persisted but they no longer shed their tears. Mist followed in its wake, rising swiftly like an ethereal tide, smothering the battlefield. The smoke from the hillside rolled into it, turning it into dense smog. He'd experienced foggy nights in Altdorf, the mist creeping off the Reik, when you could only just see the hand before your face, where visibility had been better than this. The battle had just become many times more treacherous.

It was as the grey smog clawed its way across the plain that everything began to go wrong.

AN ALMIGHTY FLASH ignited the heavens just as the Grimblades were about to engage yet another greenskin mob. Something plummeted from the sky, blazing like a falling comet.

Whether it was denial or the simple fact of distance, it took Karlich a few seconds to realise it was Sirrius Cloudcaller.

Blacktooth had won. The Celestial wizard was dead.

A bizarre after-flare was frozen against Karlich's eye. As he blinked he again saw Sirrius etched upon the clouds in agonised silhouette.

'Fight on, fight on for the Empire!' Von Rauken had seen it too and was doing his best to rally them.

Without the wizard... Karlich dare not contemplate further. The crash of blades was coming fast, so he bellowed as hard as his lungs would allow and lost himself to the madness.

* * *

WILHELM'S KNIGHTS WERE riding at the orcs' backs now. Charging along the rear of the greenskins engaged with the Empire troops, it was tempting to wheel off and gut a mob from behind. Wilhelm felt sure even the hardest orcs would crumple beneath their lances and their righteous anger. Part of him wanted to, needed to, vent his frustration at the death of noble Kogswald. It would be an outpouring of grief. Averheim demanded his attention, though. He would be its saviour. He would save the Empire and take Dieter to account for his lassitude, feathering his nest as he brokered deals with greedy Marienburgers and the rest of the Empire burned. It made the prince's blood hot that an Emperor could abandon his lands to despoliation. If he survived this, there would a reckoning. All the mercenaries and sell-swords in Tilea couldn't prevent it.

With thoughts of vengeance plaguing his mind, the prince failed to notice the shadow in the clouds growing above them. It wasn't until Ledner cried out, an oddly strangled shriek due to his old neck wound, that Wilhelm knew of the danger in their midst.

'My lord, get down!' Ledner threw himself at the prince, leaping off his own steed to do it. The two men slammed into the earth and rolled as something large and scaly raked overhead, a pair of screaming knights gripped in its clutches. It was a miracle they weren't killed or seriously injured in the fall. Several more knights were scattered across the ground, their bodies and their horses broken. Trying to heave the air back into his chest, the ache of sudden bruises from the fall muddying his senses, Wilhelm looked into the sky and saw the wyvern turn. It tossed a dangling figure from its mouth as it dove for them.

The prince rose unsteadily before Ledner tackled him again, grunting as he jarred his injured arm. Warm air and the foetid stink of the beast washed over them. Ledner yelped in pain as a talon clipped him, tearing a bloody gash in his wounded shoulder.

'It wants you,' he snarled from the agony. 'Get your wits first then face it.'

He rolled off from where he'd pinned the prince. Wilhelm nodded curtly, found his breath at last and got to his feet.

The wyvern was circling around for another pass. The shaman on its back cackled wildly, enjoying the spectacle.

Dragontooth was in the prince's hand as he took up a swordfighting stance. Since he'd been a boy, Kogswald had taught him how to fight. As the wyvern knifed through the clouds at him, Wilhelm recalled a lesson where the preceptor had tutored him in the art of engaging a horseman on foot. It required balance and timing. The prince adopted those sage tactics now.

'See this blade,' he muttered to the beast as it grew in his eye line, 'do you remember it?' They were just moments away from impact. 'It remembers you...'

Dragontooth caught an errant shaft of sunlight and flashed in agreement.

The sunlight died when the wyvern eclipsed it, hurtling at Wilhelm like a thrown spear but with all the force of a battering ram. Its eyes glinted like malevolent rubies, its claws and fangs promised gruesome death. Saliva drizzled from its open mouth as the beast savoured the scent of royal flesh.

Purge your mind of all doubt. You and your blade are as one. Kogswald was with him again, only fifteen years ago.

The rising mist swept up in front of the beast, masking it from sight. Wilhelm closed his eyes until the beat of its wings nearly deafened him, then he pivoted his body aside in a wide arc and lashed out with Dragontooth.

He was buffeted hard by the wyvern's bulk as it arrowed past him. A ribbon of heat opened up in his thigh and he realised it had cut him. Almost simultaneously he felt the enchanted blade dragging through hide and flesh, eliciting a bestial screech of agony.

Dragontooth hissed and spat as the wyvern's blood touched the blade as if whispering a curse. The wound went deep. Wilhelm knew it by instinct. Dizzy, one hand clutching his injured leg, he turned in time to see the wyvern careening off into the distance. The membrane from its right wing hung like a ragged sail. It made the beast flail in the air like a stricken ship on invisible waves. Blood threaded the earth like a red, throbbing vein from where Wilhelm had cut the wyvern to a furrow in the ground where it eventually pitched. It wasn't dead, a terrible mewling sound reverberated from its nose, but it was down and so was the shaman.

'Nicely done, my lord,' said Ledner running up beside him. Even he couldn't hide his awe at what the prince had just done.

Wilhelm was breathless with effort. 'It's a little different with horses.'

Ledner didn't know what he meant, so ignored the comment. 'Can you walk?'

The prince nodded.

'Then you can ride.' Ledner turned and hailed two of the knights.

Wilhelm paled. They numbered less than twenty. Some were injured and would never fight again. Many were dead. The wyvern's monstrous strength was awesome to behold.

Across the plain towards Averheim, whose hopes were fading like a candle at the end of its wick, several bulky shadows were plunging through the mist. The grey veil was thinnest near the city, without the powder smoke to pollute it, and Wilhelm made out a squadron of chariots heading towards them.

When the two knights reached Ledner they dismounted.

'Here, my lord,' Ledner invited.

Wilhelm frowned. 'Where is my steed?'

'Dead. Now take the saddle.'

Ledner helped the prince up and then mounted the other horse.

'Come, my lord,' he said, reining his borrowed horse towards the Imperial line. 'There's little time.'

'What are you doing?' Wilhelm didn't bother to hide his anger. 'Averheim–'

'Is lost,' snapped Ledner, 'and so will we be if we delay further. This way, my lord. The knights will cover our retreat.'

'Sacrifice their lives you mean.'

'If that makes you follow me now, then yes, they will. Don't let it be in vain.'

The proud remnants of the Griffonkorps and the Order of the Fiery Comet aligned their steeds in a long fighting line. Many had lost their lances. A lone survivor of the pistoliers mixed in with their ranks, a templar in all but name for his bravery. Those on foot stood either side of the horses. Some men were praying. More than one kissed the blade of his sword and showed it to the heavens. The shaft of sunlight that had lit up Dragontooth returned to bathe them briefly in its lustre but then was gone.

Wilhelm made to ride up alongside them, but Ledner snatched his reins and stopped him.

The chariots were closing all the while. They'd been held in reserve for this very purpose. Grom was as wily as he was obese.

'You are the prince of Reikland. You must not fall!'

Ledner's anger shook Wilhelm into understanding. His defiance crumpled into an expression of profound sadness.

'Sigmar be with you...' he murmured to the knights. He nodded slowly, almost imperceptibly, before he and Ledner rode for the Imperial line as if all the hounds of Chaos were at their heels.

It was over. Wilhelm had failed.

CHAPTER TWENTY
THE BETTER PART OF VALOUR

Outside Averheim, capital city of Averland,
483 miles from Altdorf

THE SIGHT OF Wilhelm quitting the field sent shock-waves through the rest of the army. They couldn't reach Averheim and free the Elector Count's army. A full retreat was ordered almost immediately. The orcs fighting the Grimblades seemed to sense the sudden weakness. It intensified their strength and with the burly greenskins pressing hard against them the halberdiers gave and broke.

Somewhere between running and shouting orders, Karlich fell. The damned smog was everywhere, choking the plain in a charcoal shroud. It was a curse and a blessing. For some, it meant they could retreat without fear of pursuit; for others, it meant getting lost in the darkness and stumbling into the enemy, or worse, the blades of their own panicked kinsmen.

Panic was the only way to describe it. Monsters lived in the mist and smog, some real, some imagined. Their grunting bootsteps thudded behind... or was it in front? Their snorting rage was omnipresent.

Karlich didn't know how far they'd already run. He went to get up when he was kicked in the stomach and fell down again. It wasn't a greenskin. The immediate view was hazy, but he thought he saw an Imperial uniform disappearing eerily away from him. He was suddenly disorientated. Perspective and direction lost all meaning in the smog.

He tried to rise again, this time managing to get to his feet and realised he was alone. Something came at him swiftly from the murk. He gutted it on his blade, belatedly glad it was a goblin. The greenskins too were running scared. Though entirely natural, the smog had taken on an eldritch quality. Snaps of harquebuses were muffled by it. Karlich thought he saw the vague blossom of their flaring flintlocks as the handgunners fired, and headed for them.

His sword wouldn't move. Karlich wrenched at it but it wouldn't give. It was stuck fast in the dead goblin's body. With no time to pull it free, he left it. He didn't know what had happened to the other Grimblades but, with only his dirk to protect him, hoped they were close. One moment they had been running together, trying to maintain some form of good order, the next he was tumbling into the hard earth and all was grey and dark around him.

He thought about shouting out for his comrades, but decided against it. There might be more greenskins, bigger ones, lurking in the smog and he didn't want to risk attracting them.

Warily, he trudged towards the flare of guns. He remembered it was only about a hundred feet to the rear line and safety.

It might as well have been a hundred miles.

The going was slow. Littered with fallen blades and the dead and dying, the ground was treacherous. Karlich saw the shadow of an Empire soldier rushing blindly through the smog and impaling himself on a discarded spear jutting from the earth. The poor sod gurgled once and then died. It was only when Karlich saw the hulking silhouettes drifting ahead of him, too large and broad-backed to be men, that he realised he was really in trouble.

In their eagerness to chase down their defeated enemy, some of the orcs had got in front of him. Briefly fixated on the orcs, he heard the light thud of charging feet too late.

Karlich turned, just as a black-swathed figure rammed into him. He gasped as the air was smashed from his lungs. The sergeant kicked out and was greeted with a satisfying grunt of pain. Despite the fact he was gagging for breath, he tried to shove the body off him but his arm was pinned beneath what felt like his attacker's knee. The scuffle came in flashes – a whipping cloak, black but dirty with caked mud; a silver talisman, gleaming and forbidding; the snarling face of a man he feared but barely knew. Vanhans straddled Karlich, locking his arms with his knees, and seized the sergeant's neck in both hands.

'Murdering heretic,' he snarled, his venting spittle wetting Karlich's cheek.

Karlich jarred a knee into Vanhans's back and he relented enough for the Reiklander to take a breath.

'What are you talking about, maniac?' he hissed through clenched teeth before the witch hunter reasserted his position but this time pushed the flat of his hand under Karlich's chin.

'Lothar Henniker,' he said. 'You know.'

And he *did* know. Vanhans had just used Karlich's real name.

He couldn't have known. There was no way, despite the fact they had later fought together, that Karlich could have realised the crazed butcher who had burned down Rechts's village and condemned its inhabitants to death would visit Karlich years later. The madman's name was Grelle the Confessor, a self-proclaimed title, and he was the worst of the Order of Sigmar's chaff. Death warrants were issued without cause, businesses and homes were put to the torch, innocents dangled from the noose. All of it served Grelle's paranoid fixation with purity and what he believed was a Sigmar-given duty to rid the world of the wretched and the unclean.

Grelle was the worst kind of charlatan: one who didn't know it. Karlich, then Lothar, had turned a blind eye at first, hoping that the witch hunter and his retinue would soon leave. He resented him for the burnings and the deaths, but so long as it didn't touch him or his family, he would keep his peace. Who knows, perhaps the victims of Grelle's purgings were not victims at all? Perhaps they really were heretics? That was the mentality of fear talking, the desire to avoid persecution through acceptance, no matter how abhorrent. Lothar only realised this later and to his cost.

It all changed when his wife, Helena... *my beautiful Helena...* cured an old man's sickness with a herbal panacea. It was nothing more than alleviating the symptoms of a cough but Grelle saw only witchery in her selfless deeds. When Lothar was out gathering wood for the fire, the witch hunter and his cronies took his wife and daughter… *oh, Sigmar, not Isobel*… from their home and burned them both as witches.

Lothar had seen smoke issuing from the village square and wondered why they'd lit a bonfire. A moment later he was running, the gathered firewood scattered in his wake. To that very day, Karlich couldn't explain where the sense of urgency that filled him came from but he had never run harder in his life, nor since.

Entering through the village gates, he inhaled the stench of burning meat. The fat sizzled and crackled in his ears like cruel laughter. It was too late for Helena, too late for his daughter. Battering his way through the jeering crowds, Lothar ripped at the fire-wreathed pyre, burning himself badly in the process. Rough hands seized him by the shoulders and he was hoisted off his knees where he wept and scrabbled at the smoking wood.

Two of Grelle's henchmen held him before their master.

'Conspirator!' Grelle denounced. 'Warlock!' he accused. The witch hunter's face was partially hidden behind a cage-like helmet, his skin a patchwork of self-inflicted scars. He wore little more than leather and rags. His calloused feet and hands were bare. The stink of urine and stale sweat emanated off Grelle in a pall. His breath was redolent of dung. *This* was the wretched creature that had executed his beloved family. Lothar snapped. He cried out with such anguish and apoplexy it was as if his heart were breaking.

Throwing off the minions, Lothar threw himself at the witch hunter. A charred log had rolled off the pyre and into the village square. He seized it and battered Grelle until his cage-helm was staved in and split his ugly visage. The henchmen, nothing more than bullies motivated by persecuting the weak and credulous, stood back in shock as Lothar brutalised their master. Even the rabid onlookers had lost their fervour. Stunned into abject silence, they could only watch.

Grelle mewled in pain and self pity but Lothar pounded relentlessly through the man's pleading. Red rimed his vision. When the log finally broke, he cast it aside and shoved Grelle's face into the wet mud. It had been raining since dawn, though not enough to quench the fires that had so cruelly robbed Lothar of his family. The witch hunter suffocated in the mud. His thrashing protests didn't last.

Only when it was over did Lothar realise what he had done. His hands were bloody. His wife and child were nought but blackened corpses. Lothar fled, there and then, out into the forest. He'd killed a templar of Sigmar. Others would come looking for him. Stay and he condemned everyone around him. More would die needlessly. That day Lothar Henniker died too. Feder Karlich was born in his stead.

But now his old life had returned, like an exhumed corpse. The buzzing of its flies, the stink of putrefaction gave him away. He'd been careful, leaving only a shadow of his former existence, but even shadows can be caught if they spend too long near the light.

The present rushed back to the sound of heavy guns. Meinstadt was firing the cannons held in reserve. The artillery was meant to pave the Empire army's retreat, but it was more treacherous than being surrounded by orcs. A gout of earth exploded nearby, showering the struggling men with dirt. Karlich and Vanhans were in no-man's-land, where the dead would soon linger.

'You'll kill us both,' Karlich snarled, finding it difficult to speak with the witch hunter's iron-hard palm pressing against his chin.

Either Vanhans wasn't listening or he didn't care.

'Lothar Henniker,' he declared, 'I accuse you of heretical murder and consorting with witches most foul.' He reached for something with his free hand and pushed it against Karlich's cheek.

The sergeant screamed as red-hot iron seared his face.

'See how the non-believer burns!'

Vanhans was drunk with his ravings. He'd heated his talisman in one of the many fires around the battlefield, using it to convince himself of his own deluded mania.

The thunderous retort of great cannon was getting louder.

Vanhans tore the icon away, wrenching melted skin from Karlich's face with it.

'I name you daemon, skulking in the guise of man. The order will have vengeance, Sigmar demand–'

Something hot and wet rained on Karlich's face. At the same time he smelled warm iron and felt the passage of a large object soar overhead. The pressure at his chin lessened abruptly, enabling him to look down.

Vanhans was dead. He'd been beheaded by a stray cannon ball. The bounce had taken off his skull at the chin. Lolling macabrely for a few seconds, his corpse collapsed, the Sigmarite icon still clenched in his fist. Rigor mortis would make it hard to reclaim later.

Overcoming the shock, acutely aware that Meinstadt's cannonade went on unabated, Karlich shoved off the witch hunter's body and staggered to his feet. A cannon ball whined past him nearby and he cowered for a moment before ploughing towards the flash of harquebuses again.

Shadows loomed in the smog, the orcs he had noticed earlier. Now they noticed him too, drawn by Vanhans's ravings. They had his scent and grunted in anticipation of the kill.

There were only two of them.

Unarmed, it was one more than needed to kill Karlich. He'd lost his dirk in the scuffle.

Fleeing was suicide. The greenskins were behind him and now they were in front of him, too. Something glinted nearby in the smog, catching what little light penetrated the gloom. Karlich reached for it, even as the pair of orcs closed, and his fingers gripped the hilt of a sword. It was Stahler's. He recognised the rune on the blade. Without time to wonder what had happened to his captain, Karlich took up a fighting stance.

A fight it was then.

He'd need to make it quick. Despite the smog, the rest of the greenskin army couldn't be far behind. Even deterred by the cannonade, some would still get through.

The first lunged through the grey gloom, its silhouette resolving into an ugly visage of tusks and raw aggression. Karlich let it come, ducking its clumsy swipe and slicing it along the belly. Armour and flesh parted easily and the beast was disembowelled in a single cut. The second went to cleave off Karlich's head but stopped mid-swing when it found a blade transfixed through its beady, red eye. Drooling blood, the orc collapsed a moment later.

Karlich marvelled briefly at whatever craft had wrought the runeblade. Truly, there was power in the world of which he had no comprehension.

Another explosion tinged the grey smog a fiery orange, spitting hot earth and shrapnel in a deadly cloud. Marvel or not, the rune-blade wouldn't stop him from being slain by a cannon ball. Karlich needed to get out of no-man's-land, but he was like a ship without a compass. His bearings, despite the muffled din and flare of harquebus, were off. Salvation came from an unlikely quarter.

'Sergeant Karlich! Sergeant Karlich!'

He heard Lenkmann's voice before he saw him and the Grimblades' banner. It fluttered like a beacon in the smog. Hazy and indistinct, yes, but imposing enough to be visible from a longer distance. Karlich made for it at once.

Lenkmann wasn't alone. He had Volker with him.

'Though you were dead,' the Reikland huntsman hugged his sergeant warmly, who looked awkward at the gesture. 'Sorry, sir,' he added afterwards.

Karlich smiled. 'Forgotten,' he replied. 'Where's the battleline?'

Lenkmann looked to Volker, who frowned and looked around in the smog.

'Volker?' asked the banner bearer.

'We're close,' he said. 'Hard to get a strong trail in all this smoke.'

Cannon balls and the dense impacts of mortar shells resonated around them with growing regularity.

'Can't we just go back?' asked Karlich. 'How did you find me?'

Lenkmann shrugged. 'Blind luck. I heard someone speaking through the mist and then I heard what sounded like your voice, too, sir. I followed it. Volker came with me.' He glared at the huntsman who stayed close but was becoming indistinct in the mist with every foot that he trailed a route back. 'The idea was for him to guide us back.'

'Stop moaning, Lenkmann,' Volker replied. 'Must've got turned around. If Dog was alive...' he muttered the last part.

Nearby, they could hear more greenskins closing.

'Whisper!' Karlich hissed. 'We don't want that filth finding us in all this bloody smog. If only there were–' the sergeant stopped abruptly when he saw another shadow heading for them in the gloom.

'Captain Stahler?'

It was hard to see for sure, but the figure wore Imperial trappings synonymous with Karlich's captain and nodded. Keeping his distance, he beckoned them to follow him.

'This way,' Karlich said to the others. He made off after Stahler. 'Captain,' he added, brandishing the rune-blade before him. 'I found your sword.'

Stahler's response was to plough on through the fog and smoke, always a few feet again, just barely discernible.

It wasn't long before the grey veil receded and the rugged shape of the embankment began to form. Sporadic explosions illuminated it in grainy white light, banishing the darkness briefly before it reigned again.

The heavy report of the volley gun was intense and devastating. Karlich had never seen one used in battle before. It fired with a *crank-choom, crank-choom* cadence, spitting out tongues of flame with every shot.

As they were emerging from the smog, Karlich realised he'd lost sight of Captain Stahler. His attention had lapsed for only a few seconds, drawn by the spectacle of the guns.

'Where is he?'

'Where's who?' asked Volker.

Karlich fixed him with an angry glare. 'Now isn't the time. Stahler, where is the captain? I just saw him a moment ago. He led us out of the killing field.'

Lenkmann was shaking his head. 'It was just the three of us. I thought you had found a route through the smog...' The banner bearer paled a little and looked as if he were about to vomit.

The sight of Masbrecht, Brand and Greiss running towards them prevented Karlich's immediate reply.

'Sigmar's blood, it's good to see you, sergeant.' Masbrecht clapped Karlich on the shoulder and nodded to the others.

'We very nearly didn't make it back at all,' said Volker.

They walked and talked. The rest of the Grimblades were just beyond the embankment with the rest of the Empire army. They were pulling back the entire force.

'Wilhelm's retreating,' said Brand flatly. 'The greenskins have won. So how did you get back?'

Lenkmann's eyes were hooded and he looked down.

'The sergeant found a way,' said Volker.

'And I thought you were the scout,' offered Greiss with a grin.

Volker gave him a stern look but in mild jest.

Much of the urgency surrounding the withdrawal had subsided. The spiked palisades were lowered over the abatis-filled trench, spanning them for the retreating regiments to cross. At least Wilhelm's escape plan was proving successful. The cannonade combined with the confusion of the smog had dissuaded all but the dumbest or most bloodthirsty greenskins from pursuit. The few that did make it through were soon cut down and those numbers dwindled by the minute.

Over the hill, past the slowly reforming lines of handgunners and crossbowmen, there was a scene of mass upheaval. Captains and sergeants bellowed for order, shifting banners hither and thither in an effort to achieve some kind of cohesion in the ranks. Many soldiers had been separated in the rout, those who lived were only just returning to their regiments. Horns and drums were beating in a cacophony. Runners ferried messages back and forth with frantic gusto. Waggoneers and drovers laid carts with remaining supplies. Some of the baggage train carried the dead and wounded. Hundreds would have to be left in the smog for the greenskins to eat and butcher. No one spoke of it.

Slowly, laboriously, a line of march began to form. Wilhelm was seen near the front, at a distance, marshalling his officers. The cadre had thinned distinctly since the battle. Ledner was alive, much to Karlich's disappointment. He was exchanging words with Captain Vogen, about halfway up the line. Instructions from the prince, no doubt.

Journeymen in teams of five and six hurried past Karlich and the others, bound for the war machines. The last of the army was packing up and readying to move to Sigmar only knew where. Defeat at Averheim was not fully countenanced, it seemed to the sergeant. What happened next was anyone's guess.

Karlich surveyed the milling crowds as Lenkmann led them back to the rest of the Grimblades.

'Where is Captain Stahler?' asked the sergeant. 'I want to return his sword.'

Brand looked over his shoulder. His face was cold like an iron mask.

'It's yours now, sir,' he said in all seriousness.

Karlich frowned.

As they neared the regiment he noticed a sullen-looking wagon with a bodyguard of six silent Griffonkorps, last survivors of the goblin fanatics. Three bodies were lying on it, partially covered by red blankets with gilded trim. They looked like the dead warriors' cloaks. One face was visible, the other two were shrouded.

It was Masbrecht who spoke. His tone was sombre and sepulchral. 'Captain Stahler is dead. Someone found him on his horse. His body had no fresh injuries. It was like he'd just died.'

Karlich tore his eyes off the corpse as a priest of Morr driving the wagon covered its face.

Somewhere behind the sergeant, Lenkmann threw up.

CHAPTER TWENTY-ONE
THE LONG RETREAT

Beyond the Stirland border, Stirland,
433 miles from Altdorf

AVERLAND WAS NO longer deemed safe. Harried all the way by warbands from Grom's army, Wilhelm led his troops north across the border and into Stirland. Here in peasant country, the lay of the land was no better. As in Averland, villages and towns were burning. Some of the smaller hamlets were little more than ashen husks; Grom had made bonfires out of them. Doomsayers and refugees littered the province like disconsolate sheep.

Whereas Averland was largely flat and wealthy, Stirland was rugged and poor. To the east was Sylvania, a shadow of a land that lingered like a dirty secret everyone already knew. The Carsteins had once ruled over it, a house of aristocratic fiends whose last scion had fallen to Count Martin's runefang. Strangely, in the vampires' absence, it was even more a haunted place of which few Stirlanders spoke and fewer still ventured. As for Stirland itself, it was hilly and the last tranches of the Great

Forest crept over its northernmost reaches as if to colonise it with its forbidding arbours. Rural, down to earth, Stirland's people were slow to change and quick to cast suspicion, especially on outsiders. It made for a bleak and unwelcoming vista as the army crossed the border, most of its watchtowers already smoking ruins.

On the third day of the march, armed outriders approached the column. They rode black mares that matched the colour of their hair, and carried harquebus and bows. Most of the riders wore dark caps of Stirland green. Their leather hauberks, hose and tassets were grimy. A quick parley with the leader of the fifty-strong group, a dirty-faced sergeant with an eye-patch and a dark beard, went down the line in short order. Wurtbad was the nearest, possibly the only, safe city in the province.

Despite the obvious provincial differences, Wilhelm was still a prince of the Empire and as such the Stirland outriders insisted on escorting him to their capital. Faster riders, without armour and carrying dirks, were sent ahead to bring advance word to Lord Protector Krieglitz.

All being well, the Reiklanders and their guides would reach Wurtbad in two days.

WURTBAD WAS NOT like Altdorf. Nor did it resemble Averheim. To the rest of the Empire, these were magnificent cities, shining testimonies to the achievements of man. Wurtbad, despite its bustling trade, its markets and its white walls, was a grim place. The mood was hardly helped by the greenskin hordes rampaging not so far from its border. They'd sent flocks of refugees before them, like cattle chased by the drover's whip.

Rustic, backward and generally unwashed, they lent an air of bigotry and superstition that the Count would rather leave in his hinterlands, not confront on his doorstep.

Karlich scowled back at a native Stirlander who was passing by in the near-deserted street. Though Lord Protector Krieglitz had allowed the Reiklanders entry to his capital, the army was to be billeted outside in tents. Only Wilhelm and his entourage were permitted to lodge within its walls. Forays into town by small bands of the soldiery were allowed, however, in order to drink and forget their troubles, if only for a short time. Such 'excursions' went by rote, a few regiments at a time. Karlich and the Grimblades were currently enjoying their rotation in what was regarded 'the wine capital of the Empire'.

Good news for Rechts, he thought bitterly, and wondered if a drunken stupor would ease his pain.

The sheer scale of the defeat at Averheim was barely just setting in. Fighting for your life, even trudging down the Old Dwarf Road, ever fearful of greenskin attack, tended to occupy the mind. Now, in the quiet and the solitude, the dust had begun to settle. It smelled of the grave and itched with despair. Suicides had already been reported by several sergeants. Mercifully, desertion was scarce. It was mainly Averlanders, sneaking back across the border, wanting to meet the end in their own lands. Karlich couldn't blame them. He felt a long way from home.

In the aftermath, Wilhelm's quartermasters had taken a tally. The death-books were growing into quite a compendium. He'd lost a large body of troops at Averheim, together with nearly all the knights. Middenland had almost none of its original contingent.

It gave Karlich no pleasure that the Steel Swords had not returned from the plains. Even though they had left his Grimblades vulnerable to a flank attack and were, in no uncertain terms, the biggest whoresons he had ever met, Karlich could not bear a fallen soldier ill will. For all their faults, Sturnbled had led his men bravely, fighting in a war they didn't understand or believe in. They deserved to die in the land of Ulric with their forefathers, not in some foreign field.

True survivors that they were, the greatsworders and Von Rauken still lived, though 'Carroburg Fewer' might be a more appropriate name now. At his last count, Karlich gauged there were no more than ten of the greatsworders left. They bore it all stoically, of course.

That left mainly citizen levies and those infantry regiments raised in Reikland townships and trained as professional soldiers. Then there were the few remaining Averlanders, dwindling by the day. It wasn't much.

Most of the war machines and engineers made the journey. Meinstadt was one of the few officers Karlich had met that was still breathing. Stahler was gone – it left a hole in his stomach and a chill down his back to think of it. Karlich pushed the memory of what he'd seen – *or had he?* – on the plains outside Averheim to the back of his mind. No good could come of digging there. Lenkmann had refused flat out to acknowledge it. To him, it never happened. The banner bearer was right at home with the superstitious Stirlanders. Of the rest, Hornstchaft was assumed slain in the initial charge, though his body remained unrecovered, and Preceptor Kogswald had met his end protecting the life of the prince, or so the propaganda went. Ironically, Blaselocker of Averland had died when the cannon misfired on the embankment. By seeking refuge behind the massive iron gun he had actually doomed himself. The demise of Father Untervash, Karlich had witnessed himself. The sight of the warrior priest being bitten in two still haunted his nightmares.

Thankfully no one had questioned the death of Vanhans. With the witch hunter gone, the funds from the temple dried up. Without coin, the mercenaries left the following morning. Most of Vanhans's faithful horde disbanded too with no shepherd to guide the fervent flock.

Karlich had the blood of two templars on his hands. Both were madmen to his mind. After the campaign, assuming he survived, he might have to move on again, lest the spectre of Lothar Henniker catch up with him.

Bleak. Yes, it was the only word Karlich could think of to describe their situation as he sat outside an inn with too few customers and sipped at hot ale.

'Apparently, it's the custom,' said a familiar voice behind him.

'Eh?'

Masbrecht came into view and gestured to the clay tankard Karlich was cradling.

'I've heard they use a poker from the fire to warm it.'

Karlich smacked his lips and scowled. He'd been holding the tankard so long, the heat had long since stopped emanating off it. 'Tastes like soot.'

There was a long pause. Masbrecht looked uneasy and rubbed his chin.

'Spit it out then,' said Karlich.

'Sir?'

'Whatever it is you've come to speak to me about, say it.' Karlich set his tankard down on the stumpy table beside him. The two men were alone.

'It's not right,' Masbrecht uttered simply.

'What isn't? The ale, the war, our defeat? There's much in the world that isn't right, Masbrecht. You'll need to narrow it down.'

Masbrecht barely moved. 'You know what I'm talking about.'

'Ah,' said Karlich, stretching his legs and pulling his pipe from his tunic pocket. *'That.'* The cup was already packed with tobacco. It was late, night was drawing in. Karlich leaned over to a candle stuck to the table with its own wax and coaxed his pipeweed to life.

'Are you really surprised we lost at Averheim?' Masbrecht continued. 'Even the greenskins can form an alliance. We are at each others' throats!'

'Hardly,' Karlich said through piping smoke. 'We've been left to our own protection, Masbrecht. There's a difference.'

'Someone within Wilhelm's camp, someone who could be *here*, now, wants our prince dead. How can you stand idly by and let it happen?' Masbrecht sat down next to Karlich. 'At Averheim, it was different. Surrounded by the army, the prince was safe. But here, now–'

'Ledner said he'd take care of it. We've done our part for prince and province.'

'You trust *him*?'

'Not as much as a goblin, but what other choice is there?'

Masbrecht's body language was beseeching. 'Let's tell the prince, warn him of the danger he's in.'

'We don't know he's in danger. The assassin's dead, remember.'

Masbrecht's expression darkened. 'Eber's blood was all over my hands and he's still not fit to fight. I remember well enough.'

'Look, I'm sorry. Morals are all fine and good but they're not always practical. If word got out...' Karlich sucked a breath in through his teeth. 'Well, let's just say the consequences could be ugly.'

'Or the culprits could be found and brought to justice,' said Masbrecht. 'The prince's reputation is reinforced and would-be betrayers will think twice before plotting against him. Moreover, we'd be rid of the traitors in our midst!' He was agitated, breathing hard. Karlich had seldom seen him so passionate about something other than religion. He saw it for what it really was though. Refutation. Disbelief.

That men could turn on their own, on someone as pure and noble as Prince Wilhelm, dented Masbrecht's faith. Belief in Sigmar was really all he had. Without it, he was a shadow. Karlich saw that now, just as he saw the look that flashed across Masbrecht's face when he'd regarded the cup of ale. It was *need*. The absence of one thing meant its replacement by another. Small wonder he was so puritanical about Rechts's drinking.

Karlich leaned forward and hissed: 'We stopped an assassination. I wouldn't say we rested on our laurels, Masbrecht. What more would you have us–'

The inn door slamming open interrupted him.

'What's he doing here?' a surly voice asked. It was Rechts, nursing his own hot ale, one of several he'd already imbibed by the look of him. 'I said I didn't want to drink alone, but I'd rather that than share ale with this naysayer. The mood is grim enough.'

'Drunkenness will do that to a man,' Masbrecht replied. Anger underpinned his voice. He was already in a pugnacious mood.

'Voice of experience, *brother*?' Now Rechts was goading him.

Karlich went to intercede but Masbrecht cut him off.

'Are you a heretic, Torsten, is that it?'

Karlich quickly got to his feet. 'That's enough!'

Rechts had just sat down and was about to get up again when Karlich pushed him back onto his stool. There was silence as the drummer gritted his teeth and rode out his anger.

'They were burned,' he said eventually. '*All* of them, my entire village.'

Masbrecht found he was wrong-footed. 'Wha–'

'A templar came to us, a servant of Sigmar, or so he claimed. A boy was found with a webbed toe. Fearful of mutation, the villagers took him before the witch hunter.' As darkness crept across the sky, the shadows pooling in Rechts's face made him look cadaverous. Too much drink and lack of proper sleep had worn the man down. As he spoke, it didn't appear to lessen his burden. 'I never saw the boy after that. Trials followed, then executions. Soon the trials were abandoned altogether and it was just about the burning. Our village preacher let him do it. His voice was loudest in the mob. I only survived because my mother hid me. When I came out, they were all dead. My mother, my whole family were ash. The witch hunter and his cronies had moved on. So, forgive me if I do not trust those that preach the word of Sigmar as readily as you do.'

Rechts stood up. Karlich let him, showing his palms in a gesture for the drummer to stay calm. He did. Until Masbrecht opened his mouth again.

'That boy could not have burned for no reason, he must–'

Rechts exploded. Spittle was flying from his mouth, 'Whim, brother. That was all. Whim and the will of a raving mad man, clad in Sigmar's cloth. Preaching fear and doubt, an entire village turned on itself. The hammer is not a death warrant, yet there are those who brandish it like one.' Rechts was clenching and unclenching his fists. The old pugnacity had returned. Karlich edged around the table so he could get between them if he needed to.

'*Reason*!' Rechts went on. 'Reason doesn't come into it. An innocent boy burned, an untainted village destroyed, all at the hand of our self-proclaimed protectors. Show me the reason in that.' In a much smaller voice, he added, 'I can still smell my mother's ash on my hands...'

Masbrecht was indignant. 'I still don't–' he began, Karlich already frowning and about to tell him to close his trap before Rechts interceded.

'Speak further and I'll cut out your tongue.' He'd ripped a dirk from its scabbard and held it levelly, especially considering he was well inebriated.

'Put it away, Torsten,' said Karlich in a firm voice. 'Trooper Rechts!' he added a moment later.

Rechts obeyed, looked at Masbrecht once more, who was paling a little by then, and left.

Karlich watched him wander off down the street. Come the morning, he'd send Volker to look for him. He turned to say something to Masbrecht but he was leaving too, heading in the opposite direction. That was something, at least. Karlich sat down, his bones never more weary. As he sipped at his tepid ale, he scowled.

'Definitely tastes like soot.'

CHAPTER TWENTY-TWO
FESTERING WOUNDS

Wurtbad, capital of Stirland,
398 miles from Altdorf

TWO CONCESSIONS WERE made concerning the admittance of foreign troops into Wurtbad. The first allowed a few regiments at a time, no more than two hundred men, to spend a night in town away from the pitched encampment outside the border walls. The second instructed that all injured men in need of care beyond the skill of army chirurgeons would be housed under the auspices of the temple of Shallya until such time as they could return to their regiment.

These hospitium were not merely found in the temple itself. The badly wounded and the dying were in such numbers that it would not have coped. Inns, stately abodes, barracks and even barns were given over to the ministration of the sick and ailing. Locals avoided such places; they were grim and unpleasant to look upon. The stench of necrosis and old rot made the air inside them rank and noisome. Wailing and moaning was a common, morale-eating chorus. Few soldiers emerged alive, let alone whole. Several of the town's sawbones had already earned tidy profits from the Prince of Reikland's coffers for their diligent labours over the gangrenous and diseased. Shallyan priestesses moved between sweaty cots with a tireless grace and brought blankets from the recently deceased for the newly admitted. Steamed over the hot springs which Wurtbad was famous for, the blankets were damp and reeked of latent death. Dingy, so as to hide the horror of it from their inmates and nurses, the hospitium maintained an air of the desolate and gladly forgotten.

Eber was one of the fortunate. He would live and escape with all his limbs. Strong as an ox, determined as an Ostland bull, his natural stamina and phlegmatic humour had seen him through the worst. Masbrecht had applied bandages expertly on the heath and likely saved the burly Reiklander a lot of blood, possibly even his life. The battlefield was still beyond him, but a few more days of healing and rest would see Eber take up his halberd again. He longed to be back amongst his brothers.

Sitting up in his cot, Eber bowed his head as a grey-faced priest of Morr drifted by. Cadaverous and silent within his black robes, he was more wraith than man. A quiet prayer of warding and the sign of the raven would have to keep the God of Death and Dreams at bay. At least, Eber hoped it would.

Once the priest was gone, off to perform the final rites of soul binding for some poor wretch, Eber looked around. It was almost smoky in the dim lantern light but his heart spiked painfully in his wounded chest when he saw someone he recognised just a few cots away from his.

Torveld was sitting over the edge of his cot wearing a blank expression. He was being attended by a Shallyan matriarch. Her robes were grimy and stained with blood but she still managed to look pure. She carried a candle, perfectly poised, in one hand. She was discussing Torveld's condition with one of the army's quartermasters, a slightly corpulent man who dabbed his forehead with a rag every few seconds and whose leather hauberk strained at the gut. Eber wondered how long before he was being ministered by the sisters of mercy. They spoke in low voices, but Eber still overheard them.

According to the matriarch, Torveld had lost his memory. Leastways, he had no recollection of the past few months. His head wound was well healed, though. Physically fine, he could return to his regiment and the campaign.

At this brief summary, the quartermaster nodded and went to a large book of parchments he had in his hand. Torveld was still wearing his bloodstained uniform and the quartermaster leafed through the broad pages laboriously. It was hard to see, but Eber made out heraldries, regimental markings and banner icons as the pages were turned. Having found what he sought, the quartermaster frowned.

His voice was a low murmur. Even though he couldn't hear it, Eber knew what was said: Torveld's regiment, the Middenland Steel Swords, were dead. He was the only survivor. The northerner appeared not to understand the import of the quartermaster's words. Eber imagined a mental shrug in the man's neutral demeanour.

'Well, he can't stay here in the temple,' said the matriarch. Her voice was soft but her message unyielding.

'It's a return to the army then, my lad,' the quarter-master addressed Torveld directly. 'There'll be a use for you there.'

Torveld was then led away by the quartermaster, a walking husk awaiting a soul to fill it. Confident whatever choleric intent the Middenlander harboured was lost to amnesia, Eber eased back onto his cot. The pain in his chest flared. His wounds were still raw. A gentle touch soothed his shoulder. A priestess of Shallya calmly requested that he should lie down. Eber was sweating. Blood darkened his bandages in faint blossoms of vermillion. He did as asked, turning his head to watch Torveld leave the temple and his sight.

Nothing to worry about there, he told himself, nothing at all.

THE SUN HURT his eyes as Evik Torveld left the temple. He was only half listening as the quartermaster gave him directions to the town gate. Once at the encampment, he was to report to Sergeant Hauker for duties. A moment later, the quartermaster had returned inside to assess some of the other wounded and Torveld was left alone.

He was still finding his bearings when he noticed another soldier walking through Wurtbad's streets. The uniform triggered something buried in Torveld's damaged mind. His hand went to the head wound out of reflex. Anger burned through the fog clouding Torveld's memory, a line of heat that left a core of rage and vengeance behind.

Sturnbled, Wode... all his brothers of Ulric, all dead.

'Grimblades...' he muttered like a curse.

Torveld clenched his fists until the knuckles whitened, then headed after the soldier.

* * *

For the first time in years, Masbrecht needed a drink. He felt the familiar gravel taste in his mouth, the cotton tongue behind itching teeth. Sweat soaked the back of his tunic. Just a tiny patch in the small of his back, but it told him the craving was upon him. He'd fought hard to deny it, burying the little voice inside him under the weight of faith and religion. Foolishly, he thought he'd beaten it but it was there, waiting for a moment of weakness.

The streets were quiet. Most Wurtbad residents stayed indoors after dark, fearing attack from the greenskins. Others never left the taverns, satisfied to drink themselves into oblivion until the dawn. Being insensible made it easy to forget, if just for a while. Masbrecht didn't want to go to a tavern. He wanted to drink alone, to indulge and be damned. The brewhouses were shut and bolted. He wandered down a side alley. It was cluttered with refuse and other scraps. Urine ringed the air in an invisible pall. Drunken shapes lolled in its darkest recesses.

Masbrecht walked over to one. The man was filthy and wore the remnants of a docker's garb. He was snoring loudly, clutching a grimy bottle. His pepper-stubble cheeks blew in and out with every laboured breath.

Without thinking, Masbrecht snatched the bottle. He took a quick pull. The liquor was fiery hot. It burned the back of his throat and he coughed hard, bringing up phlegm. Wiping his mouth, he took another, wincing as the liquid went down.

All the deaths, all the lies and compromises of the last few days and weeks would disappear in a fog of drunkenness. Masbrecht embraced it, tears welling in his eyes. Cold, grey faces came to him as he closed his eyes to the pain.

Varveiter, lost at Blösstadt…

Eber, brutally stabbed and fighting for his life…

Keller, hung by the neck with his own rope…

Captain Stahler, cold and lifeless on a death priest's cart…

It didn't feel right. It wasn't right. None of it was. As Masbrecht supped, filling his body with the poison he had renounced for over five years, the old docker slowly stirred. Like a child without its blanket, he missed the presence of the bottle. He awoke with a grunt, then was screaming unintelligibly at the man who had stolen his grog.

Surprised, Masbrecht pulled his dagger and brandished it at him.

'Stay there, you old dog,' he cried. 'Stay there or I'll cut you!'

The old docker recoiled, holding up his hands and pleading clemency.

'Give mercy, milord. Don't tar your blade with an old sot like me, I beg ya.'

Reality hit Masbrecht like a flood. The bottle shattered on the ground before he even knew he'd dropped it, waking up the other drunks.

'In Sigmar's name…' He fled back out into the accusing night.

'Bastard…' he heard from down the alley. 'My grog…'

Masbrecht got as far as a tinker's before he had to stop and be sick. The liquor came back just as hot and unpleasant. Putting his fingers down his throat he puked again, just to be sure he was rid of it.

Kneeling in his own vomit, Masbrecht clasped his hands together in a desperate prayer. They were shaking.

'Merciful Sigmar, guide me in my time of need. I am lost without your hand upon my shoulder.'

Somewhere in the distance, bells were tolling. Masbrecht had heard them before. They belonged to the temple of Sigmar near the town square. Salvation was close. He made for the bells at once, unaware that someone was following him.

CHAPTER TWENTY-THREE
HARD TRUTHS

Wurtbad, capital of Stirland,
398 miles from Altdorf

KRIEGLITZ'S HALL WAS empty and echoing. The blazing hearth crackled, rudely invading the quietude and casting flickering grey slashes against the walls. A portrait hung above the fire, hinted at through the passing shadows. A noble bearing suggested itself and Wilhelm, pondering over his goblet of mulled spice-wine, thought it was probably Martin, one of Neder's most famous ancestors.

The lambent light gave the room a warm impression. Thick, woollen rugs swathed the floor, a patch of flagstone visible here and there between them. Bare wooden beams stood in ranks along the walls and arched overhead like dark, embracing arms. A pair of crossed swords, a halberd and spear hung between the vertical beams. Tapestries were lost in shadow.

Wilhelm found the rustic aesthetic pleasing. It was a blessed rural tonic compared to Dieter's lavishly appointed chambers. He eased into the furs draped across the back of his chair, still leafing through a series of missives and reports.

'Averheim holds at least,' he said with a hint of bitter irony.

'The beast is moving, Wilhelm,' said Krieglitz. 'It has sated its lust for carnage in our hinterlands and seeks fresh enemies.'

Wilhelm looked up at Krieglitz, wearisome at the bleakness in the reports and returned petitions.

The two men faced each other across a table of rough-hewn oak. They had stripped out of their battle gear, in favour of light clothes and short cloaks. A change of attire was most welcome in Wilhelm's opinion, though that and a bath had done nothing to cleanse the taint of defeat and loss. Six days in Wurtbad so far for the army to regroup and for Wilhelm to decide what to do next. Several officers had requested an immediate return to Reikland. The Lord Protector of Stirland was right, Grom and his horde *were* moving, likely westward to the heartlands of the Empire. The fact remained though that Wilhelm's army, especially depleted as it was, could not match the greenskins. He needed allies. Petitions for aid had been sent to all states and provinces upon his arrival in the Stirland capital. The first replies to those missives had arrived that evening.

'No word from Wissenland?'

'Pfeifraucher hasn't changed his position, nor will he,' Krieglitz returned.

'And what about you, Neder? What's your position?'

The mounted head of a great boar, the cured and stuffed carcass of an elk caught Wilhelm's eye. The shadows and the fire gave them a strange sense of verisimilitude. The prince suddenly imagined them roaming the wild, straying into the hunter's sights... He felt an uncomfortable empathy with the beasts' plight.

'Orcs and goblins still rove my lands,' replied Krieglitz. 'Even if I wanted to, I can't join your crusade, especially not with victory so uncertain. As Dieter's regent, I can hardly go against him either.' His face darkened as he drew back into shadow. Wilhelm thought it might be shame that made him do it.

'And I cannot leave the Reikmark to be ravaged, either,' he said. 'Is there nothing you can do?'

'I don't think a prince has ever pleaded with me before.'

Wilhelm's reply was curt.

'Not pleading – *asking*.'

'Sorry, brother.' Krieglitz looked downcast. He was only a lord protector and had no right to address a royal son of Reikland like that. 'I can provide an escort to the border but that's all. Don't forget, as well as greenskins, I have Sylvania stirring in the east.'

There was no better news in the returned missives. Wilhelm stood up abruptly.

'Then there's nothing further to discuss. Thank you for the wine, but I've lost my taste for it.'

'Wilhelm...'

The prince was turning to leave and glanced back sharply.

'Save your contrition, Neder. It counts for nothing on the battlefield.'

Wilhelm was walking away, disappearing into shadow, when Krieglitz spoke up.

'What will you do?'

Wilhelm stopped.

'Try to find more troops at Nuln, rally the townships and citizen militias, whatever I can. Perhaps Dieter will deploy his armies when the goblins are at his gates, but I doubt it.'

Krieglitz left an awkward pause before replying.

'I am sorry, brother.'

'The army will be gone by morning,' said Wilhelm, then carried on walking.

RECHTS AND MASBRECHT were missing. Outside Wurtbad in the pre-dawn light, a muster was forming. The Grimblades were supposed to be a part of it. Except Karlich and a small group were still in the town square, two bodies short. It was finally time to return to Reikland.

'Find them both,' he said to Volker, his annoyance obvious. 'Bring them back here to me. We might have an hour before Vogen starts asking questions.'

With the tragic death of Captain Stahler, Vogen had taken over command of all the remaining infantry regiments. A tall order, but most of the soldiers that comprised it were veterans and could look to their sergeants for guidance. Vogen was enough of a pragmatist to let this happen and oversee where needed.

Volker nodded and jogged off into town.

'And us, sergeant,' asked Lenkmann, 'what should we do?'

Brand stood silently alongside him, together with Greiss. The rest of the Grimblades were already outside Wurtbad's gates on the mustering field, which now closely resembled a cesspool after several thousand men had been camped there. Small wonder that the Stirlanders were glad for the foreign exodus.

Karlich looked sour and he glared at the banner bearer.

'We wait.'

VOLKER FOUND MASBRECHT in a pool of his own blood. The temple of Sigmar was the first place he thought to look, but he was unhappy at the discovery he made there. Fortunately, there was no one else present save for the old priest who ministered it. From him, Volker learned that several Wurtbad folk had already seen the body. That in itself wouldn't be such a problem were it not for the fact of what was written in the blood.

Masbrecht was on his knees, as if in penitent genuflection. In death, he slumped against a statue of Sigmar, just below a set of stone steps leading up to the temple's main altar. Dried blood streaked his neck where it looked like he'd slit his own throat. The wound gaped like a red smile that was anything but humorous. The tips of Masbrecht's fingers were red too. His confession was written in blood alongside him. It told of the assassination attempt on Wilhelm, of a 'traitor in the Reikland' and his guilt in what he saw as complicity in keeping the threat of it secret.

'Incredible that he wrote so much when his lifeblood was ebbing like that,' said Lenkmann.

As soon as he'd found the body, Volker had instructed the old priest to seal the temple until his return, which he did along with Karlich and the others. They'd all been staring for almost a minute before Lenkmann had broken the silence.

'I've seen men do more than that,' offered Brand.

All except Karlich turned to regard the unsettling Reiklander.

'What's he holding in his left hand?' asked the sergeant.

'Must've missed that...' muttered Volker and crouched beside the body. It was hard to see in the murky confines of the temple. Masbrecht's left hand was also crushed up against the statue where he'd slumped.

Volker prised a scroll loose. The dead man's body had yet to rigor.

It was a map Masbrecht was clutching in his bloodied fingers.

'Where in Morr's name did he get *that*?' asked Volker.

Karlich recognised the self-same piece of parchment Ledner had showed him before they'd been charged with the prince's preservation on the heath. Except, it couldn't be. Ledner had burned it.

'Who else has seen this?' asked the sergeant.

'Several of the townsfolk. News will be spreading,' said Volker.

'Like fire...' muttered Brand, kneeling down next to Masbrecht. 'It's no suicide.'

Karlich glared at the Reiklander, demanding more.

'Too clean, too obvious,' Brand replied without even catching his sergeant's look. 'If you wanted to confess, why stab yourself in the neck and then use your own blood to write it?'

'Guilt can do strange things to a man,' suggested Lenkmann. His hollow voice reminded them all of poor Keller.

Brand shook his head. 'Doesn't feel like something Masbrecht would do. He'd go to Vogen, the prince even, confess and then await judgement. He wouldn't kill himself.'

'How can you be sure?' asked Greiss.

Brand turned and held the recruit's gaze. 'I just *know*.'

'So he was murdered,' said Greiss, 'and in his dying moments, unburdened his soul to Sigmar. Sounds like the actions of a devout man.'

No one spoke for a few moments as reality sank in.

Masbrecht was dead. Someone had murdered him.

'We can do nothing about the confession,' said Karlich at last. 'That horse has bolted. Ledner may have us all hanged on account of it. We'll tackle that in turn.' He turned to Volker. 'Any sign of Rechts?'

It was the first time anyone had mentioned the drummer's name, but long after they'd all been thinking it.

'Would he...'

'I don't know.'

'How deep did their enmity go?' asked Greiss.

'Shut up!' Karlich snapped. The two men had almost come to blows before. The argument outside the tavern had been one of the worst. What if this time they'd met again and no one had been there to stop them? Premeditated murder was not *in* Rechts, but a fight that got out of hand... and if he was still drunk?

'Lenkmann,' said Karlich, 'wait here for the watch. Vogen or even Ledner may follow.' Karlich glared at the banner bearer intently to emphasise the import of his next words. 'Say nothing,' he said, turning briefly and taking in the other Grimblades in a glance, 'that goes for all of you. We keep quiet, try and fathom what happened. Lenkmann, you found Masbrecht here and have no idea why he did it or what his bloodied confession refers to. If anyone asks, I'm gathering the last of the regiment for the muster. Understand?'

Lenkmann nodded.

'The rest of you,' added Karlich, already walking out of the temple. 'Every alehouse, every tavern in Wurtbad. Find him.'

No drunkard in all of Wurtbad would have visited as many alehouses as they had in such short order. Rechts was at none of them, and now Karlich was beginning to despair they'd ever find him. A niggle at the back of his head mooted that the drummer *had* killed Masbrecht and fled town for fear of repercussions. Karlich crushed that voice mentally underfoot and trusted in his instincts that Rechts was a good man in a bad way.

He was alone. By splitting up, the Grimblades had a better chance of finding Rechts quickly and quietly. As Karlich gazed around, something caught his eye. Like a lot of Stirland towns, Wurtbad's rugged landscape encroached within its walls. It had several hills and narrow winding lanes that led to their summits. One such grassy knoll caught his attention. A thin smoke trail emanated from it.

Karlich turned abruptly, half expecting to see someone behind him, but the townsfolk had moved on and scowled less. Putting it down to tension, he made for the hill in long, determined strides.

The knoll was at the outskirts of town and overlooked much of its rural market. Even early as it was, traders were setting up stalls and wares for the coming morning. There were many gaps. Much of the usual bustle had been dented by the invasion. People still needed to eat, though. Trade offered a sense of order and normality fearful and superstitious folk needed. Count Krieglitz was a wise ruler, not a mere peasant lord as some of his contemporaries snidely branded him.

Rechts was smoking a thin bone pipe when Karlich found him. In the other hand, he cradled a bottle of Middenland hooch. It was empty, barring the dregs.

'Come to drag me to muster?' he asked without looking back.

Karlich didn't answer but walked closer and kept his dirk within reach.

'Just needed a little peace,' Rechts continued. 'Old memories sting when they're poked at.' Now he faced Karlich. He looked crapulous and melancholic. 'I wouldn't have cut out his tongue, you know. Thumped him, yes,' he added, nodding at the idea, 'but not cut him.'

And then, as he experienced the ambivalence of feeling relief that Rechts hadn't murdered Masbrecht but then concern that his killer was still unknown to him, Karlich noticed a shadow fall upon them both. Rechts's eyes widened and he tried to stand when he saw who loomed behind his sergeant.

Karlich moved just in time, ripping out his dirk and parrying Torveld's thrust out of instinct. Another slash came at him, opening up the sergeant's shoulder. Karlich yelped aloud, dropping his dagger as a hot dark line spoiled his tunic.

'Southern dog,' spat Torveld, drunk with anger. 'They're all dead.' He lunged, and Karlich dodged aside.

Comprehending that Torveld was alive and not slain with the other Steel Swords as he originally thought, it all made sudden, terrible sense to Karlich. The Middenlander had killed Masbrecht out of a misguided fit of revenge. Blood for blood – that was the Ulrican way.

Torveld blamed the Grimblades for the death of his comrades and was here to exact the price he saw was owed.

Rechts bull-charged him, even as Karlich was backing off to try and find some even footing, but Torveld barged the drunken Reiklander aside. The drummer's momentum took him careening halfway down the hill, where he landed with a grunt.

'Your brothers died in battle. It wasn't down to us,' Karlich told him, glancing around for a weapon, anything. 'This is murder, Middenlander. Vogen will see you swing for this.' It was an empty threat considering he'd killed already. As Torveld came on, Karlich decided to change approach. 'I thought Ulricans were proud, honour-bound warriors–'

Torveld thumped his chest. 'Winter wolves are the fiercest and most honourable.'

It was the most heartfelt and tragic affirmation Karlich had ever heard.

'Then why slit a man's throat? Why kill my brother in arms and try to hide it with deception?'

Torveld's face went blank for just a second. He had no notion of what Karlich was talking about.

'I lost the other and followed you he–' was all he could manage before Greiss knocked him unconscious from behind.

'Masbrecht is dead?' Rechts was scrambling up the hill, sometimes on four limbs, sometimes two but was dumbstruck when he realised what had happened.

'Yes,' said Greiss, his iron-hard gaze fixed on Karlich. Even unarmed, the sergeant was at least sober and presented the greatest threat to his mission.

'He killed him, Torsten,' said Karlich. 'I'm sorry I ever doubted you.'

Rechts's confusion only grew. He struggled upright, still wavering. 'What's going on?'

Karlich wasn't really listening. His eyes were on Greiss.

'Who do you serve? Ledner?'

Greiss nodded, seeing no harm in the admission now. The assassin had clubbed Torveld over the head with a *main gauche,* parrying dagger. He also had a duelling pistol snug in his belt.

Karlich gestured to the weapons. 'Gifts from your master?'

'These are mine,' said Greiss with a voice so cold it practically chilled the air. Ice flowed in his veins now. 'Commendable,' he added. 'Stalling for time, devising my true nature. Your time is almost up, yours and your men's. If you don't struggle, I'll make it quick.'

'So Ledner didn't trust us to keep quiet after all,' said Karlich.

'No more words,' Greiss told them. 'Face away from me, kneel down and prepare to meet Sigmar.'

Rechts roared and drove at Greiss. Maybe it was the grog, maybe he was just slower, but Greiss was able to turn and plant his dagger into Rechts's neck before the drummer even got his hands up to try and choke him. Rechts burbled blood-flecked curses.

Karlich saw a slim chance and went for the assassin himself, but the pistol was in Greiss's hand as if it had always been there. A shot boomed across the knoll and Karlich spun with the impact of it in his shoulder. He staggered and fell. The bone was shattered and he cried out, clutching at it through his oozing blood.

Greiss withdrew the main gauche. Rechts was already dead when he slumped to the ground. Torveld was stirring too. Greiss lunged and pierced the Middenlander's eye. He died instantly.

Then Greiss turned to Karlich.

'You and me left,' he said with the hint of a smile. 'I offered you quick, you chose slow…'

'How about a third choice?'

The voice behind him made Greiss flinch.

Brand stepped from the shadows creeping back down the knoll in the face of the rising sun. 'Me.' He glanced at Rechts and his jaw clenched.

Too late to save one…

'Was hoping I'd kill you last,' Greiss replied. Karlich was in no shape to face a trained assassin but he kept half an eye on the sergeant anyway. 'Thought I'd lost *you* in the market,' he muttered.

'You're not the only one who can follow a lamb.' Brand drew his dirk.

There was the slightest of nods and then Greiss attacked.

Steel flashed in a grey blur, thrusting, lunging slashing for any of several death-wounds. Brand parried or dodged them all.

'Knew you were too good for a common soldier,' he snarled, raking his blade against the edge of Greiss's. Metal shards and sparks cascaded like flickering rain.

Greiss growled at him though his gritted teeth. 'So are you.'

They broke off, circling before leaping in again, their dagger strokes ringing like a blacksmith's anvil.

'Campaigning's made you rusty,' said Greiss, a second blade flashing into his hand from a concealed spring-mounted bracer. He plunged it into Brand's shoulder, drawing a cry of pain from the Reiklander. With the other hand Greiss pressed for Brand's throat. He dropped his dirk and held on to the assassin's wrist. 'One by one, you're all dead men. I'll gut y– *urrghh*!'

Greiss spat a gob of blood that ruined his tunic with a long, viscous streak. He looked down at the gory length of steel rammed up into his back that punched out through his chest. Karlich whispered in his ear behind him before Greiss died.

'*Grimblades fight as one.*'

Brand pushed the main gauche away from his throat and pulled the dagger out of his shoulder with a wince. Both Reiklanders backed away. Karlich left the sword embedded and watched Greiss buckle and fall. He knew he had lost a fair amount of blood but he'd be damned if he was going to lie down yet. His breath rasped a little as he spoke.

'Ledner really didn't want us to talk, did he?'

Brand had already strapped up his shoulder with a piece of cloth and knelt down by Greiss's body.

'Small wonder given he knew about the prince's killer and used our liege-lord as bait to draw the assassin out,' the sergeant added. 'Civil war be damned, Vogen is hearing of this.'

'It is worse than that,' said Brand, turning Greiss's head. There was a tattoo on the dead man's neck which exactly matched the one they had found on the Tilean assassin. 'No Marienburg gold this time.'

'That bastard...' uttered Karlich.

The killers were both Ledner's. With that truth came a chilling revelation. Not only did he know of Prince Wilhelm's assassination, he had orchestrated it. Ledner was the traitor.

CHAPTER TWENTY-FOUR

PATRIOTISM

Outside the walls of Wurtbad, capital of Stirland, 398 miles from Altdorf

BY NOW, ALL of Wurtbad and the mustering army beyond its walls knew of the foiled attempt on Prince Wilhelm's life. Most of the common soldiery were shocked and angered, others simply assumed it was the price of being Reikland royalty. Officers expressed outrage. Privately, they harboured suspicions that the prince's cousin, Emperor Dieter himself, was somehow responsible. This last rumour was perpetuated by cohorts of Adolphus Ledner. Like any good spymaster, he had many lackeys in his employ. But Ledner, usually ubiquitous in the presence of his lord, was not present when Wilhelm gave his reaction to the news.

'It changes nothing,' he said, fastening his scabbarded sword and tightening the straps on his breastplate. He was in one of Krieglitz's armouries, with the Lord Protector of Stirland looking on.

'Defy the will of the Emperor and expect consequences, is that the way of it?' he said. 'I heard the assassin's bribe was Marienburg gold. What do you think that means?'

Wilhelm glared at him as he was adjusting his leg greaves. 'You should not speak ill of your liege-lord and Emperor. As for the burgomeisters,' he added, 'who knows what those greedy merchants are up to. I had hoped Ledner would have discovered something by now.'

'Nuln's Golden Palace wasn't gilded by taxes alone, I'd say.'

Wilhelm paused in his battle preparation. 'Be careful who you say that to, Neder.' It wasn't a threat, more an expression of concern.

Krieglitz smiled thinly. He changed tack. 'Word will have reached most of the other provinces by next morning,' he said. 'You'll be a legend, Wilhelm – the noble Prince of Reikland who rode out to defend his Empire and crushed the vipers in his nest trying to stop him.'

'Am I so glorious? What have I achieved? Averland is ruined, much of Stirland is also devastated,' – Krieglitz's face darkened at this remark – 'and now I've failed to dismantle the greenskin horde and left the Reikmark open to invasion. Assassin or no, it's a bitter draught to swallow. *Legendary* is not how I would describe it.'

'Even still, you've made friends of the other electors and nobles. Backbone and courage, that's what the Empire needs most.'

'Just not friendly enough, eh, Neder?' The bitterness in Wilhelm's voice was obvious.

Captain Vogen appeared at the armoury door before Krieglitz could reply.

'Beg your pardon, lords,' he said, 'we are all but ready to march.'

Wilhelm nodded to the officer. 'Get them into order, captain. The orcs move west, so will we, and get ahead of them if we can.'

'Are we still bound for Nuln?' Vogen asked.

Wilhelm sheathed a dagger at his hip, the last of his war trappings. 'The beast will want to sack the capital and with it all but empty, there's nothing to stop the greenskins doing it.'

Vogen saluted and left to perform his duties. Just as he was going, Wilhelm stopped him.

'Have you seen Captain Ledner?'

'Not recently, my liege. But I could easily have missed him during the muster.'

Wilhelm gestured that he could leave.

'A concern?' asked Krieglitz when Vogen was gone.

'No,' Wilhelm decided. 'He'll turn up when he's needed, probably when I least expect it. Adolphus Ledner always does.'

KARLICH WAS HURRYING through the Wurtbad streets, taking side alleys and backways to avoid the commotion outside the temple of Sigmar near the town square, when he heard a sharp *click* from the shadows behind him. He stopped sharply and found a pistol trained on his torso as he turned.

'Couldn't let you run off to Vogen or the prince before we'd had a chance to talk,' said Ledner. His sibilant voice creaked like an old coffin.

'Slay me here and you'll bring the Watch running, quartermasters too and who knows who else,' countered Karlich, hiding his nerves.

'There are a hundred ways I could explain the gunshot and your corpse,' Ledner told him, stepping closer so the errant shafts of sunlight bathing the backstreet hit his face. The contrast of light and shade only made it more forbidding.

'For a man who claims to be a patriot, plotting to kill your own liege-lord seems like the deeds of a traitor,' said Karlich.

'Where are the rest of your men?' asked Ledner. 'The ones that still live,' he added without malice.

Karlich imagined wrapping his hands around the spymaster's throat and squeezing until all vitality had left him. 'Returned to the regiment, but you already knew that.'

Ledner allowed himself a small grunt of amusement. 'Yes, I did. Though, they are actually with my sergeants-at-arms, awaiting interrogation. Witnesses to murder,' – Ledner counted on his fingers – '*four* times over? Yes, the Middenlander makes four. Questions must be asked.'

'As we're about to march to Nuln? How did you explain that to the prince?'

'Wilhelm trusts my counsel, *sergeant*. You should know that.'

'Then he trusts a serpent!' Karlich spat, making fists. 'You're a snake in more than just your voice, *captain*.'

'Barbs are only painful if they're real,' Ledner told him. There were only a few feet between them. 'You're much too clever for a mere soldier–' A hacking cough stopped the spymaster. Karlich went to grab for him before the pistol came back up and Ledner regained his composure. 'Don't make me revise my opinion of you!' he snapped, still spluttering.

'Choking on your own lies?' Karlich framed a bitter smile.

'Amusing. You are quite a resourceful man. I never expected you or your footsloggers to best my Tilean, let alone kill Greiss,' said Ledner, more hoarsely than usual. 'He was from the Border Princes, not Averland, by the way.'

'Can't say I care. Dead is dead. Is this where you ask me to join your brood?'

'No,' Ledner said flatly. 'You have the wit for it, but not the moral ambiguity or ruthless pragmatism I require in my agents.' He paused to size Karlich up, gauging whether to kill him or let him live. 'I organised the assassination, the one I tasked you to foil,' he admitted at last. 'You already know this. Wilhelm was either supposed to die or be badly injured in the attempt. Either way, sympathy for our cause and that of the Empire would soar. Martyrs are potent rallying symbols.'

Karlich's anger was almost palpable. 'You said we could speak nothing of it, for fear of civil war.'

'Don't be naïve. You're better than that. Your success on the road back to Mannsgard was as unexpected as your discovery of my messenger. The Marienburg coin you found–'

Karlich interrupted, 'Was left for others to find in order to discredit the Emperor. Even my thick, *soldier's* ears have discerned some of dealings with the burgomeisters. Every sane son of Sigmar in the land knows of it.'

'By finding that wretch in the barn, you became a thorn. When my counter plan also failed, I decided to bring about the same result by killing you and letting slip that Wilhelm was attacked in the same breath. The prince's reputation will soon be enhanced. I confess, I had not thought of it originally but this is a better outcome. This way Wilhelm lives.'

'And us, my men and I, what is our fate?'

'I *am* a patriot of the Empire, but the Reikland above all else. Emperor Dieter's efficacy as ruler of our lands is questionable at best. I would also scrutinise his loyalty, for his Marienburg allies are no friends of the Empire.' Ledner dabbed a trickle of blood that had seeped from the corner of his lip. He'd coughed it up and Karlich wondered what else the man was hiding beneath his crimson scarf. 'Understand me, Karlich. Know that when I say I would do anything to protect the Empire and the Reik, I mean *anything*. Wilhelm is a brave leader but he could not challenge or overthrow the Emperor. Only as a martyr and the catalyst for revolution could he do that... until now.'

'How do you sleep with such plans twisting inside your head?'

Ledner smiled, as if the man before him had seen a measure of his soul.

'I don't want to kill you, Karlich,' he said.

'What's a little more blood? We'll all be drowning in it soon enough.'

'I hadn't thought of you as a fatalist. You're not like that shackled wolf in your regiment – the killer of killers.' Ledner raised his eyebrows, as if considering. 'Now, *he* would suit my purposes greatly, if I believed he could be controlled. No, you're a different animal altogether I think, much more savage.' He showed his teeth. '*They* don't see it, your precious Grimblades but *I* do, Lothar. I know it all too well, Lothar Henniker of

Ohslecht. That was the name of your village, wasn't it? The place where you killed a templar of Sigmar?'

Karlich's blood ran cold. He thought that part of his old life had ended with the headless witch hunter on the killing fields outside Averheim.

Ledner went on. 'I'm sure he and that brutal bastard Vanhans deserved it. Unfortunately for you, though, templars of Sigmar are a persistent, vengeful breed. They'd likely torture you first if they found you. *If* they found you. Do we have an understanding?'

Karlich was breathing hard through his nose, something between rage and fear. Compromise or death, why did it always come to those two choices with men like Ledner? After a few moments, he spoke.

'Release my men. Never approach or threaten me again.'

Ledner lowered his pistol. 'I knew you were wise, much too good to be a sergeant. I don't need to tell you what would happen if you broke our agreement. If any of you did...' He backed away until the shadows of the alley swallowed him.

Karlich waited until he was sure Ledner was gone then staggered up against the wall, hands bracing him as he retched. By the time he reached the army outside Wurtbad, what was left of his regiment would be waiting for him released from the sergeants-at-arms' custody. They'd survived Ledner's machinations, at least for a time. Now they just had to survive the green horde.

One way or another, it would end at Reikland.

CHAPTER TWENTY-FIVE
A RETURN TO THE RANKS

Stirland border, north-east of Averland,
394 miles from Altdorf

LEDNER REJOINED THE army several miles on the road out of Wurtbad. A long trail of soldiers, ranked in order of march and followed by baggage trains, streamed from the encampment site at the edge of town. A virulent scar was left in their wake, the remains of latrines, cookfires and earth churned by many booted feet. It would be weeks, assuming a cessation to the greenskin invasion, before the land could be restored.

Though the orcs and goblins were moving, bands of raiders still lingered in the province. Hunkering down in the hills and scratches of forest, it might be years before the recalcitrant greenskins were rooted out and expunged.

Krieglitz's huntsmen took the army south-east, down the Old Dwarf Road at first. They could make good time and try to forge ahead of Grom's horde pushing westward towards Reikland. Swift riders had already been sent to the province to warn the garrisons still manning Blood Keep, Helmgart and the barracks at Grünburg. Wilhelm doubted his cousin would admit, let alone heed his urgent missives. The Emperor's concerns were elsewhere, wrapped up in Marienburg gold and the charms of some courtly maidens, no doubt. Such languor while the Empire suffered made the prince sick with anger.

Barring its beleaguered capital, Averland was overrun so the southern border of Stirland was to be avoided. Nor did they wish to be slowed by the larger tributaries of the River Aver that bled into the province. In all likelihood, the crossings would be watched or even impassable. It was only a short way south-east before the army left the Old Dwarf Road and went west with the hills to the south instead. They would hug the northern border, close to Talabecland, make first for Kemperbad and any troops the prince still had there and then on to Nuln, hopefully ahead of the horde. The journey would take several days, possibly longer.

'Am I on a fool's errand, Ledner?' asked the prince as the spymaster rode up alongside him.

'Even if you were, I would keep such truths to yourself, lord. Our army is ragged enough.'

They were mainly an infantry force now with a predominance of citizen soldiers. Meinstadt's war machines were few and largely inconsequential. The knights were almost vanquished to a man. Those that remained stayed by the prince's side always, especially since the news of the assassination attempt had broken. From behind their visored helms they regarded every man who came into their liege-lord's presence as sternly as an enemy to be slain on the battlefield.

Some more Mootlanders had joined them, so too did the dwarf exiles march to Nuln, but half-breeds would hardly swing the balance of the war for Wilhelm or the Empire.

Krieglitz relented to an extent, impassioned by Wilhelm's stalwartness in the face of what he believed was Dieter's treachery. He made a cohort of his household guard available to the prince. The Hornhelms wore battered plate armour and their steeds could hardly be considered magnificent, but the knights-at-arms would accompany Wilhelm all the way to Nuln and fight for him as if he were their own lord. The huntsmen too, their guides along the northern border, would stay and fight. They were all Krieglitz's representatives while he and his army ventured forth to tackle the larger greenskin bands shed by Grom's immense horde still in his province. To the goblin king, they were just dregs. His army was formidable without them. To Krieglitz they were a pest threatening his subjects.

'Where have you been, Ledner?' Wilhelm asked after he'd allowed a brief silence to fall between them.

'With the quartermasters, dragging the walking wounded into the line of march. We'll need every spear and blade we have. Arrangements also had to be made for the dead and dying. Several of Morr's own raven-keepers had remained behind at Wurtbad.'

Wilhelm rode ahead but instructed his lead infantry officer to maintain the same pace. He also urged Ledner to follow. The Griffonkorps remnants came too, Wilhelm's armoured shadow. They would fight and die only. Ears and eyes closed to the prince's private dealings, the knights were as disciplined as statues in this conviction.

'Did you know?' he asked when they were out of earshot.

Ledner pursed his lips.

'Of course you did,' said the prince, 'you know everything concerning my business, even when I do not.' The remonstration in his tone bordered on outright anger.

'Had I acted sooner, the perpetrator would have escaped, slipped its noose,' Ledner replied. Utterly calm, it was hard to tell he'd incurred the ire of an Imperial prince, one that could have him executed with but a command to his knights. 'You'd be supping poison in your evening tonic or finding a viper in your bathwater, my lord. Perhaps a keg of blackpowder, fused and lit, rolled into your tent or a dagger in the back as you consulted your officers. Murder needn't be subtle or clean. But this I know: if you have an assassin within your grasp, you let him come...' Ledner made a fist, '...and crush him when he's close enough to touch.'

'You've made your point, Adolphus,' Wilhelm conceded, 'but if I find out you've used me as bait again, we will have words, you and I. Don't think me one of your tools to be manipulated.'

Ledner nodded contritely. 'Understood, my prince.'

'Good.' Wilhelm slowed his steed to allow the line of march to catch up. 'Now, tell me what faces us at Nuln.'

Ledner looked westward, his gaze unwavering. 'Blood, my prince. Rivers of blood are what await us there.'

EBER WAS SADDENED to learn of the death of his comrades. He rejoined the regiment outside Wurtbad, one of the many 'walking wounded' pressed back into service for what was being called the 'Preservation of

Reikland'. He had liked Rechts most of all, despite his bad temper, and Masbrecht had always struck him as a gentle soul. These men were more than his comrades; they were his family, in lieu of the one that had cast him out so cruelly when he was a boy.

He ached when he moved. His gait felt awkward and his breath came laboured after walking long distances. After the horrific knife attack, Eber was not the man he once was, the ox no longer. That saddened him too, but he vowed to stand and fight anyway, to ensure no more of his brothers in the Grimblades died if he could help it.

Something was going on. Two days of silence with Nuln growing closer all the while told him that. It was more than just grief affecting the other halberdiers. Eber had wondered if Ledner was the cause, that there was more to the deaths of his fellows than first appeared. Allegedly, the Middenlander Torveld had killed them. He'd also learned from Karlich that it was now a matter of military record that the soldier had done it out of revenge for what he saw as the Grimblades' culpability in the destruction of his regiment. A head wound supposedly afflicted the poor man, 'affected his humours' so the scrivened words of the physician went.

'Madness took him and it ended in blood,' Karlich had said, though it was clear he did not believe this fully, and that to utter the half lie rankled with the sergeant. Later, when he was sure prying eyes weren't watching, he'd spoken differently. 'Torveld was a bastard,' he'd said, whispering, 'but not a murderer, not like that.'

Eber had then learned of some of Ledner's role, at least that he was involved somehow, but nothing more.

It was another reason for Karlich to hate the spymaster. Rumours abound that witnesses had been paid off or silenced in order to foster Ledner's lie. The soldiers in the Grimblades' regiment were painted as victims of circumstance, which they were, only not in the way the spymaster had portrayed.

Eber was not gifted with the quickest wit; he knew that and accepted his limitations. Some people regarded him as credulous and gullible, but even he knew the story was a falsehood before Karlich had confided in him. He didn't dig for further answers, assuming they were best left unearthed, but it laid an uncomfortable pall over his brothers in arms that he didn't like.

He decided to do something about it and broke into bellowing song.

'The Burgher of Bögen had such girth, 'tis a wonder his mother did give birth...'

He'd learned the ditty years ago. Though his voice was not as strong as Rechts's had been, Eber gave it his all.

'...to a brute of a son without much grace, feet from the Moot and a round, red face!'

At the end of the front rank, he glanced sideways at Karlich who joined him in the second verse that added further scorn on to the Burgher of Bögen's 'legend'. Pretty soon, all of the Grimblades were singing. Volker, who became drummer in Rechts's absence, beat out the marching rhythm. It spread down the column. The Averlanders and Stirlanders in the army took up the song, too. They didn't know the words but it was unimportant. The halflings brought out pipes and spoons by way of instrumental accompaniment. Even the dwarfs *hrummed* and *hroomed* to the tune. It was a strange, discordant sound, likened to the filling and exhaling of bellows or the slow movement of earth. No man could repeat it.

Eber came to the end of the song, a rousing crescendo supplied by the enthusiastic Mootlanders and the mood lightened.

Volker laughed loudly, there was relief in the gesture, and slapped Eber on the back. It drew a wince from the burly Reiklander that he hid well behind a broad smile.

'It's been many years since I heard that marching song.' It was Vogen, touring the line on his steed, seeing to the courage and morale of the men. His task was almost done for him and he smiled, twisting his large moustaches upwards. He trotted over to Karlich, maintaining pace with that part of the column.

'Captain,' said the sergeant, and the others in the front ranks followed suit.

'Your voice would benefit from some melody, though,' Vogen said to Eber with a subtle wink at Karlich.

Eber nodded then flushed a little.

'No need to stand on ceremony,' the portly captain from Kemperbad told them, whilst adjusting the belt at his waist. 'I am not Stahler, but he told me much of the men in his command,' he added, smoothing his beard with a gauntleted hand. Vogen was so bulky and broad he had more in common with the dwarf exiles than his own kith and kin.

'Then he would've said the Grimblades respect their officers,' answered Karlich. It was the first time he'd really spoken to Captain Vogen. With Nuln looming like a black cloud on the horizon, he wondered if it would be the last.

Further down the line another marching song began.

'We'll need our spirits up for what's to come,' said Vogen. It was like he'd reached in and grasped at Karlich's thoughts. He found he liked the man at once. The captain looked down at the sergeant's hip.

'That was his sword, wasn't it?' There was sorrow in his voice.

Karlich nodded humbly.

'It's good that you keep it,' Vogen told him. 'Stahler would've wanted that, to fight with us at the end.'

'And is it "the end"?' asked Karlich, the old scars on his face starting to itch.

Vogen looked to the west, as if trying to scry their destinies. 'Of the campaign? Yes, I believe it will end in the Reik. We'll give our blood for that land, more than any other. No son of Reikland will abandon it. Our bodies would litter the fields before that ever happened.' The grim mood returned for a spell. Sensing it, Vogen changed the subject.

'We'll be joining up with reinforcements from inside the province,' he said. 'Garrisons from Blood Keep and Grünburg are assembling to the north of the city. It's mainly a citizen militia force but these are Reikland men with Reikland blood – I'd take that over hirelings any day of Mitterfruhl. The barrack houses will arm them and we must be ready to meet them near the border. Together, we'll turn back the green tide.

'We need only bloody their nose. Survival of the Reik, and by extension the Empire, is all that matters now.'

'Sir...' Volker interrupted.

Karlich shot him a stern glance before following the scout's pointing finger towards the horizon. They'd just crested a rise and the lay of the Reikland had unfolded before them in the distance. It was not all they saw.

A thin haze of smoke drifted languidly above another range of hills.

The spate of singing stopped as the other regiments saw it too.

Lenkmann narrowed his eyes. 'What is that?'

A solitary horn rang out. Captain Vogen was needed at the head of the column. He rode off without a word.

'It's Nuln,' said Brand, voicing aloud what everyone was thinking.

The capital of the Empire was already burning.

CHAPTER TWENTY-SIX
BURNING IN BLACK

Outside Nuln, capital of the Empire,
289 miles from Altdorf

A DAY LATER they reached Nuln. There was little of the city left. A flickering shell of a city danced with shadows created by the fires within. Nuln's once proud walls were ransacked and gaping, like a festering wound. A killing field littered the land outside it. Men in the black tunics of the capital lay dead in their droves, broken remains of war machines were scattered around like chaff and fat flies droned about the carcasses of steeds in noisome clouds.

Before coming to the capital, Wilhelm had almost emptied Kemperbad on the way. There was just a skeleton garrison left behind. The reinforcements were mainly citizen levies again, the prince's legend having spread to all men of the Reik, who pledged to his cause as their worthy and noble saviour. The army's stay was brief but as Wilhelm and his warriors rode through the square, children placed garlands around their necks, women gave prayers and men their strength of arms. Young and old, strong and infirm, all swore to fight for Wilhelm and the Reikland.

At Nuln, they barely reached the city's outer milestone. At Kemperbad, Wilhelm not only gained troops and goodwill, he also discovered that Nuln's army had been defeated, the city sacked. The forces due to meet them from Grünburg and Blood Keep had apparently joined up with the defenders. How many now survived was unknown. It might be none.

Grom had moved on but some of his warbands remained. They'd come to a nervous halt and the Empire column broke ranks as the men, unable to comprehend the horror of their glorious capital as a blackened ruin, wandered loose and suddenly bereft of hope.

A ragged-looking scout approached Prince Wilhelm, who rode a little way out to meet him with three of his Griffonkorps in close attendance. The boy was almost battered to the ground by a knight's armoured steed before the prince ordered them to stand back and let the poor wretch through.

'Nothing left, my liege,' he said, breathlessly. A runner from the baggage train brought him water and he drank deeply before continuing. 'The army was defeated. All except Lord Grundel, who holds the west quarter of the city...' At that the distant echo of cannon fire rang out.

'Albrecht Grundel,' muttered Ledner, close by. 'He was... *vocal* in court at the lassitude of the Nuln army. Likely, he kept his household troops well drilled, unlike the city-state forces.' He looked down at the messenger from atop his steed and gestured to the fallen soldiers in the distance. Wilhelm had ordered the column be brought up short of the city after hearing the news out of Kemperbad. 'Where are the rest, boy? This can't be it.'

'Altdorf, my lord. The rest fled to Altdorf.' The scout ferreted around inside his jerkin, pulling out a scrap of parchment. 'I was given this by Captain Dedricht.'

'Do we know him?' Wilhelm asked Ledner in a low voice.

'Commander of the Grünburg force,' he said, as one of the Griffonkorps dismounted and stalked up to the boy. Snatching the parchment, the knight delivered it to the prince a moment later before getting back on his steed.

Wilhelm frowned as he read.

Retreated across the hills. Nuln is defeated. Blood Keep and Grnburg are still at fighting strength. More regiments are arriving from Helmgart and Ubersreik. Will meet on the Axe Bite Road between Bgenhafen and Altdorf. Faith in Sigmar.

Capn. Elias Dedricht

'Faith in Sigmar,' Wilhelm muttered and clenched the parchment in his fist. The prince's face was grim. He lifted the spyglass to his eye. Nuln's gatehouse was badly breached and offered an unobstructed view into the heart of the city. His expression hardened further.

'Ranald's teeth, the Paunch will pay in blood! I see chariots roaming Nuln's streets and orcs run amok.' He put down the spyglass before he broke it in a fit of rage. The scout balked beneath the prince's glare.

'What's become of the Golden Palace?'

'S-stripped b-bare, my liege. It's nothing but a pen for the greenskins' beasts.'

The poor lad was on the verge of collapse. They'd get nothing further from him. Ledner was about to press for more when Wilhelm raised a hand to stop him.

'Enough. Go to the baggage train,' he said to the scout. The lad blinked back tears from inside a soot-blackened face. Dried blood caked his dirty hair. 'Tell them to give you food and water. You're to ride in one of the carts until we reach Altdorf. Tell them it's the prince's order. Now go.'

The lad bowed profusely and scurried off towards the distant baggage trains.

'What now?' asked Ledner. 'What of the capital?'

'Men grew fat and rested on the laurels of old glories, Ledner,' he said, 'sure in the knowledge that no foe would ever venture as far west as Nuln. Now look at it.'

The city was a wraith, looming across a sea of dead. It was a charnel house and although Wilhelm railed at leaving Albrecht Grundel unreinforced, he had no choice but to press on and try and save the city that was still intact – *his* city.

'Nuln is lost,' was the prince's dire proclamation. 'We go to Altdorf. The dead here are barely cold. There might be time enough to overtake the goblin warlord before he reaches the city.' Wilhelm considered it before he continued. 'There are passes through the hills that the greenskins won't know about. It's rugged land but fit enough for marching. We'll use one to get ahead of the horde.'

'We'll join with Dedricht's force?'

'Even our combined army can't match the greenskins,' said Wilhelm. 'I have another idea. Get three of our fastest messengers and meet me at the front. Do it quickly.'

Wilhelm reined his steed around and rode back to the head of the army. The column was reforming as Ledner went the opposite way to gather the messengers the prince requested.

As they marched on with despair in their hearts, the desolate boom of cannons raked the blood-scented breeze.

CHAPTER TWENTY-SEVEN
THE VALLEY OF DEATH

Reikland hills, on the Bögenhafen road,
34 miles from Altdorf

GROM'S GREEN HORDE swept down the Reikland hills like a contagion, defiling everything it touched. To the naked eye it appeared as if the land undulated with an obscene tempo. Orc and goblin heads bobbed in the tide, jeering and bellowing. It was hard to define tribes – the beasts massed in a stinking ruck, the larger battering the lesser and so on to the smallest creature. Like their enemies, the earth was beaten and brutalised beneath the greenskins' chariots and hobnailed boots. Their dung choked the very life from it, the once verdant Imperial fields reduced to a cesspit of filthy mud. Such was the price of open war.

A paltry force of defenders defied the orcs at the bottom of a small valley. It rose sharply behind them and would make any retreat difficult. Beyond that rise was the road to Altdorf. Grom had marched the most direct route. There would be no further delays. The Empire was within his meaty goblin fist. Altdorf represented its last defiant bastion. Every man amongst the defenders knew it couldn't get that far. They might have no choice. They were ragged and despairing in their serried ranks, so bedraggled that they looked incapable of flight even if they had to. This would be a last stand.

The valley sides were just as sheer as its mouth and the orcs funnelled into it in a screaming flood. Grom wanted Altdorf. He wanted to sack this proud city of men, the ancestral capital of Sigmar, as he had already sacked Nuln. And he didn't want to wait.

Prince Wilhelm's jaw was set as hard as stone as the greenskins came for them. He waited in the centre of a long battleline of roughly a thousand men, mounted on his warhorse. Captain Dedricht was to the east side of the valley, grim-faced and on foot, gripping his halberd like it was life itself. Aside from the Griffonkorps bodyguards, the rest of the force was also on foot. They looked worn and tired. They were – the passage across the hills had been hard. Their uniforms were ripped and scuffed, and they stank of sweaty fear. Banners dipped as the thin breeze wafting down through the valley ebbed to nothing. Even dug in behind makeshift barricades and several upturned carts, the Empire army couldn't hope to hold for long.

The noise of charging greenskin feet and rumbling chariots built to a crescendo. It was deafening, made louder by the dense, hard rock of the enclosed valley walls.

For a moment, the chariots pulled ahead but then foundered when they hit a patch of rough stones strung out in a line that extended the full width of the valley. Here was the first of Wilhelm's deterrents. The greenskin mobs behind the previously faster machineries overtook them. Picking their way through the rubble, some of the larger orcs upturned several of the lighter chariots, so eager were they to bloody their blades.

The natural funnel of the valley pressed the orcs and goblins tighter. Grom was somewhere amongst them, snarling commands and keeping order. It was hard, even for the Paunch. The greenskins recognised the Empire army in front of them was bloodied, like a wounded animal. They wanted to put it down. No greenskin could resist bullying the weak and these men were laid low. Even the goblin king could not deny his own nature. He too bayed for manflesh, held so tantalisingly before his tongue.

Deep into the valley bottom, well below the ridges on either side and with the greenskins barely a hundred feet away, a banner rose up in the Empire ranks. A chorus of muted trumpets rang out, signalling to all.

Far from holding the line and giving up their blood for the Empire, Wilhelm and his army fled.

They had seen the sheer strength of Waaagh! Grom and quailed.

It only goaded the Paunch all the more. His prize was running up the valley ridge, directly away from his horde. Urging his mobs to greater efforts, he was determined to catch the 'humies' before they reached the summit.

Wilhelm, cantering in order to keep pace with the foot troops, did not get to the valley peak, nor did he intend to. Instead, he came up about twenty feet short. Another banner went up, more clarion calls echoed on the dead air. The Empire line reformed, became much tighter, much denser than before, its ranks packed and deep. Shield walls were raised and locked, spears levelled. A ragged band of defenders became a tough and determined rectangle of soldiers. The second part of Wilhelm's plan happened a moment later.

Imperial war cries spilled down over the east and west ridges, thousands of men followed them, two flanking forces comprised of state regiments and citizen militia. The western force contained the Hornhelms, the flower of Stirland's cavalry. Several stern-faced state regiments accompanied them. The slowly-dipping lances of the knights sent a shiver of fear through the greenskins they barrelled towards. The eastern force was on foot, led by Captain Vogen. Stolid dwarfs joined the Empire ranks of swords, pikes and militia. Mootlanders ranged their flanks.

Behind the prince, who had resumed his position in the centre of the battleline, a fourth force appeared. The remnants of Meinstadt's war machines and all of the harquebuses were suddenly levelled at the onrushing green horde. The goblin frontrunners faltered in places and there was a collision of bodies. The larger orcs remained uncowed and hacked through their more timid brethren if they held them up.

Like a piece of meat, Wilhelm had dangled the prospect of a quick and bloody win before the Paunch. He was greedy, this Grom, and he had taken the bait readily. Though still outnumbered, the Empire had trapped the greenskins in the narrow defile and could attack on three aspects at once. Victory was far from assured, but at least now they had a fighting chance.

KARLICH'S SHOULDERS ACHED from heaving the carriage of the great cannon up to the ridgeline. Several regiments were positioned with the war engines, partly to defend them, partly to get them where they needed to be. The first task was done – blackpowder smoke already laced the air from the opening salvoes, and set ears ringing with *thudding* reports – the second, keeping the machines from harm, would not be as easy.

The Grimblades made ranks quickly, stationed just below one of the two great cannon. Meinstadt still had the volley gun and one of the mortars left too. The latter was aimed at the rear of the greenskin lines, where its explosive shells would cause maximum damage but pose minimum risk to friendly troops. A deadly barrage landed deep in the valley, throwing greenskins and dirt plumes into the air with brutal ease.

Lenkmann pumped his fist, thrilled at the ingenuity of the Empire taking such a toll on the beasts, but the hole in the mobs was quickly filled and his optimism disappeared with it.

'It's as if it never happened, just like at Averheim,' he said, holding onto his banner with both hands as if it supported him. 'They're endless.'

'You expected any different,' grumbled Volker, sticks held fast against his pigskin drum. The instrument still felt awkward, as if he were wearing a dead man's coat that didn't fit. Rechts had been the Grimblades' beating heart. To carry his drum felt like a transgression, not an honour. Volker wondered if it was time to leave the army.

Karlich intruded on his thoughts. 'We don't need to beat them,' he said, rotating his shoulder blade where it was still sore, 'just bloody them enough to force the greenskins out of Reikland.'

'I thought orcs liked to fight?' queried Eber. The big man was a welcome presence in the ranks, though the bindings around his chest suggested he might not have much fight left in him. 'Won't that just make them want to fight more?'

'Anything that lives doesn't want to die,' Brand told him. 'Greenskins are no different.'

'There'll be much dying this day, before it's out,' said Volker.

Karlich adjusted his shield straps, looking down at the throng below. 'Be thankful you're up here and not amongst that.'

Farther down the valley from the Grimblades' position, Wilhelm's baiting force made a slow advance. With higher ground and Imperial discipline to gird them, the ragged soldiery could effectively 'bung' the valley. They were so closely packed, they'd be hard to rout. Wilhelm's presence, shining in his gilded armour plate, would galvanise them further. Even still, it was a meat grinder.

Hope, what there was of it, seemed very far away.

'Should we make our farewells now?' asked Lenkmann with genuine regret.

Volker went to reply, when Karlich stopped him.

'Leave it unsaid. It's a bad omen to honour the dead before they're in the ground,' he added. 'Tends to end up putting them there.'

Another blast of powder smoke obscured the foot-sloggers before they met with the first of Grom's orcs. Karlich was still wiping soot from his eyes when the clash of arms resolved itself on the low breeze.

At the valley sides, on the east and west slopes, similar struggles played out. The high ridge and the backline afforded a strong vantage point from which to see the entire battle. Maybe that's why Wilhelm appointed

Ledner to marshal the rearguard force. Karlich had seen the spymaster only once after deployment. Even as he surveyed the carnage below, as the Hornhelms split off from combat and reformed for another charge, as pike and sword met with cleaver and club, as skulls were split and bodies sundered, Karlich knew Ledner was close by. It felt like a blade against his back, poised to thrust.

SMOKE ROLLED DOWN into the valley like fog. It was not so different to Averheim, but here it gathered in the valley's low trough. Wilhelm's horse fought the reins a little as the grey-white mist engulfed them. With the weak breeze unable to shift it, the smoke lingered at the valley bottom in a thick pall. It smothered the greenskins, making them appear numberless as they emerged from it in droves.

The element of surprise was spent. The fighting was fast and dirty now. Wilhelm's runefang was well bloodied as the giant black orc loomed into view. It appeared as a shadow at first, like a beast of the deep oceans slowly surfacing. He felt the Griffonkorps close protectively around him. The axe, too large and heavy for a man to wield, cut through the mist first. One of the Griffonkorps fell away with hardly a sound but minus his head. The carpet of fog swallowed him like he was just a memory.

A second knight managed to angle a sword thrust before the black orc's claw snapped out and seized him by the helmet. The Griffonkorps elicited a sort of squeak as his skull was crushed.

In the intervening seconds, Wilhelm pushed forward ahead of his protectors. The black orc emerged fully from the pooling smoke. It was huge. Eye-to-eye with the prince, despite the fact he was mounted, it snarled and bit off the horse's head. Part of the poor creature's skull remained as it collapsed to the ground, gushing blood, taking Wilhelm with it. The horse's demise was slow enough for the prince to leap free and still keep his feet, after a fashion. All around him, the desperate fighting went on. Parts of the shield wall nearby crumpled against the enemy's savagery. Spears were snapped like twigs but the Empire line held.

The shadow of the axe swept over Wilhelm, hard to discern in the press of bodies and the tumult of battle. Another Griffonkorps gave his life so the prince might live, horse and knight cleaved almost in two. Wilhelm used these seconds to get a solid footing. The black orc beast was not alone. Its slightly smaller, but no less brutal, brethren crowded out the other Empire soldiers near the prince's side. He would face the beast alone. Somewhere, probably during the fall, he'd lost his shield, so he held Dragontooth two-handed. Wilhelm knew he'd only get one chance at the monstrous black orc and he'd need all of his strength to kill it, even with the magical dwarf blade.

Obviously a warlord and one of Grom's chieftains, the orc's skin was like dark leather only more rugged. Thick mail armour swathed a heavily-muscled body that heaved with barely fettered rage. The axe was the size of a cart wheel, notched with use and stained crimson. Spiked boots added unnecessary height, while the black orc's skull was stitched with scars. Around its neck it wore a ring of desiccated halfling corpses as a man might wear a charm of wolf's teeth. The beast bellowed, showering the prince with foul spittle. Its rancid breath stank of rotten meat.

The clash of arms surrounded Wilhelm. He was in the eye of a massive storm but the war had narrowed into this one fight, this moment of kill or be killed. The prince tried to step back, telling himself it was for a better fighting stance and not because he balked at the ferocious creature, but found there was no room. It didn't matter anyway. The black orc had issued its challenge. Now it advanced, axe swinging like a deadly pendulum.

'Strength of Sigmar,' Wilhelm muttered, kissing his blade in the manner of the old ways, and went to meet the beast.

STARING INTO NOTHING was getting maddening. For the last few minutes Karlich had watched the belt of thickening smoke, alert for the first sign of a greenskin breakthrough. He blinked away several imagined horrors in the mist, before realising all was well. Sweat sheened his forehead, though he wasn't hot. With the pale cloud wreathing the field, tendrils of it reaching up to them on the ridge, a nervous tension gripped the valley. There was little to see now, even from on high, just half-shadows moving in the false fog and the sounds of battle.

It was eldritch, unsettling. Lenkmann clamped a hand over his mouth to still his chattering teeth. The grey white smoke played on his fears, reminding the banner bearer of something unnatural. Lenkmann saw ghosts in that growing cloud. In some respects, it wasn't so far from the truth. Some of the shadows were soon just echoes where once they'd been lives. The smoke deadened, evoking a sense of the strange and disquieting. It was made worse by the presence of the great cannon so nearby.

The fate of Blaselocker was put into Karlich's mind as the war machine boomed only feet above them. The baron's shredded remains had to be portioned away in separate sacks when the cannon had exploded alongside him. The raven-keepers were still removing iron shards from his flesh when poor Blaselocker was half assembled on a slab in the temple of Morr.

The cannon thundered again, rocking on wedged wheels. Karlich winced, dipping his head against the noise. When he opened his eyes, he noticed the pommel of his inherited blade glinting. It brought back the memory of Stahler. He'd be laughing at him, no doubt. Karlich drew comfort from the imagined presence of his old captain embodied by the sword. Some of the smoke had cleared a little when he looked up again and saw Stahler's replacement, Vogen, fighting hard on the east flank.

Fortunately the greenskins had yet to right themselves. The smoke added to their disorder and confusion, and they fought at a disadvantage. Without more manpower, though, the Empire couldn't press it. Attrition governed the battle at that moment. With the greenskins' superior numbers, it meant the balance would soon shift as the casualties mounted on both sides. They needed to find a way to break the orcs, and soon.

Ledner's choke-rasp shouting above brought Karlich from the throng below and back up to the ridge. He was directing some of the cannon fire for Engineer Meinstadt, picking out targets in the fog. Somewhere in the distance, a goblin chariot exploded in a shower of wooden splinters. They'd navigated the rocks intended to foul them and were roaming the flanks. There was little room, but the narrow machines snuck through.

Shifting his gaze, Karlich found the centre of the battlefield to be almost occluded but the smoke was slowly beginning to dissipate. He recognised the Carroburg Few and wished they were side-by-side. Von Rauken's men slowly resolved in the fog, fighting hard against a mob of massive, dark-skinned orcs. Something even bigger bellowed and hollered in their ranks before a belt of fog veiled them again.

Karlich said a quiet prayer that it wasn't the last time he'd see them alive.

THE IRONY WASN'T lost on Ledner. Despite his stern words to the spymaster on the road to Altdorf, Wilhelm had offered himself up as bait to draw the Paunch out. He suppressed a wry smile at that thought, allowing only a moment of reflection, before turning his attention back to the cannon. The goblin king, his death or serious injury, was key to victory. As it so often did, greenskin supremacy depended on the strength and willpower of its warlord. Without Grom, the disparate tribes would quickly fragment, lesser chieftains would vie for the leadership of the army and the Waaagh would slowly dissipate.

Bloody their nose... It was a phrase Ledner had heard much of in the intervening hours since leaving Kemperbad and before the battle.

The Paunch was shrewd, far shrewder than any goblin had a right to be, he would not be goaded easily. Wilhelm had to offer up a trophy for his rack the greenskin could truly savour. The only bargaining piece that the prince had, though, was himself. It was a risk Ledner didn't like. Using Wilhelm to reveal an assassin, with potential benefits resulting from either outcome, was one thing; the prince's death on this fog-choked field would mean the sack of Altdorf. The spymaster could see much at stake, and much that could go wrong. It wasn't a game he liked playing, when the odds were evenly stacked.

These machinations had been flooding through Ledner's mind like irritated moths bouncing off the glass of a lantern. Worse still, Wilhelm had ordered him to the ridge. War machines were dangerous, the province of madmen, but it was the fact that he couldn't be by the prince's side that bothered him the most. Ledner suspected their earlier 'words' had something to do with that. Or perhaps it was a less emotionally-driven decision than it first appeared, and Wilhelm was merely being practical. If he fell in battle, then it would be up to Ledner to rally the troops or marshal the retreat. Either way, leadership would be needed.

It didn't matter. Fate was not yet done with the Prince of Reikland, nor was it done with Adolphus Ledner.

He waited for a short subsidence in the cannonade before turning in his saddle to address Meinstadt.

'Engineer, how long can we keep this up?'

The cannons bellowed again, their iron cargo buoyed on fat streams of powder smoke spat from fire-blackened mouths.

Meinstadt hollered at one of the gunnery crew with the volley gun to rotate its barrel array – Ledner eyed the so-called 'wonder weapon' suspiciously, glad he was well away from it – before replying.

'We're low on ball and powder,' the engineer said, leaving an oil smear across his forehead after mopping his brow. Most of the gunnery crew had shed their tunics and let the sweat sheathe their brawny, smoke-stained bodies. They were as black as coal miners, and twice as grim. 'When that's done, we'll go to grapeshot. Hope you've a few coins in that expensive-looking attire you're wearing, captain,' he added wryly. 'We might need them.'

Ledner's retort was lost in the gunfire, and he gave up repeating it. Before he returned his attention to the field, he bemoaned the lack of ammunition to which Meinstadt gave the equivalent of a vocal shrug then went back to his labours.

One saving grace was that at least the prince had arrayed some decent troops around him. Though now he looked more intently, through the spyglass Wilhelm had given him to observe the field, Ledner saw the Grif-fonkorps had thinned to almost nothing and the greatsworders were struggling against a mob of hulking black orcs. Their banner dipped and swayed frantically as they tried to reach the prince. They had good reason - Wilhelm was facing an absolute monster. Ledner had only seen ogres as big. Had the beast not been green, he would've assumed it *was* an ogre.

Something caught Ledner's eye, just at the periphery of his vision. He angled the spyglass eastward and caught sight of the prince's prey. It was Grom, ranging along the flank, content to let the battle unfold and develop, so he could better read it.

Ledner shook his head, disbelieving.

Truly, this fat brute was unique – he could think! He plotted and planned like a man! Mercy of Shallya, not all greenskins are created thusly or the Empire would drown in its own blood. It might yet!

Fascinated, Ledner watched the Paunch catch and commandeer a chariot that was slow to build momen-tum after stalling on the rocks. He hauled the crew off and took their place. As he climbed aboard, the carriage of the chariot dug into the earth like a wooden plough, dragged down by Grom's heavy body. The wolves pulling it strained at their crude tresses, struggling to ferry the obese goblin king. Under his fierce goading, they picked up speed. Fear lent them vigour.

Greenskins in the Paunch's path either stepped aside or were crushed under the chariot's ironbound wheels.

Ledner guessed at Grom's direction. He followed the path suggested by his erratic journey on the chariot and found Wilhelm at the end of it. The prince was engaged with the giant black orc and hadn't seen the goblin king approaching.

A pang of something resembling anxiety twisted Ledner's gut. It was a fleeting emotion, hard to discern. He seldom felt anything but calm detachment.

'This is why I never leave your side, my lord,' he muttered bitterly. Ledner urged his steed forwards, heading for the slope and Prince Wilhelm.

CHAPTER TWENTY-EIGHT

THE VALUE OF SACRIFICE

Reikland hills, on the Bögenhafen road,
34 miles from Altdorf

FEINT. EVADE. STRIKE. The words of Kogswald entered Wilhelm's mind from the past: *remember these three rules when fighting a foe bigger and stronger than you. Move quickly and attack when your opponent tires, victory by a thousand cuts is still victory.*

But the giant black orc showed no sign of tiring, nor would it die by a thousand cuts. One chance, one cut, was all that Wilhelm would get, if that.

A small arena of dirt had grown around the two combatants, despite the efforts of the Empire troops to reach their lord. Wilhelm was glad of it; at least he didn't feel like a drowning man anymore. When the black orc attacked, it charged like a bull. When it passed for a third time, Wilhelm heard deep grunting before its bulk was reduced to a shadow in the fog. It struck a glancing blow to the prince's pauldron. Only the virtue of the armour's forging kept his shoulder from shattering. The monster came again, turning quickly on its heel and resolving through the gloom. Something hot struck Wilhelm's face. Belatedly he realised it was freshly shed blood from the black orc's axe.

This time the prince stood his ground. Dragontooth had taken on a strange, dull glow in the fog. An overhead swipe drove towards his head. He only just parried it, jarring both arms, but deflecting the blow downwards. The axe was buried deep in the ground. Pounding greenskin feet had loosened the soil at the valley bottom and the earth received the blade gratefully.

Wilhelm took his chance. The effort of parrying sent his runefang away from the black orc, but he used the momentum of the attack to carry on the swing. It went full circle in the time it took for the black orc to realise his axe was snared, and impaled the monster's skull.

The black orc shuddered, the pathetic halfling corpses around his neck quivering as if they were dancing. Wilhelm pushed hard against bone until his runefang pierced the greenskin's tiny brain. The black orc let go of its axe, still refusing to yield and acknowledge it was dead. Wilhelm wrenched Dragontooth free. The enchanted blade tore through the monster's head, decapitating it from the chin upwards. The slab of stinking skull and meat sloped off the ruddy stump like a cut from a butcher's block. Its claws stopped grasping inches from the prince's throat and the giant black orc slumped into a heap.

A spike of dissolution shot through the other black orcs, stunned at the chieftain's death. Sensing a turn in the fight, the Carroburg Few drove even harder at the greenskins. Together with a large regiment of Auerswald spearmen, they broke the black orcs and sent them reeling. Several goblin mobs which had previously been eager to join the winning side lost heart and fled too. Wilhelm ordered the line to hold and reform.

'Draw out the warlord,' he shouted. The prince was still stranded in the open, unaware that he already had.

He was marshalling his strength when a spectacular explosion lit the ridge behind him, sending burning shrapnel into the ranks below. Men standing several feet away were struck and killed. Wilhelm turned, along with others in the army, to witness a massive fireball ignite the ridge.

KARLICH TASTED EARTH as he was thrown down and scattered with the other halberdiers by a tremendous blast wave. Heat pricked the hairs on the back of his neck and despite the grubby tang of soil in his mouth, he embraced the instinct to sink his face down further.

It had come from the vicinity of the volley gun, he guessed, though it was hard to tell with his senses momentarily shredded. He still couldn't see or hear properly. Soot stained the air black, making it hard to breathe. Somewhere amidst the deafening explosion of blackpowder a horse shrieked.

'Come together, come–' Karlich's voice was choked by coughing. Smoke filled his lungs and he brought up thick black phlegm. Wiping his mouth, he looked around. Shapes emerged as the black clouds slowly cleared. He was still dazed, only vaguely aware he was alone, when he noticed dead men strewn upon the ridgeline. War machine crew and harquebus gunners were the main casualties. Meinstadt's voice rose above the panicked clamour, attempting to restore order. Karlich thought the engineer had been with the volley gun and wondered briefly how he'd managed to survive the blast before he saw the dead horse.

Though peppered with hot metal from the sundered cannon, its insides now its outsides, Karlich recognised the steed as Ledner's. Following the unfortunate beast's path, he found its master not far away, rolling on his back, dazed. He was quite far from the summit of the ridge. Ledner had been moving away when the volley gun misfired. If not, he'd surely be amongst the dead.

The world had dimmed into a narrow half-blur, as if he was seeing it through an underwater tunnel. Karlich's hearing was still affected too, but he didn't let it stop him stumbling towards the spymaster.

'On your feet,' he snarled, feeling his hate for the man anew. Karlich seized Ledner's hand, almost got him level, then slipped, sending the two of them back down again.

A bestial cry echoed from farther down the valley, tinny with the explosion still reverberating in Karlich's skull. Orcs had broken through the first line, part of the east flank crumpling when one of the militia regiments had made for the edge of the valley in utter terror. They were big, not the size of black orcs, but burly and thickly armoured.

'Get up!' said Karlich with more urgency than bile this time. His hearing came back in a crash of sound. He staggered at first, but quickly composed himself. ' said up, you bastard.'

Ledner smiled, drooling blood from where he'd lost a couple of teeth. He had a cut across his forehead, too, and held his wounded arm gingerly as he rose.

'Here's your chance, *Lothar*,' he said. 'I'm at your mercy. I can see it in your eyes!'

Karlich had his dirk and Ledner was injured and unarmed. A swift glance behind revealed they were separated from the rest of the men, a belt of thick smoke clouding the view.

No one would ever know.

All the things Ledner had done, the way he'd manipulated them. He'd cost Karlich friends and comrades, forced them to compromise their own morals to serve his shady ones. This was a man willing to sacrifice his prince and liege-lord. However noble the cause, nothing could excuse that. Karlich had him by the scruff of the neck.

It would be easy.

All this flashed through the sergeant's mind before he made his decision.

'No.' He pulled Ledner up, helped him onto his shoulder. 'I killed in cold blood before,' he said, walking him back up the ridge. 'I did it for love. I won't do it for hate, not for you. And in any case,' he added, whispering into Ledner's ear, 'your death will come soon enough. I saw the blood on your lip in the alley. Lung rot is a painful way to go.'

The mask slipped for a moment before Karlich looked away again, all of Ledner's insecurities and fears revealed to him. Let him die in agony; Karlich's conscience would be clear.

Ahead of the two men, the Grimblades were reforming. Mercifully, it looked like no casualties had been sustained in the blast, just pounding heads and grazed knees. Karlich was already shouting up to the great cannon, warning them about the approaching orcs when Ledner found his wits and pointed to the opposite side of the valley.

'No, there!'

Meinstadt never saw Ledner. His eyes were on the orc mob advancing on the war machines. Fearing they'd be overrun, he ordered up pails of coins, nails, spoons and anything else they could find to stuff the cannon with and fire grapeshot. It would render the weapon useless for the rest of the battle but at least they'd survive a little longer. The beasts were bearing down on them. By the time the cannon was turned and primed, they'd be too close for an iron ball.

Karlich followed Ledner's outstretched hand. He saw Grom, riding a lop-sided chariot, heading for the prince who'd just despatched a monstrous black orc and hadn't seen the goblin king.

He looked back down the ridge. The armoured orcs were clanking up the slope, gathering momentum. They looked tough. The Grimblades were still shaken from the explosion. Across the valley, Prince Wilhelm stood in the path of the goblin king's chariot. The cannon couldn't pepper the orcs with grapeshot *and* fire on the chariot. The latter was a risk, but without intervention the prince would be run down.

Grom was getting close...

Karlich made up his mind. He had to shout to be heard.

'Save the prince, we'll hold off the orcs.'

Meinstadt, a dishevelled, slightly blackened figure, nodded and ordered the great cannon turned about. He was already giving out miniscule adjustments to elevation and amounts of blackpowder when Karlich resumed his position in the Grimblades' front rank.

Ledner was alongside him.

'This is my captain's sword,' he told the spymaster. He drew the blade and it shone star-like in the light. 'I don't plan on dishonouring it today, nor should you.'

Ledner had picked up his own sword when they'd staggered back up the ridge. He held it in one hand, shakily due to his injuries.

'I knew you had balls, sergeant,' he rasped. 'That's why I've always liked you. That's why I haven't had you killed.'

'Sigmar be praised, then,' Karlich replied. The orcs were close enough to taste their foetid aroma on the breeze.

Ledner gave him a quizzical look, to which Karlich answered, 'That you spared me long enough for this bloody end.'

Behind them, the great cannon boomed.

WILHELM WAS ALONE when the chariot burst out from the greenskin ranks. Grom had weaved around the back of his mobs, waiting until the last moment to charge. Bearing down on Wilhelm now as it did, there was no time to mount a defence against the deadly machine. Its spinning scythed wheels were mesmerising... The cries of Wilhelm's men rushing to try and save him were moot, their desperate actions fated to always be too late.

In the wake of the fleeing black orcs, a mob of tattooed greenskins with bones through their noses, wearing animal hide and wielding crude stone axes charged into the open ground, wailing.

Caught between a goblin king and a sea of frenzied green, thought the prince.

Wilhelm saluted his forefathers and then his enemy. He levelled his runefang at Grom and prepared to meet him.

'Deus Sigmar...' he murmured, and closed his eyes.

At the sound of splintered wood and half-heard goblin curses, he opened them again.

Grom's chariot was wrecked. The Paunch was flattened underneath its carriage in a heap. One of the scythed wheels was still spinning, but pointed harmlessly in the air. The other had broken off and rolled away somewhere out of sight. The wolves were dead, crushed or impaled. A cannonball was lodged in the ground nearby, exuding smoke. It had upended the machine, flipping it dramatically to land just short of the prince.

When Grom didn't move at first, Wilhelm dared to hope the goblin king was dead. But then a piece of debris trembled atop the wreckage and fell off. Other larger pieces followed until the Paunch was back on his feet. He wrenched a stake of wood from his chest. Wilhelm's eyes widened as the wound closed behind it, and he saw all of Grom's cuts and bruises heal as if they had never been there. He recalled Ledner's words about the rumour the warlord could not be killed. Despite the evidence of his own eyes, he forced himself not to believe it.

Abruptly, Wilhelm became aware of Empire troops rushing to his side.

Grom's minions did the same. The savage orcs subsumed him into their ranks, while the Paunch's standard-bearer laughed and capered beside him. A brutal cuff from Grom to the little wretch's head curbed his enthusiasm.

Seeing the prince, Grom snarled and spat a gob of blood on the ground. He brandished his axe meaningfully before ordering the charge.

Up close, Grom looked even bigger. Eating troll flesh had done this to him, so it was reckoned. It accounted for the creature's massive belly, swollen with carnage, glutted on war.

Wilhelm allowed himself a murderous grin that narrowed his eyes. 'What do we do with trolls…' he said, before muttering a word of power that ignited a bright red flame along Dragontooth's blade.

Kogswald's reply in the war tent returned to him in a whisper as the Empire men charged.

We burn them.

Several of the armoured orcs rushing up the slope towards the war machines jerked and fell but the desultory harquebus salvo didn't slow them.

'For Reikland and Prince Wilhelm!' cried Karlich, before storming down the slope with his men to meet them.

Even Ledner roared, a hoarse unsettling noise, as a fatalistic abandon gripped the Grimblades.

Despite the fact they occupied the higher ground, the impact of the armoured orcs was brutal. Heifer and Innker, two recent stand-ins for the front rank, died at once. Heifer lost his nose and most of his face when a spiked club staved it in; Innker slipped on his own innards before realising he'd been opened up by an axe and died spewing blood down his tunic. Others, who Karlich failed to recognise in the maddened scrum of the fight, moved up from the back ranks to replace the fallen.

Eber took a blow to the stomach, more haft than blade, and grunted in pain. He stuck the orc on the end of his halberd and kept pushing until it was dead. Gore streaked the haft when he jerked it loose.

Brand abandoned his polearm completely, having dragged a hammer from the carnage and used that to bludgeon the greenskins. Bone chips and brain matter flicked off every strike he made. Stooping in the melee, he picked up a fallen sword and wielded it in his free hand. Stabbing and swiping, he was more frenzied than the savage beasts escorting the goblin king down in the valley. There was no finesse in this, no killing art. It was raw and primal with men reduced to beasts, desperate for survival.

For a fleeting moment, Karlich thought they could win. He felt determination in his troops and an overwhelming desire to live. Even injured, Ledner was devastating, a true swordsman compared to his own clumsy efforts. Stahler's sword was the leveller, though, shearing armour like parchment and cleaving off limbs like they were dead twigs.

But it wasn't enough. Karlich's misplaced optimism crumpled when Volker's lifeless body spun away from the orc chieftain leading the mob, impelled by the cleaver blow that had ruined his face and ended his life. The Reikland hunter disappeared in the mass as he fell and was trampled underfoot. Karlich wanted to reach for him and save Volker the indignity of being ground into the dirt but it was impossible.

Someone cried out. It sounded like Eber. Pain or anguish, it was hard to tell for sure.

They were losing. Karlich felt it in the surge of hopelessness that threatened to end him. A back step became three. Lenkmann looked to him for a sign. His left eye was gummed with blood. Karlich couldn't actually see it for sure. It didn't appear to concern him. Lenkmann's banner, his charge and solemn responsibility, was flecked with a comrade's blood.

Volker's dead.

'Hold! Hold!' rasped Ledner, shoving Karlich's shoulder in a gesture of defiance.

If they fled now they would not escape. The greenskins would catch them and they'd be slain to a man. Do or die – Karlich knew it was this he'd agreed to when telling Meinstadt to save the prince. No sacrifice comes without cost.

Behind them, men were running. Karlich heard the distant bootfalls getting closer and realised they weren't running away.

A burst of staccato *cracks* sounded near to his left, or was it his right? He wondered if he'd got turned around in the battle. Several orcs fell dead with smoke oozing from holes in their armour. The *cracks* came again, to much the same effect. Then a band of brawny gunnery crew led by Meinstadt slammed into the side of the orcs and laid about them with hatchets, hammers and other tools. With their machinery's ammunition exhausted, the engineer had pressganged the mortar crew into combat.

Meinstadt discharged his pistol at close range. The repeating mechanism fired three shots that sank an orc to its knees where he finished it with his sword.

Renewed hope filled Karlich, and the sergeant used it as a vessel for his anger. Armoured orcs died beneath Stahler's blade. It was the like the old captain lived on through it.

The greenskins thought they'd broken the Empire men. When they held on, rallying to Lenkmann's soiled standard, the orcs' pugnacity faded. The Grimblades had fought back the ground they'd lost, grinding the greenskins back down the slope, when a cry came from the ridgeline.

'Down!'

To a man, the halberdiers and gunnery crew dropped. Above them, a burst of grapeshot shredded what was left of the armoured orcs and broke them, but finished the last of the war machines.

None of the halberdiers gave chase. They'd hung on long enough for the great cannon to reload. Several of the Grimblades were dead, Volker with them. Karlich and Brand dragged his battered body from amongst the fallen.

They tried not to look at the dead man's face. They wouldn't have recognised it anyway. Brand shawled the poor sod with his cloak and dragged him farther up the ridge. Karlich ordered them all up there. With the cannons spent, it made no more sense to stay below them, they might as well occupy the highest vantage point where they were not so far from the ranks of harquebus. Grief was a luxury to feel later.

Karlich noticed Eber had not moved. He was on his knees, half sunk in the blood-soaked earth. His halberd rested limply in the crook of his arm like a fallen flag. The sergeant winced as he went down to him. A cut in his leg gave him discomfort, but he neither cared nor had time to staunch it.

'Higher ground, Eber,' he said, aware of the battle raging below them and that another greenskin breakthrough could be imminent. 'Come on, I'll help you up.'

He reached under Eber's thick arm but it was like heaving dead weight. Then he saw the burly Reiklander holding on to his sides. He was whispering something.

'Sergeant!' Lenkmann cried. The banner bearer's tone was urgent but Karlich waved away his concern without looking. Instead, he leaned in and listened.

'Like thread, like thread...' Eber muttered, and Karlich noticed the big man's fingers were ruby red and slick with his own blood. 'Feels like... sides splitting... I'm coming undone...'

'Lenkmann! Brand!' Karlich cried when he saw the wounds reopened in Eber's ox-like chest.

So much blood, so much blood, was all he kept thinking.

Eber was staring at him when he turned back. An incongruous look of serenity softened his face.

'I always thought of you...' he said with the last of his breath, '...like a father.'

When Brand and Lenkmann arrived, Karlich was crouched down shaking his head. His eyes were rimed with tears. It would be easy to give in then, but the battle wasn't done. A prince fought for his life, fought for all their lives in the valley below.

'Help me carry him,' said Karlich in a distant voice. Gazing down into the cauldron below, he hoped the sacrifice they'd made would be worth it.

FOR A FAT brute, Grom was quick. And he fought with the fury of a caged boar. A savage punch sent hot spikes of agony rushing through Wilhelm's jaw where the goblin king had connected. His eyes filled with white needles that threatened to turn to black. The prince shook off the nausea and disorientation that tried to overwhelm him. He bit his lip, finding clarity in pain, before fending off Grom's bearded axe with Dragontooth's blade.

Around him, the prince's charges fought so their lord might get his chance, his one chance to defeat the Paunch and end the war – at least for Reikland.

Greatswordersfrom the Carroburg Few, led by their grizzled champion, fought side by side with spearmen from Auerswald and citizen militias from countless villages and small towns. The Reikland had rallied for their province and their prince. Wilhelm was determined not be found wanting, but reward their faith in him.

Grom came again, the low *thwump* of his axe like a death knell when it swept overhead. It met Wilhelm's runefang with a dissonant *clang* and forced the prince back a step. Another swing, overhead and hard. Wilhelm parried high, pushing the axe blade out and wide, before driving into the beast with his armoured shoulder.

It was like hitting a wall of lead. Grom's flesh was as unyielding as it was obese. Though he'd jarred his shoulder, Wilhelm was close enough to yank the dagger from the belt at his hip and stab the greenskin king in the neck. He drove it deep, one-handed – the other gripped Dragontooth – until the fat brute squealed.

Grom used his bulk to drive Wilhelm off, the dagger wrenched from the prince's grasp but still embedded in the goblin's neck. Grom yanked it free with a spit of dark blood. In moments the wound closed and the Paunch smiled through spine-like teeth the colour of rust.

Wilhelm rolled Dragontooth around in a circle, tracing arcs of flame in the air that vanished in seconds.

'Just a taste,' promised the prince, but inwardly he despaired at the goblin's apparent invulnerability.

Grom snorted, belched and came at him again. One solid hit from his axe, which was no ordinary blade, and Wilhelm was sure he'd be maimed or dead. Anger made the goblin king reckless. His first strike cut thin air. Wilhelm went to counter, but Grom's wrath also lent him strength. Another punch crumpled the prince's fauld and sent lances of agony into his abdomen. This time he embraced the pain and fashioned a lunge into Grom's exposed thigh.

Dragontooth went deep and the rancid stink of burning meat clouded the air. Wilhelm ignored it, goring with his blade, dragging a deep and painful cleft in the greenskin's seemingly regenerative flesh.

Grom squealed, porcine and high in pitch. So close, their bodies touching, he leaned over to bite the prince's shoulder. Wilhelm's pain escaped in an agonised yelp, but he kept the pressure up and drove his runefang deeper. Grom stopped the biting when he threw his head back to squeal again. Wilhelm was reminded of hunting swine in the Reikwald Forest. Stuck boar made a similar noise. This was no prize to mount on the mantle, no hog roast to enjoy by a roaring hearth; it was a dire foe that had brought the Empire to its knees.

'I'll cut you dow–'

Grom butted the prince hard, stalling his vow. Wilhelm's sword didn't leave his grip as he fell back, and the blade pulled out from the goblin king's leg with the tearing of flesh. The axe blow that followed would have finished the prince were it not for the last Griffonkorps selling his life to save his liege-lord. Plate parted before Grom's crimson-edged blade, cutting the gallant knight in two and spilling him all over the field like offal.

Wilhelm feared the goblin king was restored again and back for more, but when the dizziness abated he saw the wound Dragontooth had scored was not closing. That last axe strike was the lashing of a desperate beast in terrible pain. The skin on Grom's leg was burned black, seared by a captured flame.

Kogswald had been right about the trolls, and the goblin king's miraculous healing was due to the physiology of those beasts. Fire was anathema to them, and so it was to Grom. The Paunch was in agony. Two large savage orcs held him upright as he cursed and frothed. With their overlord's wounding, the fight was ebbing from the deranged greenskins. Their berserker's fervour was almost tapped. A rank of the beasts went down to spears and greatswords as the Empire men fought to hold the advantage.

Grom looked about to rally, digging deep of his pain to find the molten anger at its core. When Wilhelm showed him Dragontooth and flared the blade into fiery life, the goblin king faltered. He shied away from the ancestral sword, fearful of its burning edge, afraid for his precious flesh and acutely aware of his own mortality.

Goblins were craven creatures, even brutes as large and cunning as Grom. He knew this was a fight he was unwilling to pay the cost to win. Snorting in the crude language of the greenskins, Grom ordered the savage orcs to withdraw and bear him away from the fire-blade into the bargain.

Across the valley, the Empire and their allies sensed the balance shift in their favour. At either flank they pressed the greenskins even harder, a final effort to send them from the field. Wilhelm led the centre, his victorious warriors butchering the orcs and goblins too belligerent to buckle with their warlord.

From the ridgeline harquebuses cracked, harrying the greenskins at every step, until their shot and powder were exhausted. As the smoke settled and the noise of battle died to be replaced by the sullen moans of dying, the Empire was left on the field.

They had bloodied Grom's nose. The Paunch was far from defeated, but they had repelled him from Reikland and kept Altdorf safe.

Wilhelm would learn later that Grom had turned northwards, across the border and into Middenland. Todbringer would have to face the greenskin horde now and see if his armoured bulwarks could weather the vented storm as he had hoped.

For Reikland's part, they let the goblins go. The battle was won but there were precious few troops left alive in the valley to savour it. Certainly, there was not army enough to follow the Paunch north all the way to Middenheim.

Instead, Wilhelm raised the army's banner. It was soiled and bloody from where it had fallen in the earth as the last Griffonkorps had died. Still, it fluttered proudly in the prince's grasp. He lifted Dragontooth to the heavens and a great cheer went up, hounding the greenskins all the way past the border.

Victory was Reikland's.

And upon the ridge, a sergeant and his men praised almighty Sigmar for that.

EPILOGUE

Reikland prairie, on the outskirts of Altdorf,
8 miles from the new capital of the Empire

THE GREY DAY matched Karlich's mood as he surveyed a steel sky from a rocky outcrop. It was a day of reunion and remembrance. Four years had passed since Waaagh! Grom had blighted the Empire and brought his country to its very knees.

Karlich was proud to have been there at the end, at least for Reikland. Tales still drifted down to southern provinces of the razing of Middenland and the destruction of a temple of the White Wolves at Middenheim. Grom's anger hadn't been sated at Nuln, that much was obvious. After that, the beast had carried on northwards to the ocean and lands far beyond the Empire's and even the Old World's shores.

It was a day of great change, too. Altdorf, in all its magnificent glory, lay below. Wagons entered the city in their droves. For three days and nights it had been thus, as the Golden Palace of Nuln was stripped of its ostentation and Dieter's ill-gotten wealth redistributed. Even years later, there was much that needed to be rebuilt. Grom's invasion had left a lasting and destructive legacy behind it. The poorer villages and hamlets felt its bite more than most. Here was where the money was needed. Wilhelm, Saviour of the Reik, would see it was spent wisely.

It turned out the assassins and the dealings with Marienburg were but scraps of a larger treachery, some of which was, admittedly, perpetuated by Ledner. Karlich didn't know many details, save what he had heard down the years. It seemed Dieter's Golden Palace, all of his accumulated wealth, had been garnered from bribes. Marienburg had recently seceded from the Empire, its independence bought through Imperial corruption. At his prince's behest, Adolphus Ledner had uncovered documents and witnesses that would attest to Dieter's role in it. Many were sick of his indolent rule and like sharks scenting blood, descended upon the Emperor. It had taken time to expose these dealings, especially in the aftermath of the war, but in the end an emergency council at Volkshalle in Altdorf had seen the then Emperor deposed. He'd fled to Marienburg, in fear for his life. Rumours abounded that an army from Reikland was headed to the Wasteland to bring him back. Wilhelm was his worthy successor. With a new Emperor came a new capital, and for the first time in many years that honour was Altdorf's again.

'Grim day for a coronation,' remarked a voice Karlich knew from behind him.

'Lenkmann!' He shook hands with his old banner bearer in the manner of a firm friend.

Since the war, the Grimblades had been disbanded. There were so few of them left that there seemed little point in going on. Even with recruits, it wouldn't have been the same regiment – not anymore.

Lenkmann wore a sergeant's silver laurels on his lapel now. Karlich had heard the lad got his own command. It was well deserved.

'Pristine as ever, I see,' he said, clapping Lenkmann warmly on the shoulders and looking him up and down. Not a buckle out of place. He was immaculate in his dress attire.

'Some things don't change,' Lenkmann replied, with a note of sadness he couldn't hide.

'And this?' asked Karlich, pointing to his eye.

He'd lost it during the battle in the valley, which the poets had dubbed 'Glory at Bloody Gorge'. Well, the bards were right about one thing.

'I think the patch gives me an air of danger.' Lenkmann laughed, not deigning to touch it. Several years without his left eye, but he still hadn't fully adjusted. Perhaps he never would. 'We all lost something that day, though.'

Karlich smiled but his face still matched the brooding sky.

'I heard you're no longer serving in the army,' Lenkmann ventured after a moment's silence.

Karlich looked to the city. Several regiments were already trooping through Altdorf's gates to observe the pomp and ceremony. He recognised the banner of Von Rauken's Carroburg Few and hoped the veteran champion was still amongst them. Their ranks, so badly battered during the campaign of four years ago, had been swelled by fresh blood.

'Not sure it's in me anymore. I only joined to escape the past. This'll be the last time I don armour and uniform,' he said.

Unlike Lenkmann, Karlich felt ill at ease in the dress attire he'd been given. The coronation not only celebrated the crowning of the new Emperor, it also commemorated and honoured those who had fallen to secure Reikland's sovereignty almost five years ago. Karlich was amongst the esteemed guests, one of few that no longer served but had survived the battle.

'Ledner's dead you know. You've nothing to fear from him or his lackeys anymore.'

He'd told them all, those who still lived amongst his closest companions, about Vanhans and even Grelle the Confessor. Not a man amongst them raised so much as an accusing eyebrow, not even Von Rauken. It was past, another life.

'Lung rot, I heard.'

'Painful way to go,' said Lenkmann.

'He'd earned it.'

'Yes he had.'

Karlich took out his pipe. Smoke drifted on the breeze after he'd fired it up, carried down to the city below them.

'Did you bring it?'

When Karlich faced him again, he saw Lenkmann was cradling a dusky-looking bottle in his arm.

'Wasn't easy to procure.' Lenkmann held it up to his eye. 'But this is it. Middenland hooch. Rechts must've had a stomach like a horse.'

'And a face to match,' added Karlich.

They laughed at that, but not for long.

Karlich surveyed the sloping outcrop behind them. It was studded with rocks and wild grass, but nothing else.

'Doesn't look like he's coming. Shame that,' he said genuinely.

'Let's get to it, then. Captain Vogen will flay me if I'm late for the Emperor-elect.'

Lenkmann offered the bottle to Karlich, who declined. 'First honours are yours, Bader.'

Lenkmann gave his old sergeant a reproachful glance, before uncorking the hooch and taking a swig.

Coughing and spluttering, he handed it over to Karlich. The ex-sergeant was more of a hardened drinker and took the pull without complaint.

'Not to your taste,' he smiled, wiping a trickle of brown liquid from his lip.

'I prefer something with *taste* other than that of neat alcohol, if that's what you mean.'

Karlich grinned, before assuming a solemn expression. He turned to the horizon and slowly upended the bottle. The dark liquid trickled out over the grass, a last drink to old friends.

'To the fallen,' he said, drawing Stahler's sword and planting it in the alcohol-soaked ground.

'Aye, to Varveiter and Eber, to Keller and Rechts...'

'To Volker and Masbrecht,' said Karlich, 'to all the Grimblades. And to Stahler,' he added.

'May Morr take them to his breast and Sigmar welcome them in the halls of heroes.'

Karlich let the bottle fall after Lenkmann had finished.

'It's done then.'

'It's done.'

Lenkmann faced him, saluted once and outstretched his hand. 'It's been an honour, sir.'

Karlich ignored the hand and hugged him warmly like a brother.

Lenkmann was taken aback at first but reciprocated the gesture.

'Come on,' said Karlich as they parted. 'Mustn't keep Emperor Wilhelm waiting.'

They left the outcrop together just as a shaft of sunlight poked through the clouds.

When they were gone, another figure came out of hiding to stand upon the rocky ridge overlooking the city, a mean looking mastiff following at his heel.

Remembrances were best observed alone, Brand always thought. Besides, a reunion would only raise awkward questions. He had no intention of returning to Altdorf or the army. An old profession had come calling again and Brand meant to heed it. This would be his last act as a Grimblade.

He regarded the spilled alcohol and the gleaming sword. He was tempted to take it, such was its craftsmanship, but that would dishonour the captain and he couldn't have that. Instead, he saluted once, a final acknowledgement to old friends and an old life.

Brand didn't linger. He was bound for the port of Marienburg where a ship would take him to Tilea. He hadn't been there since he was sixteen but had heard of openings in various guilds for men of his calibre.

The small parcel in his hands contained his old uniform. Beneath the paper, it was still stained with blood. Brand laid it down and walked away.

'Come, Volker!' he snapped, and the mastiff dutifully followed.

ABOUT THE AUTHOR

Nick Kyme hails from Grimsby, a small town on the east coast of England. Nick moved to Nottingham in 2003 to work on White Dwarf magazine as a Layout Designer. Since then, he has made the switch to the Black Library's hallowed halls as an editor and has been involved in a multitude of diverse projects. His writing credits include several published short stories, background books and novels.

You can catch up with Nick and read about all of his other published works at his website: *www.nickkyme.com*